What's a woman to do
when she finds herself compromised, but in the

Lap

of

Luxury

Relive the romance…

Three complete novels
by one of your all-time favorite authors

Dear Reader,

Cinderella lives. You heard it here first.

How else would an impoverished wallpaper hanger meet and fall in love with a charming, wealthy, handsome widower with two adorable little girls and a mother-in-law (okay, "fairy godmother") who knows what's best for everyone? That's the story of *Stuck on You*. I used to hang wallpaper, long before I sold my first book, and one particular redecorating job became the inspiration for this book.

Ever heard of Cinderella as foster mother to a group of abandoned children? Guess who shows up? Two fairy godmothers and a prince who is not at all thrilled with his domestic castle abode. But there's a ball and a mansion and it takes place in Newport, Rhode Island (an island town very close to my home), summer playground of the rich and famous. Lucky, lucky Cinderella and *The Perfect Husband*.

And then there's a jilted bride who goes on her *Make-Believe Honeymoon* to England all by herself and accidentally meets not a prince, but a duke. And what a duke! He comes complete with ancestral home, jewels, cheese-making business and a grandmother who wants him to marry anyone but an American tourist. I wrote the outline for this story on a flight home from London after eight days in England with one of my best girlfriends (we even saw the queen). We both felt rather regal after buying antique jewelry at the Covent Garden antique market and touring Kensington Palace.

By now you've realized I have a weakness for fairy tales and fairy godmothers, but I suppose that's why I write romances. "Once upon a time" and "happily ever after" just come naturally to someone who owns more books about castles than she will ever admit.

Wishing you happy endings and many Cinderella moments,

Kristine Rolofson

KRISTINE ROLOFSON

Lap of Luxury

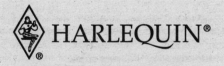

HARLEQUIN®

TORONTO • NEW YORK • LONDON
AMSTERDAM • PARIS • SYDNEY • HAMBURG
STOCKHOLM • ATHENS • TOKYO • MILAN • MADRID
PRAGUE • WARSAW • BUDAPEST • AUCKLAND

HARLEQUIN BOOKS

by Request—LAP OF LUXURY

Copyright © 2002 by Harlequin Books S.A.

ISBN 0-373-18502-2

The publisher acknowledges the copyright holder
of the individual works as follows:
THE PERFECT HUSBAND
Copyright © 1993 by Kristine Rolofson
STUCK ON YOU
Copyright © 1989 by Kristine Rolofson
MAKE-BELIEVE HONEYMOON
Copyright © 1995 by Kristine Rolofson

This edition published by arrangement with Harlequin Books S.A.

Visit us at www.eHarlequin.com

Printed in U.S.A.

CONTENTS

Live the fantasy…

THE PERFECT HUSBAND

1

STANDING on her front porch was easily the most handsome man Raine Claypoole had ever seen in her twenty-eight years. Even through the fine mesh grid of the screen door and despite the dark sunglasses that topped his finely chiseled nose, Raine could tell that "tall, dark and handsome" stood on the worn floorboards of her front entrance, waiting for admittance.

"Yes?" she managed, ignoring the dog that growled near her ankles. "Can I help you?"

Tall, dark and handsome smiled, and Raine blinked. "I'm sorry I'm late," he said in a low voice.

Charlie yapped at her heels. "Quiet, Charlie!" Raine continued to stare at the stranger. He wore beige slacks and a white dress shirt that was unbuttoned at the top, as if he'd whipped off his jacket and tie to combat Rhode Island's latest heat wave. It was two o'clock in the afternoon, and as far as Raine was concerned, no one was late for anything. What was this man talking about? "Late?"

"You know how planes are," he said patiently before slipping the sunglasses off and tucking them, folded, into his shirt pocket. His hazel eyes looked bloodshot. "And there was a mix-up with the car rental."

Car rental? Raine figured she must be missing some small, crucial detail that would help her understand why this man stood on her doorstep. Ready to protect his mistress and poised to attack, Charlie growled. Raine picked him up. All nine pounds quivered with repressed fury directed at the man on the other side of the screen door.

"I'm sorry," Raine began, "but I—"

"That's all right. The directions were excellent, by the way. Look," he said, flashing another smile. "It's about one hundred and ten degrees out here. I'd like to get settled and cool off."

Raine tried again, glancing at the latch on the door to make sure it was securely fastened. "I'm sorry, but I don't know who you are."

"What?"

"I don't know who you are." She raised her voice over the dog's growls. "And I don't know why you're here. I think there's some mistake." The mistake had been in answering the door. She'd planned to spend an hour napping. Jimmy had had another asthma attack, and the sibs' social worker was due to return the children within the hour.

The man took a step back and glanced at the side of the door. "219 Berkley Avenue, two blocks off Belle-vue?"

"That's right, but—"

"And is this the Claypoole house?"

"Yes. And you are?" she asked, fascinated despite the possibility that he could be a robber or worse. He could have read her mail to know her name. Or looked in the phone book.

"Alan Hunter."

"I don't know anyone by that name. Who exactly are you looking for?"

He frowned. "I don't understand this. Claire said she'd taken care of everything."

"Claire?" A feeling of dread started to take root in her stomach.

"Claire Claypoole. Is this the Claypoole residence?" At her nod, he brushed the hair away from his damp forehead and continued. "Could you please get Raine Claypoole for me? I'm sure she can straighten everything out."

The dread expanded. "I'm Raine. What does this have to do with Claire?"

It was his turn to look uncertain. "She arranged for me to rent the rooms on the third floor."

"That's impossible."

He held her gaze, his hazel eyes unblinking. "No, it's not."

"They're not even her rooms to rent."

"Wait right here," he ordered unnecessarily. She watched him go down the porch steps to the sidewalk, where he opened the passenger door of a large black sedan. He retrieved a briefcase, slammed the car door and headed back up the walk to the porch.

"It's okay, Charlie," she told the anxious dog, patting his fluffy coat. "You're a good watchdog."

The man was close enough to hear the last of her words and the corners of his mouth twitched. He set the briefcase upon a wicker chair and snapped it open. He flipped through several sheaves of paper, then pulled one from the pile. "Here," he declared. "This should straighten everything out."

If this had to do with her stepmother, then the man was indeed either unrealistic or an optimist. "What is it?"

"My rental agreement."

"Hold it up to the screen."

Raine scanned the words until she realized what Claire had done, to the tune of five hundred dollars a week. *Five hundred dollars a week?* "That's a lot of money."

"Yes. It includes two meals a day." He returned the paper to his briefcase and snapped it closed. "Now, could you show me upstairs? I've had a long day."

He wasn't the only one. "She has no right to rent you anything, Mr. uh, Hunter."

"You'll have to tell her that. I paid three weeks in advance. If you have a problem I'll call my lawyers—*after* I unpack and drink a couple of gallons of ice water."

She almost felt sorry for him. Alan Hunter really did look hot. His face was red, with perspiration running from his temples to his eyebrows. "How do you know Claire?"

"My mother," he said, coming closer to the screen, "is Claire's best friend. Maybe you heard of her—and I hope to hell you have—Edwina Wetmore Hunter?"

Raine groaned. She couldn't help herself. "Yes, I've heard of her. I've even met her."

He took his wallet from his back pocket and flipped it open to reveal a driver's license. "See? Alan Wetmore Hunter. That's me."

She squinted at the photograph, blurry behind the plastic. He was who he said he was. Claire would have some explaining to do. "All right," she said, unhooking the latch on the door. "You can come in."

"Good," Alan said, but turned away. "I'll bring in my luggage."

She wanted to tell him to leave it, that he wouldn't be here long enough to change his clothes, but he was halfway down the walk before she could open her mouth. For a big man he moved fast. She continued to hold Charlie in her arms, knowing the little dog would take every opportunity to dash through the open door and run down the street to look for other dogs to play with.

Within minutes Alan Hunter arrived back on the porch with three leather suitcases and a light suit jacket draped over his arm. Raine opened the screen door, despite the feeling that this was wrong. Totally wrong.

"Where to?" He looked expectantly toward the wide mahogany staircase that graced one end of the foyer.

"I'd prefer to call Claire before you start unpacking," Raine said, setting the dog down. He trotted over to Alan's feet and sniffed tentatively.

"You can talk to her all afternoon—I don't care. I just got in from London, drove from Boston in this heat and have been awake for the past thirty hours." He still held the bags above the polished tile floor. "Show me to my rooms and we'll work out any problems in the morning." His tone implied he didn't anticipate having any problems to work out.

"You might want to leave the bags, or just take one."

"Why?"

"You're staying on the third floor," she said. "It's quite a hike. And you may want to see what you've spent money to rent before you actually move in."

He set two bags down, although he looked at her for a long moment as if he were going to be tricked.

"They'll be perfectly safe," she assured him. Raine knew when she had to retreat. She didn't want a strange man in her home, but on the other hand, she didn't want an angry strange man in her living room, calling his lawyers and making a scene. Despite his bloodshot eyes and rumpled hair, Alan Hunter looked as if he still had the power to make a very big scene.

"Will this dog bite me?"

"No."

He allowed Charlie to sniff his pant leg, but he didn't bend down to pet the animal. "What is it?"

"Part Pekingese, part Lhasa apso."

Instead of following her down the hall, he turned into the oversize living room, known as the front parlor in Aunt Gertrude's day. The tall, shaded windows rejected the afternoon sunshine, and a floor fan hummed from one corner. Two new sofas faced each other, a scarred pine table between them. Building blocks lay scattered across the black-and-white-tiled floor and baskets of plastic toys lined one wall. A low shelf behind it contained colorful cardboard books made for pudgy hands and curious minds.

Raine kicked some blocks out of her path. "Be careful," she warned. "I haven't had time to clean up the mess today."

"I didn't know you had children."

"I'm a foster mother. Claire didn't mention it?"

"No." Charlie hopped onto a faded, overstuffed chair and curled up, satisfied that the stranger meant no harm.

"Well, there's a lot she doesn't mention," Raine said, then concealed a sigh. Her stepmother would have a lot of explaining to do, but first she had to get this man out of her way. There was laundry to finish, and maybe even a tiny nap to be sneaked in, before the kids returned from camp and Mindy arrived with the sibs.

"This is quite a house," he attempted.

"Yes. I inherited it from my aunt several years ago. I really love it."

"It must have been something in its day."

"Yes," she agreed politely. She supposed she would have to give him a tour of the rest of the house now. He followed her through the parlor and into the large dining room. The house possessed a Victorian lushness that Raine had always loved, which was probably why Gertrude left it to her when there were plenty of other members of the family panting after the prime piece of Rhode Island real estate. Most of the furniture was white, painted the same color year after year in thick layers. The walls and high ceilings were a soft eggshell, the floor tiled in black-and-white squares like the living room. Oriental rugs of museum quality still adorned the floor, though not with the same vibrancy as in Gertrude's day.

"How long have you lived here?"

He was trying to be polite, Raine decided, so she responded in the same tone. "Three years. I've always loved Newport."

"Yes," he said. "I know what you mean."

She preceded him into the large kitchen, glad the doors to the utility rooms were closed. A screened door led to another narrow, covered porch. Dark pine cabinets lined the walls, and a heavy wooden table took up most of the room.

Raine led Alan out of the kitchen, figuring he'd had enough of touring her house. Around the corner, fronting the main hall, was an alcove that contained the servants' stairs. She pointed to the dark wooden staircase. "That's the servants' staircase, the only way to get to the third floor."

"I thought there was a staircase at the front door."

"Yes, but it only goes to the second floor."

He turned to follow her up the stairs. "You said you were a foster mother?"

"Yes."

"How many children do you have?"

She hadn't expected the question. "Six right now, but one of them is going to be adopted soon."

"*Six?*"

She looked back at him. "I'll bet Claire didn't mention that, either."

"No," he muttered. "She sure as hell didn't tell me I'd be spending my vacation in a foster home."

"I'm sure you could call Claire and get a refund."

"I'm not going anywhere today," he growled.

They turned a corner onto a landing, and Raine stopped. "Do you need to rest?"

"No."

She thought he did. His face was even redder than before, and she could see the dark circles under his eyes. "Are you sure?"

"Positive."

The next landing should have opened onto the third floor, but Raine had installed a door to keep the children away from the third floor. They used the main staircase, which was less confusing for her. From her bedroom downstairs, the original library, she was able to hear if the children were awake and roaming around the house.

Alan breathed heavily behind her, so Raine paused once more. "We can stop if you want."

"No," he said. "The sooner I get upstairs, the sooner I'll be settled in and the sooner I can be in bed."

Well, that was clear enough. Raine shrugged, then turned and continued up the stairs. She was used to climbing—up and down all day long, but by the time they reached the third floor, Alan was huffing and puffing and mumbling under his breath.

"Here we are," she said, stepping into a dark hallway. "These rooms haven't been used in a number of years. Sometimes my brother stays here, but he hasn't been in the States much this year."

"Neither have I."

Raine peered into one of the rooms. "You can take your pick, Mr. Hunter. There are three or four bedrooms and a bathroom. There's a tub, but no shower."

"The first room will be fine."

He stepped into the room and set down his suitcase and briefcase on the wooden floor. "What about a phone?"

"There's a separate line up here. Quentin—that's my brother—had one put in two years ago."

"I assume I can use it?"

"There are quite a few things we need to talk about. For instance—"

He put up one hand as if to ward off her words. "I'm serious, Ms. Claypoole. I am ready to collapse."

Raine studied him. "I can believe that, Mr. Hunter."

"Then you understand that talking will have to wait until I can actually absorb the information you give me. Until then, I would like to be left undisturbed."

What did he think she was, the bellman at the Hotel Viking? "No problem," she replied, and turned to leave him.

"One thing," he called, as she took a step down the stairs. "Is there air-conditioning?"

"No."

He sighed. "I should have guessed."

"I'd be glad to—"

He'd already turned into his room, so Raine didn't

finish the sentence. She would have given him one of the fans from downstairs. The third floor was too stifling and dusty to be comfortable. If she'd known Claire had pulled one of her tricks and let the rooms, then she'd have cleaned them up. She hadn't expected company. Quent's band was touring Europe and wouldn't be back in the country until October. Claire always stayed with friends on the rare summer weekends she appeared on the island.

Raine heard Alan Hunter opening windows and silently wished him luck. She had to get in touch with Claire and find out what was behind her stepmother's deceit.

"I THOUGHT he'd make the most *lovely* husband for you."

"The most lovely husband," Raine repeated flatly.

"Why, of course. I've only met him once, but Edwina says he has magnificent shoulders and a charming way with women."

Raine almost laughed, but checked herself. She didn't want Claire to think that her plan was acceptable. Besides, she didn't know if they were talking about the same man. "I haven't seen any of the charm, Claire."

"You will, darling, I'm sure of it."

"I don't *want* to. Never mind. I've seen the rental agreement, though. What did you do with all of that money?"

There was a sigh. "Don't make me explain, dear."

"You have to. I'm stuck with this guy if you don't give the money back."

"I can't, darling."

"Why not?" Raine heard Alan walking through the

dining room heading toward the kitchen, so she stretched the telephone cord as far as it would go, around the corner and into a small, white-tiled bathroom.

"I spent the money."

Raine made a conscious effort to stop gritting her teeth. She took a deep breath. "Claire! You have plenty of money. Why are you turning into a landlord—and it's not even your house to rent?"

"I told you, he'll make the most lovely—"

"Husband," Raine supplied, unwilling to hear the word spoken by Claire once again. "I know. Where's the money?"

"Your sofas," Claire said. "And that nice redwood play set with the swings and slides and sandbox."

Raine could hear Alan taking the stairs, one at a time. "It was supposed to be a loan." She could probably return the couches; after all, they'd hardly been here two weeks. But the swing set was cemented in. The workmen had dug nice neat holes and filled them with cement so that the swings would be safe to play on and not tip over. She'd been pleased with the precaution. Until now.

Claire interrupted her thoughts. "All the money from your mother's trust fund goes to supporting that old wreck of a house—"

"It's not a wreck."

"You're so stubborn, never letting me use your dear father's money—God rest his soul—to buy you things. So I used your money."

"*My* money?"

"The money you made from renting the upstairs. Isn't this nice? Now you don't have to pay me back."

Raine slumped against the bathroom wall, feeling

the cool tile through the thin T-shirt. "Let me make sure I have this correctly. You lent me the money for the couches and the play set, then rented the upstairs to a strange man—"

"Not a strange man, dear, but Edwina's only son."

Raine ignored that. "A strange man who paid you in advance—"

"I would have just given him the rooms to use, but Edwina pointed out that he wouldn't like that." Claire sighed. "I understand he's rather independent."

"And then you took the money and paid yourself back, for me."

"Isn't this a relief? We understand each other."

"Yes, Claire. We do."

"Now you take good care of him, darling. He's a very important man, some kind of banker with investments or something complicated, like your father. See? You have *so* much in common. Edwina and I are *so* pleased."

Well, Raine was glad someone was pleased. She didn't know whether to laugh or cry, so she hung up the phone and made herself a tuna fish sandwich.

Alan entered the kitchen, this time carrying a laptop computer case and a garment bag. "I'm going to need air-conditioning."

"I'm afraid we don't have any."

"I must insist."

Raine was hot, tired and backed into a corner. "Look, Mr. Hunter, this latest heat wave is unbearable, but I can't produce an air conditioner. The fact that you're here in my house has taken me by surprise, so could the two of us just make the best of it for now?" He didn't answer, but simply looked at her as if she had four heads. "I'm asking you, Mr. Hunter. Could you stop acting as if I'm the bellboy and you're renting the penthouse?"

"I think so, yes."

"Thank you." She pushed the heavy black hair away from her face and tucked it behind her ear. She could feel her bangs plastered to her forehead. "Take the fan in the dining room. There's a pitcher of lemonade in the refrigerator. Please help yourself whenever you like."

"I'm going to finish unloading the car."

He clearly meant, *As long as I'm settled in, the harder it will be to remove me.*

Raine thought of her new couches and the children's play set, and attempted civility. "You brought your computer. Is this a working vacation?"

Alan grimaced. "Aren't they all?"

He turned and went back up the stairs, still moving slowly.

Raine almost felt sorry for him, but she'd tried to offer a fan, tried to dissuade him from walking around in the heat, but he was determined to do what he wanted. Including moving into this house.

THE FRONT DOOR OPENED and Raine heard Charlie yapping at the noise.

"Shut up, Charlie," one of the boys said cheerfully. "You're so funny!"

Raine headed toward the front of the house and the noise stopped. Three children, with identical blond hair and blue eyes, bounced toward her. "We went to McDonald's, Raine!"

A tall redhead followed them into the living room. Charlie wagged his fluffy tail to greet everyone, then retreated to his chair. There was only so much activity he could stand.

"You did?"

Julie's blond hair was tied in pigtails and a chocolate smudge decorated her upper lip. She held out a crayon-shaped drinking cup. "Look what I got!"

"Wow, are you lucky!" Raine turned to Mindy. "How'd everything go?"

"We had a great time. You know Joey—he's always happy, no matter what. The other two were a little quieter than usual. I'll tell you all about it in private."

"Come on, kids," Raine said. "You can go outside and play until the rest of the gang comes home." The children ran in front of the two women through the kitchen and out the back door.

Raine turned to Mindy. "Want some lemonade?"

"Please. Their mother didn't show up for the meeting again."

"What was the reason this time?" She took the pitcher from the refrigerator and set it upon the counter.

"Nothing, of course. No one has been able to talk to her for months."

Raine's heart sank. "The kids haven't talked about their mother lately, but I don't know how they're going to react if she never shows up again."

"They asked a few questions. I tried to tell them that Mom is having a hard time."

"*Still* having a hard time, you mean."

"The boys worry about her. Julie doesn't seem to care. I don't think she remembers much about her mother."

"I don't think she does, either." Raine checked outside to make sure the kids weren't by the door. "How much more do the courts need before they do something? These kids need a home. Something permanent."

Mindy shrugged and sat down at the table while Raine poured lemonade into glasses. "We're working on it, but you know how slow the process is."

"I know." Raine knew all too well. Her three years as a foster mother had educated her in the frustrations of the legal system. "They're in limbo until the court decides otherwise, right?"

"Yes, but the kids were fine. We had a great visit, lunch at McDonald's, and some pretty good conversation."

Raine handed Mindy her drink. "Good. They were looking forward to it."

"Thanks." Mindy took a swallow of the lemonade and grinned at Raine. "Who does the car out front belong to? If your rock star brother is in town, I want to meet him."

"Sorry, but Quent isn't due in town until October. The car belongs to a friend of my stepmother's. Claire is interfering in my life again."

Mindy's smile widened. "I'd like to meet her sometime. She sounds like a real character."

"Oh, she is."

"The kids told me she sent a play set. I promised I'd see it before I left."

"Well, take a good look, because that complicated piece of wood outside means I have a tenant for the next few weeks."

"I'm glad you're finally seeing my point," a male voice said from the hall doorway. Raine and Mindy turned to see Alan leaning against the frame. "Sorry," he said. "I didn't mean to interrupt."

"That's all right," Raine said. "Mindy, I'd like you to meet the man who is renting the third-floor apartment, Alan Hunter."

Mindy held out her hand and Alan stepped forward to shake it. "I didn't know Raine had an apartment to rent. It's nice to meet you."

"My pleasure." He released her hand.

Mindy continued to smile at him. "Well, I hope you have a wonderful vacation."

"Vacation and business combined," he replied, his smile once again charming. The dark circles under his eyes did little to mar his attractiveness, but his face remained flushed.

Raine cleared her throat, making both turn toward her. "Mindy, didn't you want to see the play set?"

"Oh, uh, yes," Mindy said.

"If you'll excuse me." Alan moved toward the door. "I'm going to put my car in the driveway for the evening."

"Bye," Mindy said, smiling once again as he left the room.

"You can stop drooling now. No one would guess that you're a married woman."

"Hey." Mindy grinned and finished her lemonade. "I'm not blind. But speaking of husbands, mine promised to make dinner tonight, so I'd better get going."

"Keep me posted on the kids, okay?" Mindy nodded, and Raine stood up and pushed open the screened door. "Mindy needs to leave," she called to the children. "Are you going to show her your new toy?"

The three children came running, the twins in the lead. Joey and Jimmy shoved each other through the doorway and screeched to a halt in front of the two women.

Raine looked behind them for their younger sister. "Where's Julie?"

"Here I am." The tiny version of the twins appeared behind her brothers. "Can I take Charlie out with us?"

"Not right now. You show Mindy the swing set, okay?"

Mindy grinned again. "It must be show-and-tell at Claypoole's house today."

"I don't know what you mean."

Mindy simply chuckled. "He is gorgeous," she whispered, as Julie grabbed her hand and started to tug her toward the door. "I think you should keep him."

Raine watched Mindy and the children head out. Keep him? She was stuck with him. There was no sense in trying to force Claire to refund the man's money. Claire never did anything anyone wanted her to do, at least, not since Raine had known her. That had been thirteen years now, when Claire told fifteen-year-old Raine that she was her new mother.

"Stepmother," Raine had corrected, furious because her father, always so withdrawn and preoccupied, hadn't told her he'd remarried.

"Claire," the beautiful woman had declared. "Of course you'll call me Claire."

Raine hadn't wanted to call her anything.

But Claire's outrageous laughter and extravagant ideas had brought some sunshine into Raine's life. Her father, still putting business first, allowed Claire to do what she wished as long as it didn't interfere with his work. He gave her an allowance and she threw tasteful parties and elegant dinners, but it was her personality that drew people like a magnet, including Edwina Wetmore Hunter—Wina—mother of Alan and quite a few other children, though Raine couldn't remember how many.

Best friends Wina and Claire hatched all sorts of plots, especially now that they were widowed. They traveled, they partied, they entertained and they meddled. Until now Raine had avoided most of the meddling, although Claire had sent Charlie as a gift to "keep Raine company." She'd adored him right away.

Raine had managed to convince Claire that she could manage on her own, with the house and her job, without outside financial help. She didn't want Claire's money, and she certainly didn't want her father's. Claire could keep it. Raine had paid too high a price for her father's fortune.

Raine stood at the back door and watched the children tumble through the redwood structures. If Claire figured that Alan would make a "perfectly lovely husband," Raine knew she was in trouble. Big trouble.

"THIS IS GOING TO BE SO much fun." Claire held her glass out to the waiter. "Put another martini in here, and don't forget the olive, will you, dear?"

Her companion waved the waiter away. "Don't listen to her, Frederick. She's not supposed to be drinking."

"Oh, tosh!" But Claire set her empty glass upon the table, shaded from the glare of the Long Island sun by a blue-and-white-striped umbrella. "I thought we should celebrate, that's all."

"I'll celebrate when Alan is really and truly married."

"It's as good as done." Claire removed a compact

from her purse and brushed powder onto her nose. "I'm so clever," she said to the tiny round mirror before snapping the case closed.

Edwina shook her head, and the wide-brimmed straw hat she wore tipped to one side. She readjusted it and then wagged a bony finger at her friend. "You don't know everything, Claire. You think you do, but—"

"Didn't I tell you that the Markhams would get a divorce?"

"Well, yes, but you only knew because their housekeeper told you."

"And," Claire continued unperturbed, although she frowned at the empty martini glass, "didn't I find that nice accountant for Alexandria?"

"Pure luck," Edwina declared. "Although, wasn't the wedding lovely?"

"You have to be mother of the groom this time," Claire announced. "I shall be the mother of the bride."

"And wear aqua silk?"

Claire's eyebrows rose. "Black lace."

"You can't wear black to a wedding."

"Then something red."

"Rose," her friend corrected. "It's much more tasteful."

"All right." Claire picked up her empty glass and waved to Frederick. "I insist, Wina. We must celebrate this step, and each and every step along the way."

Edwina sighed. "Alan won't like this."

"Alan will have the time of his life." Claire winked. "I promise."

HE WAS APPROACHING the landing to the second floor when he knew he was in trouble. Suddenly his feet seemed detached from the rest of his body. Black dots began to creep into his vision from the side, and he blinked to clear them.

The darkness grew.

Alan heard his heart beating, so he knew he was still alive. He felt the perspiration running down his back, in the groove between his shoulder blades. He gripped the banister and told himself that this was the last trip on these god-awful stairs in this heat straight from hell.

He could have had an air-conditioned motel room. With a bellhop and a luggage cart and cable television with remote control. That is, he reminded himself, if he'd made reservations two months ahead of time. And he would have, if he'd known there would be these kinds of problems.

Here he'd thought himself lucky when Claire suggested "her" apartment. He'd anticipated a cozy New England retreat, private and restful. He hadn't imagined carrying his belongings up three flights of stairs in the midst of a heat wave; he hadn't counted on flight delays and jet lag and a day and a half with no sleep.

Alan gripped the fan under his arm. It was his only salvation, and he planned to strip naked and stand in front of it. He reconsidered the standing part. No, he would position it so that the cool air blew onto his horizontal body while he slept.

He took a deep breath and headed for the next landing. He could do this. He could make it. His own Mount Everest, with sleep only a few minutes away.

The black dots turned into a curtain and darkness engulfed him.

2

"IS HE DEAD?" Jimmy looked at his brother as he knelt over the body of the strange man.

Joey shrugged. "Dunno."

Jimmy sniffed and wiped his nose on his T-shirt. "Is he breathing?"

"Maybe." Joey pushed Alan's dark hair away from his forehead while Julie and Jimmy watched.

"*Now* what are you doing?"

"Looking for blood."

Julie bit her bottom lip, then turned big blue eyes upon her brothers. "I better call 911."

"No, dope. You better tell Raine," Joey ordered. "Hurry up."

The voices pierced the blackness that surrounded Alan. *I'm not dead*, he wanted to explain. *I'm just very tired.*

"This is really weird, seein' a guy on the stairs," a child's voice said. "Do you think Raine knows him?"

"I dunno. I think we'd better call the police. What if he was trying to rob us or something?"

"You mean he's a kidnapper? Wow!"

Alan wished his fogged brain could order his eyes to open and his lips to move. He didn't want to be in jail when he woke up.

A vibration under his face translated itself into footsteps and a woman's voice came closer. He heard her say, "Oh, no—what happened?" before he sank back into oblivion.

Raine hurried up the stairs, Donetta and Vanessa following close behind her.

"We don't know." Jimmy sniffed again. "We just found him."

Raine knelt down beside Alan and took his wrist, feeling for a pulse. Thank God, it was strong and steady under her fingertips.

Donetta peered over her shoulder. "You know him?"

"Yes." She felt his forehead. Warm, but not feverish. "He's, uh, a friend of the family who's going to be staying with us for a few days."

"Wow! He's not a robber?"

"Or a kidnapper?"

Raine smiled, despite her concern for the man who lay on her second-floor landing. "Neither. He's a guest."

"Think he's dead?" Jimmy asked once again, hoping this time he could get an answer.

"No. His pulse is strong."

"We heard a crash," Joey explained.

Raine noticed that the dining-room fan was a few steps down. "It looks like he fainted carrying the fan upstairs."

Joey looked horrified. "Men don't faint."

"Sure they do. But just in case, I think I'd better call a doctor." She smoothed the hair from Alan's forehead the same way the boy had. "He's not running a fever, but the heat may have affected him." Raine studied the man, sprawled on the landing as if he'd fallen asleep. He didn't look like an injured person. In fact, he looked extremely comfortable, as if he thought he was in a third-floor bedroom. What had he said earlier? Thirty hours without sleep and a bad case of jet lag?

"I think he just passed out," she declared. "Maybe the best thing would be to get him into a bed and let him rest."

"No 911?" Julie looked disappointed. "I wanted to see an ambulance."

"Not this time, hon. We'll elevate his legs and put a cool cloth on his head and see what happens. Donetta, go downstairs and get a bowl of ice and a washcloth. Boys, get me some pillows off your bed." Raine unlatched the door to the second floor and carefully opened it so as not to hit Alan. When Donetta, a tall ten-year-old, returned with the ice, Raine wrapped some cubes in the washcloth and turned Alan onto his side so she could put the cloth against his head. He moaned and rolled onto his back. Still, Raine decided, it wasn't a moan of pain but more of a sigh of contentment.

The boys raced back with pillows covered with colorful pictures of football players. Raine shoved pillows under Alan's legs and waited to see if her first aid had done any good.

The children stared, waiting too, willing the stranger to open his eyes. They didn't want to miss any of the drama going on right here on the back staircase.

"You're supposed to loosen his collar," Donetta said. "I saw that on TV."

"Right." Raine looked at the white buttons on Alan's shirt and the tanned neck above it. She managed to release two buttons and discovered a thin cotton undershirt beneath the silky fabric. Crisp, dark chest hair brushed her fingertips. "That's enough," she said, pulling back. She removed the cloth and took an ice cube and ran it along his face to soothe the heated skin.

"God, that's good, sweetheart," he groaned.

"Who's he calling 'sweetheart'?" Joey asked.

"I don't know." Raine shrugged, squelching her own curiosity.

"Maybe me," Julie chirped. "After all, I'm the one who found him."

"Did not," Joey said.

"Did, too."

"Dope!"

"Stop," Raine ordered. "Let's have some quiet here."

Alan opened his eyes and blinked. "Who are you?"

"Raine Claypoole."

Alan closed his eyes again. "Never mind. I know. I'm afraid it's all coming back to me. Where am I?"

"You're on the second-floor landing. Did you fall?"

He thought about her question for a long moment. "I don't know."

"Are you hurt?"

He opened his eyes and looked embarrassed. "No. I think I simply blacked out."

"Does this happen to you often?"

He rolled onto his back. "No. This is a first."

"You'd better get some rest."

"I thought that's what I was doing," he said, his mouth turning up slightly at the corners. It was a wonderful mouth, Raine noticed. And then wished she hadn't. Claire had sent him, but that didn't mean Raine wanted a husband.

"Maybe you'd be more comfortable in a bed. Can you walk?"

"I think so."

"Good. I can't get you up another flight of stairs, so I'm going to put you into a bedroom here on the second floor."

"No—I can make it."

"Well, I can't," she said, helping him up. "You weigh twice as much as I do."

He looked at the twins. "I think my vision..."

"You're not seeing double," she assured him, still holding his arm. "Meet Joey and Jimmy. Twins."

"Thank God." He eyed the rest of the children standing around him. "Where did you all come from?"

The children looked at him but didn't answer. Raine leaned over to take his arm underneath the elbow. "Come on. There's an extra room that hasn't been filled yet."

She guided him through the doorway, with the six children following them along the hall to a nearby room. Donetta hurried to turn the bedspread down before Alan reached the bed.

"Thanks," he said, as the child scurried away. "I think I can take it from here."

Raine released his arm, glad to stop touching him. "Are you sure?"

"Yes. This has been embarrassing enough."

Julie thrust the bowl towards him. "Here."

He took it and set it upon the nightstand. "I don't know whether to drink it or stick my head in it."

Raine put the pillows upon the bed. "I'll bring you an ice pack and a cold drink."

"Please, don't bother," Alan said, sitting down on the bed. He reached down and untied his shoes. "I'm going back to sleep."

Raine shut the shades, despite the fact that the sun was on the other side of the house, then shooed the children out of the room. She edged towards the door as he peeled off his socks.

"I still think I should call a doctor."

"I saw one three days ago," he said, his hands going to his shirtfront to undo the rest of his buttons. He seemed to be accustomed to undressing in front of women.

"Are you sick?" How would she explain to Edwina and Claire that the "perfectly lovely husband" was ill?

"Not really. It's a bad case of exhaustion. I'm afraid I planned my vacation about three weeks too late. I just need some rest." He smiled, once again the charming guest. "I'll be fine in a day or two, I promise."

"All right." Raine backed out of the room, but paused in the doorway. "If you need anything, just call out. I'll be in the kitchen for a while, if you need me, and the children sleep on this floor—one of them will hear you."

"I apologize for putting you through this much trouble."

"You don't have to apologize. Just call for help if you need it."

"I'll remember."

He leaned back and closed his eyes. Raine shut his door behind her and saw the children waiting. She put her finger to her lips. "You'll have to try to be quieter," she warned. "I don't think noise is going to bother him, but just in case, keep the music down."

"What about the doctor?"

"He already went to a doctor who told him he was tired."

"Why?"

"I don't know. I think he's been really busy in London."

"What's he do?"

"Works in a bank, I think. Come on, it's time to fix dinner. Who wants to help?"

Only one hand went up.

"I do," Donetta said, her voice low.

"Well, thank you." She looked at the rest of the sweaty group in front of her. "Everyone else find something quiet to do, either downstairs or outside."

"Can we use the back stairs?"

"Okay, but only for now. Come on," she said, herding them in that direction. The fan lay where Alan had dropped it, so Raine picked it up before any of the children could trip over the cord that lay over the treads.

"Why was he takin' the fan?"

"I told him he could. It's hot upstairs." Raine hesitated on the stairs. "You go on down. Have a Popsicle—that should hold you until dinner's ready."

"What are we having?"

Raine thought fast. "Hot dogs. Now go play or I'll put you all to work. Donetta, would you set the table? I'll be down in a minute."

She went back into the hall to Alan's closed door. She took a breath and turned the doorknob, pushing the door slightly so she could peek inside. He'd managed to remove his shoes and socks before falling asleep again. He lay stretched across the bed, his shirt unbuttoned to reveal a wide, tanned chest above the deep neckline of his undershirt.

She tiptoed inside. The room was dim and stuffy. She wondered when the weather would break. The breezes from the ocean were only halfhearted, and the island sweltered, unaccustomed to the stifling heat. She plugged the fan into a nearby outlet and turned it on, adjusting it to fan air onto the bed where Alan lay asleep.

What had Claire done, sending this man into her life? Now she was stuck—oh, that wasn't very nice, but if "stuck" didn't describe her feelings, she didn't know what did—with a sick man in her already overflowing house. A house filled with kids who needed her. She didn't need anyone else to take care of, thank you very much.

And this particular "sick man" was very appealing, even though a large chunk of masculinity, unconscious in her spare bedroom, wasn't usually her idea of something to look forward to. She preferred her men standing up, capable of uttering coherent sentences, with no prior knowledge of Claire Claypoole.

A perfectly lovely husband. Claire should see Alan Wetmore Hunter now. Neither lovely nor perfect, and definitely not husband material.

Raine tiptoed out of the room and shut the door quietly behind her. She would feed the children, maybe walk them downtown for ice-cream cones this evening, then put everyone to bed. Then she would sit down and balance the checkbook and figure out if she could afford to send Alan Hunter on his way to an air-conditioned motel room.

That is, if he woke up.

ALAN DIDN'T KNOW where he was. He drifted out of sleep gently. There was no buzz of an alarm clock or shrill telephone wake-up call from the front desk. He stretched, keeping his eyes closed, hoping he'd figure out his location before he opened them. The light beyond his eyelids told him it must be day. Sultry summer heat wrapped itself around his skin, along with a sheet.

He didn't know where he was, but he liked it.

Once he'd opened his eyes, he wasn't so sure. The day started to come back to him—the long flight, the traffic in Boston, and the ebony-haired woman with the big blue eyes—eyes with an expression that had said she'd rather he slept on the sidewalk. The silly, fluffy dog hadn't liked him, either.

There were no other sounds except a fan. He remembered wanting the fan. He sat up slowly, jamming a pillow behind his head against the iron headboard. A heavy, ivory shade covered the window, a tall, walnut dresser sat in the alcove between the corner of the room and the closet door. Everything in the room was tall and narrow—even the mirror above the dresser.

He looked around for his suitcases and didn't see them. Then he threw back the sheet and looked down in surprise. He still wore his pants. His white shirt lay in a heap on the ivory rug that covered a small portion of the wooden floor next to the bed.

All at once Alan remembered. But none of what he remembered made the least bit of sense.

"WHAT DAY IS IT?"

Raine jumped, startled to hear a man's voice behind her. She turned to see Alan standing in the door between the laundry room and the pantry, the two narrow areas that lay behind the kitchen. "Thursday."

He frowned. "Thursday? It can't be."

"Okay." She turned back to dumping clothes into the washing machine. "What day would you like it to be?"

He stepped farther into the room. "I slept for... twenty hours?"

She shut the lid of the washer and pushed the button to start the machine. "That's right."

"I can't remember the last time I slept like that."

"You must have needed the rest."

"Yes," Alan agreed. "I suppose so." He shoved his hands into his pockets. "I remember being surrounded by children. Did that happen?"

"Yes. They found you on the stairs and then called me."

"How, uh, did I get undressed and into bed?"

Raine wanted to smile, but she didn't. "I helped you into bed. You did the undressing yourself."

"Oh."

"Disappointed?"

"Definitely." He grinned. "My fantasy life was in high gear for a while."

"Sorry."

"Where are the kids?"

"They're at playground day camp."

"I really didn't imagine them, then?"

"No," she repeated. Despite the fact that he was conscious, he was still pale. The man needed a few days in the sun. "I was just going to have lunch. Would you like a sandwich?"

He looked relieved. "I'm starving. I've been wondering if this time I'd faint from hunger."

"You should have said something. I would have brought you a tray."

"Should I clean up first?"

Raine shook her head. She preferred the unshaven, scruffy look. For now he didn't look like a high-powered banker or a perfectly lovely husband. "No."

He grinned, rubbing one hand over his cheek. "Now I know I'm on vacation."

"I thought you were in Newport on business."

"In one respect," he said, following her into the kitchen. "I have an important legal matter to clear up."

She sensed the rest was confidential, so didn't push. Instead she told him to sit down at the narrow trestle table while she made thick turkey sandwiches.

"Root beer, Diet Coke or iced tea?"

"Root beer."

She fixed an oversize glass with ice cubes and set the glass and a can of root beer in front of him, along with a paper plate filled with the sandwich and a handful of potato chips.

"Start," she said. "Don't wait for me." She slid the salt shaker and pine napkin holder in front of him, then arranged her own lunch. By the time she sat down across from him, Alan had eaten half his sandwich and all of the chips, so Raine stood up again, grabbed the extra sandwich and the bag of Ruffles and put them in front of him.

"When was the last time you ate?"

"I don't remember."

Raine could believe it. He ate like someone who had just washed up onshore after a shipwreck. She sipped her iced tea and nibbled on half a sandwich while she watched Alan empty the plate in front of him. When he'd demolished another sandwich and drained his glass of root beer, Raine attempted another question. "Do you work in London?"

"Yes. Or rather, I used to."

Either he was a very quiet man or he was very good at keeping information to himself. "Used to? Did you lose your job?"

He looked shocked. "Of course not. Why on earth would you think—?"

"Because you didn't say anything about yourself," she explained. "You don't remember the last time you ate, you don't say what you do or where you work, and you passed out on my stairs yesterday afternoon. You're very mysterious. And you must be under a lot of stress."

He leaned back in his chair and started to laugh. "I've never been called mysterious," he said, his dark eyes twinkling at her. "I have four younger sisters. They know everything about me and always have."

"Do they know why you're here in Newport?"

"I'm sure they've been told." He leaned forward. "Look, Raine, I'm sorry. We got off on the wrong foot yesterday. Maybe we could start over."

She shook her head. "You don't understand. You don't know why you're here, do you?"

"Of course I do. I paid a high sum, too."

"I'm not talking about why you're here in this house, although I guess that's exactly what I'm talking about."

"Are you going to eat that?"

Raine pushed her plate away with the uneaten half sandwich. "Go ahead."

He took it. "All right, I give up. Why am I here?"

"Claire and Edwina have decided I need a husband." Raine didn't like saying it out loud like that, but there was really no choice.

"Edwina. My mother, you mean?" He looked blank.

"Yes. A 'perfectly lovely husband,' Claire said." Men, for all their wonderful qualities, were sometimes not really very bright, when it came right down to subtle meanings.

He swallowed. "And?"

"She was describing you."

Alan choked. Raine stood up and pounded him on the back.

"Better?"

He took a deep breath and nodded. When he had himself under control, he studied Raine with a more serious expression. "She must have been joking."

"I don't think so."

"They couldn't possibly have thought..."

"That's why you have to leave. I can give you your money back in a couple of weeks. In fact, I can give you some of it today. I wrote a check." She stood up again, retrieved her checkbook from her purse and sat back down at the table. She ripped out the check and handed it to him.

He took it and looked at the figure. "This is only one week's worth."

"I know. It's the best I can do."

He handed it back to her. "Look, I don't want to be here if it's a big inconvenience for you. But it's July in Newport—the height of the season—and I may need a few days to find something else. I'd rather stay here. I'll even buy a small air conditioner and put it in one of the third-floor rooms because I'm tired of hotels."

Raine hardened her heart so she wouldn't feel sorry for him. "You're being set up. Whether you realize it or not, your life is no longer in your control."

He smiled. "I doubt the situation is that serious. Claire and my mother may have wanted us to meet, but I doubt that this is a full-blown matchmaking attempt."

"Not an *attempt*," she stated. "It's a scheme. A plan.

A plot. And you're falling right into their hands by staying here."

He didn't look as though he understood anything. "This is the nineties. No more arranged marriages, remember?"

"Claire has it all figured out."

"We're supposed to look at each other, fall in love and live happily ever after?" He shook his head. "That's storybook nonsense, and we both know life doesn't work that way."

"Tell the old ladies. I know Claire, and I know what she's capable of doing."

"And I know my mother. She's a sweet woman who never meddles in my life."

"No? You look like a man who makes his own reservations. Why didn't you rent a room at the Viking or take a cottage for the summer?"

He frowned. "I'd planned to, until I heard about an upstairs apartment off Bellevue Avenue."

"And where did you hear it from?"

"My secretary. Who talked to my mother."

"Right. And I'll bet she made all the arrangements, didn't she?"

His expression told her she'd hit pay dirt. "This is ridiculous!" he protested.

"I'm warning you. I've been dealing with Claire's plans since I was a teenager, when she married my father. She likes to rearrange other people's lives. It's a hobby, or maybe it could be called a compulsion, I don't know."

"Why hasn't she found you a perfectly, uh, lovely husband before now?"

"She's tried."

"Well, you've managed to defend yourself so far."

"She never sent one to the house before."

"Look, you're a perfectly lovely woman yourself. And although it would be tempting to climb between the sheets with you and spend some time sampling that perfectly lovely body of yours, I don't have the time or the inclination."

"You're gay?"

"Don't look so relieved. Not *that* inclination—I'm taking about sex with a woman who lives with a bunch of kids and a dog who looks like a cat. A woman who thinks every man who knocks on her door has been sent by her stepmother to marry her." He stood up and pushed back his chair. "I really don't think you're my type."

"Thank God."

"What?"

"Then you'll leave." She pushed the check back to him. "That's great."

"I'm not going anywhere." He ignored the slip of paper. "Except downtown to buy an air conditioner for my 'apartment.'"

"Look," she began again. "Be reasonable."

"Reasonable? *Reasonable?* I've paid to live here, at least for the next three weeks, with an option for three more if I want. That includes two meals a day—lunch and dinner." He looked at his watch and then back at Raine. "What time is dinner?"

"Six, but..."

He nodded. "Fine. In that case, I'd better get busy. I have a lot to do today."

Raine watched him leave the kitchen and heard his steps on the stairs. She picked up the check, soggy from sitting in a puddle left by the root-beer glass. The ink ran, blurring her signature in the corner. She'd tried to warn Alan Wetmore Hunter of the danger he was in. But had he listened? No.

Hardheaded, Raine decided, crumpling the check into a ball and tossing it toward the garbage can in the corner of the room. Wasn't it just like a man to ignore the obvious dangers and rush headfirst into trouble?

3

"JUST WANTED YOU TO KNOW I've talked to my supervisor. We're pushing for a termination hearing as soon as we can get a court date."

"Thanks for telling me, Mindy." Raine tucked the phone under her ear and leaned against the kitchen counter. "You know how I feel about those kids. They were my first foster children and we've been through a lot together."

"I'll be on vacation for a couple of days, but I'm going to write up the summary report, and hopefully the judge will approve the petition the first time around."

"And then?"

"Adoption, but we'll cross that bridge when we come to it. I'm even trying to be transferred into that unit, so keep your fingers crossed for me."

"You'll have to give me plenty of warning if they're to be adopted. It's going to be hard to part with those three."

"Don't worry. They're all set with you for the time being, and we won't be in any hurry to find anything less than perfect."

"Okay." Somehow Raine didn't feel any better. The thought of saying goodbye to Joey, Jimmy and Julie made her want to cry. "I'm getting ready for the boys' birthday party. They'll all be back from camp in an hour. Lily should be back any minute—she's been visiting with her new family for the past three days."

"How's that going?"

"Great." Raine smiled to herself. "They're good people and Lily's starting to get attached to them."

"We're still set for permanent placement next week, I hear. Holly's picking her up Monday?"

"Yes. At ten."

"You going to be okay with that?"

"It's never easy to say goodbye to any of them."

"This is a tough business."

"No kidding."

"Maybe that handsome tenant of yours will be around to take your mind off things."

"Don't tease, Mindy. He's not my type."

"That's the most ridiculous thing you've ever said."

Raine chuckled. "I have to finish wrapping presents for the boys' party. They requested a picnic, so we're heading over to Ten Mile Drive."

"Well, have fun."

"We will," Raine promised. She hung up the phone and surveyed the gifts spread on the kitchen table. She'd bought two of everything, only in different colors. Three years ago, when they'd felt comfortable enough in the house to tell Raine anything at all, they'd told her that they preferred it that way. Two plastic warrior turtles, two G.I. Joe action figures, two neon bathing suits, and two green and white T-shirts with Boston Celtics splashed across the fronts needed to be wrapped.

Two of everything was what the children needed. Including two parents. Mom and Dad. She couldn't provide that, no matter what she did. At least not now. She wasn't even dating anyone. There were no male role models around, either. Quentin was a fantastic uncle, but he wasn't here much. His rock and roll band kept making music and giving concerts.

Raine wished she could keep the three children with her always, but would that be the best thing? She knew that lots of foster parents adopted the children in their care. Half the kids in the state never made it up for adoption because the foster families kept them. But she was a twenty-eight-year-old single woman.

And the children, especially the twins, needed a father.

Raine swallowed hard and reached for the wrapping paper. She had a lot of thinking to do, but it boiled down to what was best for the children.

When Charlie barked at the front door, Raine had finished wrapping the last of the presents. The Damons, a young black couple, stood on the porch.

"Hi. Come on in." Raine opened the door and the Damons stepped inside. Lily, a chubby toddler with dark eyes and drooling grin, clung to the woman who held her in her arms.

"Did you have fun with your Mommy and Daddy?"

Janet reluctantly handed over the toddler to Raine. "I can't wait until next week. This visiting process is starting to get to me."

"I'm glad she's had time to adjust to the change," Raine said. "Remember how shy she was the first few times?"

Bob Damon set down the diaper bag on the tiled floor. "We're going away for the weekend," he announced, smiling at his wife. "Our last trip before we become parents."

"Bob tells me it will make the time go by faster," Janet added.

"What a wonderful idea." Raine winced when Lily

tugged a lock of her hair. "Monday will be here before you know it. The social worker is bringing her to you, so I'll have to say goodbye now. I'm sure you and Lily will be very happy together."

Janet's eyes filled with tears. "Thank you for taking such good care of her."

"We've all loved her. We're going to miss you, aren't we, Lily?" The child giggled.

"Rain, rain," she chanted. "Go."

"You'll go next week, go with Mommy and Daddy." Raine and Lily waved goodbye to her future parents. Then Raine kissed the baby's soft cheek. "Want to go swimming today?"

"Beach!"

"That's right, angel. Won't we have fun?"

"THERE HAS TO BE a way out of this."

The young attorney, his dark hair carefully combed back from his forehead, shook his head. "I'm sorry, Mr. Hunter, but I don't think that's necessarily true."

"You're going to sit there and tell me there is no way to get around a thirty-year-old will?"

He shook his head and tapped the papers in front of him. "Your grandfather was very specific."

"My grandfather was crazy," Alan muttered.

"Not legally."

"No," Alan agreed. "Not legally. This idea must have made sense in 1959, when I was four years old."

"It's actually not all that uncommon, Mr. Hunter. My father handled many unusual cases in his day."

"Which you inherited."

The young man almost smiled. "Yes. My father retired several years ago. He's probably out sailing on the bay this very minute. Do you sail, sir?"

"No." Alan preferred to swim in the water instead of gliding on top of it. "Are there any of the original lawyers left?"

"Just Benjamin Atwater. He works one afternoon a week, to keep his fingers in the pie, so to speak."

So to speak. "That name sounds familiar."

"I believe he and your grandfather enjoyed playing golf together many years ago."

Alan leaned forward. "Is this one of those situations where my lawyers meet with you for months—maybe years—to settle this will?"

The man sighed. "I sincerely hope not. That would be a big waste of time and money for all of us, and I would rather spend my time on the bay. Why don't you talk to Benjamin? He's visiting his nephew in Wyoming for a few weeks. I can call you when he returns. Maybe he'll have an idea where we could go with all of this."

"I don't want to lose the property," Alan stated.

The man shrugged. "Your grandfather was very specific. Twenty-five years after his death, the oldest married grandson was to inherit everything. Or the estate reverts to the state of Rhode Island." He snapped the file shut.

"I'm the *only* grandson," Alan growled, "and I'm not married."

Jonathan D. Horton III spread his hands, palms up, in a gesture of surrender. He grinned, as if he'd just thought of something funny. "Then maybe you'd better find a wife."

Alan stood up, unamused by the comment. "I'll make an appointment with Ben Atwater."

"Talk to Mrs. Murray at the reception desk. She'll contact you when he returns."

"Fine." The two men shook hands. When Alan left

the discreet brick building, a blast of heat hit him full force. He stood near the harbor, beside the Brick Marketplace. Across the narrow street lay the wharves and another area of warehouses renovated into shops. He was tempted to wander through the marketplace, but the heat deterred him. He hadn't forgotten the strange weakness he'd experienced on the Claypoole landing. He'd felt fine when he'd returned the rental car and walked to the lawyer's office, but the return trip was all uphill to Bellevue Avenue and Raine's house.

Disgusted with the lack of progress this afternoon, Alan shoved his hands into his pockets and headed up the hill. He'd had few illusions about easily wrapping up the legal process concerning the will. His own lawyers had warned him, but he'd decided to take matters into his own hands. He hated taking so much time from work, but he would settle the problems here—even if it took him the entire summer.

"HERE, HONEY BUN," she crooned. "It's so nice to have you back."

Alan, having entered the house without Charlie noticing, stopped in his tracks and peered into the kitchen. "What?"

Raine, kneeling on the floor beside Lily, looked up and flushed. "I wasn't talking to you."

Alan smiled. "I didn't think so." The thought of his mother trying to match him with Raine Claypoole still struck him as hilarious—as if he'd entangle himself with a woman like Raine, however beautiful she was. And all those children. He shuddered.

"How are you feeling?"

"Fine," he replied. "Mind if I join you?"

"Come on in. We're waiting here for the rest of the

kids. They should be back from day camp any minute."
Raine lifted the chubby toddler into a high chair and
tucked a bib around her neck. "There you go, Lily
May." She scattered a handful of Cheerios on the tray
and the baby picked one up carefully between two
chubby fingers and popped it into her mouth.

Alan pulled up a chair and sat down at the table.
"Aren't you going to introduce me?"

The baby's eyes widened at the sound of the strange
voice, and she craned her neck to see who was speaking.
Her big, dark eyes remained wide as she assessed the
stranger.

"This is Lily. She's almost one."

"Hello, Lily."

The baby picked up more Cheerios and reached toward Alan. He took a bit of cereal. "Thank you."

Lily grinned and reached again, her palm open.

"I think you're supposed to give it back now," Raine
suggested.

"I realize that." He handed the piece of Cheerios back
to the baby. "I happen to be an uncle."

Lily banged on the table. "Rain, rain!"

Raine put another handful of Cheerios onto the tray.
"That's it until dinnertime," she stated, then turned
back to Alan. "Lily is going to live with her new parents
next week. She's a very lucky girl."

"Is it hard to give her up?"

Raine swallowed and looked away. "Yes, but that's
part of my job. Knowing Lily is going to have a wonderful new family really helps."

"Do you really take care of six children?"

"Yep."

He gulped. "That's a lot of kids. How did you get into
this kind of, uh, work?"

"I collected college degrees for a while, trying to decide what I wanted to do with my life." She smiled. "It took me a while, but I realized I loved working with children. So I became a second-grade teacher in a private school in New York, but it wasn't exactly the way I envisioned it to be."

"And?" he prompted, curious why a beautiful young woman would turn away from New York and hole up in Newport with a house full of homeless kids.

"Aunt Gertrude left me this house and I decided—in two seconds flat—to move to Newport. I applied for teaching jobs on the island and ended up substituting until one of my new neighbors suggested I think about foster care. So I trained, got my license, and have been taking in children ever since."

"How long is that?"

"Three years."

"That's a long time." Not that there was anything wrong with children. It was the sheer quantity that shocked him. Although Raine's blue eyes, silky black hair, long eyelashes and neat little body could certainly tempt a man, there were a lot of reasons to take two steps backward. Thanks, but no thanks.

"Yes, it is."

Alan looked around the kitchen as Raine began stacking food on the counter. "This place reminds me a little of my grandfather's house." He wondered if he'd ever own it. The thought of the property reverting to the state made him tighten his lips into a thin line.

"I like old houses." Raine counted the slices of bread, then opened the oversize jar of grape jelly.

"You look as if you're getting ready to go somewhere."

"A picnic," she answered. "If you really have your

heart set on two meals a day, then you can join us. If not, feel free to stay here and order a pizza."

"I'll stay."

She didn't look surprised. "I can leave a couple of sandwiches for you. What do you prefer—tuna or peanut butter?"

"Tuna." He noticed the birthday cake on the counter. "Whose birthday?"

"The twins."

"The boys who thought I was dead?"

"Exactly. They're turning eight today, and having a picnic is their idea of heaven."

"I haven't been on a picnic in...many years."

"Your work keeps you that busy?"

He thought for a minute. "Yes, I guess it does. But I like it that way. I've always enjoyed traveling, especially in Europe."

"So, what brings you back here?"

"To the States?" At her nod, he continued. "The end of a very large project. And just in time, too." He smiled at the toddler across the table. "I have business to take care of here in Newport, and you know I needed a vacation."

"You'll have to call your mother off," she said, plopping sandwiches into small plastic bags.

"I will," he assured her.

"I've tried to call Claire, but I keep getting her answering machine."

"If she's as determined as you say she is, why bother calling her at all?"

"To tell her that you're not interested in me. She may accept that and leave you alone."

"And if she doesn't?"

"Then I have to think of a way to keep her out of Newport."

"Don't worry. My mother always spends the summer with my sister—the married one with the grandchildren—in the Hamptons."

"I hope you're right."

The doorbell rang, and Charlie barked furiously from the living room. "I'll get it," Alan offered. "I'm expecting a delivery."

Raine shot him a grateful look. "Thanks." She was too busy to wonder what he would be expecting. Some official documents, she supposed. She was amazed he didn't travel with a fax machine—at least, she hadn't seen him carry one in from his car.

"Bye, bye," Lily called.

"Bye, sweetheart," he said.

What was going on here? Busy banking types didn't play with strangers' babies. He was charming, that was certain. Claire had said he would be.

Raine opened the cupboard and took out a stack of plastic cups. She'd be glad to get away for a few hours. The children's footsteps pounded through the house. "I'm in the kitchen," she called, but they had already burst through the door. "Hi. Did you have a fun day?"

"Raine, guess what!"

"What, Joey?"

"We had a shaving-cream fight!"

Raine set a bag of ice cubes in the bottom of a large blue and white insulated cooler. "A shaving-cream fight? With the counselors?"

Jimmy nodded. "Yeah. It was so cool."

Donetta turned up her nose. "It was disgusting. I pretended I didn't know them."

"So, what did you do while they were playing with the shaving cream?"

"I was with my friends playing the mall game."

"Oh," said Raine, suppressing a smile. "That sounds fun, too." The boys' clothes were streaked with water, their blue T-shirts grimy from playground dust. Julie, who didn't look much cleaner than her older brothers, tugged on Raine's arm.

"It was so funny." She giggled. "They put the stuff on top of their heads."

Raine bent down and gave her a hug. "Where's Vanessa?"

"Holding Charlie. The man—you know, the sick one—he's getting a present."

"He is?"

"Yep. Van wanted to watch."

Joey danced around Raine. "What about the party? Can we have our party now?"

"Sure, we can. Go put your bathing suits on, get your beach towels off the clothesline and don't forget to go to the bathroom."

"Hurray!" the boys cried. Donetta and Julie raced them out the door. Raine picked up Lily and went through the dining room to find Vanessa. A shy five-year-old, she tended to forget where she was supposed to be or what she was supposed to be doing. This time she was sitting on one of the new couches, Charlie curled up in her lap. When she saw Raine and Lily, she smiled.

"Hi, Van. I heard you had fun at camp today." The little girl nodded, her long dark hair swinging across her shoulders. Sometimes Raine thought the child looked Asian, with her dark, almond-shaped eyes and straight hair. "Charlie can't be up on the new couches, remember?"

Vanessa lifted the tiny dog from her lap and set him upon the carpet. "Charlie likes the couch."

"I know he does, but he'll lie down in his chair."

They watched as the tiny dog tossed them a dirty look and hopped into the rocker. He curled up, rested his head upon his paws and closed his eyes.

"We're going on a birthday picnic, remember?" Vanessa shook her head. "Well, we are. Go get your bathing suit on."

Alan entered the living room and Vanessa stopped short.

"Did you get your package?"

"Package?"

"Didn't you just have something delivered?"

"Oh," he said. "Yes. Who's this? Another one of your children?"

"Yes. Vanessa, this is Mr. Hunter. He's visiting here at the house for a while."

Vanessa stared at him, then hurried out of the room.

"Bashful, isn't she?"

"Vanessa's been with me for six months now, but she doesn't like to speak. I don't know if she's shy or afraid."

"Where are her parents?"

"That's anybody's guess." Raine lowered her voice. "Vanessa's mother has been in and out of prison. She's out now, but no one's seen her in months. Whenever she reappears, the state attempts reunification."

Alan sat down on the couch and Charlie came over to his feet and growled. "Why does this dog hate me?"

"I think he's just being very protective."

"Well, tell him I'm not going to touch you."

"Charlie, go away." The dog trotted off to the kitchen.

Alan put his hands behind his head. "You were telling me about Vanessa. What's reunification?"

"That's when they attempt to reunite the children and the parents—to live happily ever after."

"You don't sound convinced."

Raine hesitated in the doorway. "I get that way sometimes. Sometimes it's hard to believe that the kids will go back home and live happily ever after."

"You have a very strange job."

"You're right." She smiled. "And I have to get back to it. See you later."

Ten minutes later the children were tucked inside the minivan, along with two coolers and a paper bag stuffed with picnic gear. She'd told the boys that candles wouldn't work near the ocean, so they'd consented to save dessert until they were back home again. Raine climbed behind the wheel, slammed the door and felt as if she'd been set free.

She had been, actually. From Alan Hunter and his lethal charm. She'd met enough men like him to last her a lifetime. So many, in fact, that she considered herself immune. The Wetmore Hunters of the world were wealthy, handsome, charming and confident—and not at all the kind of men Raine wanted for a mate. She wanted a down-to-earth guy who would put the family before making money, a man who would be faithful to her and would think a recliner and a television set with a twenty-seven-inch screen were the ultimate in home decorating.

She wanted a man who'd want her—with her children and her house and her secret, silly dreams of happily ever after.

But not Alan Hunter.

"WHAT ABOUT THAT GUY?" Joey set a bag of garbage upon the counter.

"He's probably upstairs," Raine said, lugging the cooler into the kitchen and putting it onto the floor in front of the sink. Everyone was sandy and covered with salt after two hours of playing by the ocean.

"Can he come to my party?"

"I don't know," Raine stalled. Then she saw the disappointment on the boy's face. "I'll ask him, but you and Jimmy need to get into the shower right away. No cake or presents until everyone is clean and in their pajamas!"

"Aww!"

"I'll set the table and put Lily to bed and we'll be ready for a party in no time at all, you'll see." Raine took the baby out of Donetta's arms and shooed the rest of the children out of the kitchen. Lily was half-asleep, so Raine quickly readied her for bed and popped her into the crib. The child had had quite enough excitement for one day. Then, remembering her promise to Joey, she hurried upstairs to the third floor.

The door to one of the rooms was closed, but a loud, humming sound came from behind the walnut door. It didn't sound like a regular fan. Raine knocked quietly on the door, then called, "Alan?"

In a minute she heard a muffled sound, so she called his name again.

"Just a minute," he called back. Then he opened the door; Raine opened her mouth but no sound came out. He looked as if he had hastily pulled on a pair of light khaki slacks, because the waistband was undone. His chest was covered with a mat of dark hair. His shoulders were as Claire had described them, broad and nicely defined. All in all, he did not look like a man who spent his days counting money behind a desk.

"Excuse me," she began, then felt cold air hit her face.

"Come on in," he said. "You're letting the heat in."

Her gaze went to the large appliance in the window. "You bought an air conditioner?"

"I told you I was going to."

"I said no."

"No, I don't think you did. You offered me a fan."

Raine tried to remember the conversation, but couldn't recall the exact words. "Is this what you had delivered?"

"Yes. I even had it professionally installed, so there would be no problems. I have no intention of living in an oven for the rest of the summer."

"The rest of the summer? I thought you were only going to be here a few weeks."

"It depends," Alan said. "Now, what can I do for you?"

"You're welcome to join us for birthday cake. The party is about to begin."

"Great." He reached for the shirt hanging on a hanger on the doorknob. "I'll be right down."

"You don't have to if you don't want to," she said, stepping back.

"I want to thank the kids for helping me yesterday," he assured her. "Are there any others I haven't met yet?"

"Probably, so brace yourself."

The children jumped around the kitchen, while Donetta poured punch and Julie arranged paper napkins on the table. Her little helpers, Raine thought, were always trying to make themselves useful.

"Is that man coming?" Joey asked, sliding into his seat.

"Yes."

"Great! Is he still sick?"

"No, I don't think so." Raine grabbed a box of candles and proceeded to arrange eight on one side of the cake, then started in on the other side. Eight each, so they could each blow out an equal number and declare an official wish.

"Can I blow out candles, too?"

Raine looked down at Julie. "Not until your birthday."

"In October?"

"That's right."

"Joey, sit down beside Jim and settle down."

"Move over, butt-head," the boy told his brother.

"Watch your mouth," Raine warned, standing on tiptoe to reach the book of matches she kept stashed above the stove. "And behave yourselves, especially in front of company." She turned around and saw Alan enter the room.

"Happy birthday," he said to the boys.

Jimmy grinned at him. "You didn't die, huh?"

"Not that I know of," Alan said, looking at the children seated around the table. "Aren't you missing someone?"

"Lily's in bed already. She's had a busy day." Raine pointed to a seat at the foot of the table. "Sit down and I'll let the children introduce themselves."

Alan smiled at Vanessa. "I know you, don't I?" The child simply stared at him without saying anything. Alan looked at Donetta. "You're the young lady who brought the ice pack, aren't you?"

Donetta nodded. "Yes. I'm Donetta."

"Thanks for the help." The girl shrugged, unsure of what to do around a stranger. The boys wiggled on their seats.

"We found you on the stairs and we were gonna dial 911, like the television show, but Raine came and said we didn't have to because you weren't dead and you didn't have a heart attack—"

"And you were just sleeping or else you fainted, but men don't faint, do they?" Joey interjected.

Alan looked surprised. "I'm sure they do, although maybe they don't talk about it much."

"You haven't met Julie, the boys' younger sister," Raine said. "Julie, this is Mr. Hunter."

"Call me Alan," he told the children. "It's easier."

Julie edged closer to Alan and looked up at him with wide, blue eyes. "Are you a daddy?"

"Uh, no."

Do you know how?"

"Probably. Why?"

"I need one."

"Jeez, Julie, shut your face," Joey commanded.

"Don't be such a dope." Jimmy groaned.

"That's enough," Raine warned the three of them as she lighted the candles. "We're going to sing 'Happy Birthday' now." Donetta turned the overhead lights off, then moved into a chair, then Raine set the cake upon the table in front of the boys.

"Ready?" The children nodded. So did Alan. Raine began the song and everyone joined in. When it was over, the boys leaned forward, blew out their candles in two identical gusts and grinned.

Raine wondered what they were up to. "Did you make a wish?"

"Yep."

"Yep."

"Good." She hoped it was something that could come true. Raine took her seat at the head of the table and scooted the pile of paper plates closer to her. "I'll cut the cake. Birthday boys get theirs first."

"Yay!" the boys yelled.

The next hour was a noisy combination of chocolate frosting, wrapping paper, homemade cards and spilled punch. The boys ripped the paper off their presents and exclaimed their pleasure over every gift.

Charlie paced underneath the table, hoping cake crumbs would fall. Occasionally he barked, hoping Raine would feel sorry for him and share a piece of cake. The boys donned their new T-shirts over their pajamas and insisted on sleeping in them. They loved the action figures and the plastic turtle warriors, ate two pieces of cake each and hugged everyone at the table. They were shocked speechless when Alan handed them envelopes with a five-dollar bill tucked inside each one.

Raine finally sent everyone upstairs to bed, with instructions to be quiet and not wake Lily. "I'll be up in ten minutes to tuck you in," she promised.

"That was quite a party," Alan said, leaning back in his chair. "Is it always like this?"

"Like what?"

"Chaos."

She frowned at him and stood up to clear the table. "I wouldn't call it chaos exactly. It's just, well, it's just the way it is with six kids."

"And a dog that looks like the working end of a mop."

Raine smiled, balancing a handful of sticky plates. "A very small mop." She dumped everything into the garbage can in the corner and returned to the table for another load.

"Why do you do this?" Alan stood up, walked to the garbage can and carried it back to the table. "There," he said. "It will save you some trips."

"Thanks. Why do I do what?"

"Take care of other people's kids."

"I love children. Why is that such a crime?"

"That's not what I meant. Your father was one of the richest men in New York."

"Meaning I must have a hefty trust fund that supports me, and allows me to have anything I want for the rest of my life?"

"Your father was a very successful man. I'll bet he never dreamed you'd have to support yourself by changing diapers and taking in kids."

"I don't think my father ever thought about it one way or another. Making money was the only thing he cared about."

"It's not a crime to make money, Raine."

"I forgot. That's what you do for a living, isn't it? Investments or something?"

"Yes, but—"

Raine went to the sink and grabbed the sponge. "The only thing I inherited was this house, from Aunt Gertrude. My mother died when I was a child, leaving me a small trust fund that pays the taxes and some of the utilities, but nothing else. I didn't want my father's money. I support myself," she declared, wiping the tabletop. "And I like it that way."

4

"HE'S NOT PLEASED WITH ME," Edwina told her friend. She hung up the phone and looked out the window toward the golf course. "Not pleased at all."

"He'll be fine," Claire assured her, holding out one tiny, veined hand. "Do you think I should have this ring reset?"

Wina studied the oversize gold band studded with diamonds. "It *is* slightly, mmm, showy. Are you thinking of something simpler?"

Claire put her hand down and drummed her fingertips on the glass tabletop. "I'm thinking of something quite complicated. I remember an excellent jeweler in Newport, on Thames Street. In fact, I can't possibly imagine trusting these diamonds to anyone else."

"Oh, no, you don't. I'm already in trouble with my son. He's accused me of meddling, which I've never done before."

"Not to him. But what about the girls?"

Edwina grimaced. "Daughters are fair game."

"It's different with boys?"

"Of course. They get so irritable and touchy."

Claire sniffed, obviously thinking that "irritable" and "touchy" people were minor matters to deal with. "I thought asking Alan to watch over her was a nice touch."

Edwina brightened. "It was, wasn't it? Especially

when I mentioned we might have to come to Rhode Island and check up on my son's health *and* your overworked, fragile stepdaughter."

Claire chuckled. "He didn't want us descending upon him, did he?"

"Alan's a private person," his mother said. "He's always been that way."

"He's about to change, then, isn't he?"

"I don't know, Claire. He didn't sound too pleased."

"She's perfect for him. He needs livening up."

"You don't even know him!"

Claire looked at her and sighed. "Well, does he or doesn't he need some excitement?"

Edwina pretended to think about it. "He does," she finally admitted. "He's going to turn into an old man before his time, stuck in his ways, giving his entire life to his work and living alone."

"Not anymore," Claire assured her. "Everything is falling into place quite nicely."

"Do you really think so?"

"Trust me," Claire declared. She held her hand up again. "Now, what do you think? Should I change to white gold?"

ALAN SHOULD HAVE KNOWN his mother was up to something. His sisters had warned him, but he hadn't taken it seriously.

Not until now. Not until Raine.

So, the old women were now attempting blackmail. *Take care of Raine or we'll arrive in Newport ourselves.* Which didn't matter to him at all. He'd planned on visiting his family in a few months. He'd spent Christmas in Denver with Stephanie and her brood, along with everyone else, six months ago. His mother had looked radiant and contented and only slightly curious about the women in his life.

Women. As if there were hundreds. He'd dated some interesting, ambitious women and become lovers with several. But there'd always been something missing. The women he'd met either protected their independence with savage ferocity, to the point of no compromise, or had looked upon him as the answer to their prayers, making him feel as if he had Rich Husband branded all over him.

He had no plans to be anyone's husband.

His last months in London had been hectic—he'd spent so much time flying between London and Moscow, he'd been relieved that he didn't have a woman in his life. Now he didn't know what he wanted anymore, or even if a woman with warmth, intelligence and humor existed anywhere. Especially one who could handle the jobs of hostess and traveling companion with sophistication and class.

Alan almost wished he'd continued talking to his mother. She usually made him laugh, even when she was interfering in his life. And it was only right, he decided as he headed downstairs, to admit to Raine that she'd been right all along.

"IF WE DON'T GET THERE early it's going to be too crowded, so eat your breakfast and then get your bathing suits off the line." Raine, dressed in a long shirt and sandals, handed the twins cereal bowls and spoons.

"Get where?" Alan asked.

"To the beach. You left your air-conditioned room? Your computer and your telephone? A miracle."

"For now," he admitted. "I was lonesome."

She shot him an amused look. "Right."

"Really," he insisted. "I've been working so long, I think I've forgotten what I used to do in my spare time." He looked around the kitchen at the piles of sandwiches and bags of potato chips. "Having another birthday party?"

"No. Just lunch."

"Sounds like fun," he hinted. Maybe if he spent the day with her he could report to Edwina and Claire that Raine was in good health—at least physically. The mental part he wouldn't even try to hazard a guess about.

She didn't pick up the hint. "Should be. Damn."

"What?"

"I'm out of bread."

"You must spend a lot of time in the grocery store."

"More than I'd like, that's for sure."

"I can go get you a loaf of bread, if you like."

"You?"

"Why not? Isn't there a store right down the street?"

"Yes, but you don't look like the kind of man who knows his way around a supermarket."

He pretended to be hurt, smiling at her surprise. "I've been a bachelor a long time. I didn't starve." Barely, he amended silently.

Donetta sat on the end of the long counter, swinging her legs and talking on the phone. The boys ate cereal at the table, while Lily sat in her high chair, banging her chubby palms on the plastic tray and screeching. The two other little girls were nowhere to be seen, but he heard shrieks from the backyard. Charlie didn't leap from underneath the table and growl, so Alan assumed he was outside guarding the girls.

"Thanks, anyway, but I think there's enough for lunch, after all." She looked over her shoulder at him as he poured himself a cup of coffee from the carafe on the counter. He edged carefully past Donetta's swinging feet and took a seat at the table.

"You coming with us?" Joey asked. He lifted the cereal bowl and drank the rest of the milk.

"I don't—"

"Yeah," Jimmy added. "Are you? That'd be cool."

"Well..." He looked at Raine. "Mind if I tag along with you?" Accustomed to a busy schedule and hectic life-style, Alan was tired of his room. Despite the frequent telephone calls from the office, he missed having adults to talk to. Going to the beach with Raine would have to do for now. He'd also get some exercise and fresh air, two things the doctor had advised.

"It could be a very long day," she said, hoping he'd say no, but hoping for the boys' sake that he'd agree to go. They didn't get much time with men.

"I need the exercise."

"True, but you may prefer peace and quiet."

"I can find a quiet place on the beach."

Raine gave up the argument. He'd learn there were no quiet places on the beach, especially on a Sunday morning in July. "Peanut butter or ham?"

"Ham. Extra mustard. What time are you leaving?"

Raine shrugged. "Whenever we get ready. Sometimes it takes longer than others."

He looked at his watch. "It's eight o'clock now. Eight-thirty departure time?"

"I don't know. We'll leave when we get in the car."

"Which should take how long?"

Raine put down the box of plastic sandwich bags and turned to face the man at the table. "Why don't you relax, enjoy your coffee, have some breakfast, and then get ready for the beach? We'll leave when we leave."

He grimaced. "I'm having trouble slowing down."

"Yes, you are."

He sighed. "This is going to be harder than I thought."

Raine almost felt sorry for him. "Well, just remember you've only been on vacation a few days. Sometimes it takes a while to unwind."

He looked hopeful. "That's true." He picked up his coffee cup. "Is this decaf?"

"No, but there's a jar of instant in the cupboard above the coffeemaker." She didn't offer to get it for him.

Donetta turned the radio on to WRX and an old Rolling Stones tune blasted from the speakers. She nodded toward Alan. "Cool oldie, huh?"

Alan nodded back. "I thought kids listened to rap music."

"I do, sometimes. Sometimes I don't."

"Oh."

Joey pushed a gaudy cereal box toward him. "You want some?"

Alan took the box and examined the side panel of ingredients. "No, thanks."

Donetta raised her voice. "I'm trying to win an hour."

He took a sip of his coffee and winced. "An hour of what?"

"Of my choice of songs—a WRX listeners' choice hour."

Raine tossed sandwiches into a paper bag. "That's why she's sitting by the phone. If she's the right caller, she wins the hour of music."

Alan looked confused, but Raine figured he'd get used to confusion if he insisted on staying here.

"What kind of coffee is this?"

"Whatever was on sale last month." She grabbed a sponge and wiped off the counter. "There," she stated, tossing the sponge into the sink. "We should have enough to eat."

Alan eyed the bags of food and the large cooler on the floor. "Yes, that looks like enough for the New England Patriots."

"You followed football in London?"

"Sure."

"You don't look like a football kind of guy."

"I played in college."

"Wow!" Joey gasped. "Can you teach us how to throw?"

"I thought you were into baseball," Raine said.

Jimmy shot her a withering look. "You can do both, you know."

"Oh, sorry." She tried to hide her smile. The boys scooted their chairs closer to Alan, who drained the rest of his coffee and looked at the half-empty carafe on the counter. As the boys peppered him with questions, Raine took pity on Alan and refilled his coffee cup.

"Thanks," he said, interrupting an explanation of a play.

"How much of this stuff are you used to drinking?"

He smiled. "Too much."

"I thought so." She replaced the carafe and motioned to Donetta. "Time to load the dishwasher."

The girl reluctantly slid off the counter and moved closer to the sink. "I can still call, can't I?"

"Sure, but while you're waiting you can do your work, okay?"

The child sighed. "I guess so."

Raine interrupted the boys. "You can talk to Alan later, guys. Go get your bathing suits and shirts on, and put your pajamas in your drawer, not on the floor."

Alan stood up and took his empty cup to the sink. "I have refrigerator privileges, don't I?"

"Of course," she said. "I can empty part of a shelf for your food."

"Good. I'll need to pick up some things."

"Are you sure you want to go to the beach with us? It could be pretty—"

"I'm sure. I need the exercise."

Exercise was not how she'd classify a morning at the beach with six children, but Raine didn't waste her breath discussing it. This was obviously a man who did what he wanted when he wanted to, and he didn't take kindly to advice to the contrary.

"I CAN'T BELIEVE how many people are here at ten o'clock in the morning." He'd forgotten the beaches. He'd grown used to swimming pools and lakes with private docks. He'd forgotten the crowds, music, lifeguards and enormous number of people.

Raine handed him a bottle of sunscreen. "Sunday's the worst day."

"Then why come?" He wished she'd take off that oversize shirt. It hung down to her knees. Very cute knees, actually, supported by smooth calves and tiny feet.

"It's fun."

"Fun," Alan repeated flatly. He looked around at the crowds of people surrounding the faded bedspread that served as command central for Raine's group. Lily, protected by a large yellow T-shirt and a wide-brimmed hat, sat in the sand, digging a hole with a plastic shovel. Vanessa, making sure she was safely near Raine at all times, sat beside the baby and helped mound hills of sand. The other four played in the surf.

Raine leaned back on her elbows and faced the ocean. "I love to watch the people."

Alan could agree with that. Many long-limbed, shapely beauties had strolled past their blanket. A few had given Alan the once-over, then seen Raine and the children. Alan figured he must look like Father Goose in sunglasses.

Still, at least he was in the process of relaxing. He would relax if it killed him. He picked up the book he'd brought and opened it at page one. Within minutes he was completely absorbed.

A shadow fell over the page. "Whatcha readin'?"

Alan looked up at Joey/Jimmy. "Nothing right now."

"Wanna swim? I know how to bodysurf."

"Maybe later."

"When?"

Alan looked at his watch. He was cornered. "How about half an hour?"

The boy grinned. "Great!"

"That was Joey," Raine stated. "In case you didn't know."

"I didn't," he managed to reply. Raine had removed her shirt and sat on the bedspread beside him in a one-piece, red bathing suit.

"He'll hold you to it, you know."

"Yes." Alan nodded, hoping his sunglasses hid his surprise. She had a lovely body—trim, neat and at the moment nicely oiled. Her black hair brushed her smooth shoulders when she turned to talk to him.

"That's nice of you. He doesn't have the chance to be around men and it's good for him." Her lips turned up at the corners and he wished she wasn't wearing sunglasses, so he could see if she was teasing him or not.

"Why?"

"You know, male role models. I'm going to enroll the boys in Scouting in the fall, that is, if they're still with me."

"Why wouldn't they be?"

She looked back to the shoreline where the older children bounced in the surf. "It depends on what the state decides is best for them. They might be up for adoption by then." Raine looked at the book in Alan's lap. "What are you reading?"

He flipped it shut so he could read the cover. *"Dealing: the Fate of American Companies in the Next Decade."*

"Oh."

"It was written by an acquaintance of mine," he said, wondering at the same time why he felt he had to defend his choice of reading material. "The reviews were excellent."

"I'm sure it's a very good book," she agreed, but didn't look at all convinced. "It sounds more like a college textbook than a beach book."

"What do you consider a beach book, Miss Claypoole?"

She turned to smile at him, then resumed watching the shoreline. "That's easy. First of all it should be a paperback. That way, if you get sand in it or it gets wet, it won't matter as much."

He tapped the glossy cover. "This isn't going to get wet."

"Oh, of course not. That's because you don't have children on the blanket beside you."

"No." He gestured toward the people on the next blanket. "I have *them* on a blanket beside me." A young man and woman lay locked in an embrace, oblivious to the crowds of people around them. Of course, Alan decided as he glanced over, he'd rather be doing something like that instead of reading a book on business deals.

"I see what you mean."

"What else?"

"It should be fiction. Something relaxing, a book you've wanted to read all winter and didn't have the time for. It shouldn't be so suspenseful that you forget to watch the kids, though."

Alan realized he enjoyed watching *her*. The tops of her breasts rounded nicely from the bodice of her suit. He'd always been partial to the color red, especially this particular cherry shade. "Of course not."

"It should have nothing whatsoever to do with what you do for a living."

"Meaning business."

"Whatever."

"The idea is to learn nothing?"

"The whole idea is enjoy yourself, to take a mental vacation."

"I guess I'll have to go to the library."

"See?" Raine sat up and helped Lily sit down on the bedspread. "You're learning how to take a vacation, after all."

"I've taken lots of vacations," Alan countered. "All over the world."

"Then why are you in such bad shape?"

He readjusted his sunglasses and stretched his legs. Lily patted him on the knee. "Hi," she said.

"Hi," he answered, hoping she wouldn't take that as encouragement to climb all over him.

"You're not answering my question."

"All right. I've spent the last ten months negotiating with the Russians and setting up several projects. It was a twenty-four-hour-a-day process, especially since we wanted to nail things down before the country self-destructed any further."

"I thought you were in London."

"Based in London." He shifted slightly so Lily could have more room.

"Are you going back at the end of the summer?"

"I don't know where the next project will be."

"Eat!" Lily cried, grabbing one of Alan's toes.

"Here, pumpkin," Raine said, reaching for the baby. "We'll have a snack."

"Uh-oh," said Alan. "Here comes the bodysurfing expert."

All four children trotted toward them, dodging between beach blankets to plop near Raine's cooler. "We're hungry," Jimmy stated, eyeing the bags of food by Alan's tennis shoes.

"May we have a drink, please?" Julie squatted near Alan and gave her older brothers a dirty look.

"Yeah," Joey said. "Please." He looked at Alan. "You promised to go swimming, remember?"

"You want to go now or have a snack first?" Alan didn't believe in breaking promises.

"Go now," Joey said, as if he couldn't risk the possibility of Alan's changing his mind in the next ten minutes.

"Okay." Alan stood up, tugged his blue polo shirt over his head and tossed it onto the bedspread. Then he removed his watch, put it inside his shoe and removed his sunglasses.

"Here," said Raine, holding out her hand. "I'll tuck them in my bag."

"Thanks." His fingers grazed hers for only an instant, but the contact of her warm skin jolted him. Alan dropped his hand quickly and turned toward the two boys.

"Alan?"

He looked back at her and thought what a pretty picture she made, sitting on the blanket. If she were anyone else, he'd attempt to get to know her better. But he already knew all he had to about Raine Claypoole, and everything he knew was a warning to stay as far away as possible. "What?"

"Don't let them go out too far," Raine said.

"They'll be fine." Alan stepped onto the sand, enjoying the sting of heat against the bottoms of his feet. Four children followed him to the water's edge, and Alan wondered just what kind of vacation this was going to be, playing male role model to such an assortment of children.

He put his hands upon his hips and four pairs of eyes stared at him. "You can all swim?"

They nodded.

"Everybody can bodysurf?"

They looked uncertain, even Jimmy, who said, "Kinda."

Great. He was responsible for the survival of four kids in the Atlantic Ocean. "Okay, here's the deal," he said, making his voice stern. "Stay with me and do as I say."

The boys nodded, Julie squealed as incoming foam tickled her ankles, and Donetta waited for further in-

structions, her hands on her hips, too. "I can do CPR,"
she said. "Just in case anyone drowns."

"I'm glad to know that," Alan assured her. "Okay,
everybody into the water!"

RAINE WATCHED from the blanket, rarely taking her
gaze from the five bobbing heads in the surf. Vanessa
sat on the shoreline and created small mountains in the
wet sand, and Lily curled up beside Raine, put her
thumb into her mouth and fell asleep. Raine adjusted
the umbrella so that the child was shaded from the
morning sun.

She'd have gone to the shoreline herself, just to be
closer, if Lily hadn't dozed off. Now she was forced to
stay here on the blanket and pray that the children
learned to bodysurf without drowning.

It seemed an eternity before they returned, skin dripping with salt water. Raine passed out towels and listened to the children's excited chatter.

"They did great," Alan said, slicking his wet hair
back from his forehead. He looked younger that way.
She wished he'd put a shirt on or cover himself up with
a towel. She handed him one.

"Thanks," he panted, and wiped his face.

There were those magnificent shoulders again.
Raine watched him quickly pass the towel over that
part of his body, rub his nicely furred chest a couple of
times, then plop onto the blanket beside her.

She inched away.

"Sorry," he said, noting her move. "I'm getting you
wet?"

"That's okay," she managed. "Thanks for swimming
with the kids."

"No problem," he said. "I'm out of shape, though."

He didn't look out of shape at all. The modest black bathing trunks topped a pair of muscled thighs. "You looked like you were having fun."

"Yeah." A look of surprise crossed his face. "We had fun. I should do this every day while I'm here."

"True. It's your vacation." She opened the cooler and lifted a can of ginger ale in the air. "Thirsty?"

"Thanks." He took the can and popped the metal tab. "I don't know how much salt water I swallowed."

Raine dispersed sandwiches and poured lemonade while Donetta opened a bag of pretzels and passed it around. The older children described the length of rides the surf had given them, proudly displayed the scrape marks on various parts of their bodies and compared their prowess to Alan's bodysurfing ability, which was, as Joey put it, "Awesome."

Raine feigned shock. "Awesome?"

"Totally," Jimmy added. "For an old guy, he's pretty fast."

"For an old guy?" Alan repeated, as if he couldn't believe what he'd heard.

"Old and awesome," Raine muttered, trying not to laugh at Alan's dismayed expression. "Wow."

"I think I'll go back to my reading," he said, rummaging through the pile of clothes until he found his book. "Old guys need their rest."

"Everyone is going to stay out of the water for a while." Raine gathered up the garbage into a plastic bag. "There are apples in the cooler. Or you can wait until later on."

"When do we have to go home?"

Raine looked at her watch. "It's after eleven. How about in another hour? I don't want anyone to get sunburned."

Alan tossed the book aside. "Fine with me."

Raine looked past his shoulder at the couple beside them. No longer silently entwined, they lay face-to-face, talking to each other. She could see their lips move, saw the smile flit across the face of the young woman. She was probably twenty; her skin was tanned evenly, which meant she was probably a college student with a job working nights. You didn't get a tan like that on weekends. The young man was lighter. Raine figured if he wasn't careful he would have one killer of a sunburn by sundown.

"People watching again?" Alan murmured, leaning close so the children wouldn't overhear. "At least they're taking a break."

Raine flushed. "I wasn't—"

"No boyfriend?"

"What?"

"It's a simple question. Do you have a man in your life—such as a boyfriend, good friend, relationship, et cetera?"

Raine pushed up her sunglasses onto the bridge of her nose. "No."

"Which is why your stepmother sent you one."

"Well, she sent *you*. You wouldn't be described as a boyfriend, good friend or relationship."

"True," he conceded. "I'm the perfectly lovely husband."

Raine groaned. "I wish I hadn't told you."

He chuckled. "It's sounding funnier every time I think about it."

"They're serious, you know."

"Who—Claire and Wina?"

"Yes."

"Don't worry, Raine. I took care of it."

She looked at him curiously. "How?"

"I called my mother yesterday and told her to back off."

"And she agreed, of course."

"Of course. She's a reasonable woman." He lay on his back and shoved a clean towel under his head for a pillow. It was obvious he was getting comfortable. She hoped the kids didn't throw any sand onto him.

Raine rolled her eyes. "Claire isn't."

"I'm going to enjoy my vacation," he murmured, closing his eyes and taking a deep breath.

Easy for him to say, Raine figured. She had the sense of impending doom she always had where her stepmother was concerned.

It was a shame, Raine thought, watching him lie there in contentment, a shame that he wasn't a different kind of man—someone not quite so good-looking or rich or businesslike. Someone who had no ties to the social stratosphere or financial wizardry. She didn't mind having money—at least, she hadn't in the past, but she'd be damned if she'd spend the rest of her life with a man like her father, a man who put dollars before family and business before his children.

What on earth was Claire thinking?

5

CHARLIE SNUGGLED CLOSE to Raine's side, taking up more space in the queen-size bed than a nine-pound dog should occupy. She moved away from the heat of his body, then, realizing there was no more room, gently nudged the dog until he moved over.

Raine readjusted the sheet and heard a noise in the hall. None of the children had been roaming around the house lately, but nothing they did would surprise her. Charlie began to snore, a high, wheezing sound that made Raine smile until she heard muffled sounds from the kitchen.

She peered at the numbers on the digital alarm clock on the nightstand. Two-thirty. Somebody was about to be returned to his or her bed. Charlie paid no attention as Raine stumbled out of bed and headed for the kitchen.

The light was on over the sink, and as Raine tiptoed through the doorway, she saw Alan standing by the counter, holding a glass. He wore light-colored shorts—nothing else.

He winced when he saw her. "Sorry," he said, keeping his voice low. "I tried to be quiet and not wake anyone."

"That's okay." Raine stood in the kitchen doorway and brushed her hair from her face. Then she realized she was wearing only a long T-shirt and crossed her arms in front of her chest. "I thought one of the children was up."

He went to the refrigerator and took out the pitcher of iced tea. "Do they do that often?"

"No, but sometimes they have nightmares. Why are you up in the middle of the night?"

He poured tea into a glass, then opened the freezer for the ice cube tray. "I was thirsty. Want some?"

Raine hesitated. The night was sultry and her skin still felt warm from the time on the beach this morning. "All right." She sat down at the table, telling herself he'd seen more of her body in the bathing suit today than he would right now, but still felt uncomfortable wearing her nightshirt in front of a strange man.

Alan quickly assembled another glass of iced tea, even going as far as to take a lemon from the refrigerator and slice two pieces into the glasses. He left the pitcher on the counter, then sat down across from Raine and handed her a glass.

"Thanks." She took a sip. "Couldn't you sleep?"

He shook his head. "No, but I'm used to it."

"Doesn't the air conditioner help?"

"The heat isn't the problem."

"Then what is?" The quiet was incredible, heavy and peaceful, and Raine began to relax, although she wished she had thought to put on a robe. She would have to remember from now on.

He took a long drink, and the only sound in the room was the ice cubes tinkling against the glass. "It's nothing new. I usually wake up in the middle of the night and then can't get back to sleep for hours, if at all."

"Why not?"

"Too much on my mind, I guess. I made a few phone

calls to the London office and ran through some numbers on the computer."

Raine wasn't surprised that Alan couldn't take a real vacation. His type never could. "I thought you were supposed to be on vacation."

"An enforced one," he admitted. "I'm supposed to rest, relax, exercise, eat sensibly and watch my blood pressure."

"And are you?"

"I've been trying, but it's not easy. I love my work." He gave her a rueful smile. His face was darkly handsome in the dim light, and Raine wondered again why he wasn't married. He seemed at ease talking to a woman in the middle of the night.

"Good luck. This place isn't exactly peaceful and quiet."

"So I've noticed."

She reached for the pile of books on the table. *Scenic Newport* was the one on top. "Are you going to do some sight-seeing while you're here?"

"Yes. I planned to sit here and make a list." He pulled a yellow legal pad from underneath the books and pamphlets and turned it around so she could read it. "I've already started."

Raine peered at the neat handwriting. "You're going to do the Cliff Walk, tour seven mansions, bicycle Ten-Mile Drive, take the railroad dinner train.... Wait a minute, there's a question mark on that one." She looked up.

"I haven't decided on the train for certain."

"Oh." She looked back at the list. "Tennis Hall of Fame. That's a good one."

"I remember being there briefly years ago."

She pushed the pad back across the table. "Sounds like quite a schedule."

He lifted it up and peered at the writing. "That's only part of it." He put the pad down again and drained his iced tea. "I might even buy a treadmill."

"You really do want to get in shape," Raine said, trying to control her smile. He was a classic Type A personality. "I thought you were supposed to slow down."

"I am."

"You're planning your vacation as if it was a battle plan. Or rather, a business strategy."

He leaned back in his chair. "How would you do it?"

"I think I'd play it by ear." When he frowned, she couldn't stop her amusement from showing. "You know, wake up in the morning and say to myself, 'Gee, what do I feel like doing today?' Then I'd go back to sleep."

"And then what?"

"When I woke up I'd think about it again and do whatever I felt like." She took a sip of her drink. "I don't think I'd worry about it in the middle of the night."

"What about you? Isn't there anything you worry about in the middle of the night?"

"Sometimes," she admitted. "But I usually don't have too much trouble sleeping."

"I can see why," he said. "Six kids wear you out."

"Five, as of tomorrow."

"What happens tomorrow?"

Raine grimaced. "Lily is going to leave in the morning. Her social worker is taking her to her new family."

He looked surprised. "Isn't it hard for you to give her up?"

Now it was her turn to be surprised. "Yes," she answered, resting her elbows on the table. "But I feel good knowing she'll have a permanent home. The people are very nice and can't wait to adopt her."

Alan nodded. "I'm glad."

"And I have two more coming in a few days."

"Two more kids?"

She nodded.

"That makes seven. *Seven.*"

"I can add."

He rolled his eyes. "So much for the perfect vacation spot."

"I didn't ask for you, you remember. And I offered you a way out. You can still take it."

Alan watched as Raine stood up and walked over to the sink to put her glass there. Her black hair looked even darker, and the delicate, womanly curves of her body could be glimpsed underneath the cotton shirt. She was definitely a temptation.

"No, thanks," he answered, wishing he could take her into his arms and see how she felt beneath his hands. "I'll stick with my original plan."

She turned and smiled. "I thought you'd say that."

"How?" He stood up, studying her face in the shadowy mixture of dark and light. She was beautiful, with a heart-shaped face, large eyes and wide mouth. Funny, in the chaos that usually surrounded her, he'd noticed nothing beyond a certain prettiness.

"Investment bankers prefer to stick to plans."

He moved closer. "You have personal experience with investment bankers?"

She looked up at him with dark blue eyes. "My father. You may have met him."

"Yes. A powerful and brilliant man."

"He liked to stick to plans, too."

"There's nothing wrong with plans." Alan really didn't want to talk about her father. He wanted to bend over and kiss that little frown from her lips.

"Perhaps." She shrugged, and the movement brushed the cotton across her breasts. "Right now I plan to go back to bed."

"Good idea." He touched her shoulder as she began to move past him. "Raine," he began, wondering why on earth he'd touched her, wondering what the hell he was going to say. "Will you be all right?"

She looked surprised. "Why wouldn't I?"

"Tomorrow, I mean. You seem very attached to that baby."

"Is there something wrong with that?"

He put both hands on her shoulders to stop her from walking away. "Not unless it gives you pain."

"Pain to see her leave, joy to have been able to take care of her. It's a mixture of both."

He shook his head. "I don't know how you do it."

"You can't keep yourself insulated from pain—no one can." She peered at him closely in the darkness. "Or can they? Is that how you live—not getting involved enough to get hurt?"

"Nonsense," he snapped. "That's not—"

"It's a nice, safe way to live," she said softly. "And I don't blame you at all. But you don't have to worry about me."

"I wasn't," he said, and realized that was exactly what he was doing. Worrying about Raine.

She took a breath, as if ready to say good-night. But Alan wasn't ready to let her go. He bent down and touched his lips to hers. He felt her surprise, sensed her hesitation, and moved his mouth across hers, slowly, seeking a response. He tightened his grip on her shoulders to hold her in place, to keep her from moving away while he tasted her lips, felt the heat strike them both.

When Alan lifted his head, he looked down into a pair of very startled blue eyes.

"What the hell do you think you're doing?"

"Kissing you."

"For heaven's sake!" she sputtered as he released his hold on her shoulders. "Don't do that again."

"Why not?"

She glared at him. "You're practically a stranger."

"Wrong." He shook his head. "I'm the man sent to be your husband."

"Very funny."

"Oh?" His eyebrows rose. "That's what you told me just a few days ago."

"And you didn't believe me."

"And I still don't," he admitted. "But I've been thinking about kissing you all day. It was," he drawled, looking at her lips again, "very pleasant."

"Well, I'm glad you enjoyed yourself." She didn't sound glad. "Just don't do it again."

Of course, he didn't plan to. Alan let her step past him and leave the kitchen to return to her bed. He'd be out of here in a few weeks, as soon as some progress was made on the inheritance, as soon as he felt rested enough to return to work. He was supposed to be relaxing—not making passes at women in the middle of the night.

No matter how enjoyably.

RAINE WATCHED the social worker swing the state-owned station wagon into the street, Lily securely fastened into the car seat in the back. Charlie whimpered at Raine's feet, so she bent to pick him up and held him in her arms until the car was out of sight and the threat of tears had passed.

"Then there were five," Alan said behind her.

"Not for long, remember?" Raine sniffed and wiped her eyes before turning around. Charlie growled, so she told him to hush and put him down. He immediately went over to Alan and sniffed his feet.

"He isn't going to lift his leg, is he?"

"I hope not. I wasn't planning to wash floors today."

"I was more concerned with my slacks." Alan moved away from the dog, careful not to step on him. "Are you sure you're all right?"

She tried to smile. "Sure. I should be used to this. I just need to keep busy today, that's all."

"What are you going to do?"

"The kids are at day camp until three-thirty." She took a tissue from the pocket of her shorts and wiped her nose. "I thought I'd clean out the refrigerator and then go grocery shopping."

"I have a better idea."

Raine looked at him curiously. "Something from your list?"

"As a matter of fact, yes."

"Why am I not surprised?" She studied him, noting the color the sun had given him yesterday. He looked better, the lines in his face less prominent, the mouth more relaxed. The kiss last night had been more pleasant than Raine wanted to admit. It had been nice to stand in the darkness of her kitchen and enjoy the nearness of a man's body, his warm lips on hers. But nothing could change the fact that he was all wrong for her.

"I've realized I'm not the only one who could use a vacation," he said.

"Meaning me?"

"Yeah."

"That's really not your problem."

He shrugged. "I could tell Edwina that I thought my landlady was worn out. She'd probably tell Claire, and then..."

"Stop." Raine chuckled. "You're trying to threaten me, Alan. It won't work."

"No? You haven't heard what I had in mind."

"Okay, what?"

"Get that animal off my shoe and I'll tell you."

"Come here, Charlie," Raine ordered, motioning to the little dog. He hesitated at Raine's feet, then trotted into the living room, heading for his favorite chair. Raine turned back to Alan. "So?"

"The International Tennis Hall of Fame Championship starts today. We could go to La Forge for lunch—I haven't been there in years. Have you?"

She shook her head. "No."

"Then we could walk over to the tournament. Do you like tennis?"

"I don't get to many of the tournaments."

He looked at his watch. "We can leave in an hour, have an early lunch, then spend the afternoon watching some of the matches."

"I really can't—"

"Get ready in an hour? Sure you can."

"No, I have so much to do."

"Like what?"

"Groceries, cleaning, laundry..."

"I'll help."

"You?"

"Of course. Why not?"

"You're not exactly a domestic kind of guy."

"You don't know what kind of guy I am."

That was a challenge if she'd ever heard one. Raine smiled. "Maybe you're right." She looked into those cool, hazel eyes of his and grinned. "You've inviting me to lunch, tennis and offering to help with the groceries. What's the catch?"

"I'm bored."

"Right."

"No, really, I don't want to go by myself. Help me out."

Raine considered the invitation. It would be good to get out of the house and not think about missing Lily. She couldn't remember the last time she'd taken the day off and done something frivolous in the middle of the week. "You're serious about the grocery shopping?"

"Absolutely."

"Okay, you're on."

He looked as if he'd known all along that she'd agree.

SHADES OF ROSE PINK and forest green dominated the long porch of La Forge. Tucked beside the Tennis Hall of Fame, the restaurant had been sitting on Bellevue Avenue for over a hundred years. One of the staff led them down the steps to the wide porch. Trimmed in lattice, with cooling fans in the ceilings and wide windows overlooking the piazza, the room was a favorite dining spot for locals and tourists alike. Two young women, dressed in Victorian tennis dresses, lobbed tennis balls back and forth on the grass court outside the windows.

"I feel as if I've entered another century." Raine thanked the waitress who helped her into her chair and gestured at the window. "Can you believe it looks the same as it did when I was little?"

"Which was not a century ago," he said, smiling.

She ignored his teasing. "Claire used to bring my brother and me here at least once a summer, in the days when we summered here."

"With your father?"

She shook her head. "No. He never liked Newport," she said. "Said it was too crowded, too full of people who had too much time and too much money."

"Claire didn't agree?"

"No. Thank goodness, her philosophy of life was completely different."

A waiter interrupted to take their drink order, but when he left, Alan resumed the conversation. "And yet they were married."

"I never figured that out. My father had been a widower for years, the kind of man who kept to himself. I asked Claire once, before my father died, why she married him. 'He needed cheering up,' she said."

"From what I've seen, Claire is the kind of woman who can do just about anything she puts her mind to."

"Yes." Raine flipped open the heavy, plastic-covered menu. "Your being in Newport is living proof."

Alan looked blank, then comprehension dawned. He smiled, a slow, deliberate, charming smile that took Raine's breath away for a moment. "As the husband, of course."

"The last thing I need. Or want." Which wasn't quite true, but Alan didn't have to know that. She didn't want to hurt his feelings, after all.

"I'd think that with all those children, you'd need a man around."

"Why?" The suggestion hit a little close to home. She'd been trying not to worry, but watching Lily leave had been a sharp reminder of what was in store if she couldn't adopt Joey, Jimmy and Julie herself.

"What?"

"Why would I need a man around?"

He opened his mouth, then closed it again while he looked at her. He shook his head and tossed his menu to one side. "I give up."

"That was fast."

"It's not my usual way of handling problems."

She decided to return his teasing. "I meant the menu. You chose lunch quickly."

"You're doing this deliberately, right?"

"Right. You were getting too personal."

"We live together. *That's* personal."

The waitress returned to deliver their drinks: iced tea for Raine and a Bloody Mary for Alan. "Would you like to order?" she asked.

Raine nodded. "I'll have the lobster roll plate."

"I will, too," Alan agreed, handing his menu to the waitress.

"We don't live together."

"I'm living with you and all those children. I'm sitting in the kitchen, I'm drinking iced tea on the porch, I'm swimming in the ocean, I'm—"

"For heaven's sake!" Raine interrupted, looking around at the other tables to see if anyone was listening to them. "Why are you getting so worked up over this? You should be pleased that you're not being considered husband material."

"Pleased is the understatement of the year."

"Then relax, or as Joey would say, 'Take a chill.'"

Alan removed his celery stick and took a deep swallow of the tomato juice while Raine sipped her tea and watched. She had to admire him—he wasn't shy about voicing his opinions. He was probably used to people being impressed with what he had to say and jumping to obey the orders he issued.

"What are you smiling about?"

"You're not used to being ordered around, are you?"

He grimaced, but his eyes crinkled at the corners in silent laughter. "No, sweetheart, I'm not."

"So, are you relaxing?"

"As much as I can."

"Good. That's an improvement."

"I'm working on it."

She leaned forward. Now seemed a good time to pry. "Why were you forced to take a vacation?"

"I collapsed at my desk." He winked. "Don't tell my mother."

"You collapsed? Why? What was wrong?"

"I told you before—overwork, exhaustion, high blood pressure, you name it—I had it."

"And on the stairs?"

"Exhaustion, I think. I talked to my doctor about that incident. You don't have to look at me as if I'm an invalid. There's nothing seriously wrong with me that a few weeks of fresh air and rest won't cure."

"I would have thought you'd want to be alone."

He shook his head. "I'd go crazy." The waitress set plates in front of them, and Alan thanked her. "I prefer people," he said. "And lobster for lunch."

Raine smiled at him. "You know, Alan, sometimes I like the way you think."

"Only sometimes?"

"Definitely only sometimes."

He picked up his fork and stabbed a thick chunk of lobster meat. "I can see I'm going to have to work harder to change your mind."

"You can try," Raine said, lifting a curly French fry. "In the meantime, thanks for the food."

THERE WAS A LOT to be said for spending an afternoon in the company of a handsome and charming man, watching other handsome and well-built men run around in shorts.

Tennis was so, well, *clean.* Despite the heat and the humidity, Raine was thrilled to be part of the crowd of spectators walking on the crunchy gravel paths behind the grass tennis courts. Alan filled in background information as she needed it, patiently answering all of her questions in a low voice. She'd forgotten how quiet the tennis matches were; the strict etiquette observed by the crowd assured the players of total concentration on their games.

The relentless heat from the sun made Raine glad she'd brought a wide-brimmed hat and worn a loose, cotton sundress. White was always a good choice for a Newport social occasion, Claire had stated more than once.

"If the heat's bothering you, we can use the box seats," Alan offered, watching Raine fan herself with her paper program.

"I'm fine," she said, pushing her sunglasses back up on her nose. The match was over, the Australian besting the young kid from Great Britain in two out of three. "I like standing here by the fence where I can see everything."

"If you change your mind, let me know." He looked at his program. "The best match of the day will be on the center court. We could go up on the bleachers and catch some of it."

He took her hand, surprising Raine with the easy gesture, and led her along a path beside a high green fence to the other side of the arena. Players warmed up on practice courts, while their coaches shouted encouragement and advice from the sidelines. Raine and Alan waited for the interval between sets to take seats in the bleachers.

"I can't believe it isn't crowded."

Alan shaded his eyes and watched the players. "It's the first day. By the end of the week, when the finals happen, this place will be sold out."

"Do you have tickets for the week?"

"My company does. If you want to come again, just say the word."

Raine smiled and looked down at the court as the next set began. She was having a wonderful time, but there was no reason to get carried away and plan to do it again. She watched the tennis players, she watched the crowd, she wiped her brow and discreetly fanned herself with the program. She promised herself she'd take up tennis again, even though it had been years since she'd held a racket. She wondered if she should give the children tennis lessons and how much they cost.

When the match ended, Alan stood up. "Let's go find the Del's lemonade cart."

"You're not going to pass out on me again, are you?"

He shook his head. "No. Despite meeting you in the kitchen last night, I managed to get a good night's sleep."

Raine wished he hadn't brought that up. It would have been easier to forget the way she'd responded to his kiss.

Alan didn't seem to notice her embarrassment. "What about you? Were you able to go back to sleep?"

"Sure," she lied. "No problem at all."

He took her hand to help her down the concrete stairs, then kept hold of it while they walked back along the path beside the fence. The green and yellow lemonade stand was three feet away when Raine stopped and attempted to tug her hand free.

"Alan!"

He didn't pay the least bit of attention and continued to hold her hand, even tighter, and smile at her as if she'd given him a secret signal. "Large okay?"

"Let go of my hand," she whispered, aware that there was a match going on nearby.

"What?" He bent down to listen to her. It was an intimate gesture, which made Raine even more nervous.

"Let go of my hand."

He looked surprised, but loosened his hold so she could pull away. "Better?"

"They're here."

"Who?"

Raine pointed to the two women bearing down upon them, parting the crowd like two ocean liners steaming up Narragansett Bay.

"*Darling*," one trilled.

"That's who," Raine said, feeling her heart sink. "The one called 'Darling' is Claire. The other one is your mother, right?"

"Yes," he managed to say. "Do you think they've seen us?"

"No jokes, please. Not now." She groaned. "They're going to eat us alive."

"We could make a run for—" But Alan was enveloped in a petite cloud of lavender cotton and gray curls before he could finish his sentence. Raine stepped back to avoid being run over, only to face Claire, slim and sporty in navy walking shorts and a white polo shirt.

Claire patted her stepdaughter's cheek. "Raine, you look a little warm."

"Well, I—"

"I'm so glad you could finally take some time away from the children. How are they?"

"Fine, Claire, but—"

"Isn't he something?" Claire lowered her voice. "And holding your hand, too. Fast worker, is he?" She winked. "I always loved a man who knew what he wanted."

"I don't think that's quite—"

"Never mind." Claire shook her head. "We'll talk later, in private. Wina is ready to catch up on all the news with her son, so we'll have the driver take us to your house." She turned to her friend. "Wina, we're going to Raine's now. Tell that handsome son of yours to lead you out of here before we totally succumb to the heat."

Wina hooked her arm through Alan's and smiled at Raine. "Raine, it's been so long. I can't wait to see Gertrude's house again and meet all of your children. You are so wonderful to let Alan stay at your place."

Raine managed a smile. "He's a perfectly lovely houseguest."

Claire arched one eyebrow. "Of course he is, darling. Didn't I tell you?"

6

"HOW DID YOU KNOW where to find us?"

Claire beamed, obviously quite pleased with herself. "I called your house, of course. You left a message on your answering machine."

Alan looked surprised. "You led them right to us."

"I can't leave the house without leaving a number, in case one of the children has an—"

"You look hot, dear," Claire said again, smoothing Raine's hair. "Are you feeling well?"

"Yes. Actually, now that I'm inside an air-conditioned limousine, I'm feeling quite cool." She crossed her legs and waved at Alan, who sat beside his mother. "Too bad you couldn't have hired something bigger."

Claire frowned. "Now, don't start with the sarcasm, Raine. You know I never learned how to drive."

"It's never too late," Wina interjected. She smiled at Raine. "I always tell her that, but she insists on hiring one of these big, silly automobiles."

Alan smiled at his mother, but steel threaded his voice. "You still haven't told me why you're here in Newport, Mother."

Edwina shot a plaintive look at Claire, then waved her tiny hands in the air as if to shoo away her son's questions.

Claire leaned forward and held out her hand. "Who is the best jeweler of all?"

"I have no idea," Alan replied. "And I have a feeling that it makes no difference whatsoever."

"Thames Street," Edwina finally sputtered.

Claire waggled her fingers. "I need to have this ring reset and there is no one else I'd trust."

Alan nodded politely in Claire's direction. "I'm sure that's true, of course," and the three women were aware he was sure of no such thing. "But," he continued, his tone even, "I wonder why you're not visiting with Alexandria and the children. Wasn't that part of your summer plans?"

"Later," his mother managed. "She's expecting us—me—later."

"After Claire sees the jeweler," Raine finished for her. She felt sorry for Edwina, who obviously hated to deceive anyone. And yet she and Claire had been friends for years. Who could tell what kind of schemes Claire had embroiled poor, flustered Wina in?

The limousine pulled to a stop in front of Raine's home, and the driver assisted the three women out of the car, then stood waiting for further instructions.

"Don't disappear," Alan told him. "They won't be staying long."

Raine watched the older ladies head toward the front porch and waited for Alan to step beside her. "Isn't that wishful thinking on your part?" she whispered.

"No, simply an accurate assessment of how long my patience will last."

"I warned you."

"Yes," Alan agreed, his eyes twinkling. "You certainly did." He took her arm. "Come on. We have to stick together through this."

Raine unlocked the front door and gave Edwina a brief tour of the downstairs as they headed for the kitchen. Lily's high chair still stood in its customary corner, so Raine quickly carried it into the utility room.

"This is lovely," Wina purred, her hands fluttering in the air again. "Simply lovely. I remember your great-aunt, of course, but I haven't been inside her home for years. Isn't it wonderful that she left it to someone who would love it the way she did?"

"Thank you." Raine set bright plastic pitchers of lemonade and iced tea on the kitchen table, while Alan retrieved clean glasses from the dishwasher and filled them with ice. It was a domestic scene, Raine noted, that would most likely send the ladies into raptures of delight. "Would you like to sit on the porch?"

Claire shook her head. "It's cool enough right here."

"Oh, I agree," Wina added, sitting down at the wide oak table. "Nice and cool."

Alan lifted a pitcher. "Who would like lemonade?"

"I would," Claire said. "With a touch of vodka."

"Me, too," Wina added.

Alan looked at Raine. "Above the sink," she said. "It's Claire's personal supply."

"Don't give me that look, Raine." Claire sniffed. "After that long trip, I could use a little sustenance."

"Long trip?" Wina asked.

"Of course it was long. Long and dry."

"Oh, yes."

Alan found the bottle and brought it to the table. "Where are you two staying? And for how long?"

Claire nodded approvingly at the generous amount

of liquid he splashed into her glass. "I simply adore it when a man makes a drink."

"Maizie Chapman's cottage," Alan's mother answered. "Just for a little while."

Raine knew that the Chapman "cottage" was a thirty-room, oceanfront showplace. She sat down at the foot of the table and watched Alan hand Claire the drink, then make another for his mother. "I'll have tea, as long as you're playing host," she said. She looked at the clock over the refrigerator. "I have to go pick up the children at camp in fifteen minutes."

"Send the car," Claire replied airily.

"That's the vodka talking."

"No," Alan interjected. "Let the ladies make themselves useful."

"Well..." Raine hesitated. "Maybe this once."

"Write down the address."

"I'll need to go, too. They've been taught not to get into strange cars, no matter what."

Claire leaned toward Edwina. "Didn't I tell you what a lovely mother she'd make?"

"Oh, yes, yes." Wina was fluttering again. She turned to Raine. "How many children do you take care of, dear?"

"Five."

Claire frowned. "I thought there were six."

"The baby left today. But I'm expecting two more this week."

"Two more? My goodness."

"A brother and sister. They've been in a temporary placement, but they need—"

"That makes seven!" Claire gasped. "Are you going to hire a nanny?"

"I *am* the nanny, Claire. It's my job."

"You're much more than a nanny. You're—"

"Drink up, Claire," Alan ordered. "And I'll make you another."

"I'm going to need it," the older woman said, raising her glass to her lips. She took a long swallow, then smiled at her stepdaughter. "Life is certainly full of surprises, isn't it?"

LIFE WAS FULL of a lot of things, Alan decided later in the cool comfort of his third-floor room. And surprises were right up there at the top of the list. He was still in shock over last night. Not about kissing Raine, she'd looked sultry and sleepy in the middle of the night, and he had no regrets.

His reaction was the problem. Her lips packed one hell of a wallop. He didn't recall a simple kiss ever arousing him quite the way that one had. Maybe this enforced vacation was responsible for more than simple rest and relaxation.

Okay, he told himself. He hadn't had time before to enjoy kissing a woman in a dark kitchen, nor the satisfaction of holding her hand on a sunny summer afternoon. He'd missed feeling warm fingers in his palm and the sweep of a woman's hair against his shoulder. He'd like more—a whole lot more—but Raine tended to dance away whenever he got too close. She'd made it clear. All right, so he wasn't "perfectly lovely husband" material; being a husband was not a job he wanted.

But what in hell was the matter with him? He was an ordinary-looking guy who still had plenty of his own hair. There were a few wrinkles around the eyes, but he kind of liked them. He could be in better shape, but he'd been working on that. He still had all of his teeth and plenty of money. His secretaries liked him. His employees didn't use his face for a dart board.

But one tiny, dark-haired woman looked at him as if he were her worst nightmare come true.

Still, she'd let him kiss her. She'd even let him hold her hand. And she'd consented to lunch, too.

Maybe that crazy stepmother of hers was right, after all: life was full of surprises. He was certainly beginning to surprise himself.

RAINE WAS FOLDING LAUNDRY in the utility room when Alan found her. He leaned against the dryer and watched her fold a pile of towels into neat squares. "Good morning."

She smiled, ridiculously glad to see him. After yesterday, she felt as if they were friends, which made living with him a whole lot easier. "Good morning. You look like you slept well."

"I got up once—looked for you in the kitchen, but you weren't there. It was very disappointing."

Raine shook her head, refusing to be embarrassed by his teasing. "I never heard a sound. Yesterday wore me out."

"Where is everybody?"

"It's late. I already took them to camp." She stacked the towels on the table, pushed a couple of buttons to start the dryer and turned the dial on the washing machine. "Come on," she said, as the machines sprang into action. "I have to keep moving."

"You're always moving," he said, following her into the kitchen.

"I'm happy when I'm busy."

"You must be happy all the time, then."

She ignored the comment and pulled the plastic garbage can close to the refrigerator before opening the door.

Alan leaned against the counter. "I've been giving our problem some thought," he began, watching Raine frown at something in a plastic bag that she couldn't identify.

"You're talking about Claire and Edwina?"

"Right." At least he knew she was listening. "I think we should go along with them."

She tossed the bag into the garbage. "You've been out in the sun too long, Alan. Why don't you find a staircase and take a little nap?"

"Very funny." He reached past her and helped himself to a handful of green grapes.

"I'm not feeling funny. I'm trying to get ready for two new children *and* clean out this refrigerator so I have room for the groceries I need to buy *and* decide what to give everyone for dinner tonight *and*—"

"Everyone meaning the old ladies?"

"Yes. Remember how Claire invited herself?" She tossed a moldy cucumber into the trash. "I don't know why I buy those things. No one eats them."

"Tell me about the new kids. What usually happens?"

"You never know. Sometimes they're scared. Sometimes they're angry."

"What do you do?"

"Make them part of the family as quickly as possible. They'll take their cues from the other kids. With luck, they'll settle down." Raine certainly hoped so. There was enough turmoil in the house right now.

Alan finished the grapes and peered over Raine's shoulder. "What are you looking for now?"

"My yogurt."

"I don't see it." She winced. "I hope no one ate it."

He grabbed a can of soda. "I'll have cookies for breakfast instead."

"So much for health food." She removed a casserole dish and set it upon the counter, then tossed an empty ketchup bottle into the recycling bin.

"It has its drawbacks." He popped the top on the root beer and took a long swallow.

She frowned at the inside of the refrigerator again, then shut the door. "No plans today? No list?"

"I'm playing it by ear."

"That's unusual. Are you sure you're feeling all right?"

"No. And I won't be all right until Claire and Edwina have left the state."

"You shouldn't say that," Raine said, but smiled anyway. "It's not very nice."

"I say we beat them at their own game."

"How?"

"They want us together. So, let's be together."

"You don't mean in the biblical sense."

He most certainly did, but wouldn't admit it yet. "Sexually? No. Unless..." He grinned at her, putting a hopeful expression on his face.

"No, thanks. And quit teasing me while I'm trying to work."

"Okay. If we go along with their plans, they'll leave."

"Why would they leave? Wouldn't they hang around and gloat?" She sat down at the table and pulled a yellow legal pad and pen in front of her.

"No. They'd be off somewhere else. Two of my sisters are still single. They could go pick on them for change."

"So, mission accomplished, they'd fly off to the Hamptons to meddle in someone else's life."

"Exactly. You're right on top of things, Raine. I admire that in a woman."

"You don't have to be sarcastic. I'm trying to make a grocery list—and by the way, you owe me a trip to the supermarket, remember?"

Alan groaned. "I was hoping you didn't."

"No way, pal."

"Want to skip out of here and go back to the tennis tournament?"

"I thought you were going to give your tickets to your mother."

"I did, but I can always get more tickets."

"Aren't you going to spend time with her?"

"No. That's not part of the plan. Spending time with you is part of the plan."

Raine rested her chin on her hands and sighed. "I have this fantasy that someday I'm going to meet a single man, maybe one wearing one of those carpenter tool belts. He's going to want to go out with me just because he wants to, and not because it's part of somebody else's plan."

"Well, you can always dream, can't you?"

"I think it's easier not to."

"Uh-oh. Cynicism."

She shrugged and picked up her pen. "Call it what you want. I'm not sitting here waiting for Prince Charming to come along."

"Would you recognize him if he did?"

"That's a strange question."

"I'll tell you, honey, fairy godmothers could line up here in the street offering to grant your wishes and you know what?"

"What?"

"You'd tell them you didn't need anything." Alan stood up and pushed his chair in. "Let me know when you want to go grocery shopping. I'll drive."

Raine watched him leave, then doodled absently on her shopping list. What would she wish for, if she was sure it could come true? She thought for a long moment. She'd wish for a man to love, one who would love her in return. Someone strong and dependable and kind and sexy.

Alan Wetmore Hunter came close, especially in the strong and sexy categories, but she'd had a preview growing up of what it was like to live with a man who put business first. She wouldn't do that to her own children. She wanted her prince to go to school plays and coach Little League and pick up a gallon of milk at the store on his way home from work. She wanted him in bed with her at night, not working late at the office, especially if the office was on the other side of the world.

Raine picked up her pen and looked at the list in front of her. Enough daydreaming—it was back to reality. What on earth was she going to feed all these people?

TOBY AND CRYSTAL stood quietly beside the front door, identical expressions of fear in their big brown eyes. The social worker wished Raine luck and left, promising to be in touch at the end of the week.

Raine touched the little boy's shoulder. "Want to see the rest of the place?"

Toby stuck his lip out. "I don't like it here."

Raine knelt down so she could be at eye level with him. "You're eight, right?"

"Yeah."

"Wait till Joey and Jimmy come back from camp. They're your age, and they can show you around."

"I don't want to."

Raine turned to his younger sister, Crystal. "Would you like to see your room? You'll be sharing with Vanessa, but she's not home right now." The little girl nodded, then yawned. Raine noticed that her eyes were puffy; she looked as if she hadn't had any rest for quite a while. The social worker had said that the children had been abandoned a week ago and had stayed in a temporary shelter until a foster home could be found for them.

"'Kay."

The children stood next to two plastic garbage bags filled with their possessions, so Raine picked them up and led the youngsters to the front staircase. Alan came out of the living room, Charlie following at his heels.

The dog wagged his tail when he saw the children.

Toby frowned. "I don't like dogs."

"I do," his sister said, her eyes lighting up as the little furry animal tilted his head to look at her. "Is he a real dog?"

"Yes, he's real. Why does he like kids and not me?" Alan said, taking the bags out of Raine's hands.

"They say dogs sense things."

"What kind of things?" Toby said.

"I'm not sure, but I think dogs know things about people that we don't."

"I'm Alan," her houseguest offered, smiling at the newcomers. "I live upstairs."

The children didn't respond with anything other than petrified expressions, so Raine headed upstairs. Toby and Crystal hurried after her, with Alan following behind them. When they reached the wide hall-way, Raine stopped at the first door.

"This is the bathroom," she said. "Anyone want to use it?" They shook their heads. "Okay, moving on." She stopped at the next open door. "Here, Toby." She pointed. "Joey and Jimmy have one set of bunk beds, and you can have the other. You can pick the top or the bottom."

"I don't like bunk beds."

"You're out of luck, then, because that's all there is," Raine stated cheerfully. "You get this dresser, too, so put your clothes away." She opened the closet and showed Toby the shelves full of puzzles, games and Lego sets.

"These belong to everyone," she explained. "Feel free to play with anything in here, just as long as you pick up your mess when you're done."

The boy looked a little less grumpy. "Yeah?"

"Private stuff is kept in boxes under the beds and no one else is allowed to touch." She took an empty box from the space under Toby's bunk bed and showed him. "See? You can put your special things in here and slide it right back under the bed so no one else will touch your stuff."

"Cool."

"What about me?" Crystal asked, tugging on Raine's pants. "Do I get a bed, too?"

"Of course you do, honey. Just follow me."

Alan caught Raine's eye and lifted his eyebrows. She shook her head and took Crystal's hand, leading the child across the hall to another bedroom, this one done in shades of yellow. Twin beds lined one wall, with a window in between. Opposite were two dressers, a dollhouse and the door to the closet.

"Which one is mine?"

"This one," Raine said, patting the yellow and white quilt on the bed on the right.

"It's so pretty."

"I'm glad you like it."

"I brought my Barbie dolls."

"Vanessa and Julie—that's another girl who lives here—like to play dolls, too. I'll bet you'll have lots of fun together." The child yawned again. "Why don't you crawl under the covers and take a little rest?" She picked up some books that lay piled on the floor and put them upon the bed. "Would you like to read?"

"Okay." The child kicked off her dilapidated sneakers and climbed into bed, gingerly stroking the pillow as if she'd never seen one before. She looked afraid to touch the books until Raine handed her one. "I'll be downstairs when you wake up."

"What about Toby?"

"He'll be with me," Raine promised. "You can meet the rest of the kids, too." Raine smoothed the dark hair from the child's face and stroked her brow as she snuggled under the sheet.

Alan stood in the doorway and watched the whole thing. It was amazing to him that children would not have beds or pillows or private places for their special toys. It was hard to believe that these children didn't have parents to take care of them, a roof over their heads or enough food to eat.

These kids had nothing except Raine and what she could give them.

Alan Wetmore Hunter III was impressed.

"COME ON. It'll be fun."

Raine tossed two heads of lettuce into the grocery

cart. "You said that on Monday, and I ended up with Claire and Edwina drinking vodka in my kitchen."

"This will be different. Look, didn't you say they might be coming over to the house today?"

"Claire mentioned it, yes. But I'm not sure when."

He looked at his watch. "It's only ten. We'll be out of here in what—twenty minutes, tops?"

Raine looked at the pile of groceries in the cart. "Pretty close."

"Then we race home, put the food away and bail out."

"And go where? Someplace on your list?"

"As a matter of fact, yes. Touring a mansion or two is right up there at the top. I want to see how my ancestors tried to outspend each other."

Raine picked through the mushrooms and selected the freshest ones. "Which ancestors—the Wetmores or the Hunters?"

"Wetmores. One branch of the family owned Château sur Mer. My parents used to take us there years ago, but I've never seen any of the other mansions." He halted the cart when Raine stopped at the milk section. "How many?"

"Four," she said, trying to make room in the cart. "Then we're out of here."

"No ice cream?"

"It will be soft by the time we get home."

He opened the freezer door in front of the shelves of ice cream. "I'll risk it."

"What happened to yogurt?"

Alan tossed three half-gallon cartons of ice cream into the overflowing cart. "The boys and I are addicted to Heavenly Hash."

"I noticed. If you're going to sneak ice cream you'd

better learn to rinse the bowls and put them in the dishwasher."

"Or buy paper."

"Good idea. How do you eat ice cream without the girls knowing about it?"

He shook his head. "I'm not telling. We made a secret pact."

Raine could believe it. In the last couple of days Alan had seemed more comfortable with the children, going out of his way to talk to them. Even grumpy little Toby, pleased to be included in Alan's secret ice-cream parties, had responded.

Just like me, Raine realized, *responding to the man's quiet charm despite my better judgment.* The children would take their cues from her, and so far no one had found any reason to avoid the houseguest. He'd relaxed into something almost human.

"We're going to have some fun," Alan stated, taking over the steering of the shopping cart. "I'm getting the hell out of here now. Then we're going for a tour of...what—The Breakers, Rosecliff, Marble House?"

"It's the busy season. There might be lines."

"I don't care. The kids won't be back until three-thirty, right?"

"Right."

"Then we have plenty of time." He started jogging toward the checkout stand. Raine hurried after him. He was difficult to argue with once he'd made up his mind.

She continued to hurry after him for the rest of the day. They put the groceries away in record time, with Alan looking at his watch while attempting to organize the placement of canned goods on the pantry shelves.

She reheated leftovers in the microwave while he read the Newport guidebook aloud.

She accused him of being obsessive. He told her he was simply trying to bring some diversity into her existence. Raine didn't argue. Having a gorgeous man live in her house and direct her social activities was certainly different from her usual summers. She just had to remember that he'd be donning his business suit and flying off to the real world soon.

RAINE TRIED TO KEEP UP as they toured The Breakers, the Vanderbilts' summer mansion, with a large group of tourists eager to see an authentic home of the Gilded Age. Alan looked intrigued, seemed to absorb the information given by the tour guide, and asked several polite questions.

"Alice Claypoole Gwynne Vanderbilt. Any relation?" He stood in front of a large painting hanging above the second-floor landing.

"I doubt it," she whispered. "I think my father would have told me, but maybe not. He didn't talk much about himself."

"Maybe you should have inherited all of this," he teased.

She leaned closer. "Do you think it's too late?"

"It's never too late to go after what you want." Alan took her hand and tugged her toward their group, which was disappearing through a wide doorway. The guide allowed them a few minutes to admire the view of the green lawn and the ocean from the upper loggia before hustling the crowd through the rest of the huge mansion.

Raine was impressed most by the massive dining

room. Red-damask-covered chairs lined the walls and surrounded a huge teak table.

"Above you, on the vaulted ceiling, is an oil painting of Aurora, Roman goddess of Dawn," the guide explained. "The Baccarat chandeliers were designed by Richard Morris Hunt and contain thousands of crystal beads."

Alan, several feet away on the opposite side of the table, winked at her. She knew he was thinking of her chaotic group at dinnertime. She couldn't quite picture anyone but royalty eating in this dining room. When the crowd moved toward the kitchen, Alan waited by the door.

"I keep losing you in the crowd," he said.

She was surprised that he said it as if he missed being with her. "Don't worry. I'm not sneaking off."

"Promise?" His grin was infectious.

"Promise."

"Can you get a sitter tonight?"

"Why?"

"How about an elegant seafood dinner somewhere, just the two of us?"

"Why?"

He frowned. "What do you mean—why?"

The guide gave them a pointed look and asked for quiet before describing the Vanderbilts' kitchen. After the tour, the group was led outside and invited to go downstairs to the basement souvenir shop.

"That was fun," Raine said, ignoring the signs for the gift shop. "Want to walk out on the front lawn?"

"Certainly," he said, taking her hand. "I don't want to miss anything."

They strolled across the wide expanse of grass toward the ocean, then headed through the high, cast-iron gates to Victoria Avenue. "Now, let's discuss dinner," Alan said.

"We can discuss it, but—"

"Didn't we agree to at least pretend to go along with the old ladies' plans for us?"

"Yes, but..."

"Then let's get them to baby-sit tonight while we go out for a romantic evening. They won't be able to refuse."

"A romantic evening will thrill them."

"What about you?" His voice was low.

"I've nothing against romantic evenings, but..."

"But not with me."

Raine didn't know how to deny the truth. "You're not my type." She looked sideways at his handsome profile. "No offense, and besides—I'm not your type, either."

"Really? And what exactly *is* my type?"

"That's easy," she replied. "Sophisticated. Elegant. The kind of woman who gives lavish parties without one single anxiety attack."

He looked uncomfortable, so Raine knew she'd been accurate in her description of the future Mrs. Wetmore Hunter. He cleared his throat. "Do you know anyone like that?"

"Claire." Raine laughed as they turned off Bellevue Avenue and headed toward her home. "The perfect wife for a tycoon."

"Kiss me," Alan demanded, turning to take her into his arms.

"What?"

"Just do it," he whispered. "They're watching."

Alan's mouth closed over hers before she could utter a word of protest or assent. He urged her lips apart and deepened the kiss until Raine moaned. She didn't realize her arms had gone around his neck, or that her body had leaned into his until he lifted his head and the demanding pressure of his mouth on hers was gone.

"Thanks," Alan said, his eyes dark. A trace of a smile flickered across his mouth as he stared down at her. "That was almost as good as in the kitchen."

"Who's watching?" She slid her arms from around his neck and eased onto the soles of her feet. She'd been standing on tiptoe and hadn't even known it.

"Wina and Claire are waiting for us on the front porch."

"So?" For a banker, he sure could kiss.

"The plan, remember?"

"Oh, yes. The plan. Dinner."

"Smile at me and take my hand."

She did, wishing just for a second that there wasn't any plan—or, for that matter, that there were no matchmaking mothers or seven kids due home from camp. Raine took a deep breath and looked at the front porch. "Oh, no!" She raised her voice. "Don't open—"

In a flash Charlie swept past Claire's feet and out the screen door. He flew down the sidewalk and past Raine as she lunged to catch him.

"Charlie!" she called. "Come! *Come!*"

"What the hell—?"

"He runs away," Raine said, turning to race after the speeding little dog. "There are two female beagles down the street. I don't want him to get hit by a car!"

Raine shot down the sidewalk after the dog, cursing both him and her sandals. He hadn't run away in months, but she hadn't given him any opportunities, either. She'd fenced the backyard, so he was allowed to play outside with the children, as long as everyone understood that no gates were to be opened on any condition.

Alan caught up with her quickly. "I'll find him," he said.

"You don't know where he's going," she panted, her breathing labored.

"Tell me."

"Brown house, three stories, green mailbox with pineapples painted on the side."

"Got it. If I can't catch up with him, I'll grab him when I get there." Alan sped past her, and Raine slowed down, keeping her gaze on Charlie, who was running away from them as if it was all a game.

"Damn dog," she muttered. Who'd think a spoiled little lapdog would turn into a gazelle the minute he smelled freedom? She worried about him being hit by a car. After all, he was her best friend, the little ball of fur that slept on her feet in the winter and kept her toes warm. Raine kept jogging toward the brown house on the corner and watched Alan attempt to catch up with Charlie.

The next thing she knew, she landed facedown on the pavement.

7

ALAN THRUST the squirming bundle of fur into Raine's arms. "Take him before he bites. This idiot dog growled at me."

Charlie licked Raine's hand. "Bad dog," she scolded. "Only bad dogs run away."

"Come on," Alan said, reaching down with one hand. When Raine didn't take it, he frowned. "Why are you sitting on the sidewalk?"

"I'm not sure." Raine winced and tried once again to move to an upright position. "One minute I was running, the next thing I knew I was on the pavement. I think I may have twisted my foot or something."

"You're hurt?"

The concern in his voice amazed her. "I'm afraid I am. This is so embarrassing."

He knelt in front of her. "Which foot?"

"The right one." Alan touched her ankle with tentative fingers, then moved them lower, to the top of her foot where an ugly scrape oozed blood. "Ouch," she said. "There."

"I can't tell if anything's broken. Can you stand?"

"I think so."

"Well, hang on to that idiot animal while I help you up."

"Then what?"

"Either I carry you or we call an ambulance."

"I'm only one and a half blocks from home. I think I can hobble—ow!" She stood with his arm around her waist. Charlie whimpered and put his head upon her shoulder.

"Don't fight me, Raine. Just this once, don't fight me." Alan swept her up and into his arms, and Raine found herself tucked against his warm shirt. Charlie remained silent, which, Raine figured, showed a lot of sense. She decided to follow the dog's lead.

They rounded the corner to see Edwina and Claire waving goodbye to a large station wagon, the other half of the neighborhood car pool for day camp. The children stopped in the middle of the yard and stared at them for a moment before they broke into a noisy babble of questions.

"Oh, good," Claire called. "You caught him!"

Edwina hurried out of the yard. "Are you hurt, my dear?"

Vanessa started to cry. "Raine's hurt?"

"No," Raine called as they approached the gate. "Well, maybe a little, but I'll be okay."

Vanessa sniffed and joined the kids surrounding Raine asking questions.

"Somebody take the dog," Alan ordered, his voice rumbling above Raine's head. Jimmy rushed to obey him. "Everyone else out of the way so I can get Raine in the house." The children parted like the Red Sea.

Joey held the door, the ladies fluttered behind them, and Alan carried Raine to her bedroom.

"No—the living room. The couch is fine."

He sighed and reversed direction. Once in the living room he set her gently upon the couch. "Don't move."

"I don't intend to, at least not yet."

"Oh, dear," Edwina moaned, wringing her tiny

hands. "I had no idea the little dog would run out the door."

Claire patted her friend's shoulder. "Now, Wina. You mustn't blame yourself. Raine will be fine. Alan here will see to it."

Raine adjusted her leg so that her foot rested on the arm of the couch. "He will?"

Edwina sniffed. "He will?"

Alan frowned at all of them. "I will," he stated emphatically. "Would the two of you take the children into the kitchen and give them milk and cookies or something while I get some ice on this foot?"

"Here," Donetta said, standing nearby. She handed him the ice pack. When she saw his look of surprise, she added, "I got my first aid badge in Girl Scouts."

Alan nodded. "I believe you." He took the ice and held it on Raine's foot.

"I'm really fine," Raine insisted, wishing everyone would quit making such a fuss. She didn't like being the center of attention, especially since it had meant being cradled in Alan's arms for a block and a half. It had been altogether too irresistible, being held against that wide chest. She'd even rested her cheek against his shirt for the briefest of moments—until she'd realized what she was doing.

"How does that feel?"

"Very, very cold." She gritted her teeth, unwilling to admit that her foot was starting to hurt like hell.

Alan lifted the pack, and he and Donetta examined Raine's injury. "It's still swelling," he said. "Think we should get X rays?"

Donetta's eyes glowed. "Yes—just to be safe."

"I don't need—"

"Where's the hospital around here?"

Raine told him. "But I don't need to go there."

"You're a very cranky patient." He left the room, and Charlie hopped onto the couch next to Raine and snuggled against her.

"I'm not cranky, am I?" she crooned, petting Charlie's head.

"Yes, you are," Donetta said, perching on the couch across from Raine. "You're not cooperating."

"Okay, Doc." Raine smiled despite the shooting pains in her toes. "I promise to do better."

Alan returned to the room. "The mothers will watch the kids while I take you to the emergency room. We'll take the van. Where are the keys?"

"In my purse, but I don't think I need—"

"Don't move. I'll be right back."

He sounded as if he had it all figured out. Here was a man who liked to be in charge, and since he'd been on vacation he'd had no one to boss around. Until now. The man was in his glory, giving orders and expecting that they would be followed without question.

And there wasn't a darn thing she could do about it, except grit her teeth and pray.

"NICE BEDROOM." Alan looked around at the floor-to-ceiling bookcases and the tall windows in the octagon room. "I gather it used to be the library?"

"Go away."

"Can't," Alan said cheerfully. "I'm your nurse."

"This is a nightmare, right?" She threw one arm over her eyes as she lay on her bed, her foot in a thin, putty-colored cast and propped up on a pillow.

"Not exactly." He poked at a couple of the books that filled the shelves. "You have quite a collection."

"It's my hobby. Help yourself to anything you like."

Alan turned away from the shelves and sat down beside Raine on the wide bed. "Do you need one of the pain pills the doctor gave you?"

There was silence before she finally admitted, "Yes."

Alan opened the vial of pills on the nightstand and shook one into his palm. "Sit up a little," he said, waiting for her to lean back on her elbows before handing her the glass of water and the white capsule.

"Thanks," she murmured, then took the medicine. She handed the glass back to him and her smile was rueful. "I hate being dependent on anyone."

"I noticed."

"It's just that I don't know what I'm going to do, cooped up in this room with seven kids...."

"I'll take care of everything."

She pressed her lips together. "It hurts when I laugh."

"Really," Alan insisted, hearing himself say the words but not believing them. "I can handle everything around here. The doctor said nothing was broken, the ligaments are torn and are going to be painful for a while, but—"

"But I'm in a cast."

"A soft one."

"Still..."

"You have me and two grandmothers available, too."

Raine rolled her eyes. "I hope your mother is more maternal than mine. Where is everybody?"

"Out to dinner," Alan confessed. "Claire put everyone in the limo and headed to her club."

Raine groaned. "Why couldn't she have just gone to McDonald's or called out for pizza?"

"I don't think that's the way her mind works."

"Were they clean?"

He knew she was talking about the kids and not their respective parents. "I don't know. They were gone when we got back. My mother left a note."

"I feel rotten," Raine confessed. "And stupid."

"Speaking of stupid, here comes Charlie."

He hopped onto the bed, shot Alan a disgusted look, turned his back on him and curled up by Raine's knees. Alan envied the dog his position. He wouldn't mind curling up anywhere against Raine's delectable little body. Kissing her was just the beginning.

"What can I do to make you feel better?"

He knew she wanted to say "Go away" again, and wished he hadn't given her such an obvious opening to get rid of him. This was a rare moment. After all, they were alone. In bed.

The scene had its charms.

"Could I have a washcloth?" She pointed to a door on one side of the room. "There's a bathroom in there. I'd really like to wash my face."

When he returned with the cloth she reached for it, but he didn't give it to her. "Let me," he said.

"Alan," she began, but he didn't wait for her protest. Instead he took the warm, damp cloth and passed it lightly over her forehead, moving back her bangs as he did so. He traced the lines of each eyebrow, while Raine closed her eyes and sighed.

"Okay?"

"Mmm," she murmured.

He needed no further encouragement, and gently wiped her face with soft strokes of the cloth until he reached her lips.

The temptation was too great. Alan lowered his head and touched Raine's lips with his own, the forgotten cloth still gripped in his hand. He felt the gentle pressure of her fingertips across the nape of his neck, then her lips parted. He tasted the sweet warmth there, and he heard the little moan in the back of her throat, an entrancing sound that made him long to stretch beside her on the bed and take her right there.

But making love to an injured woman who couldn't get away was not exactly a noble idea, no matter how willing the lady appeared.

Alan lifted his head and looked down—into the surprised expression in Raine's blue eyes. Surprised, but not angry, he was glad to see. There was hope, after all.

"Do it again," she murmured, her lips turning up at the corners. Her hands slipped to his shoulders.

It was the last thing he'd expected to hear. "Why?"

"It makes my foot stop hurting."

"Well, that's a good enough reason," he answered, bending over her again as she twined her fingers around his neck.

This time he couldn't be gentle. This time he needed to explore the tantalizing textures of her mouth, feel the warmth of her lips parted only for him. Raine sank back against the mound of pillows and Alan followed, his chest touching her breasts, his hands braced at her sides. He felt her fingers glide through his hair, and her touch made him long to lie beside her and continue making love to her until they were both naked and sated.

He lifted his lips from hers when he heard the excited chatter at the front door. Raine opened her eyes and smiled at him. "Thanks," she murmured, her voice sleepy.

"Thanks?" No woman had ever thanked him for kissing her until now. *"Thanks?"*

"Mmm," she said. "For the pill and the kisses. I'm feeling better."

Claire poked her head into the bedroom. "We're back," she informed them unnecessarily.

Alan shot Raine a look filled with regret and slid off the bed.

Claire tiptoed into the room. "How's your foot, dear?"

"Feeling much better, Claire. There's nothing broken."

"But isn't that a cast?"

"Torn ligaments," Alan supplied. "More painful."

Raine looked at her leg. "'Fraid so. I'm supposed to stay off of it for two weeks or until it doesn't hurt."

"But however will you manage—"

"I'll call the social worker in the morning. Maybe I can arrange something."

"You won't need to," Claire stated. "I'm here to help."

"You are?"

"Well," Claire said, twisting her rings, "of course."

Edwina knocked on the open door. "There are some worried people who need to see that you're all right."

Raine waved at her. "Bring them in."

The seven children surrounded the bed, their eyes wide at seeing Raine lying there.

"Does it hurt?" Julie wanted to know.

"A little."

"Do we have to go away?" Donetta asked, examining the cast carefully without touching anything.

"Why would you think that, honey?"

Donetta shrugged. "It's happened before."

Vanessa's eyes filled up with tears, and Raine pulled

her close to her. "No one is going anywhere. Grandma Claire is going to help."

"And Auntie Edwina, too?"

"Yes, Nessa. I'm sure she will." Raine looked past the children surrounding the bed, but Edwina and Claire had left the room. Alan still remained beside the bed, his hand close to the headboard. "Tell me about dinner," she said to the children. "Where did you go and what did you have to eat?"

Toby edged close to the bed. "We rode in a *limousine*," he whispered, as if confiding a secret. Crystal nodded, her dark eyes huge.

Joey added, "It was so cool."

"Totally awesome," his twin agreed.

Julie edged close to the bed and Raine put her arm around the child. "What did you have to eat? Hamburgers? French fries?"

The little girl shook her head. "Lobster," she informed Raine.

"*Lobster?*"

Donetta nodded. "To 'broaden our horizons.'"

Alan made a strangled sound, then covered it with a cough.

"I'm almost afraid to ask what you had for dessert," Raine finally said.

Joey shrugged. "Anything we wanted."

"From a—" Julie stopped and wrinkled her brow.

"Cart," Jimmy supplied. "We picked what we liked and the guy came back and gave it to us."

"And you all said 'Please,' and 'Thank you,' I'm sure."

All seven heads bobbed up and down.

Alan stepped forward. "Okay, everyone. Time for

Raine to rest, so go play or whatever you do after dinner...."

"They take showers," Raine told him as the children gave her kisses and hugs. "And play outside in the backyard—before the showers, that is."

"Bedtime?"

"Seven-thirty for the little girls, eight-thirty for the boys, and nine for Donetta, but everyone can read in bed."

"I'll be right out," Alan told them. He sat back on the bed and faced Raine. "How's your foot?"

"Better." She yawned. "I'll be running around here in no time at all. But Alan, I don't think Claire and Edwina are up to taking care of this crowd."

"What about me?"

She shook her head. "It's a big job for a paying guest."

"It will help me get back in shape for the real world." He kissed her lightly on the lips before sliding off the mattress. "Call me if you need anything."

"Thanks." She watched as he left the room and closed the door quietly behind him. From a mansion to the emergency room, it had been quite a day. She hadn't expected Alan would take care of her, hadn't known that his arms would feel so good when he carried her back and forth from the car to the hospital and home again.

It had been a heady sensation, having this man all to herself for a change. His lips had felt wonderful against hers, warm and demanding. She didn't want to think about how different they were, or who he was or, or anything important at all. She'd felt safe from the minute he'd lifted her from the sidewalk and swung her into his arms.

He'd be returning to his "real world," but it was tempting not to think about that particular departure. Alan Wetmore Hunter might prove to be Prince Charming, after all. A Prince Charming with an office half a world away.

"THIS IS GOING VERY well," Claire declared.

"It is?" Edwina followed her out of the kitchen and into the small bathroom.

"Of course. Shut the door." Edwina did, and turned to face her friend. Claire looked at herself in the mirror and smoothed several gray hairs into place. "I'm so smart."

"Yes, Claire, you are, but..."

"All we have to do now is get out of the way."

"I thought we were going to stay and help. We promised, didn't we? And the children are so much fun. Did you see Jimmy's face when he saw the chocolate cake?"

"That was Joey, Wina. Jimmy took the raspberry torte. Did you see Vanessa? She buttered both sides of her bread." Claire turned away from the mirror and put her hands upon her hips. "We are going to *pretend* to help Alan, of course. But we're only going to get in the way."

"Oh," Edwina said, frowning. Then comprehension dawned. "He'll have to do everything all by himself, including taking care of your lovely stepdaughter!"

"Your future daughter-in-law," Claire corrected with a wink.

"I can hardly wait. Do you think they'll have one of those long engagements?"

Claire shrugged. "You tell me—he's your son. Does

he take a long time to make up his mind about things like this?''

''I don't know. I don't think he's been in love for years. But he usually goes after what he wants, once he's decided what he wants. Just like his father, bless him.''

''Did you see the looks on their faces when we walked in? They'd been kissing—I'd bet my diamonds on it.''

''I know,'' Wina said with a sigh. ''She looked a little stunned, didn't she?''

''Surprises are good for Raine,'' her stepmother declared. ''Especially passionate ones. She's much too set in her ways.''

''Unlike us.'' The future mother-in-law reached for the doorknob. ''Two mature women who have experienced our share of passion.''

''Edwina! You make us sound positively exciting!''

RAINE LEANED ON Aunt Gertrude's old oak cane and limped toward the kitchen. Spending yesterday in her bedroom had almost driven her crazy. Despite the frequent rests on the couch, she'd always felt as though she was missing out on everything. It wasn't easy being bossed by three people—three people who didn't have a clue how a household with a lot of children operated. They expected her to sit in bed and read magazines and drink iced tea as if she had nothing better to do, for heaven's sake.

Thank goodness they asked a lot of questions. She could answer questions. She *liked* answering questions. She would, if she wanted to, sit in the kitchen and answer questions all day long. She heard the familiar tones of Alan's voice and peeked through the door-way.

"No," Alan insisted. "Absolutely not. In fact, I think the two of you need some time off."

"Time off?"

"You're going to wear yourselves out," he declared, slapping peanut butter onto a slice of bread. He picked up another slice of bread and repeated the motion.

"Well..." Claire hesitated. "If you insist."

"I do." He turned to the women; each held a little girl on her lap. "Grape or strawberry?"

"Grape," they answered in unison.

Edwina sighed. "Maybe we'll head up to Alexandria's for a few days. What do you think, Claire?"

"If Raine doesn't need me, I suppose I could go with you."

"Go. Have fun. I don't need you," Raine said from the doorway. She smiled at her stepmother to soften her words. "Really."

"Darling," Claire called. "What are you doing out of bed?"

"My foot doesn't hurt," she fibbed. "I thought I could help out here."

Alan finished putting sandwiches in wax paper bags. "Everything is under control."

"I see that," she murmured, strangely unsettled. He looked so strong and handsome, standing there in his black bathing trunks and white T-shirt. "What are you doing?"

"Fixing lunch for the gang."

"Where is everybody?"

"Upstairs getting dressed, I hope." He glanced at the clock. "They have to leave in fifteen minutes, right?"

Raine nodded and hopped over to take a seat at the

table. She couldn't believe Alan had made lunch for the kids.

"I got the dirt out," Donetta said, entering the room with the cooler in her arms. "Hi, Raine! Are you feeling better?"

"Why are you wearing a dress?"

Donetta shrugged. "Everything else is dirty."

Raine's heart sank. She'd forgotten about the laundry.

Claire noted the expression on Raine's face and quickly spoke. "I'll take her shopping after camp."

"Uh, that's not quite the solution, Claire." Raine started to get up from her chair. She grabbed the cane and lifted herself to her feet. "I'll just go throw a few things in the washing machine."

"It's under control," Alan said. "You're supposed to stay off your feet."

"But..."

"The doctor said."

"When did you get so bossy?"

"I learned from you." He put his hands upon her shoulders. "Go on. We're doing just fine."

Alan watched her limp off, every muscle in her body shouting reluctance at having to walk away from the running of her household and her seven little charges.

Doing just fine? Now *that* was a joke. He'd spent hour after hour trying to keep kids fed and clean. He hadn't had time to answer several important calls from New York or examine contracts expressed from Frankfurt. Claire and Edwina were practically worthless, complicating the simplest chore with advice and endless details to discuss. If they just left, he'd be better off.

This fatherhood business was enough to drive a man crazy.

"Phone, Alan!" his mother called.

He gave Raine's backside in those cute yellow shorts one last, longing glance before turning back to the kitchen. He took the receiver from Edwina as Vanessa walked past him, her hand in a box of cereal. Donetta was putting nail polish onto her fingertips, and the boys were nowhere to be seen. "Could you make sure they're all ready for camp?"

"Of course, darling." She motioned to Donetta to put the polish away and follow her.

Alan sighed and turned towards the wall. "Hello?"

"Mr. Hunter? This is Atwater, Brenner and Horton calling. Can you hold for Mr. Atwater?"

The Benjamin Atwater who could help him with the will? Alan couldn't believe he'd forgotten about that problem for a few days. "Gladly."

Within seconds, a man's voice boomed through the receiver. "Mr. Hunter, I understand you're unhappy with your grandfather's will."

"That's an understatement. I've come to Newport to see what could be done to speed up this inheritance."

"You're not close to marriage, I hear."

"No." Somehow Alan didn't sound as emphatic as he'd hoped. A vision of Raine leaning against the bed pillows flashed in front of his eyes. He quickly banished the idea. Marriage was not the solution, especially to Raine. He'd be required to make peanut butter sandwiches for the rest of his life.

"That *is* the easy solution, but if it's not an option, then we'll have to consider the alternatives. Your lawyers have been in touch with us in the past six months, but your grandfather's will is very clear."

"There's no other way?"

"The property still reverts to the state if there is no married grandson to inherit."

"I was afraid you'd say that."

"You can challenge the will and tie up everything in court for years, though. I'm sure you know that."

"I had hoped it wouldn't come to that."

"So did I. I enjoyed your grandfather. He was quite a character." There was a brief pause. "Proceedings will begin August 19, the twenty-fifth anniversary of his death. I'll look forward to meeting you, Alan. Come by the office any Tuesday and I'd be happy to discuss this with you."

Alan thanked the man and hung up the phone. There didn't seem to be anything else he could do about the will, except leave it to the lawyers to settle. Right now he had more immediate problems. He leaned against the counter, his hip soaking up a puddle of milk, and surveyed the disaster before him. The sink was full of cereal bowls, the table covered with boxes of cereal, spoons and bits of frosted cornflakes.

So much for his plan to make love to Raine. He'd been so consumed with kids and food and everything else in this crazy house, he hadn't had time to devote himself to the very intriguing woman who liked his kisses.

Well, Alan decided, picking up a sponge. It was time to make some changes around here.

8

RAINE FELL ASLEEP watching "Regis and Kathie Lee" interview a pet psychologist on their morning talk show. When she awoke, the familiar ache in her foot had subsided. The fan blew air gently across the bed, and the lace curtains moved slightly in the Atlantic breeze. She picked up the remote control and flicked the television off, then listened to footsteps in the hall.

"Alan?"

The door opened slowly. "Raine? You're awake?"

"Come on in."

Alan stepped inside and smiled as he crossed the room to the bed and sat down next to her. "How are you doing?"

"Much, much better."

"Is that the truth?"

She nodded. "Cross my heart."

"Want some lunch?"

Raine hadn't felt hungry until he mentioned lunch. "Yes, but you don't have to wait on me. I can come to the kitchen."

"Don't move," he ordered, sliding off the bed. "I'll be right back."

Raine hobbled to the bathroom and washed her face. She looked at her pale face in the mirror, quickly brushed some blush onto her cheeks and combed her hair. She climbed back into bed, wishing Alan would come back and kiss her again, the way he had yesterday.

Raine mentally shook herself. She was in danger of falling in love with this man, and she'd better watch out. He was charming and sexy and kind—qualities she'd given up hoping to find in a man, especially one with designer suits and an international life-style. But he spent too much time with his computer, and openly admitted he put business before pleasure, even at the expense of his health.

Alan didn't look like a banker when he returned in less than ten minutes, carrying a tray filled with sandwiches, two glasses of iced tea and a bowl of fruit salad. His T-shirt was stained with strawberry jam and Charlie trotted behind him.

"I can't believe this," she said, as Alan placed the wicker tray over her lap. Charlie hopped onto the bed and snuggled against her knees.

"Enjoy." Alan sat down facing her. His thigh brushed her legs, which, Raine decided, added an extra pleasure to the lunch in front of her. He picked up one of the glasses. "Mindy called. She's the social worker I met last week?"

"Yes. For the twins and Julie."

"She said to tell you she hopes you're feeling better, and if you need anything, just let her know and she'll see what she can do. She said she'd call when she gets back from her vacation."

"Okay. Anything else?"

"Your neighbor brought over a chocolate cake and thanked Claire for letting her kids ride in the limousine. And someone named Janet Damon called."

"She's Lily's new mother. Is anything wrong? What did she say?"

"She said to tell you that Lily is doing fine. She left her phone number."

"That was really nice of her." She always felt better if she knew that "her" children were doing well in their new homes.

"Eat up," Alan suggested. "And I'll tell you where our mothers are."

"Where? Out shopping for designer children's clothes and picking out lobster for dinner?"

He grinned at her and raised his glass in a mock toast. "I convinced them to take some time off. They've gone to Long Island to visit my sister."

"That should calm things down around here, but it leaves you with all the work," Raine protested.

"Don't worry about it. They haven't been much help, anyway. You'd never know my mother had raised five children."

"Tomorrow's Saturday. I should be able to be up and around all weekend. I need to get to the bank. You must have had to put gas in the van, and I want you to keep track of everything, so I can pay you back. The kids usually do as they're told, even Toby and Crystal. It's the grocery shopping that's the major problem. And the driving—"

"Raine," he interrupted. "Enjoy your lunch. I've taken care of everything."

She frowned at him, but picked up a fork and speared a melon ball. "You keep saying that."

"Well, you don't have to do everything. I have it all figured it."

"You do?"

"Of course. I've given it a lot of thought."

She picked up half of a sandwich and looked to see

what kind it was. "Bacon, lettuce and tomato. Very nice."

"Claire told me you liked BLTs."

Raine put down the sandwich. "Why are you doing all of this?" Alan shrugged and looked uncomfortable, but Raine held his gaze. "You should be at some fancy hotel, and we both know it."

He glared at her. "That's the trouble, sweetheart. You think you know everything about me, just because you labeled me the first afternoon we met. Yes, I admit to working long hours and making a great deal of money, and I'm not going to apologize for it. I earn every dollar. And yes," he continued, leaning closer to her, "I desperately needed a vacation, and I'm fortunate to be able to take the time off and stay in this old house with a very beautiful and desirable black-haired woman who doesn't have the sense—"

"That's not true. I have plenty of sense."

"—to realize how attracted I am to her."

"You are?"

"Constantly." He stood up and took the tray off Raine's lap, then set it upon the floor. Then he reached over her and lifted Charlie.

"What are you doing?"

"Creating some privacy," he muttered, walking to the door and putting the little dog out. He shut the bedroom door, oblivious to Charlie's whimpers of complaint. "Pretty soon seven children are going to be traipsing into this room to tell you all about their day. I want you first."

"That's really not—"

"Where were we a few days ago?" He sat down on the bed and faced her once again. "I think we were kissing, don't you?"

"Do you realize how much you interrupt me?"

"Do I?"

"Yes," she whispered as he leaned closer. "It drives me nuts."

"Good," he said, touching her lips lightly with his. "Then we're even."

Raine hadn't the faintest idea what the man was talking about, especially after his lips captured hers once again and all thoughts left whatever brain she had left. It was natural to lift her hands to his shoulders, natural to respond to the pressure of his lips. His mouth was insistent upon hers, his tongue teased her lips. Raine felt herself transformed into lazy heat, unwilling and unable to move. Heaven, she decided, was kissing Alan Hunter. Raine wished she could go on kissing him for the rest of the hot July afternoon.

His lips finally released hers, but only to skim along her jawline, nibble one earlobe and move down her neck, which suddenly turned into tingling warmth as his lips trailed a path to her breastbone, visible in the open neckline of her shirt.

This was crazy, Raine thought, but she didn't want to think about common sense or reality; she simply yearned to feel this man's touch. Alan's fingers slid underneath her shirt and caressed her skin, sending ripples of pleasure throughout her body. His hand cupped one lace-covered breast in his palm.

He lifted his head and looked into her eyes. "You have a gorgeous body."

"You told me that once before."

"I did?"

"Yes. The second day you were here. You said I wasn't your type."

"I don't remember. I guess I changed my mind." His

thumb teased the nipple through the lace, sending warmth streaking through her body now, settling in a very specific place. "You're very much my type, after all."

Raine touched his face, running her palm along his cheek and touching his upper lip with one finger. "Which is?"

"Smart."

"But you must have known a lot of intelligent women in England."

He looked thoughtful, then added, "None as funny as you are."

"Funny like ha-ha or funny-weird?"

He thought for a minute. "Both."

"Oh."

"And loving."

"You don't know that."

Alan shrugged as if her observation didn't affect him. "And sexy."

"You don't know that, either."

"Sweetheart, I can tell."

"How?"

"A man just knows."

She didn't really believe him. "And are you my type?"

"I doubt it, sweetheart." He sighed and withdrew his hand, leaving Raine with a sense of loss. Then he grinned at her. "Unless you'd prefer designer clothes and penthouses in three cities to grocery shopping in Newport?"

She knew then that he was kidding. "You'll have to keep looking for someone like Claire."

Alan grimaced and moved off the bed. "Please,

don't mention that name," he said, then walked out of the bedroom, smiling as he shut the door behind him.

She wasn't his type. He wasn't hers. Raine told herself that it was for the best, that being caressed by this man could only lead to heartache and pain.

She wasn't willing to welcome either one into her life.

"OKAY, EVERYONE. Pick up your own mess."

This Saturday evening there was a lot of mess to pick up, Raine decided, looking around the living room from her position on the couch. The children had talked Alan into letting them eat hot dogs on the front porch, but the mosquitoes had driven them inside, where the little girls had insisted they eat in the living room.

"A real picnic," Vanessa had whispered. Raine had watched Alan melt as he'd looked into the child's big dark eyes.

Now the oriental carpet was littered with potato chip crumbs and even a few blobs of dried ketchup, but Joey appeared in the doorway with the vacuum cleaner.

Raine looked at him in amazement. "Do you know how to work that?"

Joey grinned. "No problem. Alan told me to just plug it in and start moving it around."

Crystal curled up beside Raine on the couch and yawned.

"Sleepy, honey?"

The child nodded and Raine put her arm around her. Raine wished she could take her up to bed, but for now they had to be content to snuggle together on the couch. The noise from the kitchen was incredible.

"WRX Classic Rock and Roll" blasted from the radio.
The vacuum cleaner roared to life and Charlie hurried
out of the living room, presumably to take refuge on
Raine's bed until the noise died down. Alan entered
the room, a dish towel tied around his waist, protecting
his obviously designer jeans from ketchup and mustard.

"We're eating in the kitchen from now on," he
stated, wielding a sponge against a ketchup splatter.
"You should have warned me."

"I did," Raine said, trying to stop herself laughing.
Alan conquered the stain, then sat down on the couch
and stretched his long legs in front of him. He watched
Joey turn off the vacuum cleaner and carry the machine out of the room.

"Great job, Joe!"

The boy grinned. "Thanks."

Raine yawned. "Who's doing dishes?"

"Nobody."

Raine had visions of mounds of dirty plates littering
the counters. She wondered if she wanted to go into the
kitchen and see for herself. "Nobody?" she squeaked.

"We don't wash. We throw them out. I bought a couple of cases of paper plates, cups, plastic silverware,
things like that."

"A couple of *cases*? I'm only going to have this cast
on for another ten days."

"It makes life easier."

A typically male solution to a problem. But a solution, nonetheless. She bit her tongue and decided to
change the subject. She looked at Crystal. "Time for
bed, honey. Would you tell Donetta that I need her
help getting you ready?"

Crystal's eyes filled with tears. "My mommy went away. I don't know where she went."

"You must miss her." Raine stroked Claire's hair and met Alan's shocked gaze over the child's head.

"Sometimes—" the child thought for a minute "—sometimes Toby gets mad."

"At you?"

"Uh-huh."

"I know," Raine said, choosing her words carefully. "But I think Toby gets mad at everybody. I think he has a lot of 'mad' inside."

"He likes it here."

"You think so?"

"Yup. He told me to be real good and not wet my bed anymore so we could stay."

"You can stay, even if you wet the bed."

"Really?"

"Really. Now go get Donetta for me, okay?" The little girl jumped off the couch and ran through the dining room to the kitchen.

"Do they always come out with things like that?"

"Yes. You never know when they're thinking about their families or worrying about what's going to happen to them next."

"I never thought of it that way," he said. "And I've never asked you much about why these kids are here." Alan lowered his voice. "I guess I figured the kids didn't know their parents and didn't care."

"Oh, they care all right. Very much."

"I see that." He moved over and put his arm around Raine's shoulders. "What about Crystal's mother? Do you know where she is?"

"No. I don't think anyone does. She left the kids

alone in an abandoned car. One of the neighbors noticed and called the police."

Alan swore softly under his breath. "At least they're safe now."

Raine leaned back against his arm, grateful to have his strength beside her, warm and solid. "That's the whole idea."

One of the boys screamed from the kitchen. "Sounds like a food fight to me," Alan muttered, leaving the couch. "Guess I'll go kick some butt."

It really was remarkable that a stranger could take over her house, with her children and everything else involved. All day Raine had paid close attention to the children's behavior and had not noticed that they were nervous or upset by the changes in the house. Maybe there was a lot more to Alan than she had given him credit for.

RAINE LEANED against the sink and eyed the ancient, claw-footed bathtub with longing. Claire had helped her with a sponge bath, but that had been less than satisfying. Raine longed to soak in the deep tub, preferably for two or three hours, and read the historical romance she'd bought six months ago and hadn't had time to open.

If she could step into it with her good foot, she could hang the right one over the edge of the tub, keeping the cast safe and dry.

It was worth a try, she figured. She'd kissed all of the children good-night. Alan, in some strange imitation of boarding school, had made sure everyone was in bed with their lights out. No one had griped too much, except Toby, and no one knew what he would do if he couldn't gripe.

Alan hadn't come downstairs again, so Raine assumed he had gone up to the peace and quiet of the third floor and would remain there until morning.

So, it was just her and the tub. Raine leaned over and turned on the faucets, then found the bottle of foaming bath oil Claire had given her for Christmas. After squirting some into the water, the scent of apple blossoms filled the black-and-white-tiled bathroom. Raine retrieved her book from the nightstand and stripped off her clothes before limping back into the bathroom. She tested the water, added more hot water and carefully eased herself in.

It was heaven on earth, she decided, drying her hands on a towel. Her foot was propped out of harm's way and her body luxuriated in the silky water. She reached for her book and opened it to the first page, ready to enjoy every minute of steamy silence.

An hour and a half later, Raine yawned and tossed the book onto the tiled floor. The water had cooled and her leg had grown stiff. She couldn't wait to curl up in bed and continue with the story of love in Montana. Unfortunately she couldn't figure out how she was going to get out of the tub.

"Raine? I just thought I'd say good night," Alan said from the hallway.

"Oh, okay. Good night."

"Are you okay?"

"I'm in the tub, that's all."

She heard the bedroom door open and his footsteps cross the room to the bathroom door. "In the tub? How'd you do that?"

"It's kind of hard to explain, but I'm fine. In fact, I'm ready to get out." To prove her intentions, she nudged the stopper with her toes until it popped out of the drain, releasing the water.

There was silence. "I'll wait here to make sure you can manage."

"I can manage," she insisted, but looked at her outstretched leg and naked body and tried not to laugh out loud. She wasn't sure she could get herself out of this, after all, though all she had to do was turn around, so that her good leg was on the outside of the tub and she could swing it onto the floor.

"Raine?"

"What?"

"Why is everything so quiet?"

"I was thinking."

"You can't get out of there, can you?"

The last of the bathwater gurgled down the drain. "Of course I can. I'm planning the best way, that's all."

She heard an impatient male sigh, then Alan's voice. "That's it. I'm coming in."

"What? You can't!"

"Sure I can. Can you reach a towel?"

"Yes, but—"

"Then cover yourself with it, because I'm not going to let anything happen to you."

"Nothing's going to happen to me," Raine grumbled, but reached for the towel, just in case he meant what he said. She dried herself as best she could, then wrapped the towel around her body, carefully covering herself in pink terry cloth.

The door opened a couple of inches. "All set?"

"Yes." Raine began to think this whole bath idea had been crazy.

Alan stepped inside, walked over to the tub and

frowned at her. "How did you think you were ever going to get out of there?"

"I had it planned," she said, relieved that the towel covered so much of her. "I was going to turn around so that my good leg was on the outside." She made a face and looked back at her foot. "I thought that would be easy, but I'm not sure where to start. I didn't count on stiff muscles."

"Obviously." He put his hands onto his hips. He'd obviously showered, because his dark hair was damp on the ends and his short-sleeved, button-down shirt looked crisp and fresh.

"Are you going out? You're all dressed up."

He put his hands into the pockets of his linen slacks. "I was going to the movies."

Raine felt a stab of jealousy. Did he have a date? "Sounds fun. Don't let me make you late."

"You won't." But he didn't sound convinced; he stepped closer and peered at her.

"Don't step on my book."

Alan looked down and picked up the paperback. "This is the reason you were in here so long?"

"So?"

He shrugged, then set the book upon the edge of the sink. "I should have known. My sisters used to do the same thing."

"Didn't your girlfriends read?"

His eyes twinkled. "Sometimes. But I've never had to help a lady out of her bath before."

"And you don't have to now." But she was getting chilled. Tiny goose bumps dotted her bare arms. "What are you looking at?"

"Your gorgeous little body. I'm also trying to figure out how to lift you out of there."

"Lift me? I just need a shoulder to lean on, I think."

"You need a hell of a lot more than that," he muttered.

"I don't—"

"Hold on," he ordered, leaning over the tub. "I have to brace myself."

"I don't weigh that—" She inhaled sharply when his hands touched her skin. He slid one arm behind her back and under her arm, his thumb grazing the side of her breast. "You can't touch me there—"

"I *have* touched you there," he growled. "Or pretty close." His eyes darkened as he looked at her. Raine was entranced with the raw hunger in his gaze. "And chances are I'll do it again. So shut up and hang on," he ordered, ignoring Raine's protests. "Unless you want to sleep in the bathtub." His other arm cupped the backs of her knees.

Raine had no choice except to put her arms around Alan's neck, all the while hoping desperately that the towel would stay in place.

"I'm going to get your clothes wet," she said.

"That's the least of my problems." He adjusted his grip on her body, lifted her over the edge of the tub and into his arms. "There," he said, sounding pleased with himself. He smiled down at her and then looked at the towel. "It's slipping."

Raine blushed and looked down, grabbing a corner of the towel to keep it in place. "Put me down."

"No 'Thank you, Alan'?"

"Thank you, Alan," she repeated, clutching the towel. "Now put me down."

"Right." He carried her out of the bathroom and across the dimly lit bedroom to the bed, its ivory quilt smoothed neatly into place. He lifted back the covers to expose the flowered sheets underneath, then plopped Raine onto the bed, her head against the lace-edged pillows.

Charlie, curled up at the end of the mattress, lifted his head and growled at Alan.

"Quiet," Raine told the animal. She quickly adjusted the towel and attempted to slip her legs under the sheets, but the weight of Alan's body prevented her from hiding under the covers. "Would you hand me my robe, please? It's on the chair by the desk."

Alan's arms were still around her. "I think I like you better naked."

"Alan..."

He bent to kiss her, and she reached for him. She had to admit that she loved kissing him, even though it wasn't the smartest thing in the world for her to do. Raine touched his face, feeling the freshly shaved skin under her palms. He smelled good, too. "Did you have a date tonight?"

"No. I thought I'd get out of here so I wouldn't end up here, in your bedroom."

"What made you think you'd end up in here?"

"Lack of willpower."

"That's not very flattering."

He kissed her lips once again, then lifted his head to smile into her eyes. "Of course it is. Means you're irresistible."

"I'm also naked," she grumbled. "And very embarrassed."

"I prefer it," he murmured, kissing her neck. His hand dropped to the towel. "Your skin feels like silk."

"Apple blossom bath oil."

He nuzzled her neck. "I'll remember the fragrance for the rest of my life."

"You shouldn't say things like that."

"Why not?" He lifted the terry cloth barrier and his lips drifted lower to the top of her breast. "I mean it. I'll remember the feel of your lips and the softness in your eyes when I touch you like this...." His fingertips stroked her breast. "And I'll remember the first time we made love."

"We're not making love," she protested softly.

"We will. If not tonight, then sometime soon." He smiled at her as his hand cupped her breast, and Raine's breath caught in her throat. "I can wait."

Raine wondered if she could. Still, she fought to maintain a grip on her defenses. "You're not the kind of man I expected to—to have in my life."

"I guessed that. I didn't expect you, either."

"I guessed that," she echoed. His lips met hers for a long, searing kiss, until all thoughts of any other kind of man vanished—just like the towel between her body and Alan's. She didn't know how she moved onto her side or how Alan's body came to lie facing hers. She felt pillows drop to the floor, heard Charlie whimpering outside the bedroom door, but nothing mattered except the feel of Alan's hard body against hers, pressing closer, and his mouth, pleasing her, touching her, tasting her.

Finally he released her, but his mouth still hovered above hers. "This is your last chance to send me out in the hall with Charlie."

"Well, we haven't known each other very long." She kissed his chin.

"Not a very long time at all," Alan agreed, sliding his hand along her side, dipping at her waist and lingering at her hip. "But I don't remember ever feeling like this."

"Me either," she murmured, leaving a trail of tiny kisses along his jawline.

Alan grinned. "Stop that. I'm trying to be serious here."

"You can be serious if you want to." Raine smiled, reached for the buttons on his shirt and began to undo the first one. She'd reached the third before Alan took over the job himself.

He moved off the bed and dropped his shirt onto the floor. His chest was bare and tanned, with a tantalizing path of chest hair that disappeared into the waistband of his slacks. "Don't move. I'll be right back."

Raine sat up, keeping the sheet around her, but knew she couldn't move even if someone removed the cast from her leg and paid her a million dollars. But there was still something important to settle between them, before this went any further. "Alan? Wait, I—"

He turned, the planes of his face shaded in the dim light. "I have something upstairs," he said, as if reading her mind.

"You don't have to—"

Alan shook his head. "Of course I do. I always use—"

"There's a box in the bathroom, in the medicine cabinet. I think Claire put it there a few days ago."

"Smart old witch." Alan locked the door and went into the bathroom. He switched off the bathroom light, leaving the room lit only by the moonlight behind the flowing lace curtains.

Nerves fluttered in Raine's stomach when Alan returned to the bed. It was one thing to be lifted out of the bathtub—quite another to be making love with a man who was practically a stranger. But when Alan leaned forward and kissed her, Raine's fears disappeared; the passion between them exploded into something she didn't want to stop, wouldn't stop even if she could. They clung together while he removed the last of his clothing and the pink towel fell onto the floor.

There was no longer a reason to go slow, no longer any way to hold back. He followed her down and onto the mattress, skin against skin, hard seeking soft in a tangle of sheets and pillows. When he would have slowed to touch, explore and caress, Raine slid her hands to his hips and urged him against her.

When she would have taken him inside her, he hesitated. "I want it to be good for you."

"It is," she whispered. "It will be."

He entered her, surely, hard and deep, and her hands slid along his back to hold him close. He thrust slowly, letting her grow used to him. Raine trembled as his lips grazed her neck, found the quivering pulse at the base of her throat and moved to claim her lips once again. She hadn't expected to want him this much.

He made love to her with complete absorption and passionate skill. Raine moved with him, sensing what pleased him, until there was nothing left to hold back. The exquisite tension built until she climaxed around him, holding him in her tight warmth while sensations rocked her body. Answering tremors shook Alan's body, then his hoarse cry touched Raine's lips and took her breath away.

Later, tucked in the curve of his shoulder, Raine wondered what had possessed her. She'd had three dates in as many years, and none had come close to turning romantic in her own brass bed. She hadn't needed or wanted anyone in her life until lately. Had Claire really cast some sort of spell over this summer?

She snuggled up to Alan, pleased with the way he

filled up her bed with his large masculine body. Whatever magic had been woven around them, Raine
hoped it wouldn't disappear. At least not for a while.

"You have driven me crazy," he groaned.

"What?"

"I've fantasized about making love to you for weeks,
since the first time I saw you holding that stupid dog.
Raine..." He paused, choosing his words carefully. "I
never intended to make love to you tonight."

"I know. You were going to the movies."

"Yes."

"What were you going to see?"

"What difference does that make?"

She ran her fingertips along his shoulder, enjoying
the play of muscles underneath his skin. "I just wondered."

"I didn't really care. Just as long as it was something
violent. Something to take my mind away from wanting you."

"Interesting the way a man's mind works."

"Yes," he said. "Men are very smart. We remember
things, important things—like the smell of apple blossoms on a woman's skin."

"Is that what you'll think of when you're back in
London or New York or wherever your office is?"

"I don't want to talk about London or anything else
right now. I want to make love to you again," he murmured. "Maybe I should stay in this room for the rest
of my life, watching your eyes light up when you smile
and I'm inside of you."

"You sound more like a poet than a banker," she
said.

"That's a compliment, isn't it?"

"Of course. No one's ever told you you were poetic before?"

"No."

"A banker with the soul of a poet," she teased. "That's an odd combination."

"Maybe I could be good at both."

She lifted her head so she could give him a wicked look. "You're good at a lot of things."

"True," he drawled, smiling into her eyes. "I could think of five or six."

Her hand found him, she smoothed her palm across the hard, satin flesh and felt him swell against her fingers. "Shall we start with the first one and work our way up?"

"Sweetheart, I'm beginning to like the way you think."

9

"GOOD MORNING."

Raine opened her eyes to see Alan walk across the room, a mug of coffee in each hand. She couldn't prevent the blush that heated her cheeks as he approached the bed. He wore white shorts and a navy polo shirt and looked as if he were ready to play a few sets of tennis. "Hi."

"I brought coffee," he said, carefully setting the mugs upon the nightstand. "But you can go back to sleep if you like."

"Uh-uh. It smells wonderful." She sat up, bunched her pillows behind her and looked at the clock. "I slept until ten-thirty?"

He handed her the coffee. "We had a late night."

Alan didn't have to remind her. Last night's memories were all too real. Making love with him had been an unexpected pleasure, an experience she would always treasure, even if she wasn't sure how it fitted into the general picture of her life. Raine attempted to sound casual, as if she accepted coffee in bed all the time. "You've been awake a long time?"

Alan sat down on the edge of the bed and smiled at her. "I sneaked out early, before the children woke up."

"Thank you."

"You've very welcome." His smile seemed to mock her politeness.

"Don't tease. I'm not very good at this morning after talk," Raine admitted, sipping her coffee. It was hot and strong, just the way she liked it.

"There are several variations of morning after," Alan suggested, his dark eyes twinkling.

"Such as?"

"The man leaves while the woman is asleep and is never heard from again."

"What if she wakes up?"

"He says he'll call her."

"And does he?"

"No."

"That doesn't sound very nice. What else?"

He reached for his coffee, took a swallow and thought for a minute. "They have breakfast together. They make small talk. If he's still attracted to her, he might panic and start backing off. He says he'll call her."

"And does he?"

"Maybe. It depends."

"Are there any alternatives, such as *she* leaves first, says she'll call and doesn't?"

"It happens."

"None of this sounds like a happy ending."

"You believe in happy endings? I'm shocked." Alan waited for Raine to defend herself, but she merely drank her coffee. "Of course, I haven't mentioned one other scenario."

"Which is?"

"He has pursued—and won—the woman of his dreams, and wild horses couldn't tear him away from her side."

Raine laughed. "In fairy tales, maybe, but not in real life."

Alan shook his head. "What am I going to do with you, sweetheart?"

"Help me take a bath?"

He stood up beside the bed. "If that means that I can get my hands on your body again, then of course."

"I don't think the children would understand."

"I rented five movies this weekend. They won't even leave the television set."

"That's not good for their eyes."

"It's ninety-nine degrees already, it's Sunday, and the tourists have jammed traffic all over the island. I don't think that this once we need to worry about their eyes. In fact, they're well taken care of. Everyone has had breakfast and the kitchen is cleaned up. All I have to do is take you to the tub."

She set her empty cup upon the table, swung her bare legs over the edge of the bed, then realized she was naked and her robe was still across the room. Fortunately the sheets were tangled, so she grabbed one and preserved her modesty. She tested her foot on the floor, leaning part of her weight upon it to see how it felt. Some soreness, but not much. She looked up; Alan was hovering close to her.

"You're an amazing man," she said, making a face at him. "But I can't figure you out."

"You don't have to," he said, swinging her into his arms. "I have everything figured out for both of us."

Raine was afraid he was right.

SUNDAY PASSED in a haze of heat, sunlight, secret glances and shared smiles.

Alan offered to move the air conditioner into Raine's room, for the fortieth time, and she refused once again.

Raine insisted on helping cook lunch, and Alan took her up on it. She sat at the kitchen table and grated cheese, while he fried the hamburger for the taco filling. The children spent a quiet day watching movies, then ate Popsicles and played games on the shaded back porch. Donetta listened to the radio, hoping to win tickets to the Michael Bolton concert in Providence, and beat the twins at Monopoly. Vanessa, Crystal and Julie spread dolls and doll clothes all over the living room while Toby complained that there was nothing to do.

This was what it would be like, Raine realized, watching Alan pile food onto paper plates. This was what it would be like if they were a real family. If these kids were really hers and if they had a real father.

If Alan stayed. Raine hardened her heart. She was thinking like a love-struck idiot, when she was a mature woman who should be able to handle a summer love affair.

"ARE YOU SURE everyone's asleep?" Raine whispered.

Alan opened the refrigerator and took out a bottle of white wine. He set it upon the table in front of her. "You don't have to whisper. And yes, I'm sure."

"Good."

"That's an understatement." He winked at her and pulled the foil from the top of the bottle. "This foster father business is wearing me out."

"This isn't the vacation you had planned."

"But I think it's the vacation Claire and Edwina planned." He poured the wine into glasses and handed one to Raine. "Here. The best California has to offer. And not in a paper cup, either."

"Thank you."

"Drink up. I'm going to ply you with alcohol and then make love to you." Alan kept his voice light, but his body hardened at the thought of having Raine beneath him once again.

She didn't look concerned. "Is that how bankers seduce women?"

"Hey!" He touched her glass with his. "Whatever works."

"Last night was..." She hesitated, and Alan's heart stopped beating.

"Was what?" he asked carefully, concentrating on loosening his death grip on the fragile crystal. He watched her take a deep breath and he braced himself.

"Incredibly...special," Raine answered. "But I don't want you to think that *I* think it...meant anything."

"You don't want me to think *what?*" In the interest of safety he set the glass down. *What the hell was she talking about?*

Raine drained her glass. "You know what I mean."

"No," he answered through gritted teeth. "I don't."

"You don't have to get angry about it." Her eyes were very large and very blue as she looked at him. Alan was glad there was three feet of pine separating them. "I just wanted you to know that—"

"Our making love didn't mean anything," he finished for her. "Is that right?" She had the gall to nod. He wanted to wring her neck. "It meant something to me."

"It's temporary."

"I know." He frowned. "But that doesn't make it meaningless."

"I don't know why you're getting so upset. We're mature adults. Neither one of us has any commitments," she began.

"Honey, the last time I counted you had *seven* of them."

"Don't interrupt." She took the bottle, refilled her glass and took a sip. "This is really wonderful wine."

"Don't change the subject. You were talking about commitments?"

She turned her gaze back to him. "Yes. Maybe I phrased that badly. Neither one of us *needs* any more commitments." Her grin was lopsided. "Is that better?"

"Yes." He finished his own glass. "But what's your point, Raine?"

"I just wanted you to know I understood that."

"Well, that makes one of us." He would never understand women, not even after growing up with four sisters. "Drink up, sweetheart, because I want your body."

"I want yours, too."

That was all he needed to hear. Alan kicked his chair back and stood up, reaching for Raine's hand. He lifted her to her feet and kissed her, his lips insistent on her warm skin. She lost her balance, and Alan gripped her shoulders to keep her from falling, but didn't move his lips from hers. His hands slid to her waist, feeling the tempting curves underneath the cotton shirt, and lifted her onto the counter.

"Spread your legs," he whispered, and as she did, he stepped into the V between her thighs.

The cotton barriers between them were the most exquisite torture Raine had ever known. She wrapped her arms around Alan and pulled him closer, and his tongue played with hers as heat burned lower and centered between her legs, where his body was pressed so intimately against her own.

She'd thought she'd melt when his fingers teased a trail along her thighs, then higher, to slide under her baggy shorts.

She was so glad she was wearing baggy shorts.

His fingers gripped the tops of her thighs, holding her legs open while his thumbs caressed her burning skin, teasing the edges of her nylon panties, turning her legs to butter and her skin to fire.

"We can't do this here," she moaned; his thumbs caressed the moist scrap of fabric until she felt as if she wasn't wearing anything at all.

"But we are," he countered, his lips finding her earlobe and tugging gently on the soft skin.

Raine groaned and reached for the buttons on his shirt. "We shouldn't. Someone could come in."

"I locked both doors," he whispered, sending shivers of need through her body as he eased his lips under the collar of her shirt.

"Do you always think of everything?"

"I do my best," he admitted. Raine finished unbuttoning his shirt and slid her palms across his hard chest, loving the feel of his skin under her hands. "Now yours," he demanded, keeping his hands high on her thighs, his thumbs continuing to create a heat Raine no longer wanted to deny.

"This is crazy." She unbuttoned her shirt and released the front clasp on her bra, pushing the fabric aside to invite him to move his heated skin against hers.

"We could go to the bedroom," she whispered, at the same time wondering if her knees would hold her if she tried to jump down from the counter. She reached for the waistband of his shorts and released the clasp.

"Too far away."

He was right. Raine didn't want to wait to feel him inside her. Her fingers hurried to find the zipper tab and tug it downward. His mouth melded with hers again, a hot, arousing kiss that raised the temperature in the kitchen to a record high. "What about the kitchen table?"

"Next time," he promised, leaving Raine with erotic visions of future August nights.

"The floor?" She slid her hand under the elastic waistband of his underwear, wanting to do what he was doing to her. Her fingertips touched the hard length of him, feeling the taut, heated satin; Alan groaned.

"Tomorrow," he said, his breathing ragged as he lifted his mouth from hers. He slid his hands down her thighs and away, leaving her with an empty longing.

She wanted him inside her, wanted that delicious, hard length of him filling her.

She didn't care anymore how he did it or where. Nothing mattered except wanting Alan, loving Alan. It didn't surprise her when he pushed one of the legs of her shorts high, when his fingers tugged the damp scrap of satin aside, when he moved into her and filled her with such pleasure that it took her breath away.

When she gasped he claimed her mouth, his tongue moving with hers, her breath catching in her throat as he took her. She wrapped one leg around his waist, holding him to her, and urged him deeper. Her clothing seemed to capture him inside her. It was wild and hot and frenzied; she had never felt such crazy need in her life. Perspiration ran between her breasts, slick against Alan's chest, as she gripped his shoulders. He filled her, thrusting again and again with such raw need and power that Raine could no longer deny her body's greedy reaction. She tightened around him, felt him pull the very climax from deep in her body until endless spasms shook her. Shook them both.

He lifted his mouth from hers, and Raine could feel the bruising her lips had taken. His arms cradled her, but neither moved. Or could move. Raine felt the rapid pounding of his heart under her breast and knew he could feel hers in equal rhythm. For long moments they clung together in the dim light of the kitchen, neither willing to move.

Raine put her head upon his shoulder and willed her heart to slow its beat so she could pull away, pretend this was only a brief interlude of heated sex and not the dangerous, illogical behavior of a woman in love.

CHARLIE BARKED at the front door when a black limousine pulled up in front of the house. Raine peered out of the living-room window and saw a plump, middle-aged lady dressed in black step from the car. She watched in amazement as the chauffeur took three bags from the trunk and followed the tiny woman up the sidewalk.

Charlie yapped in unison with the doorbell, bringing Alan from the kitchen while Raine, barely limping, went to answer the door. Alan hurried past, taking the suitcases and setting them inside.

"I won't need you for another hour, at least," Alan told the uniformed man. He nodded and strode down the steps.

The gray-haired woman stood patiently. "Mr. Wetmore Hunter?"

"Yes. You must be Miss Minter."

Her sweet, round face burst into a radiant smile. "Wonderful of you to send for me! I told Mrs. Alex it was so lovely of you. Of course, Mrs. Alex's brother would have to be lovely, now wouldn't he?" She turned to Raine as if seeking confirmation.

Alan spoke first. "She means my sister, Alexandria."

Miss Minter's gaze went past Alan's shoulder toward the staircase. "Oh, these must be the little lambs! Hello, duckies!"

"Duckies?" Raine looked at Alan. "What's going on?"

"What's a duckie?" Joey asked.

Jimmy was not about to be outdone by his twin. "Are you from another country?"

"England, my dear. A very long time ago." The children came down the stairs and gathered around the tiny woman. Her head barely topped Donetta's. "Why don't you show me where your kitchen is and we'll cook up something for breakfast?"

"Come on." Julie took Miss Minter's hand. "Where's England?"

Joey rolled his eyes. "Don't be such a dope, Julie. Everyone knows where England is."

"Come, come," Miss Minter clucked. "We mustn't call each other names. I'm Miss Minter, and that's what you shall call *me*."

With that, she led the children down the hall, the eight of them chattering together happily as they headed toward the kitchen.

"Alan, who was that woman?"

"Miss Minter. Isn't she wonderful?"

"Answer my question first. Who is she?"

"The new housekeeper."

"I don't have an *old* housekeeper."

Alan looked very pleased with himself. "You have one now. I called Alex days ago, and she promised to help me find someone who could take over running this household."

"I run this house."

"Not lately. And not on one leg, you don't. Besides, I thought you would enjoy a little time off."

"This is my job, Alan. I can't afford to hire someone to take care of things around here. People like that cost a fortune."

"You don't have to worry about that. I've taken care of everything."

"In other words, you just have to wave your check-book around and everything falls into place."

"I don't know why you're so angry."

"If you didn't want to help with the kids, you should have told me. If you were sick of it you should have packed your bags and left."

"I didn't—don't—feel that way. But I've got work piling up upstairs. And the children can't continue to eat hot dogs off paper plates for another week or two, and if you go back to walking around here full-time, your foot is going to take forever to heal. I thought sending for help was the best solution."

"You should have discussed it with me first."

"I wanted to surprise you."

"Surprise me? This is my house, my children. And my problem."

"It's been my problem, too, or haven't you noticed? I can't stay here indefinitely—we both know that." With that, he pushed open the screen door and went onto the porch.

"I don't want her to stay!" Raine called, hurrying after him. She didn't want to think about him leaving. "You hired her, you tell her to leave."

"No way." He stopped and smiled at her. "We need her."

"I don't—"

"Need anyone?" He kissed her lips briefly, then shook his head. "Of course you do. You just haven't realized it yet."

"ARE YOU FALLING IN LOVE with him?"

Raine's heart sank. Her stepmother would never leave the subject alone. "Who I'm in love with—even if I'm not—is none of your business, Claire."

"Of course it is," her stepmother replied. "Whose business would it be?"

"Mine." Raine glared at her foot as she rocked in the porch swing.

"How is your foot, dear?"

"Much better. It hardly hurts. I'm going to call that doctor and see if he will take the cast off sooner."

"When do you think you'll be up to dancing?"

"Dancing? Are you kidding?"

"No, darling, I'm not." Claire took a pad and pen out of her purse. "I'm planning a party. A birthday party."

"It's not your birthday. In fact, your birthday is in November."

"Close enough." Claire shrugged. "Besides, I feel like celebrating early."

Raine decided not to try to figure out Claire's logic. She'd always been a little strange about birthdays. "All right. I'll ask the doctor when I can dance."

"Can't you tell for yourself?"

"Okay. I hardly limp, unless I've been walking around for a long time. I'm sure I could dance, at least a little."

"In ten days? There was a cancellation at Rosecliff—I love the ballroom. The bride called off the wedding. I have to make definite plans and let them know today."

"Claire, do whatever you want. Just write the date on my calendar, if it means that much to you."

"I want it to be a special evening."

Suspicious, Raine glanced at her stepmother. "Special for whom?"

"You and—"

"Don't say it. What's between me and Alan is none of your business."

"None of my business? I *sent* him to you! You should be thanking me, you should—"

"Should not speak to you," Raine finished.

"Why? He's wonderful."

"Yes, right now he is. Because he wants to be. He's on vacation and it's a lark to play uncle to seven children. He's made it clear that this isn't his kind of lifestyle, not permanently."

"And what do you think he's playing with you? House?"

"I don't know. He hired a housekeeper without telling me, and he's sending the kids back and forth to camp in a limousine, for heaven's sake."

"A stroke of genius."

"You would agree with him."

"What good is having money if you don't use it to make your life easier? Why should he spend his time wiping noses when he can hire someone to do it for him?"

"Is that how my father looked at parenthood—as wiping noses?"

"You have a blind spot where your father is concerned. I loved that man, so watch what you say about him."

"He loved you, too." Raine smiled at her stepmother. "I always thought that was the nicest thing, even though I probably wasn't very kind to you at first."

"I thought you were, darling. So serious and scared."

"That house wasn't fun until you arrived."

Claire beamed. "What a lovely thing to say! Your father was good for me, too. I wasn't used to staying in one place. Your father settled me down, gave me a place to call home. Opposites attract, they say." Claire pulled a linen handkerchief from her purse and dabbed her eyes.

Raine thought of her weekend making love with Alan and couldn't disagree with Claire. Despite their differences, they'd made a lot happen in a few short days. It terrified her. She'd fallen in love with him, which was the stupidest thing she'd ever done in her life.

"Anyway, I think you've fallen in love with Alan Hunter, even though you don't want to admit it," Claire declared. "It's made you cranky. A party is exactly what you need to lift your spirits."

"MISS MINTER?" Raine peered into the kitchen and was amazed by the transformation. The floor sparkled, the table gleamed with fresh polish, and the counters were cleared of dirty dishes and clutter.

"In here, duckie!"

Raine followed the sound of the lady's voice into the laundry room and saw Miss Minter sorting clothes.

"Here, I'll help with that," Raine said, feeling guilty that someone else was sorting her dirty laundry.

"The little lambs are very lucky, aren't they?"

"Lucky?" Raine started a pile for blue jeans.

"To have a home like this, and a sweet girl like yourself to love them and take care of them," she declared. "I didn't hesitate a bit when I heard about them." She winked at Raine. "Retirement is no fun, my dear. No fun at all."

"Do you mind my asking where you came from?"

"Heavens, no! One of those little retirement places in Florida. God's waiting room, they call it. Now I know why. Thank the good Lord Mrs. Alex called me. I took care of her husband's family, you know. Worked for them for years. Mrs. Alex wanted me to help with her little ones, but I thought I might be too old for babies. My hearing isn't as good as it used to be." She smiled again. "I can hear your children, though. They speak up quite well, now, don't they?"

"Uh, yes, they do. How long are you able to stay?"

"Just as long as you need me, duckie." She switched on the machine and shut the lid. "Just as long as you need me."

That was the trouble, Raine decided, going back into the gleaming kitchen. She needed too much all of a sudden.

How could she fire Miss Minter? She needed someone with two good legs to deal with the children. How could she bear to think of Alan leaving? She needed his arms around her at night—or any other time, for that matter. And Claire? She could tell her stepmother to mind her own business, but Raine even needed

Claire's antics to cheer her up. Still, she needed to back off a bit. Self-preservation.

Alan poked his head in the door. "Still angry with me?"

"No. I'm sorry I yelled. I don't like surprises."

"You're allowed. I should have asked you first." He looked around the kitchen and whistled slowly. "It pays to hire the best, doesn't it?"

"I still can't believe it," Raine groaned.

"Are you talking about sending for Miss Minter or what happened on the kitchen counter last night?"

"Both, I guess."

"Me, too." He came over to her and kissed her, pulling her into his arms.

"Miss Minter is in the laundry room," Raine warned.

"Okay. The counter's safe, for now."

"The bed wasn't bad, either."

He grinned and attempted to slide his hand under her shirt. "Not bad at all."

Raine stopped him, unwilling for the housekeeper to find them groping each other. "Tell me about the chauffeur. You hired him, too?"

"His name is Harry, and yes, I hired him, too."

"That's a waste of money. I have a perfectly good van in the garage."

"Someone else can deal with Newport traffic," Alan explained. "I have better things to do with my time."

"Such as?"

"Come upstairs to my room and I'll show you."

"I can't," Raine said, smiling at him. "Your mother and Claire will be back any minute to discuss their party."

He swore under his breath. "They're back?"

She nodded. "Claire came by a while ago, after you stomped off."

"I didn't stomp off. I walked down to the Wave café for breakfast."

"Whatever. They're planning a little party and have rented the Rosecliff ballroom."

"Why?"

Raine decided to protect her stepmother's privacy. "For Claire's birthday party. I have a feeling it's going to be very fancy and very romantic."

"Romantic? I like the sound of that."

"They hadn't given up, you know. They're still matchmaking."

"I'm not complaining."

"You should be," Raine said, before his lips touched hers. When the kiss ended, she stepped back. "This has gone too far, Alan."

He let her go. "How?"

"The bathtub, the bed, the *kitchen counter*, for heaven's sake. I'm not used to...behaving this way. I think I should go back to wiping noses and you should go back upstairs and do whatever it is that you do."

"I hired Miss Minter so you would have some time off."

"No, you hired me so that *you* would have time off." She shook her head when he would have protested. "Let's take a break, okay? You're going back to London soon and I don't want to get hurt." Raine didn't know how much clearer she could be.

Alan hesitated before he spoke again. "Fair enough. I'll go back to being the boarder, but we have a date for Claire's ball. Fair enough?"

"Yes." She wouldn't admit, even to herself, that she'd already fallen in love. There was nothing fair about that.

10

"WHO'S THE SMARTEST friend you have, Edwina?"

"Martha VanDoorn," the tiny woman replied from the neighboring chaise lounge Maizie had so thoughtfully provided for their comfort.

"*Martha VanDoorn?*"

"Last year she won eleven thousand dollars on Wheel of Fortune."

"That doesn't count." Claire sniffed. "I'm not talking about *buying vowels*, for heaven's sake."

Edwina held out her glass and Claire poured another martini from the pitcher placed conveniently on the table between them. "You're talking about the party, I suppose?"

"I'm talking about matchmaking, Wina. The party will create the perfect evening for romance. Our children won't be able to resist each other. I have it all planned. Raine will wear a lovely Halston I just happened to see downtown, and of course your son will look outrageously handsome in a tuxedo. Don't forget to remind him to send for one."

"I won't."

"And also remind him about flowers."

"I will." Edwina took a delicate sip of her drink. "These martinis aren't as good as the ones Miss Minter makes for us."

Claire agreed. "She's a gem. That was a stroke of genius on *your* part."

Edwina was pleased to have received a compliment from her friend. Claire didn't give compliments often. "Well, dear, I have my moments."

"I've never understood how you raised five children, though."

"With a housekeeper, a cook and a nanny, of course. While you were traveling all over the world with your first husband, I stayed in New York having babies."

"I envied you," Claire said with a sigh. "Roland never wanted children."

"Well, it's a good thing you divorced him and married John Claypoole. You ended up with Raine and Quentin."

"And I love them dearly. So much that I can't bear to see Raine living her life alone."

Edwina reached out and patted Claire's hand. "Now, now, darling. We've taken care of that, haven't we?"

"No, you're not going to get out of it."

Edwina winced. "Now, Alan..."

"Don't use that maternal voice on me, either." Alan took his mother's elbow, led her onto the front porch and guided her to the swing. "Sit."

"Of course, I'd love to chat with you," Edwina began, her hands fluttering uselessly in the air. "But the three little girls are waiting for a story and I promised..."

"They can wait a little longer," Alan said, sitting down beside her. He planted his feet on the floor to prevent the swing from rocking and turned to his mother. "What is this crap about a party at Rosecliff?"

"Well, it was Claire's idea...."

"Don't give me that innocent look, Mother. You and I both know it won't work."

"Well..." She sniffed. "*Sometimes* it does."

"You're matchmaking with that woman. You've never meddled in my life before, until now."

"And it's about time, too." Edwina smiled at him encouragingly. "Claire and I thought a little party might be just the thing to make you and Raine see each other in another light."

"I don't get it."

Edwina shrugged, as if to say *Men!* "It's supposed to be romantic, darling." It was time for a little white lie. "I've noticed that Raine isn't exactly falling in love with you."

"That is my business."

"Well, is she?"

"I don't know."

"Well, there you have it. You need help."

"Mother, I don't know how you got into all this in the first place, but you and Claire arranged for me to rent these rooms, didn't you?"

"Of course."

"Because you thought I'd be a good husband for Raine?"

"Yes." She wagged a finger at him. "And I know you need a wife. My father's will was very specific."

"I can't believe the old man was allowed to make a will like that."

"It wasn't so unusual in that day and age. My father was a little eccentric, but he held strong opinions and he lived by them."

"Couldn't anyone talk him out of it?"

"Whatever for? Darling, you were just a small child.

Men and women married young in those days. They certainly didn't wait until their mid-thirties, for heaven's sake. Who would have known that it would cause this much trouble?''

"It's caused a great deal of trouble," Alan declared, thinking of the lawyer's fees he'd paid over the past eighteen months, and so far all for nothing.

"Marry the girl, Alan. You're in love with her. I can see that without your having to tell me."

Alan opened his mouth, but no words came out. How could he deny something that was staring him in the face? And what on earth did he want to do about it?

Edwina patted him on the cheek. "Close your mouth, darling. You'll be all right in a moment."

Alan took a deep breath. "Don't get your hopes up, Mother. Raine and I are as different as night and day."

· "You have to convince her that you're the perfect man for her, my dear. With more than words, of course."

"WELL?" Raine twirled on the landing. "What do you think?"

Anything Alan hoped to say stuck in his throat as Raine paused on the staircase. Seven children surrounded him and watched the black-haired beauty in the shimmering pink dress walk toward him.

The twins started a war whoop and the rest of the children joined in, even Vanessa.

"You look like a princess," Julie declared. "Like in a book."

Donetta held the Instamatic camera and focused it. "Smile," she ordered. Raine stopped on the bottom step and did as she was told. The flash popped and Raine turned her gaze toward Alan.

"You look very impressive," she told him. He looked very nonchalant and elegant, as if he wore tuxedos every day. She'd certainly been to many parties with tuxedo-clad men, but somehow this was different.

Tonight was different.

She couldn't put her finger on it, but something special was happening. Raine met Alan's admiring gaze and tried not to blush.

"It's true," he murmured, taking her hand and lifting it to his lips. "You do look like a princess."

"Thank you." Her skin burned where his lips had touched.

Raine felt like one, too. She'd argued with Claire about the gift of a dress until she saw what Claire had purchased. In the end, as Claire had known would happen, Raine hadn't been able to resist. With the strapless bodice trimmed with silver accents, its elegant simplicity was just too tempting.

"Shall we?" Alan held on to her hand as if he was afraid she would disappear forever if he let go.

"I want a picture of the two of you together," Donetta said. "Everybody get out of the way."

The rest of the children reluctantly moved away from Raine so the couple could smile obligingly for the camera, then Raine knelt to hug the children. "Everyone be very good for Miss Minter, okay?"

"'Kay." Crystal yawned.

Jimmy sneezed, Vanessa hid behind Alan's legs, and Toby looked upset.

"Are you comin' back?" he asked, his brown eyes dusted with suspicion.

"Of course we are," Raine promised, suddenly realizing that this was the first time since they'd moved in that she'd left Toby and Crystal at night. "But it will be very late, so we'll see you in the morning."

The little boy nodded and sidled up to Joey, who tried to reassure him. "We'll watch a movie and eat popcorn," he told his friend. "We'll have fun, you'll see."

"And so will we," Alan said, tugging Raine toward the door.

Harry stood at the curb, the limousine door open for them. As they approached, Harry presented Raine with a large spray of white roses tied with a silver bow.

"They're beautiful," Raine said, touching the velvet petals with gentle fingertips.

"White roses seem to fit you," Alan murmured, helping her into the car.

"Thank you," Raine said, setting the bouquet upon the opposite seat. "You didn't have to do that."

"I know I didn't. It's something I should have done weeks ago."

Raine didn't know what he meant by that, but she didn't pursue it. "You didn't notice anything different?"

"What? Your hair looks the same to me."

"It is the same."

"The diamond earrings are stunning."

"A birthday present from my father many years ago." She crossed her legs in a deliberate motion. "But that's not what I'm talking about."

Alan glanced down to see that silver sandals decorated her feet. "The cast is gone." He looked up at her again and smiled. "When did that happen?"

"This morning. The doctor told me to be careful with how much dancing I did tonight, but he didn't see any reason to keep a bandage on it." The dress deserved more than flat sandals, but Raine wasn't going to complain.

"Congratulations," he murmured, bending close to her ear. "How does it feel?"

"Wonderful," Raine breathed as his breath tickled her ear.

"I've missed you."

"I needed to slow down." She'd tried to give herself time to fall out of love with Alan, but that plan hadn't worked. Just looking at him every day was enough to make her heart beat faster. Not making love to him had only made her want him more.

"I know, but these past ten days haven't been easy." His lips grazed her cheek and then brushed her lips softly. "Did you miss me at night?"

"Yes, but Charlie kept me company."

"I would have gladly kicked him out of your room. I've done it before, remember?"

She shook her head and looked into his eyes. "That was a weekend of...madness. I've come to my senses and you should, too."

"You're always telling me what to do," he chided, kissing his way to her other ear and sending shivers along Raine's skin.

"I thought it was the other way around."

He lifted his head as the limousine came to a stop in front of an enormous, white mansion. "See? We're good for each other."

She shook her head and laughed. "I'm not so sure about that."

"I'll do my best to convince you, then."

Rosecliff's wrought iron gates were open to admit Claire's guests, and Raine and Alan stepped inside the white-marbled vestibule. Alan presented his invitation to a butler, who bowed and waved them forward.

Raine slipped her fingers through Alan's as they passed the heart-shaped staircase, with its red carpet and iron railing, into the crowded reception room. Music poured through the wide doors and conversation hummed everywhere. Raine didn't recognize anyone, although several older women nodded politely.

"We'd better find Claire and let her know we've arrived," Alan said, guiding Raine toward the ballroom. "She'll hunt us down if we don't."

"You make her sound like such a witch."

"Isn't she?"

"Not all the time." *Unless she's casting spells, like the one I'm falling under tonight.*

"Watch yourself. You're mellowing."

She was mellowing, all right. Wearing a beautiful evening gown and diamond earrings could have that effect. If that wasn't enough, stepping back into the early 1900s would be the crowning touch. "There they are," she said, waving toward the west wall of the lavish white ballroom where Claire and Edwina were receiving guests. "Holding court."

"Why am I not surprised?"

He wove through the crowd, keeping a careful grasp on Raine's hand. Dressed in antique white lace dresses, Claire and Edwina stood amid a fragrant bank of white hydrangeas, roses, orchids and lilies of the valley. Silver bows decorated the flowers, and matching silver threads sparkled in the ladies' dresses.

"Well, darlings," Claire trilled as they approached, "you're right on time. And the two of you look absolutely wonderful."

Alan released Raine's hand and touched her on the

back, urging her toward her stepmother. Raine kissed the cheek Claire offered. "So do the two of you." She turned to Alan's mother. "Hello, Edwina. Where did you find dresses like that?"

"They've been in the family for years," Edwina confided. "My mother never threw anything away."

Alan looked around the room. "Who are all these people? Two hundred intimate friends?"

Claire tapped him on the arm with her fan. "I don't know most of them myself, but I think they're having a wonderful time, don't you?"

"Yes," he said, surveying the crowd. "But how did you convince two hundred strangers to attend your birthday party?"

Edwina answered instead. "It was genius. An absolute stroke of genius. You wouldn't believe what she did."

Alan smiled. "Maybe we would."

"'Stroke of genius' is a bit of an overstatement, Wina." Claire shrugged. "I simply contacted the local Make a Wish foundation and offered to throw a ball. These lovely people bought tickets, and all the money goes to finance fulfilling the dreams of ill children."

"Why, Claire..." Raine began, touched by her stepmother's thoughtfulness.

"It's nothing," she demurred, shaking her head slightly. "So darlings, what do you think of my *Ball blanc*?"

Edwina lifted her cheek for Alan's kiss. "She modeled it after Tessie Oelrich's white ball in 1904, right in this very ballroom. Isn't that a breathtaking idea?"

"It's absolutely gorgeous, Claire," Raine agreed. She couldn't help teasing her stepmother. "It's another stroke of genius. You've done wonders in such a short time.''

Claire beamed, obviously pleased with Raine's approval. "Oh, yes, I know." She and Edwina exchanged a smug look. "It's one of my specialities."

"LOOK AT THEM." Edwina sighed. "So perfect."

"Yes. Just as we imagined." The conspirators watched the tall, dark-haired man and the tiny, dark-haired woman dance in each other's arms against a backdrop of arched French doors and silver pots filled with flowers. The enormous chandeliers sparkled above the crowd as Claire and Edwina strolled around the outer edges of the room.

"This must be the most beautiful ballroom in Newport," Claire added.

"My grandmother used to tell stories about the balls here." Edwina adjusted the lace on her sleeve. "I never dreamed I'd celebrate your birthday here."

Claire made a face. "I suppose I have to pretend to enjoy my cake."

"I think that would be a nice touch, dear."

"I'll do it later," she promised, hoping Wina would forget. There was enough food and refreshment in the reception room to satisfy the most discriminating palates, so she needn't feel guilty about delaying the cake. Claire kept a careful watch on her stepdaughter between greeting acquaintances and nodding to strangers. She and Edwina paused again when they had another clear view of their favorite couple.

"The rose dress was an excellent choice."

"Your son is playing the part of the perfect gentleman."

"He's not playing a part, my dear. Alan is truly in love."

"Did he tell you?"

"He doesn't have to tell me in words. A mother knows these things."

"And Raine loves him, too."

"Do you really think so?"

"Yes, I do. But the question is, will she admit it?"

ALAN HELD RAINE in his arms and they waltzed to the strains of Strauss. Somehow he knew Claire had selected only the most romantic music for the evening. He was unreasonably and illogically pleased. It fitted his mood.

Tell the woman you're in love with her.

It wasn't that easy, even though he'd had days to examine how he felt about her. He'd missed her body, of course. But he'd missed other things as well. He'd attempted to concentrate on work he shouldn't have been concerned about, while Raine had immersed herself in the children's activities.

Tell her you've fallen in love. The top of her head barely came to his shoulder, her cheek grazed his lapel. Her perfume, some light scent she'd worn before, wafted into his nostrils and drove him crazy with desire. Which, he supposed, was exactly what perfume was supposed to do.

Well, it was working. *Tell her you love her.* Alan's hand tightened around Raine's waist.

"Raine?" he tried.

She looked up, her blue eyes sparkling. "Isn't this fun?"

He promptly forgot what he was going to say. "Yes," he managed.

A little wrinkle appeared between her eyebrows. "Aren't you having a good time?"

"Why would you think that?"

"It's not like you to be quiet," she replied. "You usually have something to say and you haven't said a word for three waltzes."

"Have I told you how beautiful you look tonight?"

Her cheeks flushed. "Yes. And thank you."

Have I told you how much I love you? "It's true," he growled, pulling her close to him. "Do you want to stop for a while?"

"No. I'm not tired and my foot doesn't hurt and I could dance all night in this beautiful ballroom."

"I guess that answers my question." He twirled her in front of the open French doors as a cooling breeze drifted from the ocean. "But I think people are beginning to leave. Claire's birthday party is almost over."

"She loved it. I loved it." Raine gazed into his eyes. "I'm going to dream of crystal chandeliers and champagne tonight. What will you dream of?"

"That's a leading question, sweetheart."

She laughed. "I know. You looked so serious, I had to tease you."

Serious? He was serious, all right. "I don't intend to dream tonight, because I'll be making love to you until dawn. I've had enough of this separation."

"Until dawn? It's after midnight now."

He pulled her tighter against him. "Which doesn't give us much time."

"Only four or five hours."

"Not nearly enough." Raine melted as he looked at her with passion in his eyes. She'd managed to resist the physical attraction between them for almost two weeks, but this was too much. The night, the music, and Alan's masculine charm had all combined to work an irresistible magic around her. She couldn't fight it any longer and didn't want to. The summer would be over soon enough, Alan would return to London, and Raine would return to her seven children.

Life would return to normal. A very lonely normal life, Raine was afraid.

"Would you like some champagne?"

"We'll have some later," she promised.

"Later?"

"At dawn."

ALAN UNDRESSED HER in the semidarkness of the bedroom. He stood behind her and released the zipper, then kissed the nape of her neck and the soft, ticklish place where her neck sloped to her shoulders. He slid the heavy dress down her body, Raine wriggled out of it and draped it over the desk chair. She stood naked, except for thigh-high, sheer stockings and ivory silk panties.

Raine turned to face him, her breasts brushing the tiny pleats in his shirt. He took her into his arms, hummed something that resembled a waltz, and danced her slowly around the dark room.

"I didn't know you were so romantic."

"I told you that you didn't know me very well," he murmured, tucking their clasped hands to his chest. His fingers brushed her breasts and sent tingling shocks along her bare skin. "You don't even know that I've fallen in love with you, do you?"

"No."

"Are you in love with me, Raine?"

"Yes. But I didn't want to be," she confessed.

"I know." His hand tightened on the smooth curve of her waist.

She smiled at him. "Then how do things like this happen?"

"Coincidence. Fate. Magic." He stopped dancing and bent to touch his lips to hers. "I don't know which one," he said before he kissed her. It was a kiss full of love and promise and longing, and Raine felt as if she would shatter into tiny pieces from sheer happiness. Somehow she managed to unbutton his shirt and he shrugged it off his shoulders. She fumbled with his clothing in the darkness until she was the only one left with anything covering her body. He was hot and hard against her as his lips sought a trail along her neck and moved down to tease her breasts. He knelt before her while his fingers eased the tiny scrap of silk over her abdomen and along her thighs in a slow motion. The whispering trail of silk glided down her thighs to her ankles, until Raine lifted her foot and kicked the garment aside.

He treated her thighs the same way, caressing her skin with his lips as he slowly removed each fragile stocking. When he stood once more, Raine, trembling and needy, reached for him and held his hard length in her hands. She smoothed the satin skin and marveled that there could be such passion in her life, in her bed, in her body.

Alan groaned and swept her into his arms, carrying her the few steps to the waiting bed.

He made love to her with his hands and mouth and with all the words he hadn't yet spoken.

She made love to him with her fingertips and her lips and with all of the love she'd stored in her heart.

And when he joined his body with hers, when he

filled her and she held him, they moved together in a timeless rhythm of love and passion, until the world exploded into shards of crystal, shimmering through the ebony night.

"MARRY ME." Alan lifted his head from the pillow and peered at Raine. Her eyes were closed, her breathing was even and soft. She lay cuddled against him, her round backside pressed against his groin in a most satisfactory way. Alan cleared his throat and tried again, this time a little softer. "Marry me."

It wouldn't hurt to practice, he decided. He moved strands of dark hair from her cheek. "Marry me," he whispered into her ear, hoping she would awaken and put him out of his misery.

But Raine didn't move, not even an eyelash. It was growing lighter as dawn greeted the room. He knew he should slide out of bed and tiptoe up three flights of stairs before Miss Minter or the children woke up, but he didn't have the heart to leave Raine yet.

He wanted her to open her eyes and smile. He wanted to make love to a sleepy woman on a Sunday morning. He wanted the scent of apple blossoms on his pillow at night, he wanted to hear her laughter in the afternoon. He wanted her to marry him and stay part of his life forever, because he couldn't imagine spending the rest of his life without her.

Alan put his head upon the pillow and closed his eyes. He would let Raine sleep as long as she needed. He would still be here when she woke up.

RAINE HEARD THE SOUND of little footsteps hurrying down the stairs and pulled the sheet over her head to block out the noise. She started to stretch, but her toes bumped someone's warm shins.

Alan.

Raine opened her eyes and struggled to wake up. Alan shouldn't be here. But he was, snoring softly near her ear, his larger body warm against hers. She wouldn't, shouldn't explain this to seven little children on a Sunday morning. Seven little children who always brought her the Sunday paper and climbed into bed to fight over the comics.

Charlie whined at the door and Raine groaned. The little dog wouldn't give up until he got into the bed. He scratched and whined louder, until Raine was afraid he'd bring all the children to the door, worrying that something was wrong.

She slid carefully out of bed, tiptoed to the door and unlocked it. Then, hiding behind the door, she opened it enough to let the dog inside before locking it shut behind him. Charlie gave her a pained look, trotted across the room and jumped onto the bed. Raine hurried after him, afraid of what the little dog would do when he saw Alan.

But Charlie just padded up to Alan's face, sniffed and turned away to return to the foot of the bed.

"Good dog," Raine whispered.

"Mmm?"

Raine climbed back into bed and pulled the sheet over her. She touched Alan's rough cheek and smoothed a lock of dark hair from his forehead. "Nothing. Go back to sleep."

He opened his eyes. "Did that damn dog just kiss me?"

"Sort of. That's what happens when you don't go back to your own room."

"I'll risk it." He slid a warm palm over her skin. "I'll risk it anytime."

"Well, I won't. We have to sneak you up the back staircase."

"Couldn't we have coffee first?"

"Later."

He kissed her shoulder. "Then couldn't we make love before you send me away?"

Raine snuggled against him. "The children will be knocking on the door any minute now. I heard them downstairs a few minutes ago."

"Marry me, then."

Raine froze. "What?"

He smoothed her hair and looked into her eyes. "I'm serious, Raine. Marry me. Let's wake up together for the rest of our lives."

"Alan..."

"You know I love you. And you've said you loved me."

"I do," she whispered.

"Then spend the rest of your life with me."

"I can't..."

"Yes, you can. Just say yes."

Her heart resumed beating with a rapid pounding, and Raine took a deep breath while Alan waited for her answer. "I can't," she finally stammered again.

"Will you think about it?"

"What are you asking me to do, Alan?"

"It was a simple question."

"No, I don't think it was." Raine eased herself out of Alan's arms, away from the warm comfort of her bed. Minutes later, safely behind her locked bathroom door as the shower spray soaked her skin, Raine blinked back tears. Marry Alan? It wasn't simple at all. Was he asking her to give up her home? Her job? Her children? Was she supposed to pack up and follow him to London, host parties in fancy gowns and attend charity luncheons?

She'd seen that life. It was her mother's life and Claire's, but it wasn't hers.

11

"LET ME TRY asking you again," Alan said, entering the kitchen. Raine missed the tuxedo, but at least this was the man she knew, one in beige slacks and a jade polo shirt. He came to the table and smiled at her. "By the way, you look beautiful in yellow."

"Thank you." After her shower, Raine had changed into a bright sundress and drank two cups of coffee, all in hope of taking her mind off Alan's proposal. Nothing had helped, she realized, but at least now she was wide-awake.

Alan sat down beside her at the kitchen table and pushed two empty cereal bowls out of his way. "No comment?"

"If it's about what you asked me an hour ago, I wish you wouldn't," Raine pleaded as he leaned closer. "Someone could walk in at any minute."

"If they do, I'll change the subject," he promised. "Why won't you marry me?"

"I think I need some more coffee," Raine said, rising from her chair and heading to the other side of the kitchen.

"Not a good enough answer. I'll take you out for breakfast," Alan offered. "We can talk privately and you can have all the coffee you want."

Raine hesitated, unwilling to discuss marriage in the middle of the kitchen, while Miss Minter folded clothes in the next room and little girls played dolls on the back porch.

"Besides," he continued. "Edwina and Claire could drop in anytime now to recap last night's party. Maybe you don't want to miss their visit."

"You're playing dirty."

"Yeah."

The last thing Raine needed this morning was Claire's scrutiny. She'd seen the triumphant expression on her stepmother's face when they'd left Rosecliff. "All right."

"We'll walk to La Forge," Alan said, looking pleased. "They serve brunch on the porch."

Raine told Miss Minter where they were going, then stepped outside with Alan into the sunshine and headed down the street toward Bellevue Avenue, where traffic was already heavy. Alan held her hand while they walked the three blocks to the restaurant.

"This will be over after Labor Day," Raine said as they dodged the crowds.

"I may have to go to New York next week," Alan said. "But I'll be back within a few days."

"You're certainly well rested now. Your vacation was good for you."

He smiled at her. "Yes, in many ways."

"When do you start back to work?"

"I haven't decided yet. I need to make a decision soon, though." He pushed open the heavy wooden door and ushered Raine into the restaurant's cool darkness. "A lot depends on you."

She wished her stomach wouldn't drop to her toes at the thought of him leaving. She loved him, but couldn't live with him. And he knew it, too, despite all his masculine insistence to the contrary.

They walked down the narrow hallway to the other end of the restaurant, where a hostess showed them to a small table near the window overlooking the grass court. A jazz quartet played a bossa nova in the middle of the porch, lending a festive mood to Sunday morning.

After they'd ordered coffee and the waitress had told them to help themselves to the buffet in the other room, Alan turned back to Raine. "Now, where were we?"

"Could we have coffee first?" As if on cue, the waitress stepped to the table and filled their cups, giving Raine no more excuses.

"Why won't you say yes?"

"Why do you keep asking?"

"Because I love you." He smiled at her again. "And I don't give up easily."

"I know. That's why you're still living in my house."

"Right. You're beginning to understand me."

"No. I don't understand you at all."

"But last night you said you love me—or was that just passion speaking?"

Raine looked around, hoping no one could hear them. Fortunately none of the other people in the room were paying the least bit of attention. When she turned back to the man waiting for an answer, she couldn't help hearing the love in her voice. "Of course I love you."

"Of course," he repeated, shaking his head. "But not enough to marry me."

"Not enough to give up everything I've worked for, everything that's important to me."

"I wasn't aware I had asked you to do that." He frowned at her and, realizing they weren't making any progress, stood up. "Come on. Let's call a truce and have breakfast."

During breakfast they discussed the weather, the summer, the traffic, music, his sisters and her brother. He revealed he spoke three languages. She confessed her love for country and western music.

He asked her to marry him in German, French and Russian.

"Stop," Raine demanded, setting her empty plate aside for the waitress. "You're teasing about something important."

"Well, at least you admit it's important. This morning you flew out of the bed in the middle of my proposal. At least here you've had to stay in one place long enough to listen to what I have to say."

"What are you asking, Alan? What role does the wife of Alan Wetmore Hunter, international financial wizard, play? What do you expect of me?"

"Just love, sweetheart."

She shook her head. "Nothing's that simple, and you know it. Would we live in London? Would we have to travel? Entertain?"

"Not necessarily."

"Could you be more specific?"

He took her hand. "I can't, not until I've met with people in New York next week. All I'm asking is for a chance to work it out together."

"What about the children?"

"Raine, I love what you do."

"I can't take them with me." Her eyes filled with tears. "If I leave with you I leave them, too."

"Don't make me into a monster. I'm not asking you to leave the children."

"You're not?"

"No. Marry me, the sooner the better, and we'll work out the rest."

"There's more to this than you realize." Raine took a deep breath. "Julie and the twins are going to be up for adoption soon. Are you ready for instant fatherhood?"

"You're going to adopt them?"

"If the state agrees."

He leaned back in his chair. "I admit, it would take some getting used to, but..."

"But what?"

"I'm not shaking with fear, if that's what you mean. We can work this out, Raine."

She wanted to believe everything was as simple as Alan thought. She wished she could fall into his arms and give him the answer he wanted. "What do you want me to say, Alan?"

"I'd prefer a yes, but how about a maybe?" He smiled at her and held her hand tightly within his.

Raine allowed her romantic little heart to hope. After all, he hadn't run screaming out of the restaurant. Maybe he'd grown more accustomed to family life than she thought. "Okay. I'll definitely think about it. But you have to think about this, too."

He smiled at her, a smile full of promise and confidence. "How could I think of anything else?"

"THAT'S THEM coming down the road, isn't it? What's going on, Claire?"

She stood at the door and peered out. "I don't know."

"Why, Claire!" Edwina gasped. "I don't think you've ever said that before."

"They don't look as happy as they did last night."

She turned away from the screen and shrugged. "I think they've reached some sort of crisis."

"*Crisis?*" Edwina wrung her hands. "They're supposed to be falling in love, not having a *crisis!*"

"Shh! They're coming up the walk now. You don't want them to hear you shrieking." The two women arranged themselves on the porch swing and picked up sections of the Sunday newspaper.

"Hello, ladies," Alan said as he opened the door and he and Raine stepped inside. "Enjoying your Sunday?"

"Very much, darling." Edwina lifted her cheek for his kiss. "Did you enjoy the party last night?"

"Yes," he replied and turned to Claire. "It was certainly an evening to remember."

"That's what I'd hoped," Claire replied, watching him with narrowed eyes. If there was a crisis going on here, this young man could certainly hide his feelings. She would never find anything out from *him*.

Edwina held out the sports section. "Would you like part of the newspaper?"

"No. You'll have to excuse me, ladies." He moved towards the door. "I have some packing to do."

"Packing?" his mother echoed, but Alan had already gone into the house.

Claire turned back to Raine, who sank into a wicker chair like a wilted yellow flower. "Something wrong, darling?"

"I'm just tired." She avoided Claire's curious gaze and looked at her watch. "It's almost noon. Miss Minter has the rest of the day off, so I'd better change my clothes. I think I'll set up the sprinkler in the backyard. The children would like that."

"We could go to Bailey's," Claire suggested, determined to spend the afternoon with her stepdaughter and discover what was going on. "I still have my membership."

"No beach for me today. The sprinkler in the yard will do just fine." Raine stood up and smoothed her skirt. "Besides, it's about time things around here went back to normal."

After she'd left, Edwina turned her anxious gaze toward Claire. Newspapers slid off her lap and onto the floor, but neither noticed or cared. "He's packing, and she's talking about going back to normal. I don't like the sound of that. I don't like the sound of that at all."

"*Back to normal,*" Claire scoffed. "That's the silliest thing I've ever heard."

"Oh, I agree," Edwina said. "We've never been *normal* in all of our lives."

THE REST OF SUNDAY passed peacefully, so peacefully that Edwina and Claire finally grew restless and returned to Maizie's. Alan stayed upstairs in his air-conditioned retreat. Miss Minter went to the movies with an old friend she'd discovered summering across the bay.

Raine played in the sprinkler with the children, squirted them with the hose to make them shriek, fixed chocolate milk shakes and egg salad sandwiches for supper, and at sundown tucked seven sleepy children into their beds. It was dark before her foot began to ache; she walked through the silent house and into the kitchen for a cold drink. The Sunday crossword puzzle and Charlie waited on her bed.

Alan, naked to the waist and wearing shorts, closed the refrigerator and set a platter of leftover ham upon the counter.

"Hi," he said when he saw her. "I was going to look for you. I made reservations on the early-morning shuttle to New York."

Her heart skipped a beat. "Oh?"

"It's perfect timing. You wanted time to think and I need to make plans. I'll be back in a couple of days, so don't give my room away."

"I won't." Raine told herself it was foolish to feel so disappointed.

He opened the wrapping on a loaf of bread. "Want me to make you a sandwich, too?"

"No, thanks," she replied, stepping up to the counter to watch what he was doing. "I'm going to bed."

Alan turned to her and touched his lips to hers. "I take it that's not an invitation."

She shook her head. "Sex just confuses things."

Alan looked at her, an amused gleam in his eyes. "Sweetheart, if that's true, then we must be the two most confused people in Rhode Island."

IT WAS WEDNESDAY afternoon before Raine finished cleaning the house. Miss Minter had been a big help— she had to admit it—but no one person could keep up with seven small children and all of the chores involved in keeping a house clean.

She'd given Miss Minter a few days off, knowing the kindhearted lady would never leave unless Alan told her it was all right to do so. It felt good to be back at work, to be able to fix breakfast, stop squabbles, braid Vanessa's hair and take the children to camp. It kept her from missing Alan too much.

All seven children had complained when Alan left. He'd promised to return, which they'd tried to believe.

They'd all heard too many false promises to believe one more, no matter how much they longed to.

Raine wanted to believe, too. This summer hadn't been what she expected, that was certain. From the time Alan Wetmore Hunter appeared on the doorstep, her life had been turned upside down, no matter how hard she'd tried to resist. She could have done without Claire and Edwina's interference, and maybe she could have resisted Alan if she hadn't torn the ligaments in her foot and needed a bath, but Raine wasn't positive. Miss Minter and Harry and a magical evening at Rosecliff were part of a summer that would never be forgotten.

The summer when she fell in love.

The summer when she fell, period. She sat on the couch, flexed her foot and wiggled her toes. Almost as good as new, thanks to everyone's help. She didn't know what she would have done without Alan. She missed his teasing. She missed his body beside hers in the night. If she married him, how would he stay here? Would life go on the way it had for the past few weeks? She'd dreamed it would go on like this forever, until they were old and gray and rocking on the front-porch swing. Perhaps they'd plot romances for their grandchildren and watch the happy endings from a discreet distance. When he returned, Raine decided, she'd let him ask her again.

And this time her answer would be yes.

"IT'S OFFICIAL."

"What is?" Raine cradled the telephone receiver against her ear and took a box of Popsicle ices out of the freezer. She counted out seven and passed them out. She motioned to the children to take them out to the backyard so she could talk to Mindy privately.

"I've spent all day in court and just returned to the office, but I wanted you to know—the judge terminated parental rights for the three kids."

"Thank goodness. Will you tell them or shall I?"

"I will. I'll be down next Friday, if that works out for you. We need to talk about this, Raine. I need to know if you're thinking about adopting them."

"I don't think I can bear to let them go."

"That's not the same thing. Do you want to be considered?"

Raine looked out the screen door and saw the kids sitting in the shade of the elm tree. "More than anything, but *could* I adopt them?"

"Legally, as their foster mother, you have that right. Since they've been with you so long, staying with you would be seen as in their best interests. Can you handle it?"

"I handle it now."

"True, but you're a single woman. A young single woman. Is this something you want to do? And I have to be honest, Raine. Those children, especially the twins, have been without a father all of their lives. I think they need one."

An image of Alan running out of the surf with two little boys behind him popped into her head. Yes, they needed a father. What child didn't? "They'll have one, Mindy."

"Oh?" Mindy's voice lost its official tone. "Are you trying to tell me something?"

"Unofficially. I can't go into it now." *Not until Alan returns and we settle everything.*

"The handsome houseguest, right?"

"Right." Raine turned around as Claire, holding Charlie in her arms, stepped into the kitchen. "Give me some time to get things straightened out here, okay?"

"You've got all the time you need."

The trouble was, she needed a lot more than time. She needed Alan to return and tell her he was going to stay with her forever, children and all.

"What was that all about, darling?"

"Joey, Jimmy and Julie," Raine said, trying to sound nonchalant. "They're going to be available for adoption. I knew it was coming—their social worker has been trying to get a court hearing on this for ages—but I guess I wasn't as prepared as I thought."

Claire sank into a kitchen chair, the dog still in her arms. "I can't picture them anywhere but here."

Raine leaned against the counter. "Neither can I."

"They'll need a father, too," Claire reminded her. "Especially as they get older."

"I know." Raine smiled to herself. The dream was becoming more real all the time, but she didn't dare tell Claire until she and Alan had talked.

"Alan's in love with you."

"Yes."

"And you're in love with him."

"Yes."

"Good. He'll be a wonderful father for those three children."

"You're getting ahead of yourself."

Claire shrugged. "Perhaps. What's going to happen to the others?"

"I don't know," Raine admitted. "Vanessa is making progress and isn't as bashful as she used to be. At one time the state thought they'd located a grandmother, but I haven't heard anything since. Donetta's social worker thinks she's found an aunt who wants custody, but it will take a while for the home study to be done. Toby and Crystal just entered state care, so no one knows what's going to happen to them. That's seven lives, Claire. Seven lives to think about and take into account when a man like Alan tells me he loves me."

"Eight lives," Claire said, "counting yourself. And what do *you* want?"

"I want it all—Alan, the children, everything," Raine answered. She smiled an upside-down smile. "Do you think it's possible, Claire?"

"If you believe in yourself—and each other—then anything's possible, darling. Anything at all."

"SHOULD WE TELL HER?"

Edwina hesitated at the front door. "I don't know, Claire. It could be risky."

"It could be just the thing, too. One never knows in matters of the heart."

"You may be right, but perhaps Alan should be the one to tell her. After all, it's his—"

"Tell me what?" Raine asked, pushing open the door so they could enter. The two ladies exchanged nervous glances, then looked back at her.

"How about a martini?" Claire suggested. "I think we could all use a drink."

"I don't drink martinis," Raine said. "I hardly ever drink. Besides, I'm making dinner."

"We'll keep you company," Claire offered. "Where's Miss Minter?"

"She'll be back tonight. I gave her a couple of days off."

"Was that wise, dear, considering your foot and all?"

"My foot is perfectly fine. I was waltzing in the Rosecliff ballroom, remember?"

"And beautifully, too," Claire agreed.

"Did Alan say when he'd return to Newport, dear?"

"He said he'd only be gone a few days. Maybe he'll call tonight."

"Maybe he will."

Edwina began. "Claire told me about your predicament with the children, dear. I hope you don't mind."

Raine poured spaghetti into the pot of boiling water and picked up a wooden spoon. "That's okay."

"We have a possible—"

"Claire..." Edwina was fluttering again. "I still don't think..."

"We have a possible solution," Claire went on, unaffected by her friend's stammering. "Go on, Wina. Tell."

Edwina opened her mouth, but no sound came out. Raine stirred the pasta until it softened, then turned the heat down. She looked at Edwina. "Would the two of you like to stay for dinner?"

"That would be lovely," Alan's mother said, brightening. "Perhaps the children would like to hear a story while you're cooking. I could go—"

"Tell her now, Edwina."

Raine set the spoon upon the counter and turned her full attention on the women. She was beginning to grow accustomed to their fractured conversations.

"Well, Claire said you need a husband. A father for those children, so you can adopt them."

"Well, it's not that simple." Raine wished she could tell them that she and Alan were going to go along with their matchmaking plans permanently. Where was Alan, and why didn't he come home?

"That's the lovely part of all of this," Edwina said, her face bursting into a smile. "Alan needs to get married, too! He needs a wife."

"Look," Raine said, holding up one hand as if to stop Edwina's unbelievable words. Why would Alan need to get married? "This isn't—"

"Oh, yes, it is," Claire insisted.

Edwina looked confused. "Is what?"

"Any of your business," Raine said gently. "Even if I believed you."

"Of course it's my business." Edwina sniffed. "I'm his mother. Whose business would it be but mine?" She pointed to the steaming pot. "You'd better stir."

"Thanks." Raine did as she was told, wishing for the hundredth time that Alan was here to help control the ladies. Their schemes had gone too far this time.

Edwina leaned forward. "Now, here's the best part. Listen carefully. Alan really does need a wife. It's in the will."

"What will?"

"His grandfather's. It's very complicated, dear, but Alan can't inherit my father's estate unless he's married. The property reverts to the state at the end of the year, and of course no one wants to see that happen because they'll put a road through it."

Raine stopped worrying about sticky spaghetti and faced the two women. "Alan *needs* a wife?"

Edwina nodded. "Yes! See how easy this is! Almost as if it were meant to be. You need a husband, even though you didn't need one before, of course. But now you do!"

Raine struggled to understand the meaning behind Edwina's words. Surely she couldn't have heard correctly? "Is this why Alan came to Newport?"

"Oh, yes. He wanted to talk to the lawyers in person, but he couldn't accomplish a *thing*. They simply told him to get married."

"*Who* told him to get married?"

"Atwater, Brenner and Horton."

Claire nodded. "Of course, that idea was totally ridiculous until he met you, darling."

"Totally ridiculous," Edwina repeated.

"What's totally ridiculous?"

At the sound of Alan's voice, the three women froze into silence and saw Alan enter the room, Charlie growling at his heels. "Hello, ladies. I thought I'd find you here." He smiled and loosened his tie before stepping to the stove to kiss Raine.

She managed to resist throwing her arms around his neck. "I didn't know you were coming back tonight," she managed to say.

Alan frowned. "I wanted to surprise you, so I had Harry pick me up at the airport. What's wrong?"

Claire and Edwina stood up and picked up their purses. "We'll just be going, darlings."

"Oh, no, you don't." Raine glared at them. "You can't just drop a bomb like this and then tiptoe away."

"What bomb?" Alan said, looking at his mother, then at Raine.

She stared at him, wondering if she knew him at all. Was this another trick Claire had conjured up to throw them together? Could she have been so wrong? "Claire and Edwina have been telling me a story about your grandfather's will. Is it true?"

Alan frowned again, at his mother this time. "What's going on here?"

Raine spoke before Edwina could explain. "We've

been discussing our marriage, Alan. Or rather, your marriage. Is it true?"

"Is what true?"

"I told her about Father's will," Edwina whispered. "I thought it would help."

"Is it true you need a wife?" Raine repeated, willing him to say it was another crazy matchmaking scheme. She couldn't possibly have fallen in love with a man who would use her as a legal loophole. He couldn't be that good an actor, but then again, what did she know?

"Yes. That's why I came to Newport, but it doesn't have anything to do with us."

"Sure it does," Raine declared, hardening her heart against those warm, hazel eyes. Her fingers shook as she lifted the spoon to stir the spaghetti. She had to remember she had a family to feed. "Especially if *I'm* supposed to be the wife."

"Raine..."

"I've decided I don't need a husband, after all, so I'm not accepting your proposal." Raine looked into the face of the man she loved and felt her heart break into jagged pieces. Suddenly it was hard to breathe. "The answer is no."

12

CLAIRE GASPED. "You mean he's asked you already?"

"Yes," Raine said, tearing her gaze from Alan's frown. "Last weekend."

"I think we've made a slight miscalculation," Claire whispered. She grabbed Edwina's arm and attempted to get her out of the kitchen.

"The answer is no?" her son repeated. "Just like that? *No?*"

"Yes," Raine told him. "And dinner is ready."

"I don't give a damn about dinner." He moved out of the way of the steaming pot as Raine lifted it toward him. "I just want to know what the hell is going on around here."

She smiled sweetly as she passed him on her way to the sink. "I've finally come to my senses, that's all. Would you tell the children to come inside for dinner?"

"No."

"Fine. I'll do it myself." She set the pot into the sink and started toward the back door. "Hey, everybody!" she called. "Time to wash up for supper!"

Alan turned back to Claire and Edwina, who were attempting to sneak out of the kitchen. "Where are you two going? And why isn't Miss Minter cooking dinner?"

Raine answered for them. "I gave her a few days off. She deserved it."

"I think she's here now," Edwina trilled. "Charlie's barking at the front door."

"I'll be right back," Alan muttered.

When he'd left the room, Raine looked at the two women and shook her head. "Don't say a word."

Claire looked worried. "Darling, I'm not sure this will business is why he wanted to marry you."

She shook her head. "Don't be so sure, Claire. Somehow everything is beginning to make sense."

Raine didn't know how she made it through dinner, or why she'd served spaghetti and meatballs. By the time the meal was finished, the children looked as if they'd bathed in tomato sauce. Claire and Edwina escaped before dessert, claiming a prior date at the movies with Maizie Chapman.

Miss Minter, undisturbed by the chaos, told the children stories of her girlhood adventures in Liverpool with one of the Beatles' mothers until they'd finished their dinner.

"I still don't know what's going on around here," Alan muttered, standing up and waiting for Raine to leave the table with him. "But I'm damn sure going to find out. Come on."

"No," Raine stated, rising to her feet. She hoped she could make it to her room before tears overwhelmed her. Now that the shock was wearing off, she didn't know how she would be able to control herself. "There isn't anything else to say." She turned to Miss Minter. "Would you mind overseeing baths and putting the children to bed without me? I'm not feeling well."

Miss Minter nodded. "No problem, duckie. You take good care of yourself."

"Raine, wait!" Alan moved toward her.

"Good night, everybody," she said, then hurried to her room and locked the door before Alan could catch up with her. She turned on the faucet over the tub, hoping the rushing water would drown the sound of her sobs. What had she done? She'd thought Alan really loved her. Well, she should have known better. Great sex had clouded her judgment.

We'll work it out had been his words. Now she understood. Working it out had meant he'd get what he wanted, what he had come to Newport to accomplish. No wonder he hadn't minded adopting the children. He hadn't intended to be around long enough for that to matter, one way or another. Besides, he'd hire whomever he needed to deal with them.

Everything had happened so fast. Now she knew why.

ALAN STOOD OUTSIDE Raine's closed bedroom door until he felt a tug on his hand. Julie peered at him. "What's the matter, Mr. Hunter?"

"I wish I knew, honey."

"We're going to have ice cream. Miss Minter said."

"Sounds good."

"Want to have some?"

Alan took the child's hand. There didn't seem to be any other choice but to leave Raine alone. "Okay."

"Want to hear a secret?" Julie motioned to him to bend down. "We're gonna be adopted."

He didn't have any idea what he should say. "You are?"

She nodded. "Joey heard Raine talking to Grandma Claire about it. Raine's gonna be our mom."

Alan straightened, still holding Julie's sticky hand.

He let her tug him down the hall, but his mind was whirling.

He'd thought Raine loved him. Now he wasn't even sure about that.

"Raine! You have to come out sometime," Alan called. "The kids have to leave for camp in ten minutes, and I need to be back in New York by eleven."

"Go."

"Not until we talk." He jiggled the doorknob. "I don't know what kind of game you're playing, but I'm not into it. Open this damn door or I'll take it off the hinges."

"It's no game," Raine said, opening her bedroom door and backing away as he entered the room.

"Since when do you think you have to lock your door?"

"I needed some time to think." A long, sleepless night had given her the hours she'd needed to decide how to say goodbye to Alan.

"And?" He stayed on the other side of the room.

"We need to start being honest with each other."

His eyebrows rose. "I won't argue with that. Are you going to tell me what happened yesterday?"

"Why did you suddenly decide to marry me? It wasn't because you realized you couldn't live without me, was it?" She crossed her arms in front of her chest and wished she had dressed before letting Alan into her room.

"If I said yes, you wouldn't believe me, anyway." He sat down on her unmade bed.

"I was going to say yes," she muttered. "I thought we'd be one big, happy family." This was no time to tell him she loved him. She wouldn't admit she'd been a fool. "And then I found out you have a small legal problem. You need to marry before you can inherit your grandfather's estate. How am I doing so far?"

"You have your facts straight."

"I thought so." She waited for him to defend himself. Waited for him to tell her he loved her, that this whole thing was a ridiculous misunderstanding. Waited for him to take her into his arms and make this nightmare disappear.

He stood up, his face expressionless. "Is there anything else?"

She shook her head, tears clogging her throat so she couldn't speak. *Tell me you love me.* A muscle clenched in his jaw, but his hands were gentle on her shoulders as he kept her facing him.

"Are you through?" he asked.

She nodded. "You can go to New York now."

"No way. It's my turn." He looked down, holding her gaze. "It's easy to believe the worst, isn't it? That I would marry you for money." He took a deep breath before continuing. "I'd do a lot to keep my grandfather's house—in fact, I've spent a small fortune in legal fees to do just that—but I wouldn't get married for it."

"But..."

"No, just listen. You've had your chance to talk." Alan dropped his hands and turned toward the window. "I don't know why an old man made a will the way he did, but I'll be fighting it for years."

"That doesn't seem fair," Raine said.

Alan shrugged and shoved his hands into his pockets. "That's not the point, is it?"

"No."

"Sweetheart, you didn't want to believe that what we felt for each other was real. You didn't want to take a chance by loving me, so you jumped at the first thing that got in our way."

"That's not true."

"No?" He shook his head, as if he couldn't believe she'd deny it. "You were waiting for an excuse, Raine. You're so afraid of loving me, needing *me*, that you couldn't wait to find something, anything, to believe it wouldn't work out."

"Raine?" Donetta's voice came from the hall. "We're going to camp!"

"I'll see you later," Raine called. "Have fun!"

Alan waited until the front door slammed shut and the house grew quiet. "Those kids out there are a lot braver than you, sweetheart. At least they give people a chance. No matter how screwed up their lives have been, they're willing to love again."

"And what about those kids, Alan? What would I have done with them if I married you? Tossed them back?" She blinked back tears as she stared at him.

"Is that what you think?" She didn't answer, so he went to the door and put his hand upon the knob. "You asked me once if I avoided getting involved with women because I played it safe." He shot her a rueful smile. "I thought you hit a little close to home on that one."

"I never meant to hurt you."

"No, it was true. I had played it safe. Until I fell in love with you and gave you everything I had to give— and you didn't notice. I got pretty involved with this family, too. Or didn't you notice that, either? Well, sweetheart, I'm not the only one playing it safe around here. You'll hide in this house, not risking a thing, instead of sticking your pretty neck out and trusting me." He shook his head and his smile was wry.

"You're right about one thing, Raine. You don't need anyone. You'll always do just fine by yourself. I just hope someday, when you wake up, you don't regret the choices you've made."

Raine watched in silence as Alan opened the door and left the room, shutting the door behind him with a careful, final click. She listened to his footsteps disappear down the hall, but didn't move. She stood there as if turned to ice, wondering if the numbness in her body would ever leave.

"WE'RE RESPONSIBLE," Edwina moaned, wringing her hands as she faced Claire in the limousine. "We have to do something."

"We will," Claire assured her. "I have to give it more thought."

"More thought? He's been gone three days! And Raine hasn't spoken a word to either one of us since that horrible spaghetti dinner. Miss Minter says she's been very quiet with the children, too. What do you think happened?"

"It doesn't take a genius to figure out that they had a disagreement."

"A disagreement! He's flying back to London this week, for heaven's sake! Right after the hearing."

Claire sat up straight. "What hearing?"

"About the will, of course. On Wednesday. The anniversary of my father's death. I told you I ordered special flowers for the grave site and—"

"Alan's coming to Newport?"

"He has to." She frowned. "At least, I think he does."

"You're going to call him and tell him he has to, Edwina. Tell him it's some legal problem you don't understand, but it's very important."

Edwina chuckled. "You're thinking up something clever, aren't you?"

"Of course I am. Now all I have to do is figure out what to do about Raine."

Edwina patted Claire's arm. "You'll think of something. You really *are* the smartest of all my friends."

"YOU CAN'T JUST SIT around the house and mope."

Raine ignored her stepmother and plugged the vacuum cleaner cord into the outlet. "This place is a mess."

"So is your life, darling."

Raine looked up, exasperated. "I really don't need this, Claire. Miss Minter went to pick up the kids from camp, Jimmy's upstairs asleep because his asthma is acting up again, the social worker just left, and I have a lot on my mind."

"Like what?" Claire bent down and put Charlie into her lap. "How would I know what you're thinking about? You haven't talked to anyone in days."

"Which has been a pleasant change, believe me."

"I don't believe you." She patted the place beside her on the couch. "Come here. You look like death. You're not eating, are you?"

"It's too hot," Raine lied. Food stuck in her throat when she tried to swallow. She left the vacuum cleaner in the middle of the floor and joined Claire on the couch. She knew her stepmother wouldn't give up until she'd said what she came to say.

"There," Claire said, turning to face Raine. "This is much better. Did the worker come to discuss your adopting Julie and the boys?"

"Yes."

"What are you going to do?"

"I don't know." She hugged her knees to her chest. "I love them and I want to keep them, but is it fair?"

"If it makes all four of you happy, then that's what matters."

"It isn't that simple."

"You shouldn't have sent Alan away."

Raine didn't know whether to laugh or cry. "He sent himself away."

"Because of the children?"

"No. He said that I was so afraid of loving him that I was waiting for an excuse to believe it wouldn't work out between us. He was so angry with me, and he had a right to be. I thought he just wanted his grandfather's property, not me."

Claire looked as if she wanted to cry. "You never really trusted him, did you? You thought he was too much like your father."

"Isn't he?"

"No. Your father was not a demonstrative man. He held his feelings inside, dear, but he did have feelings. He should have spent more time with you and Quentin, should have given more of himself, but he did the best he could. Maybe he would have lived longer if he hadn't worked so hard."

"He loved his work. He didn't love us."

"No, darling. I'm afraid that's a bit simplistic. And unfair, too. Your father just didn't know any other way."

"And Alan does?"

"If I were you, I'd give it a lot of thought before I lumped your father and Alan Hunter in the same category."

"It doesn't matter. It wasn't the happily-ever-after romance you and Edwina had envisioned. Alan isn't Prince Charming, either."

"Prince Charming? You wouldn't recognize Prince Charming if he waltzed naked across your bedroom."

Raine closed her eyes against the memory of dancing with Alan in her room. "Stop it, Claire."

"Wake up, darling. Happily ever after doesn't simply *happen*, my darling. Two people who love each other *make* it happen."

"We're not talking about love, Claire."

"We're not?" She put Charlie onto the floor and stood up, brushing dog hair from her navy skirt. Then she reached for her purse and opened it. She handed a packet of photographs to her stepdaughter. "I had these developed for Donetta. Look at them and tell me we're not talking about love."

Raine took the envelope and lifted the flap. She looked through them until she came to the pictures taken on the staircase before the ball. Alan and herself stared back at her, giddy expressions of love on their faces. Identical, love-struck expressions. No one could fake that kind of radiance.

Claire touched Raine's cheek. "If you love those kids, keep them. If you love Alan, take a chance and go after him."

"It's too late, Claire. He was furious."

"He'll get over it."

"I can't go to New York."

"You don't have to." Claire looked at her watch. "He's in Newport for the reading of the will. Edwina said he's driving to Boston afterward and catching a plane to London."

Excitement curled in the pit of her stomach. "He's here now?"

"Until four. Which gives you twenty minutes."

"I can't leave..."

"Of course you can. Take the limo. I'll stay here in case Jimmy wakes up."

"You'd do that for me?"

"Darling, I'd do anything to make you happy."

Raine looked at her worn denim shorts and wrinkled, blue shirt. "Do you think I have time to change?"

"Definitely, darling." Claire hid her sigh of relief. "Put on some makeup and wear something white."

"HERE WE ARE, miss." The driver stopped the car in front of the brick entrance to the historic Hotel Viking.

"I thought we were going to the law office," Raine said.

"Yes, miss," he agreed. "But first I have to pick up something for Mrs. Claypoole."

"Is it going to take very long?"

"No, miss."

Raine waited for the chauffeur to return, grateful for the extra minutes to question her sanity. What on earth was she doing? Was she wrong to put her faith in a couple of photographs? What could she say that would make Alan stay? What if he didn't want her, after all? What if he wouldn't even speak to her? What if—? Suddenly the possibilities were overwhelming. She breathed faster, unable to stop herself from worrying.

Feeling faint and dizzy, Raine leaned over and put her head between her knees, hoping the blood would come back to her head and she could tell the driver to take her home. This was not the best idea she'd ever had.

The door beside her opened, letting a blast of muggy heat hit her legs. A familiar voice said, "What the— Raine?"

She tried to lift her head, but the dizziness returned. "Alan? Oh, my God."

"What are you doing here?"

"Hyperventilating, I think." She heard him ask the driver to go inside for a bag of ice.

"Don't move."

No chance of that. Her legs had gone numb, whether from nerves or hunger she didn't know. "What are *you* doing here? You're supposed to be at the lawyers' office."

"That particular meeting ended an hour ago. My lawyers bought me some more time."

"Then it's not too late?" Raine dared to hope her stubbornness wouldn't cost Alan his inheritance. "You can still inherit the property?"

He didn't answer. "Why are you here, fainting in the limousine I ordered—?"

"I know—to take you to the airport. To London," she moaned.

"London?" He brushed her hair from her face. "I'm not going to London. Who told you that?"

"Claire. She gave me the car to use, too."

"My dear mother sent this car for me. She said Claire had taken care of everything."

"Here we go again." She should have known Claire and Edwina wouldn't give up so easily.

"Can you lean back? I have the ice."

"I'll be okay. I think the heat got to me." And the sleepless nights and a sporadic diet of Cheerios and Snickers bars. Alan put the bag of ice against her forehead, and Raine closed her eyes and let the cold soak into her skin. "This is so embarrassing."

"I know."

"This isn't the way I had it planned."

"Move over," he said, sliding into the seat beside her. His thigh touched hers, but Raine didn't mind the heat. "Had what planned?"

"Finding you. Saying I'm sorry. Telling you that were right—I am a coward. I *was* a coward. At least I'm trying not to be. Not anymore."

Alan shut the door and spoke to the driver. Then he put his arms around Raine, all the while keeping the ice pack on her head. "Sweetheart, are you trying to tell me something?"

"Yes." Then she felt the car move. "Where are we going?"

"A few miles north of here, to Portsmouth. I'm going to show you my grandfather's estate." His arm tightened around her. "Just close your eyes and take deep breaths until we get there."

She did as he instructed, grateful for the quiet minutes and the cold blast of the air conditioner. When she felt the car slow down, she took the ice pack away and opened her eyes. The car had stopped in front of an enormous field. Several black-and-white cows chewed grass behind the weathered fence.

"This is it?" Raine asked.

"That, too." He pointed to a mammoth barn and the tiny house that sat in front of it. "My grandfather made a lot of money in his lifetime and he married a woman with even more, but he never forgot where he came from. Two acres of rocky farmland isn't worth much, not even to developers. There's no ocean view. The state of Rhode Island wouldn't mind getting their hands on it, though, in case they want to add another highway."

"But you won't let them?"

"I'm going to try." He leaned forward. "Back to the Viking," he told the driver. Then he looked down and replaced the ice pack on Raine's forehead. "You look better. Are you sure you're okay?"

"Why are you being so nice to me?"

"I'm always nice to women I plan to marry. I'm not—"

She moved the ice aside and stared at him. "What did you say?"

"I'm not going to London," he continued. "I'm not leaving the country or even the island, for that matter. I don't give up that easily."

"But your work—"

"Can change. Can be done from Newport. I've spent a lot of time in New York, arranging things the way I want them."

"They let you?"

He looked surprised. "It's my company. You never did know me very well."

Maybe not, Raine realized, but she had the rest of her life to take lessons. "I'm learning."

"Good. The first thing you'll learn is that I don't make decisions based on money. There are other important things in life, sweetheart."

She reached up and caressed his cheek. She wondered if it was possible to burst with happiness. "Like what?"

"Like spending the rest of my life making love to a woman who lives in an old house with a bunch of kids and a dog who looks like a cat."

Raine smiled, remembering Alan's protests. Had it

really been only a few weeks ago? "A woman who thinks every man who knocks on her door has been sent by her stepmother to marry her?"

"Yeah," he replied, pulling her into his arms. "That's the one."

JULIE SQUIRMED on the couch next to Vanessa. "What happens next, Grandma Claire?"

Claire turned the page of the storybook, and all of the children waited quietly to hear her read. "The prince took the princess into his arms and kissed her, a long and tender embrace that caused the flowers to change from gray to red, the birds to sing a sweeter song, and the sun to shine a golden yellow upon them all."

"That's nice," Vanessa said. "Turn the page."

Crystal snuggled closer to Claire. "Then what?"

"That's easy," Edwina replied. "Isn't it, Claire?"

The women shared a secret smile, then Claire turned the last page.

"And they lived happily ever after."

Seven children cheered.

She wasn't ready to decorate a nursery...

STUCK ON YOU

MAGGIE MCGUIRE slid a check onto the counter next to the cash register. "Here's my contribution for the week, Greg."

"Great. Every little bit helps." He nodded toward the buckets she held. "Paste for the condo project?"

"Uh-huh." She set the buckets on the floor and scrawled her initials on the invoice. "I'm scheduled to work there next week."

"The paper isn't in yet. Didn't they call you?"

"No," she said with a sigh, "they didn't. That company does everything at the last minute. Is it back-ordered?"

"Probably, but your other job is ready."

"What other job?" Maggie didn't like surprises. She'd had too many of them in the past few months. "Tell me you're kidding."

The balding man shook his head. "Nope. The note on the order says to call M & M when the paper comes in. There're a million rolls of paper back here. Fanny must've bid the job weeks ago."

"*What* job?" Maggie repeated. She didn't like talking about Fanny too much, either.

"Winslow."

"Winslow who?"

Greg tore off a copy of the bill and handed it to her. "Not 'Winslow who.' Sam Winslow. Millionaire. Old

New England money. Lives in one of those houses on the ocean that the tourists drive by and gawk at."

Maggie nodded, shoving the receipt into the pocket of her work pants. "I know who you mean. I'll call him."

"Better yet, go over there. You'll earn enough money on this job to make us both forget about this damn account. I don't want to bug you too much about your bills, but—"

She sighed once more. "It's okay, Greg. You've been really patient. A big job like this could solve a lot of problems."

"Ever hear from Fanny?"

Maggie laughed, but there was no humor in the sound. "Nope. I think she's too consumed with passion to write postcards." Unwilling to talk about her former partner any further, Maggie stooped to pick up the paste buckets.

"Why don't you pull that battleship of yours around to the side and I'll have one of the boys load Winslow's wallpaper in the back." He gave her a yellow slip. "His address is on this invoice."

Maggie pinched the paper between her fingers. "Thanks."

Fifteen minutes later she was on her way out of Wakefield, headed toward the ocean, the sea air whipping her dark curls around her face. The summer traffic was especially heavy on Fridays, but Maggie was used to it. She'd lived in the oceanfront Rhode Island town for eight years, since she was twenty-two and a newlywed. There'd been many changes since then, and not just with the town. She slowed down to watch for Winslow's driveway.

So this is the house. She parked the station wagon in

front of a gray-shingled, four-car garage and peered out the side window. The long smooth driveway led to an enormous three-story home that rose from a carefully tended lawn. She could hear the ocean in the distance when she switched the car's engine off.

She sat there for a full minute, finally admitting to herself how tired she really was. Her cotton slacks were covered in dried glue; her once-white sneakers were decorated with touches of dried cement. Her pale-blue denim shirt was wrinkled and sticky, the sleeves folded up to reveal her slender wrists. She reached across the hot vinyl seat and extracted her tape measure and notebook from the plastic tool carrier. Supposedly Fanny had taken measurements already, but it wouldn't hurt to double-check. She'd give a lot to know what her partner had bid this job for.

She opened the heavy car door and stepped out onto the immaculate driveway. A friendly-looking collie loped over to greet her.

"Hello there, puppy," Maggie murmured, slamming the car door. She didn't trust big dogs, especially big dogs she didn't know, but this collie seemed safe enough. She awkwardly caressed its long nose with the hand that held the notebook, then walked past the garage to what looked like the back door. She rang the bell and waited.

The door swung open and a plump fiftyish woman with short red hair and a round smiling face answered. "Yes?"

"I'm Maggie McGuire, from M & M Paperhangers. Greg from Paper-To-Go—"

But before she could finish explaining, the woman said, "Of course, of course! Come in. We're getting desperate. Sam was starting to pace. I'm Lou, the house-keeper."

Maggie followed the chattering woman through a maze of hallways, past closets, a washer and dryer, up several polished oak stairs and through open French doors to an enormous light-oak kitchen. She looked around at the large open room. Where there weren't oak cupboards of windows there was white tile, very expensive and certainly in no need of wallpaper. A blue cotton rug lay in front of a massive fireplace flanked by a blue-and-white patterned love seat. Off to one side, in a sunny glassed-in alcove, was a gleaming dining-room table and chairs.

"The rooms to be done first are downstairs, in the guest wing. Have you been here before?"

Maggie shook her head. "No, my partner, Fanny Maine, bid the job." She followed Lou down gray carpeted steps to a partial basement. Bright artwork hung on textured white walls and the effect was one of style and comfort. "How many rooms are there?"

"Three bedrooms down here, but they haven't been used in a few years. A bathroom, too, but the paper wasn't ordered for that. You'll have to tell Sam how much he needs, just in case he changes his mind and wants to have it papered, too."

The rooms had the faintly musty smell of disuse, but they were clean and furnished with classically simple furniture. The windows were large and curtainless.

"We're having a lot of company in a few weeks and we just finished getting the ceilings painted a few days ago. The paper seems to have taken forever to get here."

"I probably have most of it in my car, so don't worry. We'll need to sort it out so I'll know what goes where."

"Sam should be home soon. He can tell you what you need to know."

"I'll just double-check the measurements of these rooms and then I'll start bringing the paper in."

"Great! Call me if you need anything, okay?"

Lou turned and disappeared around a corner of the hallway and Maggie stepped into one of the bedrooms, pulled the pencil from her notebook, the tape measure off her back pocket and said a prayer that whoever had measured these rooms knew what he or she was doing. She sighed. It was always a nightmare if someone else measured the room and ordered the paper. Owners, trying to save money, usually didn't order enough. Wallpaper stores used the measurements in the back of the wallpaper book, which were standard, and didn't take into account any unusual characteristics of a room. And of course the hanger was to blame if there wasn't enough paper or—heaven forbid—if there was too much left over. Fanny, for all her faults, knew how to measure a room. Maggie sighed and began to check the ceiling height. She knew she was too tired to figure out the requirements right then; she'd wait until she was home, cleaned up and had a tall diet cola in front of her. Then she'd compare how much paper she needed to how many rolls she had.

SAMUEL WINSLOW drove up his driveway and stopped his white Volvo when he saw the monstrosity barring his way, then edged carefully around it. He hadn't seen a station wagon like that since he was a kid and one of the gardeners had one. What was this doing in his driveway? The silver-blue Pontiac had to be eighteen feet long.

He turned off the engine and stepped out of the car.

On closer examination, he discovered the Pontiac held a couple of ladders, buckets, plastic pails, assorted tools and long rectangular boxes. He breathed a sigh of relief; the wallpaper hangers had arrived.

Sam patted his shirt pocket, looking for his cigarettes. Normally he didn't smoke very much, but lately—well, lately he needed to. The summer was beginning to get out of control and the season hadn't even started yet. He lit a filtered cigarette and took a thankful drag in the fresh air. The girls were at swimming lessons and couldn't nag him about it. He looked around the yard and frowned; the tennis courts needed tending.

Crossing his legs in front of him, he leaned against his car. For some reason he was in no hurry to be inside again. He frowned, tossed the cigarette onto the pavement and crushed it with his leather loafer, then bent to remove the evidence of his lapse by picking it up and tossing it onto the grass where he hoped the girls wouldn't find it.

Where was the dog? Lassie was supposed to greet the master when he came home after a hard day at the drawing board. Sam went into the house, hung up his jacket and found Lou stirring something on the stove.

"Hi, Sam!" she called gaily.

"Hi, yourself. Don't tell me you bought another car," he teased.

"Nope. Good news—there's a paperhanger downstairs and she even brought the paper with her. We may be ready for the symphony hoopla yet."

"No comment. This all the mail?" He picked up a few envelopes from the tiled work island and began to glance at the addresses.

"That's it."

He threw the mail back on the counter. "Another letter from Buffie, probably with more instructions in it." Who in the world would have a mother-in-law named Buffie? Somehow it suited the old gal, though. "What are you making?"

"Cheese sauce. For that chicken dish you like so much."

"You spoil me. What would I do without you?"

"Get married." She tossed him a grin before turning to switch off the burner.

Her comment didn't faze him. "I will when you do, sweetheart."

Lou grabbed the can opener and a casserole dish. "Why don't you get out of my way and go talk about wallpaper?"

Reluctantly he slid away from the tiled work area. "Okay. By the way, where's Lassie?"

Lou shrugged. "Probably busy peeing on the tennis court again."

"Damn dog." He didn't really want to deal with this wallpaper business, he told himself as he went downstairs. He didn't give a damn about color and texture and patterns. Anne had loved that sort of thing, but hadn't had time to renovate the house the way she'd wanted to. It seemed they'd barely had time to move into the house before the babies had come. Then Anne had been so busy with her music and the children, and the "Someday I'm going to completely redo this place" had never happened. A drunk driver had ended a lot of plans.

Sam winced. He hated self-pity and tried to avoid it. But—damn it—he didn't want to talk about wallpaper. Anne should have done it. Or the fancy New York decorator Buffie had hired a few months ago.

The light was on in the bathroom, so Sam stopped and looked inside. A short, dark-haired woman stood in the bathtub. She snapped her tape against the wall above the tile and muttered through the pencil held between her teeth, then hooked the tape onto the back pocket of her jeans while she wrote in a notebook. She wasn't at all what he'd expected, which was someone taller...with muscles. And despite her delicate profile, she looked as if she'd just hopped off a freight train.

Maggie sensed his presence and turned around. She smiled, absently tucking the pencil into her back pocket. "Hello."

"Hello." Sam noted that this gorgeous hobo had deep-blue eyes fringed with lashes the same dark shade as her hair. She looked about twenty. He had the uncomfortable feeling he'd seen her before, or someone like her. In a magazine centerfold, maybe, when he was a teenager. She looked like the kind of woman who wore denim but had French lingerie underneath. That had always turned him on. *Ridiculous.* He frowned. He was thirty-six years old, a supposedly mature widower, too sensible to be fantasizing about this voluptuous elf who was standing in his bathtub.

Maggie wondered why he was staring. She was used to having an audience when she worked—people found the paperhanging process interesting, especially if they'd ever tried to do it themselves—but no one had ever watched with any enthusiasm while she measured a room. The man just leaned in the doorway as if he owned the place—which he did, of course. "Mr. Winslow?"

He nodded. "'Sam.'"

He looked exactly the way she'd thought he would: tall, lean, with light-brown hair glinting gold under the fluorescent lighting. His eyes were an aristocratic gray, his face handsome and unlined, hair waving perfectly over his forehead in a casually sexy droop. An authentic "I landed on Plymouth Rock, first bank in Rhode Island" Winslow. Maggie stepped out of the tub and extended her hand. "I'm Maggie McGuire, from M & M Paperhangers. It's nice to meet you."

There were dark circles under her eyes. Maybe she was twenty-five, he guessed. Sam grasped the fine-boned hand briefly. "Where's the other M?"

"Hawaii."

She watched his eyebrows rise.

"Was she the one I talked to about doing this job?"

"As far as I know, yes." He seemed to be waiting for more information, but Maggie hesitated to supply the details. The explanation was not going to sound very professional.

"I've run into a lot of problems trying to get this project finished," he said slowly. "If I'd known what I was getting into, I probably wouldn't have started it at all. The painting crew never showed up and I had to hire another company, so I'm already in a bind. How soon can you start?"

"How many rooms are we talking about?"

"Three bedrooms plus the bath down here, then the three bedrooms, a small bathroom and master bath upstairs."

"I'm not sure." Nine rooms, some she didn't even know the size of, never mind the kind of paper or print she was to hang, made her cautious. She liked to know what she was getting into before making any promises. "Will any of the rooms have borders?"

"Borders?"

"Strips of wallpaper that accent the ceilings or separate two different wallpapers about halfway across the wall," she explained patiently.

"Yes, I think so."

She sighed. "They take more time."

"I understood you have a crew?"

It would have been just like Fanny to exaggerate. "*Had* a crew. The other half eloped to Hawaii with a painting contractor, probably yours. I haven't had time to hire or train anyone else yet."

"This could really screw things up."

Maggie's voice was brisk. "Well, her husband and kids weren't too thrilled about it, either." He looked at her sharply, but she continued in a businesslike tone, "I'll be glad to figure out a bid for this tonight and drop it off Monday. Did Fanny tell you how much paper to order?"

"Yes, she did. At least, she left a list with Lou, which I gave to the decorator." He looked at her uncertainly before backing out of the doorway and into the hall. "But I think that under the unusual circumstances I should hire a larger company."

Maggie stopped walking and looked up to stare at him. "You can try, but you'll never find anyone on this short notice. This is one of the busiest times of the year."

"Why are you available?"

"I've been honoring all the jobs Fanny committed the company to, plus the paper on two jobs is back-ordered indefinitely, so I have the time right now." *And I owe Paper-To-Go several thousand dollars.* Not only had Fanny absconded with M & M's money, she'd taken the business records, too. Probably so Maggie would have a hard time trying to prove exactly how much money had been stolen. Up until Greg had showed her the unpaid invoices, Maggie had trusted that her partner was handling the bills properly. Now the other "M" stood for "mess," because that's what she had been dealing with for the past month.

"Bottom line—can you finish the house in two weeks?"

Maggie thought quickly. Sam Winslow was obviously a man used to getting his own way. And a big job like this one would make her solvent. If she worked weekends, if she could find someone to help her with the sizing...

He spoke into the silence. "I'll pay double if the work's done on schedule." With a trace of casual arrogance, he added, "And if you start tomorrow."

Double? She was stunned. Visions of a brand-new steaming hot tub floated temptingly before her eyes. But tomorrow? At this pace she'd be dead before she could enjoy her first soak. She flipped the notebook to a new page and drew a simple sketch of the downstairs. "All right. Which paper goes where?"

THERE WAS TIME to regret her decision when she climbed back in her car a few minutes later. But managing to turn the car around without driving on the grass took all her concentration. And as she drove home, she felt only like celebrating.

Her spirits lightened even more the closer she came to a hot bath. There was pizza in the freezer, plenty of diet cola and chocolate-chip ice cream, and a *Miami Vice* rerun on television. Don Johnson was definitely the working girl's man, unlike the clean-shaven "silver spoon" Samuel Winslow, the first intriguing man she'd met in months. He was elegance and class. She wasn't. She was just plain old Maggie McGuire. Short, divorced and covered with dried paste. But, she grinned to herself, switching on the radio, her financial problems were just about over. She'd do whatever she had to to keep the business going.

She needed a crew, though. Employees were scarce in Rhode Island these days. She couldn't afford to pay the high wages construction workers demanded, even if she could find someone willing to work for her.

The dilemma continued until she heard her sister's voice on the answering machine in the kitchen.

"Call me when you get in," Patsy said. "I just wanted to know if you made it through the week."

Maggie listened to the beeps signifying there were no other messages, then enjoyed the next hour soaking in scented bathwater. Afterward she changed into a long terry-cloth robe and turned the oven on before dialing Pat's number.

The phone rang twice, then Patsy's harried "Hello" sounded over the receiver.

"Hi," Maggie answered. "It's just your little sister returning your call."

"Oh, good. I was hoping you'd get back to me before *Miami Vice* came on."

Maggie looked at the clock on the stove. "It's only seven."

"You usually work until dark, and don't pretend you don't," Patsy chided. "We're all worried about you. Dad thinks you should sue that Maine woman."

Maggie laughed. "It's not that simple." She stretched the phone cord so she could reach the refrigerator, then plucked a pizza from the freezer section. Her shoulder muscles ached in protest. "I haven't seen Mom or Dad all week, and now I'm stuck working this weekend. They okay?"

"Oh, they're fine. I saw them Tuesday at the health club. Dad beat me at racquetball again. They're expecting you for Sunday dinner, you know."

"I know. But I've been so busy you might as well be eight hundred miles away instead of just eight. I'll try for Sunday. Are Joe and the kids okay?" She unzipped the cardboard tab from the box and ripped the plastic off the pizza.

"The girls are fine, but Ben's driving me crazy. School's out next week and he thinks he's going to the beach every day."

"Wait a minute, Pat—" It was a perfect idea. The pizza sat forgotten on the Formica countertop.

"Except Mary thinks she needs to wear a bra, and since she's only ten, I said—"

"Patsy, give me Ben. I need a crew for a big job I just got today. Just for a couple of weeks."

"Ben? You're joking. He's only thirteen. He's too uncoordinated to be a crew."

"Just ask him. He could fetch and carry. Save me getting up and down the ladder a million times." And he'd be good company, she added to herself, thinking of the weeks ahead at the Winslow house. Thinking of the long, lean body of Samuel Winslow. She blinked, willing away the attraction. With Ben around she'd have a distraction. And a helper. "I'll pay him *and* feed him. I'll try not to work him too hard, I promise. Mostly he'll just be doing the sizing."

"I'll pack his lunches. He's expensive to feed."

"I'm not exactly a pauper," Maggie protested.

"Well, you didn't get much out of Tony in the way of alimony and you work like a horse," Patsy pointed out.

"I have my little house and I'm just fine," she replied, unconcerned.

"Okay, I'll shut up. Hold on and I'll ask Ben if he wants to work for his favorite aunt."

Maggie could hear her sister's voice in the background.

"Maggie? He thinks it's great. Joe does, too. Are you sure you need him for only a couple of weeks?"

"That's what the Winslow job should take."

"Winslow? The one who lives in that great old house on Ocean Road?"

"That's the one. He's in a hurry, too. Fanny measured for the job, but I didn't find out about it until today."

"Do you know who he is?"

"Not really, except he's descended from the founding fathers and he has a tennis court."

"Samuel T. Winslow. Wakefield's most eligible bachelor. His picture was in the paper last week because he's involved in some symphony thing from New York. Or was it Newport? I'm not sure. Anyway—" Pat paused for breath "—he was voted the town's Man of the Year last year or the year before. His wife was killed in some bizarre car accident about five years ago. He has a couple of kids."

"Two girls," Maggie supplied. How sad about his wife. She vaguely remembered hearing about the accident.

"Don't you ever read the newspaper?"

"No." The only time she had to read was in the tub, and it was difficult to read a newspaper with wet hands.

"You should. Are you dating anybody?"

"'Dating' as in going to the movies or 'dating' as in a relationship?"

"Either."

"No."

"Damn."

Maggie laughed. "That's not the way I feel about it."

"Met anyone nice?" Patsy asked hopefully.

"Not since you asked me that same question last weekend." She slipped the pizza onto the oven rack. "My dinner's ready, so I'd better hang up," she fibbed.

"School's out Wednesday. You'll have your 'crew' Thursday morning."

"Great. Thanks."

"And try to make it on Sunday. Bobby's bringing a girl."

"Our little brother's serious about someone?"

"Come and see for yourself."

Maggie said goodbye and hung up the phone. She loved her large, boisterous family and didn't know what she'd do without them. One elder sister and three brothers, all but Bobby married and producing grandchildren for her parents to adore, got together for enormous family gatherings. And she would have loved nothing more than to have produced a carload of children, too, but it hadn't worked out that way.

Maybe she was destined to be the world's greatest aunt. If so, she'd better get her act together.

She opened the cupboard door to examine the calendar that hung there. No family birthdays coming up. Thank goodness she hadn't missed anybody in the past weeks. Pat would have reminded her, anyway, she hoped. Workdays were scheduled in pencil; she knew better than to write them in pen. Paper was delayed; jobs ran over; clients changed their minds on the dates. She picked up a pencil and drew an arrow through the next two weeks—weekends, too—and ended with dollar signs and exclamation marks on the final day.

Later, when she'd demolished the pizza, and a bowl of chocolate-chip ice cream and *Miami Vice* had satisfied her craving for excitement, Maggie grabbed a magazine and crawled into bed. She was too tired to figure out the Winslow invoices or the room measurements. She'd just have to do it in the morning. *What a day.*

She thought of Ben's visit with happiness. He was a good kid and he made her laugh. For the first time in three years she admitted to herself that she was lonely. And, she decided, snuggling into the overlarge bed, she didn't like it one bit.

2

EARLY SATURDAY MORNING Maggie poured herself a fresh cup of coffee, found her pad, calculator and pencil and started to figure out a bid for the Winslow job. Then she called Greg and double-checked the amount of paper on the original order before filling in a standard bid sheet. She used her usual pricing, plus a slightly higher figure for the striped decorator print in the master bedroom.

No way could it work. She shuffled and rearranged days and figures until her eyes blurred. Four cups of coffee didn't help the situation, either. If everything went off without a hitch, if the paper wasn't flawed and didn't have to be returned, if the two other jobs she was committed to didn't take up too much time, if Ben's help saved her a lot of energy, if everything in the entire world ran smoothly for the next fourteen days and nights she *might* meet Sam Winslow's deadline.

It was almost nine-thirty and she needed to be at Winslow's house soon, with a bid and a convincing, confident manner. She hated to be rushed. The perfectionist in her liked to do a good job, something that couldn't always be measured by time. She needed this job. She needed the money. There was no getting around it. She would try to talk Sam out of his demands, but he seemed like a man who knew exactly what he wanted, and when.

Outside it was a foggy June day, but there was a touch of warmth in the damp morning air. Maggie took a deep breath of salt air and thought of the beach. One of these days she'd pack a lunch and sleep on a blanket in the sand all afternoon.

Ten minutes later she parked the Pontiac in front of the Winslow garage. To her surprise, Sam answered the door when she knocked. "Oh, hi." She thrust the bid sheet at his tan, short-sleeved shirt.

"Didn't expect me to answer my own door?" He ignored the paper aimed at his chest and opened the door so she'd have to come inside. He thought she looked like a Gypsy princess in her baggy pants and pink tank top. The tangle of black curls that fell to her chin looked less moppish today and her eyes were unclouded by the tiredness he'd noticed the night before.

"Not really, no."

"I heard you drive up."

"Oh." She followed him through the entry again, into the empty kitchen. For a man with two children, he sure had a quiet house, she thought. "I brought the bid sheet for you. If you agree to the terms, sign it and I'll give you a copy." Was he even listening to her?

"Coffee?"

It was tempting. The house was cool and elegant and the coffee smelled heavenly. "Okay."

"Take anything in it?" he asked while he poured. "No."

He handed her a white mug decorated with little ducks with bows around their necks. She knew Sam Winslow hadn't selected the design.

"Have a seat," he offered, "and I'll sign this."

Maggie handed the paper to him again, this time with success. He reached for a pen. "Don't you want to read it first?" She slid onto a padded white stool at the work counter and sipped the steaming coffee carefully.

"It looks fine." He scrawled his initials on the bottom.

She had to smile. "I thought you were a business-man."

"I'm a desperate man," he said in a matter-of-fact tone. "At the mercy of women."

She laughed. "You shouldn't admit it."

"My daughters have trained me well." He slid the paper over to her. "You didn't charge me double."

"Not yet. And I won't unless I finish in two weeks. Wasn't that the deal?"

"You're starting today?"

"I'd planned to."

"Good."

She longed to ask him what the big deal was. The place looked pretty finished to her eyes. A large fire-place stood in the middle of the house; a pewter bowl filled with flowers rested on its mantel. The kitchen was shiny clean; the dining-room table gleamed with fresh polish. "I like your house."

"Thank you. We tried to keep the New England fla-vor in the remodel. Let me show you the rest of it."

She took her coffee and followed him past the stone chimney that divided the dining area from the living room. French doors led onto a sun-dried gray deck and Maggie guessed that on a sunny day a view of blue ocean would streak the horizon. The walls were smooth and painted a soft white that looked wonderful with the wood floors. The overstuffed furniture combined drift-wood gray and a sunbleached blue that contrasted with peach and shellpink accents. There were no curtains on the long row of windows. "It's beautiful."

Sam pointed to a narrow room off to one side. "The library. Actually, my office now. I do most of my work at home."

Maggie looked through the opened door and saw floor-to-ceiling bookcases, framed maps and an antique desk and leather chair. She wondered what kind of work he did, but she'd bet her last cutting blade the desk cost more than the down payment on her house. "Very nice."

"The walls on this floor will remain white for the time being. Fortunately that's something that doesn't have to be decided right away."

He led her around a corner and up to an open, carpeted staircase. Instead of framed artwork, the decorations on the walls changed to family photographs. Maggie wished she had time to look at them—she always liked to look at other people's pictures—but she hustled to follow him to a maze of rooms and hallways.

The place was a mess. There was a very faint sound of television, but Maggie didn't have any idea which room it was coming from.

"The girls must be around somewhere." He opened one of the doors and gestured for her to look inside. "This is Justine's. She's eight."

Maggie saw an assortment of toys, books and clothes strewn over a bright rectangular room before following Sam to another doorway.

"Julianne's. They share a bathroom, but the paper for that was just ordered. My mother-in-law, who started this project, left a list stating which rooms get paper and what kind."

"Good." The mess in this room was worse than the one before. But it was comforting to know that rich kids could be slobs, too.

Sam turned and strode down a hallway. Maggie hurried to keep up with his long-legged stride. She caught a glimpse of her station wagon from one of the windows.

Nothing in the house was ordinary. The small-paned windows were uncurtained and skylights were placed in unusual areas, keeping the hallways from feeling narrow and closed in. When Sam opened the door to another bright room, the sound of cartoons grew louder.

"What are you two scamps doing in here?"

Maggie heard answering guilty giggles as she followed Sam into the bedroom. Two blond-haired children lay in a tangled heap of pillows, blankets and stuffed animals on a king-size bed. A very old rocking chair stood tucked under the slanted ceiling in one corner of the room. Maggie guessed these children had been rocked to sleep there many times. Framed family pictures were everywhere: on the nightstand, a round table and on top of a massive chest of drawers.

"Well?"

Sam sounded amused. Maggie looked over at him and noticed the smile he didn't try to hide.

"We're watching *Muppet Babies*," one laughing girl replied.

"Why in here?"

The other little girl stood, bouncing gently on the mattress. "Cuz we just love your water bed."

"Well, I do, too, so go easy." The child tumbled back onto the mattress and landed on her stomach. Sam turned to Maggie. "This, in case you haven't guessed, is my room and—" he pointed to a door near the dresser "—that's the bathroom. Do you need to measure in here?"

"No." Her figures had matched with Fanny's estimates. But she looked into the bathroom, anyway. Good. There was nothing unusual about the room to make the paperhanging difficult. It was a starkly white, masculine room. Taupe towels were folded over brass rods by the *Jacuzzi*. A flourishing fern hung from the ceiling, but that was the only decoration besides the caricature of a tennis player on the wall opposite a tiled shower stall.

Maggie stepped out of the bathroom and smiled at the girls, who stared back curiously. If Sam Winslow entertained female guests, he certainly didn't do it upstairs. Which, she realized suddenly, might be why finishing the guest rooms was so important. "If you'll show me that list, I'll get to work downstairs."

"Fine. Meet the girls first. The one on the left is Julianne. The other, with the stuffed bear, is Justine. Girls, this is Ms. McGuire. She's going to be hanging the wallpaper. Make sure you stay out of her way."

Twin voices politely said, "How do you do."

Maggie didn't want them to stay out of her way. There was a special place in her heart for children. "Fine, thank you," she replied with a smile.

IT ALL CAME DOWN to walls, she thought later as she unloaded her tools from the back of the station wagon. Just walls. Walls that needed to be stripped and sanded, primed and papered, washed and dried. That was it. The houses were different, sometimes the paper. And there was always a different owner, nervously wondering how those walls were going to look when the job was finished.

But this job was something else. She told herself it was because she was used to working with women. Aside from contractors, who basically left her alone, expecting her to do her job while they got on with theirs, Maggie normally worked with women who were vitally interested in how their decorating project was going to turn out.

But she'd never worked with anyone like Sam Winslow. He hadn't even bothered to look at the paper he'd paid for. There was something intriguing about him, something charmingly masculine that reached into a very deep part of her and touched her heart.

She made a third trip through the outside door leading to the guest rooms and stacked the tools in the hall. The best thing she could do for herself, she decided, was to keep her mind on her work.

JUSTINE DECIDED this was better than television. Much better. The child edged closer to the doorway. She didn't want to miss anything. Maggie pulled another piece of wallpaper from the box of water and began to fold it in half and roll it up. Justine couldn't help herself. "Why do you do that?"

Maggie looked over to where one of Sam's little girls knelt in the doorway. "To let the paper soften. To give the glue a chance to get nice and sticky."

"Oh. Now what?"

Maggie slid her small stepladder over a few feet, tucked her tools in her pockets and picked up the roll of paper. "Now I hang it on the wall." She stepped on the ladder, gently peeled the paper apart and, starting at the ceiling edge, carefully matched the pattern of silver leaves and cranberry flowers. She leaned over to pick up another tool.

"What's that?" The child scooted farther into the room.

"My level. It tells me if all the lines are straight." Maggie put it down and, unsatisfied, moved the strip of wallpaper up a fraction of an inch. Then, touching the matching edge of paper with firm fingers, she smoothed the rest with a Styrofoam brush. She knew Justine was fascinated and didn't mind if the child watched. It felt good to have company. Little noise penetrated to the lower level and Maggie wished she hadn't forgotten her radio. Some Charlie Daniels music would pep her up. She stepped down from the stool and pushed it aside with one foot while continuing to smooth the dripping paper.

"That's pretty neat."

"Thank you," Maggie said, reaching for a bucket of water. She squeezed the excess water out of the sponge and stood. Her arms were tired already and she'd only been working for three or four hours. If she could get most of this room finished today...

"Now whatcha gonna do?"

"Come over here and see." Maggie pulled the ladder back to the wall. She grabbed her drywall blade and made sure her knife was tucked in her pants pocket before stepping on the stool. "I'm going to trim the top edge." Which she did easily, letting the wet strip of paper fall to the carpet.

Justine quickly picked it up. "Yuk. It's all goopy."

Maggie gently washed the ceiling edge and the paper, using her roller to seal the seams before wiping the extra glue. "Where's your sister? With Lou?"

"She's playing Barbie. Lou's cooking." She picked up more scraps of paper littering the carpet, before telling Maggie importantly, "Daddy doesn't like messes."

Maggie hid a smile, wishing she could tease Justine about her messy bedroom. And if Daddy didn't like messes, he wasn't going to enjoy the upheaval of having his house redecorated. Once again she wondered why he was doing this. Still, there wasn't time to be curious, and it wasn't any of her business, anyway. She stepped off the stool and carefully trimmed the paper along the edge of the carpet, tucking the ends behind tufts of carpet. She took a few more swipes with the sponge and threw it back into the bucket, absently wiping her hands on her thighs. Then she stepped back and surveyed the wall critically.

"Looks good to me," Justine said.

"Me, too."

"This is *Grandma's* room, you know."

"I'll make sure it's just beautiful." Maggie went back to work, while Justine watched silently.

"Do you need the sponge now?"

"Not yet, but I'll tell you when." She trimmed the excess paper at the ceiling and held out her hand. "Okay."

The child moved the bucket and pulled the sponge from the water. She handed it to Maggie with a satisfied smile.

"Thanks. That saves me some steps."

"Justine, you shouldn't be in here!" a deep voice rang out from the doorway.

Maggie turned from her perch on the ladder to see Sam Winslow frowning at his daughter.

"But, Daddy, I'm helping." She squatted near the bucket and triumphantly picked up a wet strip of paper from the floor and tossed it into the garbage bag. "See?"

Sam looked over at Maggie, a question in his eyes.

"It's okay." She felt uncomfortably dirty and rumpled standing up on the ladder, especially when Sam could have stepped out of an ad from *Cosmopolitan*. She gulped and looked away, flattening the seam with her roller, then sponging invisible glue from the pattern of little silver leaves three inches from her nose.

"Well, just make sure you don't get in Maggie's way."

"*I won't*, Daddy."

Justine was obviously losing patience over her father's interference, Maggie decided as she wiped the ceiling edge and tried to keep from laughing.

"Maggie, Lou has lunch ready, and I have a paper sample for the girls' bathroom. I'd like you to see it."

Maggie looked over at him. "Sure. Just let me finish this seam." She stepped down from the ladder, rolling and sponging, until she felt cool water surround her foot. She looked down, and saw that she'd stepped into the bucket of water Justine had so thoughtfully moved closer to the ladder.

"Uh-oh." Justine stared at Maggie with wide eyes.

"Well," Maggie said with a sigh, removing her dripping foot from the water. "Looks like I really stepped in it this time."

Sam's eyes twinkled. "I thought that only happened in Laurel and Hardy movies."

"Me, too." She balanced herself on the stool and sat on the step, pulling the sneaker off her foot. "Not very professional, is it?"

"Does this happen often?"

She peeled off her sock, feeling silly. "Believe it or not, this is the first time."

Justine didn't know whether to giggle or cry. "I'm sorry, Maggie."

"It's not your fault," she reassured the girl. "I should have looked first."

Sam walked over and held out his hand. "Give me your shoe and sock. I'll have Lou throw them in the dryer."

When she handed them to him, she could see the amusement in his eyes. "I feel ridiculous."

"You're going to feel cold. I'll get you a pair of slippers." He could barely control his laughter, and fought the surprising urge to tuck Maggie into his arms until her embarrassment faded. What on earth was the matter with him?

"Please don't bother. I'll just go barefoot." To prove her point, she began to unlace the other tennis shoe.

"Oh, no! Did she break her foot?"

Maggie looked up to see Julianne standing breathlessly in the doorway.

Justine answered. "*No*, dope. She just got wet."

"Don't call your sister a dope," Sam replied automatically. He handed his elder daughter the sneaker and sock. "Make yourself useful and give these to Lou to dry. And say please."

"Did she fall off the ladder? Does she need Band-Aids? I know where they are. I fall off my bike all the time in the driveway and I always know where the Band-Aids—"

"Julie, please. This is not a medical emergency." He turned to Maggie to explain. "She's in a nurse stage."

"I'm going to be a *doctor* when I grow up," the child corrected. "Justy's gonna be the nurse and have to do what I say."

"Good luck," Sam muttered, and was pleased when he saw Maggie's answering smile. "Right now everyone has to do what I say, and *you*—" he looked at Julie "—should tell Lou we'll be ready for lunch in a few minutes."

"Okay."

"Come with me." He turned to Maggie. "It's too cold down here for bare feet."

Maggie stood and reluctantly followed him out into the hall. It felt like a parade, with Julianne leading the way up the stairs and into the living area. But Sam didn't stop there; he rounded the corner and climbed the flight of stairs to the third level, with Maggie behind him.

But when Sam went into his bedroom, Maggie lingered in the hall to look at the family photographs. The beautiful blonde must have been Sam's wife. Justine had the same quiet smile. A younger Sam Winslow laughed back at his wife, tennis racket in his hand, ocean in the background. Other pictures showed the young couple with their infant daughter or with others who, Maggie guessed, were friends or members of the family. She thought she recognized Anne—wasn't that the name Sam had used?—with a former mayor of New York City, and Sam playing tennis with the governor of Rhode Island. The happiness between the handsome young man and the elegant woman practically leaped from behind the framed glass.

A dramatic black-and-white photograph drew Maggie's attention away from the family portraits. Anne was in profile, wearing a long black dress and seated at a grand piano. Jewels sparkled at her throat and on her hands as her long fingers caressed the ivory keys. On her face was an expression of deep contentment.

"That's my wife, Anne," Sam murmured, coming up beside Maggie. "But I guess that's obvious, isn't it?"

Suddenly Maggie felt as if she'd been caught trespassing. "She was very beautiful."

"And very talented. I hope the girls will take after their mother that way. They both start piano lessons this summer." His face was expressionless as he looked down at Maggie. "I can't believe it's been five years since she died."

"I'm sorry," she said simply. "It must be difficult raising two children alone."

Sam shook his head. "Lou's been a godsend. And we have a pretty regular routine."

That wasn't what she meant, but she didn't try to explain. It was obvious he was easily in control of his household. And liked it that way. But she thought it would be lonely without someone to share the days—and nights—with.

He handed her a pair of white athletic socks. "Here. You can put these on for now. Lou will find you some slippers. My mother-in-law left a pair around somewhere."

She took the socks. "Thanks. I'd better go back to work."

"Lunch is ready."

"I brought a sandwich."

"Lou set a place at the table for you. She has soup and homemade muffins. And I'm going to turn the heat on downstairs. The fog's making the house feel damp."

She was uncomfortable. "I really don't expect you to feed me. I always bring my own lunch to the job."

He gestured toward the stairs. "You don't want to hurt Lou's feelings, do you? Besides, you'll work better after a hot lunch."

She didn't tell him she'd probably want to curl up in a corner and *sleep* after a hot lunch. "Okay. For today. I'll clean up and join you in a few minutes."

Sam followed her down the stairs reluctantly. Part of him—the common sense division—suggested he place as much room between himself and the gorgeous little paperhanger as he possibly could. He'd seen enough. Despite the foot in the bucket, she was strong, competent and completely sure of what she was doing. Her graceful movements wasted no time. Then again, he supposed she couldn't afford to.

When he went into the kitchen, Lou was removing a pan of muffins from the oven.

"I'm leaving," he called to her back as he strode toward the door.

"Before lunch?"

"I need to do some work from the office. I'm behind on those designs for the community center." He countered Lou's skeptical expression with a bland smile.

"You've never been late with a project in your life."

He shrugged. "And I'm not starting now."

Sam drove away from the house very slowly and cautiously, peering into the mist. He hated the fog. The mist clung to his skin. Besides, he liked to know exactly where he was at all times, liked to be sure what lay ahead. It didn't always work that way, though. He knew from painful experience.

MAGGIE TRIED NOT TO LOOK at herself in the expanse of mirror in the guest bathroom while she washed her hands and thought of the pictures of Sam's wife. She'd been such a beautiful woman and it was obvious she and Sam had been very much in love. Maggie winced at her own reflection, then smiled ruefully. She'd been about to make comparisons.

3

THERE WERE GOOD SUNDAYS and bad Sundays, Justine
decided. A good Sunday meant going to the beach or
staying in your pajamas all day or going to a friend's
house and putting on her mother's makeup. A bad
Sunday was just like today, because it was raining and
Daddy was in his office and wouldn't even go rent a
movie for them to see. There was nothing to do. She sat
dejectedly on the kitchen counter, watching the rain
puddle on the driveway. She was wondering if she
should ask Daddy about a movie again, when she saw
the big car pull up. When the beautiful lady named
Maggie knocked on the back door Justine figured this
Sunday might be getting better. With any luck, Maggie
would let her help with the wallpaper again. "She's
here."

"Who?" Julianne stopped coloring and looked up.

"Maggie."

Julianne slid from her chair and hesitated in front of
the French doors. "Should I let her in?"

"Sure, you dope." Her sister sighed. "Why not?"

"Lou said I had to get permission before I opened
the door and let anybody in the house."

"But she's the paperhanger, remember?" Justine
hopped off the counter. "Never mind. I'll do it myself."

"Race you!" Julianne got a head start through the
opened doors to the hall, but her elder sister caught up

near the washing machine. From there on it was an even race to the finish.

Maggie was opening the door when the girls reached for the knob. "Hi, ladies."

"Hi," they answered, panting.

Maggie stepped into the entryway and looked down at the giggling children blocking the hall. Their cheeks were flushed. "Who won?"

"It was a tie," Justine said. "But Julie got a head start."

Maggie set her lunch and radio on the floor, then removed her hooded jacket and shook the extra moisture from it. "Mind if I hang this up?" She gestured toward the row of wooden pegs on the wall.

"No, that's okay," Justine said, staring at Maggie's hair.

"You got wet."

"Yep." After hanging up the jacket, Maggie retrieved her belongings, fluffed her damp curls with her fingers and followed the girls into the kitchen. "What are you two doing today?"

"Looking for trouble," Sam answered. He set his coffee cup in the sink and leaned against the counter, his arms folded in front of his chest.

"Oh, Daddy." Justine sighed in disgust.

Maggie couldn't help staring at him. All male, in white shorts and a gray sweatshirt that matched his eyes, he looked very much like the master of the house. She felt her cheeks warm. "Good morning."

"Afternoon," he corrected.

She shrugged. "Whatever." She'd be damned if she'd apologize for sleeping late, especially after having worked until late Saturday evening. For some reason it had been hard to fall asleep last night, despite the comforting patter of rain.

"How's it going?"

"Just fine." She looked away from him and headed through the kitchen toward the stairs, glad to escape. The gray rain at the windows seemed to shrink the large house, giving it an unsettling cozy atmosphere. Hurrying down the steps, Maggie heard Sam refuse the children permission to follow her down to the lower level. Too bad, she thought. Their chatter would probably slow her down a little, but at least she'd have company on such a dreary afternoon.

She wasn't alone for long. By the time she'd flicked on the lights, plugged in the radio and booked several strips of paper, the children had joined her.

"Are you supposed to be down here?" Maggie fiddled with the radio dial until the country-western station came in clearly.

Julianne shook her head. "No."

"Daddy's back in his office again," Justine explained. "Can we stay? If we're very quiet and don't move the bucket or anything?"

Maggie pretended to consider the question and kept her expression serious. "You two like Willie Nelson?"

Their faces went blank. "Dunno," Justine said. "Do we?"

Maggie laughed. "Sure you do. He's a really good singer. Listen." She turned the volume up, stuck her tools in her back pocket and unrolled a wet strip of paper. This room would be finished in no time at all. As long as Daddy stayed safely in his office, Maggie knew she could concentrate on her work.

By the end of the afternoon the first room was finished and ready for the decorative border to be applied. Maggie took a break, ate her lunch and taught the girls to make designs from the unused wallpaper scraps. Then she showed them how to cut the silver leaves from the paper and glue them onto their fingernails while she measured the strips for the border.

"Maggie," Sam called. He entered the room and stopped short.

Maggie smiled over to him. She gestured toward the covered walls. "What do you think?"

The girls proudly held up their hands. Grotesque fingernails twinkled silver as the children waggled their fingers at their father. "Very impressive," he managed.

"Don't mind them," she said. "The glue will wash off."

Sam took a step forward and looked at Maggie. "I fell asleep," he said sheepishly. "The children weren't supposed to be down here. I hope they weren't too much of a hindrance to you."

"They weren't." Distracted, Maggie dropped the tape measure. Justine picked it up and handed it to her. "Thanks."

Sam stayed in the doorway. He seemed ill at ease and shoved his hands in the pockets of his shorts. "I'm going to make a pot of coffee. Can I bring you some?"

Maggie kept a firm hold on the tape measure this time. "Sure."

He smiled. "Black. Right, Maggie?"

She nodded. "Thanks...Sam." It was the first time she'd felt comfortable enough to use his name.

MONDAY WAS OVER. Or almost. Maggie piled her tools neatly into a corner of the room, drying the wet ones on a rag first. More than half the second room was finished, thank goodness, and the job was going smoothly. She'd almost believe in leprechauns if this good luck held.

"Okay, girls. You'll have to take this stuff upstairs now."

Justine and Julianne did not look up from their project. Intent on their work, they sat cross-legged on the unmade bed pushed into one corner of the room. Intricate paper dolls and bits of wallpaper surrounded them.

Maggie shrugged. She guessed it was okay if they stayed where they were. She switched off her radio and tried again. "See you tomorrow, ladies!"

"Bye, Maggie," they chorused.

Julianne added, "Tomorrow we'll have a thousand."

"Great. You'll have to show them to me as soon as you get home from school." The making of paper dolls had been a big hit with two little girls, who hadn't known what to do with themselves.

"You're coming back, right?" Justine looked almost worried.

"Sure. I can't leave this room looking so funny, can I?" Maggie grabbed her thermos and went out through the downstairs door, avoiding Lou in the kitchen. She would only insist that Maggie stay for dinner, and Maggie didn't want to do that. She was tired and dirty and didn't feel like sitting across the dining-room table from Sam. Not that someday it wouldn't be a great idea, she had to admit, but she'd like to have paste-free fingernails and be wearing something a little fancier than dirty denim.

Sam was sitting behind the steering wheel of her car when she came around the front corner of the house. The car door was open, and when she walked up to it she noticed he had adjusted the seat to accommodate his long legs.

"Having fun?" she asked.

He wasn't the least bit embarrassed. "I just washed my car. I was going to do yours, too."

"It rained yesterday. Why would you want to wash my car?"

He shrugged. "You should take better care of it. In a few years it will be a classic." He eased out of the car and grinned down at her. "Why don't you take me for a ride in this old battleship?"

"Why?"

"Because it's Monday. And I almost washed your car. And would you quit asking questions?"

Maggie laughed. She liked this side of him. "Where do you want to go?"

"That's the spirit." He patted the front hood on his way around to the other side. "I like a willing woman."

"You're just used to chauffeurs." She slid behind the wheel and readjusted the seat before Sam joined her, then started the engine. "Now what?"

"We cruise."

She looked at the gas gauge, just to make sure it wasn't on empty. "Where?"

"Did you grow up around here?"

She nodded and backed the car around. "Graduated from South Kingstown High School, went to the university for a couple of years after that." She reached the end of the driveway. "Left or right?"

"Right. To the Pier."

"What about you? The Winslows were summer people, weren't they?"

"My aunt and uncle brought me here every year. From New York."

She wanted to ask him about his parents, but didn't want to appear nosy. The road wound along a privately owned beach for a couple of miles until it led to a shorefront resort area. Introduced by twin stone towers bridged in an arc, it was known as the "Pier." There was no pier, just a long seawall—a perfect place for teenagers to sit and watch the cars cruise by—and a sidewalk wide enough for people of any age to walk. At one point a leap over the seawall led to the town beach. There people sat and watched the surfers on their boogie boards.

"Do you come from a big family?"

"Not really." He looked around at the busy Pier area. "I loved this place when I was fifteen." He looked over at Maggie and smiled. "I used to envy the local kids who lived here all the time."

"Well, now you do, too."

"I'm lucky. I inherited the property from my uncle—he didn't have any children—and my wife and I always intended to remodel the old place." He switched on the radio, as if to change the topic of conversation. Beach Boy music blasted from the speakers.

"I think I'm having a flashback," Maggie said. "How do you like the car so far?"

"You should preserve it. You might have a son someday who'll drive it on dates."

"Or in parades."

"True."

The fresh sea air gave Maggie new energy and a renewed awareness of how hungry she was. "I'll make the circle, then head back to your house."

"Do me a favor and stop at the supermarket for a minute? I promised Lou I'd get a couple of gallons of milk."

"Okay." That was fine with Maggie. It would save her a trip to the store later. She hoped this market had a deli that made Italian submarine sandwiches. She could just unwrap the wax paper and dinner would be ready.

The parking lot was crowded; summer had barely begun and already the tourists were arriving.

"I'll just be a minute," Sam told her.

"Oh, I'll come, too. I'll get something for dinner."

It was strange to walk across the parking lot with Sam beside her. As if they walked across pavement together once a day.

She missed being part of a couple. Glancing sideways at him, she wondered if he missed being married. Yet he seemed to have his life running smoothly. Was he always this calm? This self-contained? He pushed open the heavy glass door for her and she brushed against his arm as she entered the store. There was the briefest feeling of warmth and strength and then she was alone again, under glaring fluorescent lights and chilled by air-conditioning.

"Do you need a cart?" he asked from behind her.

"No. Should I meet you here at the checkout?" She stepped out of the path of a woman laden with grocery bags and turned to him. "I need to find the deli section."

"Over here." He motioned toward a corner. "Follow me."

To Maggie's surprise, Sam waited patiently while she stood in line to be served, then as the oversized sandwich was assembled.

"Is that dinner?" he asked.

She thought he looked almost envious. "Yes," she admitted. "I'm not much of a cook."

"You live alone?"

She nodded. "Cooking for one person isn't exactly inspirational."

He smiled. "I know what you mean. I'm strictly a take-out Chinese cook. On Lou's nights off, I just call and have it delivered. The girls are happy and I don't have to clean up the kitchen."

She could not picture him eating chow mein with his kids. Images of candlelight dinners with women wearing diamonds were better suited to the Winslow mystique.

But she wouldn't have pictured him in a grocery store, either, and here he was lifting two gallons of milk from the refrigerated shelf.

"Meg?" An all-too-familiar voice cut into her thoughts. There was only one person who ever called her "Meg." And she didn't particularly ever want to hear his voice again. She looked over to see a stocky black-haired man standing near Sam.

Maggie felt as if all the blood in her body had sunk to her feet and turned to ice. She couldn't have moved from her place on the dull yellow linoleum without falling flat on her face in the attempt. She tried to keep her expression casual.

"Hello, Tony," she replied. "How are you?" But she could see how he was. A drooling baby, nestled comfortably in a bright blue carrier, peeked over Tony's shoulder. A small brown-eyed boy clung to his father's hand. The same dark hair matched father to son's.

"Just fine, Meg. You look great. I hear you have your own business."

Maggie was aware she had glue stuck to her work clothes and hadn't combed her hair in hours. But she looked like a hardworking contractor, and for that she was grateful. "Yes. It's been pretty busy lately."

"Well, that's good," Tony answered awkwardly.

He seemed to be trying to make the best of a difficult situation, and Maggie was surprised. Sensitivity had never been one of his strong points.

Sam stepped closer, returning one of the gallons of milk to the shelf before reaching for Maggie. She looked as if she were going to faint. He didn't know who the joker with the kids was, but obviously the guy didn't have sense enough to move out of the way.

"Maggie?" Sam put his free arm around Maggie's shoulders, noting how stiff they were. "Have everything you need?"

Why did Sam have his arm around her? she wondered. "I'm done," she told him, but looked at Tony's children, instead.

"Well, it's nice to see you again, Meg. Take care." With one curious look at Sam, Tony reached for a carton of milk, then turned and walked away. The baby twisted to stare at Maggie, and one little fist opened and closed in a goodbye wave.

Sam led Maggie up the aisle to the express checkout and threw a few bills on the counter, ignoring her protests. When she handed the sandwich to the teenage checker, there were fingerprints etched in the bread. Sam took the milk and the bag and led Maggie away.

Fate had a cruel streak, Maggie decided. She ought to be grateful for Sam's strong arm—after all, he was almost holding her up—and she should be thrilled that she could walk out of the store in such a pleasant manner. Instead she just felt cheated.

When they reached the car, Sam opened the passenger door and tucked Maggie into the seat. Then he went around the front of the car, climbed in, moved the seat back and asked for the keys.

"I'm okay," she protested. "I can drive."

"I don't think so."

"Nobody drives this car but me."

"Look, I don't know what happened back there, but I'm not about to let you drive me home after you almost went into shock in the dairy section."

"It was just a meeting between old…acquaintances, that's all." Embarrassed, she fished through her purse for the car keys and handed them to Sam.

The expression in his eyes was kind as he studied her. "You're getting more color in your face now."

"I'm embarrassed, that's why."

"Why would you be embarrassed?" He turned the key in the ignition and the motor roared to life. "You didn't exactly cause a scene."

"It was just unexpected, that's all."

He drove out of the parking lot to the road past the seawall before speaking again. "Who was he? A married lover?"

She looked over at him, surprised. "I don't have married lovers." It took a few seconds to realize he'd only been teasing.

"Old boyfriend from your high-school days?" Sam kept his voice light, trying to joke with her, wanting her to talk to him. He barely knew her, but he recognized pain when he saw it.

"Something like that." She shrugged. "How about ex-husband?"

So that was it. But the guy had two kids, one of them about three years old, so the divorce must have happened quite a few years ago. "Still hurts, does it?" He kept sympathy out of his voice. Somehow he knew she'd hate that.

"Some things you don't get over easily." She hoped that would end the conversation.

But Sam was curious. He couldn't connect her to the heavyset man in the supermarket. "Do you still love him?"

It was an easy question for Maggie to answer. Three-and-a-half years ago every member of her family had asked her that at least once. "No."

Somehow the simplicity of the answer convinced him it was true. She didn't still love her ex-husband. But there was more to the story. He pulled into his driveway, put the car in Park and opened the door. Before sliding out, he touched Maggie's shoulder, resisting the desire to pull her to him. "Are you okay?"

"I'm fine. Honest." They both heard the slight quiver in her voice.

He hesitated then, deciding he was being overprotective, grabbed the milk and got out of the car. Lassie trotted over and wagged her tail expectantly, but Sam paid no attention. He watched Maggie drive away, a helpless feeling haunting him. The temporary employee had turned into a vulnerable, intriguing woman.

"In other words, Lassie," Sam told the panting animal, "we have trouble."

The dog flattened her ears and, tail between her legs, slunk toward the tennis court.

THINK ABOUT THE MONEY. *Think about work. Don't think about the baby's chubby fist waving goodbye.* A car honking behind her jolted Maggie into moving forward through the green light in Wakefield's downtown intersection. She drove the remaining mile home with a white-knuckled grip on the steering wheel.

Her little yellow house had never looked so good. It sat near the center of Wakefield, across from the Village Green. Called a "starter home" by the real estate agent who'd sold it to her and her husband seven years earlier, it was a one-story box with a white front porch tacked on by a previous owner almost as an afterthought. Daffodils bloomed in its tiny yard each spring, and every other week in the summer Maggie pushed a lawnmower over the square of front lawn.

It was a house meant to be lived in by a young couple such as they had been—a husband who was starting his own landscaping business and a woman who would work with him until she could finish her teaching degree. The second bedroom was to be the nursery for the baby that never arrived. And never would.

Which had been the major problem with her marriage. Maggie sighed, unlocking the front door. No babies.

She walked through the living room to the kitchen, tossed the sandwich on the counter and looked out the window over the sink to the backyard. Thick hedges gave privacy to a brick patio and Maggie wondered if she had the energy to wipe the dirt off the chaise lounge out there and fall into it for a few minutes.

Knowing she'd be eaten alive by mosquitoes in five seconds, she decided that a long soak in the bathtub would be more relaxing. Then she'd tear into the sandwich and pretend the pain had gone away.

"WOULD YOU TURN that radio down?" Sam strode into the bedroom, papers clutched in one fist. How Maggie could listen to Willie Nelson at ten o'clock in the morning...

But the scene that greeted him was not what he'd expected. In the middle of the room Justine and Julianne were sitting on a bed with their Barbie dolls, while Maggie knelt on the floor, cutting wallpaper. Oblivious to his protest, all three were singing at the top of their lungs. And it didn't sound much like music.

He looked around the room and saw a paint-stained radio plugged into a socket in the corner. He waited for the final chords to end the song and then cleared his throat.

Three pairs of eyes turned to look at him.

"Daddy!"

"Daddy!"

"Hi, Sam." Maggie was hesitant. She hadn't seen him since the embarrassing scene in the supermarket two days earlier. She'd tried to avoid him, and wondered awkwardly if he sensed that. She stayed kneeling on the floor and busied herself rolling the strips of wallpaper inside out and fastening them with rubber bands the girls were in charge of holding.

Sam glanced at the radio, then back to the girls' happy faces. "I, uh, just wanted to see where you two had disappeared to," he told them. "You're not getting in Maggie's way?"

"Oh, no." Justine shook her head solemnly. "We're not allowed to touch the bucket anymore."

"That's true," Maggie agreed. "We made a deal."

"You have a lot of patience," he shouted as another rowdy song blared from the radio. "When it wears out, send these future country-western stars up to Lou."

"Sure."

He left them there and went back upstairs, the estimates for the community center project still clutched in his fist.

Lou raised an eyebrow as he walked past. "How's the Grand Ol' Opry coming?"

Sam shook his head. "How anyone can get work done in the middle of all that noise, I'll never know."

The housekeeper just smiled. "That's *happy* noise, Sam. You've got to learn to tell the difference."

"I'll work on it." He shut the office door with a firm click and tossed the papers onto the desk.

"HERE, BEN, take these, too." Maggie handed the gangly teenager a sponge and a brush. "And fill the bucket with clean water, okay?"

"Sure." Ben dumped the dirty water into the toilet bowl, then began refilling the bucket from the bathtub faucet.

Maggie perched on top of her ladder and rested for a few minutes. Saturday morning already, the end of a long week, and the downstairs would be finished as soon as she washed the final section of border on the newly papered bathroom wall. "We're halfway finished, you know that, Ben?" There was satisfaction in her voice.

"Think you're gonna make it, Aunt Maggie?"

"You mean finish this job in one more week?" She took the clean sponge he held up to her.

"And the answer?" asked Sam from the doorway.

"The answer," Maggie replied with a touch of defiance, "is yes, of course."

"Of course," he mimicked, folding his arms across his chest and leaning against the doorjamb. "How are you doing, Ben?"

"Just fine, sir." Ben wiped his wet hands on the back

of his jeans and waited nervously to see if he'd be noticed again.

But Sam was looking at Maggie. He hadn't seen her for days, he mused, and she had those shadows under her eyes again. What did this make—the sixth day in a row she'd been working? He felt uncomfortably as if he should be wielding a whip. "The room looks good. You do nice work."

"Thank you. It would have been done sooner, but the two kinds of wallpaper and the border in between took a lot of extra time."

"Are you done here for the weekend?"

Maggie made a final swipe with the sponge and began to climb down the ladder. When she reached the floor, she turned and smiled up at Sam. "Yep. The upstairs can wait until Monday morning, can't it?"

"Sure. But I'd better warn you. Company starts arriving next week. I'm having someone come in here tomorrow to clean, hang the curtains and make up the beds."

"Sam, I've never asked you before, but why the big hurry?" She tossed the sponge to Ben, who caught it neatly. "You can wash up the tools now," she told the boy, "and I'll take you home."

Sam waited until she'd turned her attention back to him. "Have a cup of coffee with me and I'll tell you the whole sordid story."

It was tempting. She hadn't brought her thermos this morning, knowing that the border would take less than an hour to apply. She wouldn't have bothered Ben if she hadn't needed more than two hands to do the job. "Okay," she agreed, "but don't leave out any of the details."

Before she left the room she stopped. "Sam, where should I leave my tools for the weekend?"

"Ben, put them up in my room."

"Which one is that, Mr. Winslow?"

"Top of the stairs on the left. If the girls are in there watching television, tell them not to touch anything."

"Sure." Ben nodded and turned back to his cleaning.

Upstairs in the kitchen, Sam poured two cups of coffee and handed one to Maggie. "Want to sit on the deck?"

"Okay."

He opened a set of French doors and led Maggie onto a deck with a spectacular view of the ocean.

She took a deep breath of the salt air. Summer had finally come to Rhode Island. The breeze held the tangy smell of the Atlantic, and the air was so clear Block Island was easily visible across the water. She sat down in an overstuffed wicker chair and rested her sore arms on the armrests, being careful to balance the coffee mug. "It's wonderful out here."

Sam sat in the chair beside her and stretched out his long legs. She looked over at him and decided he looked right at home. He wore white cotton slacks and his feet were bare. The navy-and-white striped shirt made him look like a wealthy sailor.

"There's a beach past the hedges over there," he said, pointing. "Feel free to use it while you're here."

"Well, thanks, but I don't think I'll have the time." She sipped her coffee and began to relax. After all, she had the whole afternoon ahead of her. Maybe going to the beach was a good idea. She'd pack a lunch or buy fruit at the stand near the pavilion—

Sam's words interrupted her daydream. "Do you always work this hard?"

"Sometimes. Just not this many days in a row." *And I hope I live to tell about it.* "Why are you going through all this? And what's the big hurry?"

"You'd have to meet my mother-in-law to understand. She engineered this project." He chuckled. "Then the girls got into it and decided they just had to have their rooms decorated, too. Buffie—my mother-in-law—was only too happy to agree."

"And?" she prompted, curling up in the chair to face him.

"And it was supposed to have been finished weeks ago, before Buffie's visit. She's bringing guests for the first annual symphony performance in Narragansett. Have you heard about it?"

"No, not really."

"It's been organized for over a year, with Buffie engineering most of the fund-raising from New York. For some reason she got it into her head that this house needed to be remodeled and she's talked me into letting a magazine take photographs for an article."

"It looks finished to me."

He smiled, his gray eyes warm as he looked at the tiny woman nestled in the chair across from him. What would Buffie make of her? And why was *he* so intrigued with this woman he'd met only eight days ago? "Vanderberg standards require intensive redecorating every few years."

"Which is good news for paperhangers, isn't it?"

He laughed. "Especially now. Justine and Julianne are demanding equal decorating rights, and Buffie's decorator insists my rooms be done, too, or the entire project won't 'coordinate' properly!"

"Speaking of coordinating, your bedroom paper is

still back-ordered. That could be a problem." She wondered if it would affect her bonus.

"Aunt Maggie? I'm finished."

Maggie turned to see Ben standing uncertainly in the doorway. "Oh, good, hon. I'm coming." She stood and so did Sam. "Thanks for the coffee. I'll see you Monday."

"See ya, Mr. Winslow."

"Goodbye, Ben. Has your aunt let you drive that tank of hers yet?"

Ben grinned. "Maybe she will when I'm sixteen."

"Maybe." Maggie took his elbow. "But now I get to take you home. See you Monday, Sam."

Remaining on the deck after they left, he sat back in the chair, his coffee forgotten. He heard the Pontiac start and listened as the sound of the engine faded, and thought that it was going to be a quiet weekend. He didn't know whether that was good news or not.

4

"YOU WANT to let me off here?"

Maggie looked over at her hopeful nephew. "Why?"

Ben gestured toward three bikini-clad teenage girls walking along the seawall. "That's why."

"Oh." Maggie adjusted her sunglasses and slowed the car. "You want me to see if they need a ride, or what?"

"Jeez, no! I just wanted to check out what's goin' on down at the Pier." He slumped in the seat as if to hide.

"Your mother would kill me if I left you here. And how would you get home?"

He gave her a lopsided grin. "You'd pick me up later?"

"Sorry, pal, but I'm going home and staying there."

He sighed. "Okay. Guess I'll see if Dad will drop me and the guys off at the movies tonight. But you gotta understand, summer is for *romance*, Aunt Maggie. And I'm missin' out."

She tried not to laugh. "You've only been out of school a few days. You have plenty of time."

He looked skeptical. Maggie knew how he felt, though. Fifteen years ago she would have been excited about the first Saturday night of the summer, wondering what the new summer kids would be like, who she would meet on the beach, if she would fall in love with some tanned surfer with gorgeous shoulders and a smile that could charm a shark. Maggie could almost smell the cocoa butter.

When Maggie left Ben at his house, she noted Patsy's car wasn't in the driveway. The rest of the weekend stretched out in front of her like an empty beach, which could be good or bad, depending on how she wanted to look at it.

The traffic was miserable, even for a humid Saturday afternoon when everyone should have been at the beach. With relief and a perspiration-soaked back, Maggie drove into her driveway. She peeled her body away from the sticky vinyl seat and cursed the humidity before going into the house for a lukewarm shower. She slipped on a loose cotton sundress and lay across the bed to enjoy the peace. A hot breeze ruffled her hair, and her cheek stuck to the pillow. But when she closed her eyes, she could see the rooms of Sam's house. Not the rooms with the patterned paper, but the blank walls that needed to be covered. She told herself not to worry, that time was not a problem yet. So far she was on schedule and blank walls shouldn't be bothering her or keeping her awake. Her worries faded as she dozed in the hot summer silence of the bedroom.

There's a saxophone in my ear. Maggie burrowed her face deeper into the pillow and tried to get away from the sound. A few minutes later she gave up and reluctantly opened her eyes. It was after seven o'clock, she noted, and there was no musician in the room, but the sounds of an enthusiastic band could be heard clearly.

Tonight would be the first night of a series of free concerts on the Village Green, Maggie realized. Another sign of summer, open concerts were a New England tradition that drew people with blankets, coolers and kids to the public lawn to listen to music, see old friends and discuss the effectiveness of various mosquito repellents.

Maggie stretched, sore muscles complaining, and listened to the band. The room was stuffy, and knowing it would be cooler outside, she got up, found her sandals and left the house. The song, a ballad this time, grew louder as Maggie followed the sidewalk to the Green. Oblivious to the entertainment, children dangled from the playground equipment off in a corner of the lawn. Adults of all ages sat in beach chairs or on blankets.

Maggie looked for Joe and Patsy or her parents, but didn't see them in the crowd. She sat on the grass, stretched her legs in front of her and leaned back on her hands. She wasn't in the mood to be with her family, anyway, she decided. She had never been what they'd expected her to be, including a divorced woman. But they'd been kind and supportive, if confused about the problems in her marriage. Maggie had thought she was over it all until she saw Tony and his children in the supermarket. It was a miracle she hadn't run into him before. But the town had grown in leaps and bounds; she hardly ever ran into people she knew. She looked around the crowd and didn't recognize anyone.

The band leader introduced the female singer. She had a pleasant voice and sang a popular rock song that both the band and the audience were having fun with. Maggie was laughing as the singer wove through the crowd, around blankets and chairs, to pull hesitant spectators to their feet for a quick dance, when she felt a pair of warm little hands press against her eyes and block her vision. The hands were too small to belong to her nieces.

"Guess who!" a girl's voice chirped.

"I give up," Maggie said.

Little giggles erupted behind her back. "You hafta guess first."

That infectious giggle could only be Julianne's, Maggie thought. But who was with her? Surely Sam wouldn't attend a free concert on a Saturday night. Probably Lou had brought the girls over to play. The thought was strangely disappointing. "Are you going to be a doctor when you grow up?"

Another giggle. The hands slipped a little, but before Maggie could turn to face the child, larger hands took their place to cover her eyes. The hands were warm, the skin slightly roughened, yet gentle palms captured her face. One thumb sent a decidedly unsettling tingling to her earlobe.

"*Now* guess who." The low masculine voice held a chord of laughter.

She forced herself not to shiver as his breath tickled her neck. "This isn't your style, Sam." She tugged at his hands and he freed her face immediately.

"My children are teaching me new tricks."

She turned around to face him as he knelt behind her. The girls had their hands over their mouths to keep from laughing.

"We dared Daddy to do it," Justy said.

Sam waved them off. "Go play for a minute while I talk to Maggie." They did as they were told, running off to join the mob on the monkey bars. Sam watched to make sure they were safe, then turned to Maggie. "Are you here alone?"

She nodded. "I live down the street. I heard the music and walked over to see what was going on."

He stood up and held out his hand. "Come over and sit with us. Lou gave me an old blanket."

He looked gorgeous, in pale clay-colored slacks and a taupe cotton shirt. His face was sunburned and his smile so friendly Maggie couldn't resist letting him pull her to her feet. Feeling foolish, she immediately released his hand to brush the grass from her white skirt.

"Is Lou here, too?"

"No. She said she'd enjoy the quiet at home."

Stepping carefully around the other spectators, Maggie followed Sam to an empty blue bedspread. If they were any closer to the playground, she noted as she sat down, Sam would be sitting in the sandbox.

It was a seductive movement, Maggie thought as she watched Sam stretch out on the blanket beside her. It was as if they were a couple, as if relaxing casually on blankets were something they did together every night. Maybe that's why summertime had its own sexual magic, she thought. It wasn't the heat, after all, or even the amazing amounts of exposed flesh. It was because people were lolling around next to one another on blankets. She slipped off her sandals and nervously rubbed her feet on the grass, tucking her dress around her as if it would fly away in the breeze like an errant tablecloth.

The exuberant band continued to entertain the audience. Justine and Julianne left the swings and danced with other children off to one side of the stage. They looked thrilled to have the freedom to dance and the open space to do a cartwheel if the music deserved one.

Sam sighed. "I shouldn't let them run wild like that."

"Why not? They're having fun and not hurting anyone."

"True. But..." He crossed his legs at the ankles and leaned back on his elbows.

"But?" she urged.

"They're wild enough as it is. I hate to encourage it."

Maggie stared at him, wondering how he could be serious. The girls were perfectly normal. "If you'd seen my family you'd know what wild was."

"You have brothers and sisters?"

"Three brothers and one sister—Ben's mother, who might be around here somewhere."

"That's a big family. What about your parents?"

"They live outside of town, in the house where we grew up. I think they're spending their retirement recovering from raising five wild Irish kids."

"You don't seem wild," Sam said, surveying the ladylike woman beside him. Actually, he was lying. Sam thought Maggie's blue eyes held a very interesting gleam. There were times he wished he knew what she was thinking, then felt relief because he didn't.

She smiled. "I've mellowed with age." She turned away from him, tapping her feet to the music. *He's getting too personal*, she thought nervously. *Just because I'm sitting next to him on a blanket in front of a couple of hundred people doesn't mean I have to bare my soul.*

Sam wasn't about to give up so easily. "Does your sister look like you?"

Maggie pictured tall athletic Patsy. "We have the same blue eyes and black hair, but she's much taller."

"I know it's rude to point," he said, pointing past Maggie's shoulder, "but there's a woman over there who fits that description, and she's been waving at us for the past few minutes."

Maggie swiveled to look, and saw Patsy struggle to her feet and begin threading her way among the blan-

kets toward them. "You're right." Maggie waited for
Patsy to join them, wondering what her sister would
do or say. There was never any way to predict Patsy's
reactions and no sense worrying about it, either. Sam
could take care of himself.

Sam began to stand as Patsy approached the blanket,
but she shook her head. "Don't get up. I won't bother
you for long." She knelt on the blanket near Sam and
stuck out her hand. "Hi. I'm Pat Farrel, Maggie's sister."

"Sam Winslow." Sam shook her hand and sat down
close to Maggie to make room on the blanket.

"I guessed that," she said. "I've seen your picture in
the paper." She turned to Maggie. "I called, but I didn't
get any answer. I was going to ask if you wanted to join
us tonight, but I see you made other plans."

Maggie wished her sister wouldn't look so thrilled.
"I heard the band and walked over."

"Lucky for me my children found her," Sam added.

Patsy looked as if she would swoon with joy. Maggie
decided to change the subject. "Ben's working out
well. I won't have much more work for him at Sam's,
but I'll be able to use him again on some other big jobs
if he wants to earn some money."

"You're working all summer?" Sam asked.

Maggie nodded. "The busy season, remember?"

Patsy agreed. "She never stops working. We're all
worried about how hard—"

Maggie stopped her. "Don't forget, Pat, you're talking to my latest employer. He's glad I work hard."

But Sam looked concerned. "You're taking tomorrow off, aren't you?"

"I'd planned to." She didn't add she was bidding a
restaurant renovation in the morning and helping an

elderly neighbor select paper for her bedroom in the afternoon.

"I bet it will be the first day off in weeks," Patsy told Sam.

Maggie shot her sister a "mind your own business" look, and Patsy grinned. "Guess I'd better go back to Joe." She stood up and added, "Nice to meet you, Sam. Don't let Maggie work too hard."

"I'll try."

"Bye, Pat."

Sam stayed where he was, close to Maggie. He was, she decided, incredibly handsome. He moved his arm and grazed her shoulder. She could almost feel the warmth of his thigh when his slacks brushed against her cotton skirt. It might as well have been skin touching, so delicate was the sensation. Maggie clasped her hands tightly around her knees and wondered if she could make herself small enough to avoid the brief contacts. It wasn't easy.

"Any other relatives in the crowd I should be aware of?"

She smiled at him. "I doubt it. Patsy would've told me. Or they'd have been over here by now. What about you?"

"I'm an only child in an unprolific family, which is why I inherited the house you're working on."

"That must have been a quiet way to grow up."

"It was—" he hesitated, searching for the right word "—organized."

"And you organize your daughters." She meant it as a question, but it didn't sound that way.

Sam winced. "I try not to, but it does come out once in a while." He searched for the girls in the crowd at the playground. "They're going to hurt themselves."

Maggie looked over to see the girls hanging upside down from the monkey bars. "I doubt it. The only things that are going to take a beating are those designer outfits."

He relaxed. "Maybe you're right."

The band continued to play as shadows filled parts of the Green. Maggie swatted mosquitoes and enjoyed the last song, a Broadway medley. As the final round of applause faded Sam turned to Maggie. "That was fun."

"I thought you were more the classical type." Was there a special woman in New York, or closer, across the bay in Newport, who would accompany Sam to more elegant performances?

"You're referring to the symphony?"

She nodded. "Aren't you in charge of it?"

"My mother-in-law likes to thinks she is. I'm just along for the ride. If you'd like to go I can—"

"We're ready!" Justine ran up and tugged on her father's arms, trying to pull him to his feet. He slowly obliged as Julianne prodded Maggie.

"Don't forget. You promised," Justine reminded him, the expression on her face serious.

Maggie said, "Promised what?"

Sam answered. "Ice cream. We parked about half a mile away, near Baskin-Robbins. A tactical error."

Maggie put her sandals on. "Well, good night. And thanks for the seat."

Sam looked as if he would have forgotten the blanket if she hadn't mentioned it. He reached down and scooped it up, rolling it into an awkward ball.

"Can Maggie come, too, Daddy? Please?" Justine jumped up and down and Julianne nodded excitely.

But Maggie refused. "I'd better be going home."

"Please?" asked Sam. "It's still early, and I'll drive you home afterward."

It was hard to say no. What harm could there be in having an ice cream cone? The man was attractive, yes, but not lethal. With two noisy little girls around he wouldn't be able to get a word in, anyway. Besides, she decided, giving in to temptation, it would be fun to walk along the sidewalk on a Saturday evening and pretend life was just one lawn concert after another.

"Okay," she agreed, winking at the girls. "As long as I can have chocolate sprinkles."

Sam gestured toward the street. "Wild Irishwomen may have whatever they want."

They mingled with the rest of the crowd and walked along the sidewalk toward the main section of town.

"Where's your house, Maggie?" Julianne asked.

Maggie pointed across the street. "Right there."

"It looks like a dollhouse."

Maggie laughed. Her tiny home would indeed seem small to children who lived in a Victorian showplace. "It's big enough for me."

Justine was fascinated. "Do you live all by yourself?"

"Sure."

"And nobody else?"

"That's right."

"No cat?"

"No dog?" Julianne added.

"Nothing at all," Maggie answered, sorry to disappoint them. Maybe she should think about a pet, but what kind of animal kept itself clean? After a long day on a construction site, the only thing Maggie wanted to clean was herself. She had no desire to curl up on the couch with an animal, looking for fleas or ticks or whatever else animals brought home.

"Maybe we could give Lassie to you," Sam added in a low voice.

Maggie laughed. "You forget, I know about Lassie's little problem."

"But you don't have a tennis court."

"I still wouldn't trust her. Besides, Lou would miss her."

A horn honked and they saw Patsy drive by in her car, waving as she passed. The girls waved back.

"Who was that?"

"My sister," she told them.

"How many do you have?"

"Just one. But I have three brothers."

They both looked astonished. Julie finally said, "I don't think I'd like to have three brothers. Maybe just one. But Dad says no."

Sam tried to stop the conversation. "You just don't order them from Neiman-Marcus."

"Grandma would. She orders everything from there."

"Brothers are different," Sam said.

"It's that sex thing again," Justine whispered to her younger sister. "Daddy won't dee-scuss it."

"That's right," said Sam. "Daddy won't."

Good for Daddy, Maggie thought. She'd consented to ice cream cones, not a birds-and-bees lecture. Still, she couldn't resist teasing, "Daddy doesn't discuss these things?"

"I'd be happy to try to answer any questions you have, Maggie. Privately." He grinned wickedly.

"That's *so* nice of you, but I think I'll pass."

"Too bad."

Maggie just laughed. She liked this side of Sam, easygoing and relaxed.

Later, after they'd eaten their ice cream, Sam dropped the girls off at the house so Lou could put them to bed, then drove Maggie home. She enjoyed the dark luxuriousness of the car as it hummed through the Pier area. She rolled down her window to smell the ocean as they drove slowly along the seawall road.

They approached an oceanside restaurant, its top deck crowded with people. Hard rock music blasted from somewhere inside. "Do you want to stop for a drink?" Sam asked.

"No, thanks." She thought he'd be relieved. The place looked like a college hangout and she felt a lot older than the kids she saw dancing on the upper deck.

"Do you mind if I take the long way and we just drive along the ocean for a while?"

"No, that sounds wonderful." She leaned back against the headrest, enjoying the luxury of being driven, it was a lovely feeling. She wanted to curl up on the seat, tuck her legs under her and close her eyes against the headlights bombarding them from the other side of the road. But she didn't. She didn't feel quite that comfortable with Samuel T. Winslow.

"Good," he said, a satisfied note in his voice.

He turned the car closer to the shore, and the ocean breeze sent a cool, delicious shiver down Maggie's arms, leaving a salty trail on her skin.

"Are you cold?" he asked.

"No. I like the feel of it."

Sam glanced over to her wondering if she'd like the feel of him. He wanted to pull off into one of the parking lots fronting the beach and, in a dark corner, take her into his arms. She had that effect on him. He'd wanted her from the first moment he'd seen her, he couldn't blame this feeling on the night or the ocean or even that swirly white dress she was wearing. The woman was a voluptuous little bundle who tantalized him. It was hard keeping both hands on the steering wheel.

Sam sighed. He didn't want to scare Maggie away. But one more week of looking at her and he would go mad. The symphony organizers would find him staggering along the beach, muttering to himself. Or maybe roaming around the yard, peeing on the tennis court.

One kiss, he decided, *to get this obsession out my system. She couldn't possibly taste as good as I imagine.* The thought cheered him up so much he was whistling when he parked the car along the curb in front of Maggie's house. Before she could protest, he turned off the car's engine and hopped out, determined to walk her to the front door.

Maggie didn't know what she should do when Sam walked with her to the steps of the front porch. Dating was an experience she'd successfully avoided for years. Should she ask him in for coffee? Was the living room clean? No, she decided, she really didn't want him to come in. That might make this evening seem like a date.

"Would you like to come in for—coffee?" she heard herself ask. *Say no.*

"No," he replied. "I know you must be tired. You were at the house pretty early this morning, weren't you?"

"The job's important," she said, reaching for the unlocked door. She hadn't planned on being out for such a long time, so the porch light was off. They stood together in the shadows while she waited for him to leave before she opened the door.

"Maggie."

His voice stopped her from turning the knob, and she looked up at him. "What?"

He stalled. "Short for Margaret?"

"Yes."

He reached out to touch her chin and lifted it with determined fingers until her dark blue gaze met his. He was going to kiss her and he intended to make it last, because he doubted there would be a second time. She remained quiet as he bent closer to her, and her light breath mingled with his before his lips brushed her closed mouth. His fingers slid from her chin to her nape and he pulled her closer, deepening the kiss, as he silently willed her mouth to open for him.

He had to taste her, just once, here in the darkness of the June night. "Open your lips for me," he whispered against her mouth.

Stunned by the feelings he was evoking inside her, Maggie obeyed. She leaned against the door and allowed sensations to seep through her as the gentle invasion of her mouth continued. His hands swept through her hair as though to keep her from pulling away from him, but she wouldn't have tried. Intimate parts of her body pulsed for more, yearning to feel his hands.

He released her and stepped back. She didn't move. She couldn't. Her knees would buckle and she'd end up falling into the shrubs—not a great way for a thirty-year-old woman to end a good-night kiss.

"I won't come in," he said.

"No." She watched him walk back to the car and drive away, before she entered the dark house and collapsed on the couch without turning on a light. She hadn't been kissed that way in a very long time, if ever. She frowned, trying to remember a time when a mere kiss had made her tremble, but her mind remained blank.

Why, for heaven's sake, had he wanted to kiss her, anyway? Maggie knew she wasn't the kind of woman who inspired lust just by walking through a crowded room, although she'd silently admired women with that quality. And she certainly wouldn't raise a man's temperature by swatting mosquitoes in time to music, as she'd done that evening.

She got up off the couch and went into the kitchen. Briefly fighting the sudden craving for frozen Oreo cookies, she grabbed a handful from the bag in the freezer compartment of the refrigerator, poured herself a glass of water and leaned against the counter while she finished her snack.

She didn't know what to think about tonight. Maybe Sam Winslow could treat casual ice cream encounters with intoxicating kisses, but she couldn't. Besides, what if he hadn't felt what she had? He hadn't kissed her twice. She sighed. She'd be better off sticking to wallpapering his home. At least she was good at that.

"MAGGIE!" Lily McGuire waved at her daughter through the window on the kitchen door of the large ranch house. "We were hoping we'd see you today."

Maggie opened the door and was enveloped by the smells of garlic and tomato sauce. She gave her mother a hug. "I'm in time for Sunday dinner, aren't I?"

"You sure are, but we looked for you at the beach this morning." Lily's eyes narrowed. "You didn't work again today, did you?"

"Just bid a couple of small jobs, that's all." Maggie was glad she'd changed into a sundress before driving to her parents' home. She threw up her hands to ward off her mother's concerned frown. "Honest, today's been a very easy day."

"All right," Lily said with a sigh. "I'll believe you. I won't worry about you anymore and you can go help your nieces set the table."

"Where's Patsy? I didn't see her car in the driveway." With luck Pat wouldn't have told her parents about whom she'd seen her sister with at last night's concert. The last person in the world Maggie wanted to talk about was her latest client. She didn't want to think about him or remember his kiss or discuss what color wallpaper he'd ordered for his bathroom. Maggie sighed. *I'm getting crabby in my old age.*

"She should be here any minute. She had to stop at the market and pick up garlic bread." Lily moved to the stove and began to stir the sauce bubbling in a large pot. "How was the concert last night?"

"Energetic." Maggie edged toward the hall.

"Don't forget the boys will be down at the Pier next week."

"What day?"

"Tuesday."

"I'll try to make it. Where's Dad?"

"He was around here a few minutes ago. And I think Ben and Bobby went next door to shoot baskets." Lily moved to the sink to fill a pan with water. "See if you can find everyone and tell them we'll eat in about fifteen minutes."

Maggie slipped through the doorway and around the corner the large L-shaped room that served as both dining and living room. The table was haphazardly set for dinner, but Patsy's daughters were nowhere in sight. Patrick McGuire sprawled in his brown recliner, the Sunday paper forgotten on his lap while he snored softly. Maggie tiptoed past her father to the open front door and saw Patsy's car pull up in the driveway. She braced herself. Garlic bread and gossip had just arrived in a red Toyota.

Fortunately Bobby bore the brunt of the dinner conversation, good-naturedly taking a lot of teasing about the girl he'd brought to dinner the week before.

"I'm only twenty. That's too young to get serious," he said, grinning. "Somebody pass the meatballs over here."

"Her name is Heather," Patrick told Maggie.

"How many Heathers have you dated, Uncle Bob?" Ben asked, passing the bowl. "Watch out—the bottom's hot."

"Three or four, I think. I've always liked that name."

"Didn't I drive you and someone named Heather to the movies a few years ago?" Maggie wiped her mouth with her napkin and pushed her empty plate away.

"Yeah, I think so. The first Heather. She dumped me for an actor in the high-school drama club." He took a large bite of spaghetti. "Broke my heart, too."

"Then what?" Ben asked.

"Your Aunt Maggie fixed me up with Uncle Tony's cousin."

"*Ex*-Uncle Tony," his mother reminded him.

"Well, he wasn't an 'ex' then."

Ben elbowed his young uncle. "Then what?"

"She dumped me, too, for a guy with a driver's license." He grinned at his sister. "We're not lucky in love, huh, Mag?"

"I think you're doing all right."

"What about you, Mag? Goin' out with anybody hot?"

"What kind of talk is that?" Patrick sputtered.

But Maggie just laughed. "You should be on construction sites with me, Dad. I get propositioned all the time."

Patrick McGuire was a large, handsome man with a thatch of silver hair and a ready smile. "You work hard, Maggie, my girl. And I'm proud of you." His blue eyes twinkled as he affected an Irish brogue. "But don't go telling me what goes on with you and the men in yer life—a father's heart is easily worried."

"WELL?"

Maggie looked at her sister, up to her elbows in soapy dishwater, and began to dry a bowl with a faded blue dishtowel. "Well, what?"

"Don't look innocent, Margaret Jean." Patsy waggled a soapy finger in her younger sister's direction. "How did you end up on a blanket with the Bachelor of the Year?"

Maggie winced. "Would you like to keep your voice down? If Mom and Dad hear the word 'bachelor' they'll get too excited."

"I didn't volunteer to do the dinner dishes just because I'm such a nice person. Now that the family dinner is over, I have you all to myself. C'mon, Mag." Patsy grinned. "Spill your guts."

Maggie set the bowl on the counter and grabbed a dripping saucepan. "He's gorgeous."

"True."

"He has a sense of humor," Maggie said, silently acknowledging a weakness for men who made her laugh.

"Really? He looked serious to me."

Maggie shook her head. "He just looks that way at first. When you get to know him you realize—" She stopped.

"Realize what?"

Maggie shot her sister a warning look. "This is not a romance. I repeat, this is not a romance."

Patsy shrugged. "Sounds like it could be."

Maggie remained silent. If she didn't know better, she'd guess it did have the makings of a hot summer romance. The signs were there. Sam Winslow had looked at her with interest, not unlike the cool sexual appraisal of a passing beach boy. But his kiss had held more experience than any beach boy's. And packed more of a wallop.

Patsy dumped the dirty water down the drain and sponged the dishpan dry. "No reply?"

"His attention is flattering. But I could live without it." Maggie handed her sister the towel so Patsy could dry her hands.

"But why should you? Don't you get lonely, Mag?"

"Lonely enough to have an affair with the first handsome man who comes along? No."

Patsy shook her head. "That's not what I meant. But it's *nice* to have a man around sometimes. Wouldn't you like to go out just once in a while?"

"If that's all it is, sure."

"Meaning what?"

"Meaning I don't need—or want—any more than that."

Patsy looked doubtful. She opened her mouth as if to argue, when Ben opened the kitchen door.

"Hey, Aunt Maggie," he yelled. "You or Mom want

to play boccie ball? Grandpa's challenging us to another championship."

The women shook their heads.

"I really should go home," Maggie said.

"You should relax and enjoy your evening," Patsy countered. "Do you have plans?"

"You don't let up, do you?"

Lily stepped into the kitchen. "Dear," she told her younger daughter, "you don't have to do any more dishes if you have a date tonight."

"She doesn't," Patsy answered. "But she should."

Maggie laughed. "I give up. It's two against one, so I guess it's time I went home." She hugged her mother. "Thanks for dinner. I'll see you on the Fourth. Let me know what kind of food you want me to bring."

Maggie's mother wasn't ready to change the subject. She followed her daughter to the door. "There are lots of nice men at the health club. You could join us at Riverbend one evening, Maggie. Your father would love to play racquetball with you."

"I've never even held a racket, Mother."

"You're small, but you're strong," Pat offered.

Maggie ignored her sister. "I don't really want to meet any men, whether they're healthy or not. And I get all the exercise I need right now."

"I don't think you've ever looked better, honey," Lily said. "Whatever you've been doing lately I think you should continue."

Maggie thought of the previous night. "Thanks, Mom. I'll try."

"Just as long as you don't work yourself to the bone while you're at that Winslow man's house. I'm glad you hired Ben to help you."

"Me, too. He's saving me a lot of steps."

"And what is Mr. Winslow like?"

"We were just discussing him," Patsy drawled.

"Well, if you really want to know," Maggie said, winking at Patsy, "he's gorgeous, funny, charming, wealthy and...kisses like Rhett Butler."

She could still hear them laughing as she closed the kitchen door and walked around the house to the backyard. She interrupted the boccie game briefly to say goodbye to the rest of the family.

"Don't you go working too hard, my girl," Patrick said. "You need some sun on your face."

"I'll get freckles."

"So?" He gave Maggie a huge hug. "Take good care, and don't be a stranger."

"I won't." She turned to her eldest nephew. "I'll pick you up at eight o'clock tomorrow. Bright and early," she added cheerfully.

Ben groaned. "Are you sure you mean that?"

"Yep." She could hardly wait.

5

"OH, NO!"

Maggie turned to see Justine looking out the bedroom window. The child had great dramatic potential, she decided. "What's the matter?"

"She's *here*."

"Who?"

"Grams. She wasn't s'posed to be here until tomorrow." She looked solemnly at Maggie. "Daddy's gonna have a fit."

Daddy could probably take care of himself, Maggie thought. She hadn't even seen him this morning, although she'd wondered where he was. Lou, bustling around the house gathering laundry, hadn't offered the usual household information.

Justine scrambled down from the stepladder. "Be careful..." Maggie cautioned.

The child raced through the jumbled furniture to the door. "I've gotta make my bed. She'll check."

"Oh, no," Lou's voice echoed Justine's as she toted a load of dirty laundry out of the girls' bathroom.

The horrified expression on the woman's face made Maggie smile, and then she grew curious. No one in the house ever seemed overly concerned about cleaning. Except for the kitchen and dining room, which were Lou's domain, the house would never pass any kind of inspection. Now a grandmother's arrival was causing an uproar.

"What's going on, Lou?" Maggie stopped measuring for level lines and watched Lou struggle with the laundry. "Do you need help?"

"Oh, yes, but that's nothing new!" Lou tossed Maggie a quick grin and squeezed through the door.

Maggie heard Sam's voice in the hall. "Would everyone please stop panicking and go greet Buff—your grandmother?" He stopped in the doorway and looked in. "Hi, Maggie."

"Hi." Maggie kept her voice casual. It wasn't easy. Sam looked wonderful, even though he was unshaven, his hair was rumpled and his clothes—an old brown T-shirt and beige jogging shorts—were sweaty. She guessed he'd either been out playing tennis or running around the yard with Lassie. "Busy morning?"

Sam seemed confused for a minute, then smiled. "Oh. I've just been out running. The traffic's so bad on Ocean Road I'm lucky to be alive." He stepped into the room and went over to the window.

Maggie stopped pretending to measure the wall. The morning was growing more interesting by the minute. "Getting company?"

"Even worse, family." He ran his hand through his hair. "Wait until you meet my mother-in-law. I really like the old gal, but she certainly causes a commotion." He turned back to Maggie. "Come see. Her limo is almost as big as your Pontiac."

"Limo?" Maggie envisioned a wizened, very proper old chauffeur in a sedate black car. She couldn't resist going over to the window to look.

The limousine was glossy black, and a tall uniformed chauffeur was lifting an assortment of suitcases from the trunk. A stocky woman in a white suit pointed to the suitcases, while Julianne stood nearby. The dog paced around yapping, but no one paid any attention to her.

"Pretty impressive," Maggie said.

Sam snorted. "You haven't seen anything yet. She's a day early, but I should have guessed she would be."

"I'd better get back to work." Maggie decided she would stay out of family politics, but there was a feeling of dread in the pit of her stomach, making her wonder if Buffie's arrival was going to affect her work in any way. Somehow she knew it was, and the thought wasn't a cheerful one.

"She'll be up here to inspect in just a minute."

There was a warning in Sam's voice that accentuated Maggie's nervousness. When he left the room she let out a sigh and went back to work.

The paper was a tiny flower pattern, the kind that took forever to hang; the little petals had to be lined up perfectly for the pattern to look consistent. And this paper had a white background, the worst color to hang, Maggie had decided. She'd put up two strips, which gave her a feel for the paper and the pattern. Now that the level lines were finished she would begin cutting. Ben was sizing Justine's room, so he would be busy for a while. She gathered up rolls of paper and went out into the hall to begin cutting, hoping Sam's mother-in-law would approve of the wallpaper the decorator had selected.

"We're running behind schedule, Sam." A woman's gravelly voice floated up the stairs. "Photographers will be here Friday. You know how important this publicity is."

Sam's voice was calm, as if he'd heard it all before.

"The magazine won't even publish them until next summer."

"Which is free publicity for next year's festival." She sighed impatiently. "And I so want everything perfect in time for the party. You have hired gardeners, haven't you?"

"Thousands of them. Why don't you let me take you to your room? It's not as bare as last summer."

"The children are down there unpacking my suit-cases, so I'd prefer to leave them alone to the task. Show me what isn't finished so I can get my bearings."

Maggie was on her knees, unrolling paper, when Sam and Buffie came up the staircase.

"I approve of the paint," Buffie said, "but we must have these carpets cleaned before the festivities begin."

Maggie hid a smile and used her scissors to slice through the paper. The layers of dust had been noticed immediately by the sharp-eyed visitor. Maggie wondered if Lou was hiding in the laundry room.

"Buffie, I'd like you to meet Maggie McGuire, the woman hanging the wallpaper. Maggie, this is my mother-in-law, Buffie Vanderberg."

Scissors in one hand and busy with the roll of paper, Maggie chose to smile and nod. "Good morning."

Buffie nodded in return. "Wonderful" was her comment, but her gaze was focused above Maggie's head. Clearly surprised, she lowered her voice and said, "You've rehung the pictures."

"I thought you'd be pleased," said Sam.

"I'm just—surprised." She patted Sam's arm. "Life must go on, my dear."

Maggie looked up at the woman, who had aged ten years in just one moment. It must be terrible, Maggie thought, to lose such a beautiful and talented daughter. What a waste.

Sam said nothing, but he took Buffie's elbow and guided her to Justine's room. He cleared his throat and invited, "Come see what we've done in here. The sky-lights and windows were installed months ago. I think you'll like the effect."

As he ushered Buffie ahead of him, stepping care-fully over the wallpaper on the floor, he passed Maggie and touched her shoulder. He seemed to want to reas-sure her everything was fine. Maggie froze, surprised by the contact. Her eyes were level with his thighs as he walked by, which was an uncomfortably intimate position. She thought about Saturday night. Had Sam been remembering that kiss, too? He followed Buffie into the other room, and Maggie stood, reluctant to spend time daydreaming. She stacked the cut paper neatly inside Julianne's room and continued to work.

"Aunt Maggie?" Ben poked his head in the door-way. "I'm done."

"Great. Make sure you take a clean sponge and wipe off the ceiling and the window trim. Then you can do the same thing in the girls' bathroom."

"Okay." He hesitated. "Are we gonna be here all day?"

"I know *I* am. After you finish the sizing you'll be free to go."

"Great." He grinned and disappeared.

She could hear the murmur of voices in the other room. Hopefully a distracted Ben wouldn't acciden-tally sponge Mrs. Vanderberg. Maggie longed to open her thermos and pour a fresh mug of coffee. It was only ten o'clock, but she'd been at the house since eight-thirty. She didn't want to look as if she were resting on the job, though. Besides, knowing Sam was around was unnerving. Add a load of caffeine to her system and she'd be falling off her ladder by noon. Yesterday hadn't been the quiet Sunday she'd planned, so she'd tried to go to bed early, but thoughts of Sam kept her from sleeping very well. It had been one hell of a kiss.

With one last glance at the thermos, Maggie switched on the radio and began to soak paper in the water tray. She should be soaking her own head, she decided. She should have had sense enough to stay away from this project and its incredibly charming owner. The dollar signs had been her downfall. Soaking *Fanny*'s head in the water was an even better idea.

Maggie had finished one wall, when it was time to cut paper again. Opening up a new package, she saw that the fourth roll was flawed, its yellow flowers smeared every few inches. She sat back on her heels and counted the rolls left. Then she grabbed her notebook and made some calculations.

Sam came up the stairs. "Trouble?"

"Just thinking." Maggie pointed to the paper stretched in front of her on the floor. "I have a flawed roll. I'm going to open the rest of the paper and pray this is the only bad one."

He frowned. "Will there be enough to finish?"

"I don't know. There should be if I'm careful. I'll just have to make sure I make the most of every inch." She saw his concern. "Don't worry. You'll get your money back for this and I should be able to stretch the rest." She didn't add that this would slow her down, but it wasn't unusual to have a bad roll now and then.

"I'm not worried, Maggie." He sat down on the carpet across from her.

But Maggie thought differently. The lighthearted Sam of Saturday night was missing. "Rough day?"

"Just wondering if this will ever be over, that's all."

"Oh, it will," she replied cheerfully. "You have a contract from me that says so."

He smiled. "I'm not concerned about that, although we're starting the second week. This summer is already out of control."

"What do you mean?" How could anything get out of control with Lou taking care of the girls, Sam never seeming to work and having plenty of money to do whatever he wanted?

"Buffie arrived a day early. But I should have guessed she wouldn't be able to stay away from the action. Two more people, including the guest conductor, arrive tomorrow. I'm hosting a party here in a couple of days. The symphony is Saturday, and magazine people arrive Friday to photograph my 'showplace' home for *New England Life*. If I'm lucky I'll be through with them in time to run in the ten-mile race that evening."

"The one through the Pier?"

He nodded. "To celebrate Old Narragansett Days. Of course, Buffie didn't know about it when she scheduled the photographers."

Maggie began to roll up the paper. "*New England Life* is a ritzy magazine."

"It's a pain in the neck, if you ask me, but Buff has her heart set on promoting the symphony. They promised to give her a plug if I let them in here to see the changes."

"Has it really been that drastic a remodel?"

He nodded. "The downstairs was completely redone last year. Plus a new roof, shingles, windows.

This winter Buffie decided to hire a decorator to pull all three floors together."

"If it's any consolation, it's beautiful."

"It'll be beautiful when it's finished and my life is back to normal. I didn't mind the changes when they were on the drawing board."

"Come see Julie's room," Maggie said, standing up. "See if you like the paper."

Sam climbed to his feet, stepped over her tools and entered the room. "It looks good. I like the yellow." He went to the window. "The gardeners are supposed to be starting work today. I hope they show up. The yard has to be done before the lawn party."

"What if it rains?" Even wealthy people couldn't control the weather.

He turned back to Maggie and smiled, suddenly looking younger. "God will have to answer to Buffie Vanderberg."

She laughed. "Then what?"

Sam shrugged, looking over to the woman holding a pair of scissors and smiling. She was beautiful, he realized once again, and he searched for an answer to her question. "I'll have three hundred people in my house." *And I really want only one.* The thought surprised him so much he walked quickly out of the room without saying anything else.

HOURS LATER Lou poked her head in the door. "Come have a late lunch with me. I won't take no for an answer."

The desperate look on the housekeeper's face made Maggie feel sorry for her. She wanted to agree, but didn't want to spend any more time with Sam, especially with his stern mother-in-law looking on. "I don't know, Lou," she said, hesitating. "What's going on downstairs?"

Lou's face brightened. "They're gone—all of them. Gone to the caterer, I think, and more errands to do with this whole music thing." She looked around the room. "Looks nice, especially for a little girl."

Maggie dried her hands and surveyed the walls. "Not an easy paper to hang, but it looks good when it's dried."

"Come keep me company. I have turkey sandwiches and fruit."

"Okay. Sounds good." Maggie liked the idea of getting away from yellow flowers. "I'll be down as soon as I've washed up."

THE SUN POURED THROUGH the living-room windows, but the dining-room ell was shaded and cool. Lou set the table with paper plates in wicker holders and red gingham napkins. A small platter of sandwiches and a basket of potato chips sat in the center of the table.

"It's pretty quiet down here."

Lou chuckled and handed Maggie a glass of iced tea. "Don't remind me. They'll all be back soon and Mrs. Vanderberg will have more things for me to do."

"Does she give you a hard time?"

Lou shook her head. "Oh, no. We understand each other. I helped out with the babies when Anne was alive, then stayed on to help Sam. Mrs. V. gets nervous about the symphony and having everything go right. And," she added, passing a bowl of fruit to Maggie, "Sam drives her crazy."

Maggie put the bowl on the table and sat down. "Why?"

Lou joined her. "She worries. She thinks the girls

should have a mother, thinks Sam spends too much time alone. Have a sandwich."

Maggie obeyed. This conversation was getting interesting. "And does he? Spend too much time alone?"

Lou shrugged. "Maybe. But just in a content sort of way. He's not loaded down with grief or anything like that. He worked through that a long time ago." Lou took a sandwich and put a handful of chips on her plate. "But Mrs. V. thinks Sam should get on with his life. That's why the big rush to redo the house. She pushed him into it, right down to the last decoration. Wanted him to change things, to shake him up a bit."

Shake him up a bit? Maggie was intrigued. The man acted as if he couldn't wait to retreat right back into a world of peace and quiet. She'd sympathize with the mother-in-law, though, because she thought Buffie was right. "I think he's shaken now, don't you?"

Lou eyed her shrewdly. "Well, we'll have to wait and see. Things have gotten pretty interesting around here."

Maggie tried to look innocent, although she'd thought the same thing earlier that morning. "What's that supposed to mean?"

"It means I've never seen Sam spend so much time at home."

"Oh."

"He goes to the office once in a while, and he jogs around town and works up a sweat, but other than that, he's been hanging around the house." Lou looked pointedly at Maggie. "I can't wait to see what happens next. This could be better than the movies."

"And you have front row seats, right?"

Lou chuckled. "Right. Wait until you see who arrives tomorrow. They're not what you'd expect."

"Who's not?" Sam called from the kitchen. He walked over to the table and sat down beside Maggie. He had shaved, showered and changed into casual clothes. Expensive-looking clothes, Maggie noted. The delicious smell of after-shave clung faintly to his skin. Maggie tried to move her chair a few more inches away from him.

"You're not what I expect of a man who has a business to run," Lou retorted. "You're not even cleaning yourself up until after noon!"

Sam winked at Maggie and helped himself to a handful of potato chips. "Business is slow."

"Architects have off seasons, too?" Maggie asked.

"I started off as an architect."

"And?" she urged.

"And then I had an idea that would help people design their own floor plans—something to make an architect's job easier, I thought." Sam finished the chips and poured himself a glass of iced tea.

Intrigued, Maggie asked, "What was that?"

"A kit with plastic pieces of furniture, appliances, doors, windows—you name it. And a grid to stick them on."

"I've seen them."

"The idea really caught on. Now we have a whole series of them and we ship from Narragansett." He grabbed another handful of potato chips and leaned back in the chair.

Maggie thought she remembered seeing Sam carry blueprints. "And what about architecture? Do you still design?"

He smiled. "Not as much as I'd like to. I do some volunteer work or something that really interests me. Otherwise I don't bother."

Lou laughed. "You're a spoiled millionaire."

"Why don't you call me a spoiled millionaire play-boy and really cheer me up?"

"Hah! That'll be the day!" She left the table. "I have work to do."

Sam looked at Maggie. "Guess she doesn't think much of my playboy tendencies."

Maggie wasn't quite sure how to reply. "Do you have them?"

"Yep." He reached for an apple. "I just don't get to use them very often."

"You don't seem too concerned."

He grinned at her. "I have my moments."

Their gazes locked, and Maggie thought she knew what moment he was referring to—the particular moment on her front porch. She felt her face grow warm but refused to look away. If he could mention it, then she could ignore it. Her eyes challenged him to say more, but he bit into his apple, instead. She thought he looked as if he wanted to laugh.

Cocky. But she noticed an uncertain look in his gray eyes, as if he wasn't sure he should tease her or not. *Good*, she thought. *Let him worry.* She finished her tea and carried her dishes to the counter. "Thanks, Lou. I'm going back to work, too." Through the arched window over the sink, she watched as a cherry-red sports car pulled into the driveway. "Where's Mrs. Vander-berg?" she asked Lou.

Sam answered, coming to stand uncomfortably close to Maggie. "With the girls, meeting the piano teacher. I'm not sure who's interviewing whom."

Maggie pointed to the window. "Then she wouldn't be the piano teacher, would she?" A tall blonde climbed gracefully out of the passenger seat of the car.

Sam uttered a low oath.

"More early arrivals?" Lou asked, coming closer to look out the window.

"Franco."

Maggie peered out the window for a better look at the man who'd draped his arm on the hood of the car and paused dramatically. From behind mirrored sunglasses, the bald robust man seemed to look right through the kitchen window. He waved, his smile gleaming.

"Who's Franco?"

"Franco Christofaro, the conductor," Lou supplied. "The woman must be Elena March. I wonder if Buffie told them to come early, too."

Sam grimaced. "Watch out, Maggie. Christofaro thinks he's irresistible."

Maggie was left wondering what was going on as Sam went outside to greet his guests. She watched, fascinated, as Sam greeted Elena, kissing her on both cheeks, European style. Then he shook hands with the smiling conductor. As Sam led them toward the house, Maggie escaped upstairs.

She forced herself to concentrate on her work. The rest of the afternoon stretched ahead in silence. She'd let Ben go home—Patsy had picked him up at the end of the driveway—and Maggie missed the girls. She hoped they would come to tell her about their piano lessons.

She was on the ladder, hanging a strip of paper, when Sam and Franco entered the room.

"Excuse me," Sam said to Franco. "I need to give Maggie a message."

"Of course." Franco smiled at Maggie, who tried not to stare.

He was very large, very tall and bald, and he looked like a wealthy pirate, Maggie thought, noticing the gleam of gold on his left earlobe. He wore loose white pants and a black body shirt that barely covered his muscular chest. Either the man had just returned from the Caribbean or he spent many hours in a suntan parlor.

"Maggie?"

She looked over at Sam. "What?"

"Paper-To-Go called and said the paper for the girls' bathroom is in."

"Oh, good. That was fast. I'll pick it up on my way home tonight."

Franco glided closer to the ladder. "You are going to introduce me to this beautiful little gypsy?"

Maggie liked being referred to as a gypsy, but was skeptical of "beautiful" and aggravated with "little." His words held a tinge of a foreign accent that made her smile.

"Maggie, this is our new guest, Franco Christofaro," Sam said stiffly. "Franco, Maggie McGuire. She's involved with the remodeling project."

Franco's eyes were warm as he reached to take Maggie's hand. He held it gently, ignoring the sticky glue, and said, "Ah, Sammy, I see. This is the woman who is to turn your house upside down? Of course." He made a courtly bow, released her hand and smiled blandly at Sam. "How lucky you are."

Sam looked as if he could commit murder. Maggie decided it would be a good idea to trim the ceiling edge. She pulled the cutting knife from her back pocket and gave Franco a brilliant smile. "It was a pleasure meeting you." She meant it, too. This had turned into an interesting day.

"We'll surely meet again," he purred. "This old house is not that big, is it, Sam?"

"It's getting smaller all the time," Sam muttered, then followed Franco from the room.

"Now, Sammy, do I have time to beat you on the tennis court?"

Maggie couldn't hear Sam's response, though she wished she could. She glanced at her watch and went back to work on the ceiling edge.

"Ms. McGuire?" Buffie poked her head into the room. "May we disturb you a moment?"

As if I could say no. "Of course. Just be careful— there's an awful lot of stuff piled around this room." She stepped down from the ladder and rinsed out her sponge.

"My granddaughters don't take very good care of their possessions, do they?"

Maggie decided not to reply. Anyway, the answer was evident.

"Elena, darling, come in. This is Julianne's room."

The other houseguest, the tall blonde, walked carefully into the room. She wore fashionably faded pencil-thin jeans and a glittery T-shirt. Her silver-blond hair hung smoothly to chin length and she nodded politely to Maggie as Buffie made the introductions, then went on to explain the renovations Sam had made on the house.

"It's lovely, Buffie. You must be very pleased."

Maggie guessed Elena was only being polite and had little interest in decorating. Was she involved with Sam? It didn't seem likely. Maggie wondered what musical instrument Elena played.

Buffie was pleased. "So much work! And it was so hard to convince Sam it needed to be done." Satisfied with her guest's reaction, she turned to Maggie. "We won't disturb you any longer, dear. Tell Lou when you've finished and she'll see to the cleaning up."

She left, Elena trailing wearily behind her, and Maggie heard Buffie's voice continue down the hall. It would be tempting to lock the door now. She could explain that she was hanging paper around it. But that wouldn't be true. That wall might have to wait until morning. Still, she'd managed to accomplish quite a bit today, despite the flawed paper. She decided to work for another hour, then start cleaning up.

It was after five when she'd finished. She knew she had to scrub her tools before she left, but suddenly she was very weary. The humidity had sapped any stamina she might have had. She thought a swim in the ocean might be more appealing than cooking Lean Cuisine at home, but then she canceled the idea—even swimming sounded too much like work.

She dumped the dirty water into the toilet in the bathroom, then sat on the edge of the bathtub to clean her tools. She was rinsing the brushes under the faucet, when she heard Sam's voice.

"Maggie?"

"In here," she called. She was too tired to get up to see what he wanted. She dried her brushes on a rag, then rinsed her hands.

He stood in the doorway. "The room looks good. Julie wanted to see it, but I told her to wait awhile."

"You'll have to be careful about moving the furniture around. Make sure no one touches the walls. I'll finish it up and put the border on tomorrow."

"Are you okay?"

She smiled. "Just a little worn out."

"Join us for dinner."

She started to laugh, until she realized he was serious. "No, thanks." She looked down at her filthy pants. "I don't think I'm dressed for it."

He folded his arms in front of his chest. "Go home and change. I'll pick you up in an hour."

"I don't think so, Sam." She knew he wasn't pleased, but she didn't expect him to walk into the bathroom and sit down on the toilet-seat lid. Their knees bumped.

"Are you sure you won't change your mind? I missed you yesterday."

Maggie didn't know what to say. She wiped her hands on an old towel, reminding herself to do laundry tonight.

"What do you look like dressed up?"

"Stunning," she said.

Sam nodded and took her hand in his. "I thought so. Come to my party Thursday. Be my date and we'll dance under the stars."

Maggie closed her eyes to temptation. "No."

"For heaven's sake, Maggie, why not?"

She pulled her hand away, knowing she'd hurt his feelings, but unable to stop. "C'mon, Sam. Look at yourself! We don't have anything in common—"

He gripped her shoulders, leaned forward and kissed her, shutting off her protests. His lips were hard and warm, demanding a response from hers. Sensations of heat coursed through her until she thought she'd slip off the edge of the tub. When he released her, she gripped the porcelain and stared at him.

He looked shocked, then pleased. "I've thought about kissing you all day. Yesterday, too."

"Kisses don't change anything, Sam."

His voice was a seductive growl. "It should. We both know how good it feels."

She stood up and began stacking her tools in their carrier. "Sorry. You'll have to come up with a better reason than that."

"Have dinner with me, anyway, while I think of something."

"Thanks, but no, thanks." She knew how right he was. It had felt wonderful to be kissed. One kiss had been an interesting experience. Two kisses meant she had better start backing off. The sooner the better. She wanted to leave before she was too tempted to stay.

Sam followed her out of the bathroom and down the stairs. "This is your last chance, McGuire."

She left him standing in the kitchen, his hands in his pockets.

BY THE TIME she arrived home Maggie decided she needed to get Sam Winslow off her mind. She attacked the dirt in the living-room by dusting, vacuuming and throwing piles of magazines in the trash can. Next she put on her favorite Bruce Springsteen tape and scrubbed the bathroom until it sparkled, then moved on to the kitchen, dumping anything suspicious-looking from the refrigerator into the garbage.

When she was finally finished, Maggie felt satisfied. She could forget about cleaning for another month and she hadn't thought about Sam for almost two hours. She would take a shower, fry a couple of eggs, wash some clothes and try to forget that she would be back in the Winslow house in less than twelve hours.

"AREN'T YOU HUNGRY, SAM?" From her place at the foot of the table, Buffie watched her son-in-law pick at his serving of lobster casserole.

"I suppose not," Sam said, setting his fork on his plate with a gesture of finality. He pushed the plate away and leaned back in his chair. For some reason, and he didn't know why, he felt unsettled, as if he were waiting for the other shoe to drop. *Ridiculous*, he told himself. *There is nothing to feel uneasy about.* It was a quiet evening, the children were settled in their beds and Franco's latest album provided soft background music.

Lou entered the dining area with another basket of hot French bread and set it on the table next to Buffie. "Here you go, Mrs. V. I fixed plenty of your favorite."

"Thank you, Lou. Everything is delicious." Buffie beamed at her guests. "I'm just so thrilled we're all here together like this."

Franco lifted his wineglass. "To you, Buff, for urging us to arrive early." He shifted toward Sam. "And to you, Sammy, for your kind hospitality to me and my lovely Elena."

Sam smiled politely and lifted his glass in acknowledgment before finishing the last swallow of his wine. It briefly warmed the hollow pit in his stomach. "You've always been welcome in this house, Franco. When Anne was alive—well—" he hesitated, choosing his words carefully "—she considered you one of her closest friends."

"I wish I'd known Anne," Elena murmured. "I met her briefly once years ago at a party my mother gave. She was very beautiful."

"Yes, she was, wasn't she?" Buffie said. "I never understood how Harry and I produced such a beauty."

"A beauty in face and spirit, do not forget," added

Franco. He sighed. "And now this house is all changed around. Things are different now."

Sam surprised himself by agreeing with the dramatic conductor. "You're right, Christofaro." *Things are different now.* There was no pain in the realization. Sam leaned forward and picked up a bottle of wine. He refilled his guests' glasses and his own, then held his up in the air. "Let's drink to that."

"To what?" demanded his mother-in-law.

Franco lifted his glass. "To the wonderful changes you have made in this house!"

"To music," added Elena.

Sam nodded. "To the symphony."

Buffie shook her head and clinked her glass against Sam's. "To love," she said, her voice like gravel before she sipped her wine. "I'm a sentimental old fool."

MUCH LATER, after Lou had served strawberry shortcake and coffee to everyone, after the guests had watched the sun set over the Atlantic and then retired to their rooms, Sam poured a snifter of brandy and sat alone on the deck. The breeze came off the ocean and rushed around the house. Sam could hear the familiar sound of waves rushing onto the beach and slapping against the rocks. He lit a cigarette and relaxed into the cushioned chair. He'd been alone since Anne had died, and he'd been lonely—the gut-wrenching loneliness of grief had accompanied him for a long, long time. Then a numb feeling had replaced the pain, until, Sam knew, he'd grown complacent, thinking this was what his life would be. Now, for the first time since he'd fallen in love with Anne, he was physically attracted to another woman. A tiny, black-haired dynamo who made him laugh, talked back to him, kissed passionately—

whether she realized it or not—and who had secrets of her own.

Things are different now. Sam downed the brandy and felt the knot in his gut tighten. He just didn't know if he was ready for the changes.

6

"Ms. McGuire?"

"Yes?" Maggie stood alone in Julianne's room and examined the paper she'd hung the day before. It had dried nicely, with little shrinkage, and looked crisp and clean in the morning light.

Buffie entered the room. "We need to discuss the schedule."

"Whose schedule, Mrs. Vanderberg?" Maggie picked up her cutting knife and stuck it in her pocket. She was anxious to begin working.

"Yours, dear." Buffie put her hands on her square hips and surveyed the room. "This is lovely work, Ms. McGuire, but naturally I'm wondering how much longer this will take."

"Naturally." Maggie picked up an empty bucket, hoping to escape into the bathroom. "Have you discussed the schedule with Sam?"

"Not specifically, no." She attempted a smile. "But, then, he lacks a certain enthusiasm for the decorating, don't you agree?"

That was putting it mildly, Maggie thought, but kept silent.

Buffie added, "Now that I'm around to take charge of things, I need to know how much longer you intend to be here."

"Well, let's see." She put down the bucket and

pulled her notebook from the tool carrier, flipped through the pages, then closed the book. "I should finish this room this morning and start on Justine's this afternoon. Tomorrow I should finish Justine's and begin the girls' bathroom. Sam's bathroom shouldn't take long on Thursday. If the paper is in for his bedroom, I'll do that on Friday." She thought for a minute. "It's a big room though, and the stripe will take a little longer than usual, but possibly it can be done in one long day."

"Has Sam told you about the magazine people coming?"

Maggie nodded. "Yes, he has."

Buffie frowned. "The photographers arrive on Friday. I had *so* hoped we'd be finished by then."

"Sorry, Mrs. Vanderberg. There's no way." Maggie tossed the book back into the carrier and picked up the bucket once again.

"Couldn't you hire more people?"

"I already have."

Buffie waved her hand. "I don't mean that young boy who washes the walls. Perhaps we should bring in another professional paperhanger."

Maggie sighed. The woman was wasting her time, but Maggie tried to keep her patience. "I already had that discussion with your son-in-law when he hired me. This is an extremely busy season. Actually, I think you're fortunate to be finishing this quickly." Maggie turned away and took a step toward the bathroom door.

"Could you possibly work faster?"

Maggie whipped around. "What?"

"You do lovely work, my dear, and I don't mean to sound critical, but time is of the essence." She waved a jeweled hand at the remaining bare walls. "Could you work into the night?"

"No, because the lighting becomes unreliable. It's hard to see air bubbles in the paper when there are shadows." Besides, Maggie thought, even the working class deserved a few hours' sleep at night.

"I see," Buffie said, but Maggie knew the woman still wasn't satisfied.

"Mrs. Vanderberg," Maggie said firmly, her Irish spirit rising. "I'm sure you will understand my position. I was hired to do a job, I was given a time limit and I have remained on schedule. You are also getting the quality work your son-in-law is paying for." Maggie didn't mention the bonus; it was none of Buffie's business, anyway. "If you have any problems, please talk to Sam."

"Thank you, dear," Buffie said. "I'll do that." Maggie could tell the woman was determined to have the last word. "I'm certain you're doing a very nice job. I'm *so* glad we had this little chat."

To Maggie's amusement, Buffie swept out of the room like visiting royalty. Little chat? More like a battle of wills. She'd been told to work faster, work longer hours, and subtly threatened with being replaced. Maggie chuckled to herself as she shut the bedroom door and turned the lock. There would be no more interruptions this morning, not if she had anything to say about it.

SAM CAUGHT LASSIE by the collar and dragged the reluctant animal around the corner of the garage to the doghouse. He snapped the chain onto her collar. "You should stay in the shade, anyway, old girl." It wasn't eleven-thirty yet and the temperature hovered at ninety degrees. Sam was glad he'd gone for his run early in the morning. Even at seven-thirty the heat had made itself felt. By nine, when he'd returned home, the sun was uncomfortably strong on his back.

He lit a cigarette and leaned against the garage. One cigarette a day shouldn't hurt his running too much, he rationalized. Tuesday already, yet he felt this week would never be over.

Maggie McGuire would be finished with the house by Friday and that would be that. He'd mail her a check and most likely never see her again. He couldn't seem to convince her to go out with him. Maybe he needed to brush up on his rusty dating skills. "Face it, Winslow. The woman is dangerous." Sam smiled. How could a sassy little woman like Maggie cause him to stand outside talking to himself? He could go to the office, he thought, but it wasn't necessary, and he'd only end up making the junior partner nervous. The younger man needed the experience of handling things his way and Sam kept in touch by phone every day, which was enough.

He threw the cigarette down onto the gravel and headed back to the house, ignoring Lassie's frustrated yips. There was still a lot of summer left. The girls would be off to camp in a few weeks; he could accept one of several sailing invitations and spend some time at sea. There was the cabin in Maine if he decided on a more rustic vacation. Or else, he thought with a grimace, he could sit in his big, empty house and look at the new wallpaper.

Maggie was on the other side of the screen door when he pushed it open. She appeared cool in faded denim shorts and a yellow tank top. She carried a small

Styrofoam cooler and looked more as if she were heading for the beach than worrying about work.

"Where are you going?" he asked. He wished she'd
take off the sunglasses. Early today she'd arrived without Ben and had worked in Julianne's room all morning with the door closed. He figured she wanted to be
left alone. Maybe he shouldn't have tried to bully her
into dinner last night.

Maggie stopped, surprised. She thought he'd left for
the day. "Just going out for lunch."

He glanced at the cooler. "You're bringing your
own?"

She didn't understand why he was so interested in
her lunch. "Yes, that's the idea." Maggie looked pointedly at the door, hoping he'd move and let her out, but
he stayed where he was. "Don't you have work to do—
like a normal person?"

"I'm not normal. I'm rich." He grinned.

She shot him her best give-me-a-break expression,
the one that made her nieces and nephews nervous.

He held up his hands in defense. "C'mon, Maggie.
It's not my fault everyone does his job too well."

He sounded almost sad about it. "Well," she said, re-
lenting, "you don't have to hang around here making
sure I do mine." This time when she stepped forward
he moved to let her pass.

"I know I don't, but you're fun to look at." He
pushed the door open for her. "Why haven't you worn
shorts before?"

"I was afraid I'd drive you mad with passion." She
swept past him and out into the sunshine.

"It's a thought," he said to her back, following her to
the driveway. "Why'd you shut Julianne's door today?"

"Your mother-in-law had a little talk with me this morning about working faster."

"Don't pay any attention to her. I'll see that she doesn't bother you again." They reached the Pontiac at the same time. "Going shopping?"

Maggie shook her head and got into the car, putting the cooler on the seat beside her. Sam opened the passenger door, put the cooler on the back seat and climbed in.

"Please?" he said.

His expression was hard to resist. Maggie could feel herself giving in, despite her intention of having a quiet lunchtime away from Sam's house. "For heaven's sake, Sam, you don't even know where I'm going."

"As long as I'm out of here."

She turned the key in the ignition. "What about your company?"

Sam stretched his arm along the back of the seat and relaxed. "Franco had orchestra business to attend to and left early this morning. Elena is sleeping late, then going to a rehearsal. Buffie has the girls. She said something about buying clothes for camp. Lou's out shopping for food and supplies. It seems Franco has developed an alarming thirst for margaritas." He shot Maggie a smile. "So you see? I'm all yours."

Thanks a lot. Maggie kept the car in Park. Sam's smile tempted her, plus the fact that he looked too good to kick out of the car. He wore a burgundy polo shirt she'd never seen before, gray shorts and tennis shoes. She was glad the car was so wide that Sam was safely seated several feet away. "Okay, pal, you get your way." She backed the car around, then headed out of the driveway.

"Where *are* we going?"

She switched on the radio. "You'll have to wait and see." He almost deserved this, she thought. It was her chance to get even with him for the kiss in the bathroom and trying to con her into staying for dinner.

As they drove past the ocean toward town the road grew crowded with summer traffic. Away from the water and set in a hollow, downtown Wakefield was stifling. Maggie dropped by Paper-To-Go and picked up the bathroom paper and more cutting blades, then stopped to buy a couple of sandwiches, before driving back toward the ocean to Narragansett Pier.

"That was quick," Sam said.

She ignored him, turned into a back street and parked the car in the shade. "You can carry the cooler. I'll get the beach towel."

"And then?"

"We walk along the sidewalk together until we get to Gazebo Park. Don't worry," she said as he hesitated. "You're going to love this." *He'll be begging for mercy within the hour.*

They crossed the busy intersection to the park, an island of grass directly across the street from the town beach. Surfers bobbed in the water, but Maggie thought they were optimistic about the waves. The ocean looked too calm.

"Good," said Maggie. "We're early." She led Sam far away from the makeshift stage perched near the gazebo and ignored the small crowd of spectators gathered nearby when she spread her oversize beach towel on the grass.

"More music?" asked Sam. "My ears are going to be worn out by the time this summer is over."

"Wait until after this," she muttered.

Sam shaded his eyes and peered at a hand-lettered sign on the stage. "The Shanty Boys," he read. "Who are they?"

"Two of them are my elder brothers. The third is a friend."

"What are they going to do?"

"Sing," she said with a sigh, gesturing toward the towel. "Make yourself comfortable. You're going to love it."

He sat down and eyed her speculatively. "Somehow I have the feeling you don't mean that."

She just smiled and pulled the lid off the cooler. "The show is part of a series called 'Brown Bag Lunches.' It's only an hour and features local talent every Tuesday." She handed Sam a can of diet cola. "It's a good thing I packed extra drinks."

"Thanks for the lunch."

She tossed a bag of corn chips on the towel and gave Sam a wrapped sandwich. "I hope you like tuna fish."

"I do. See, Maggie?" He opened his sandwich. "Isn't this better than working?"

She swallowed a bite of food. "Tell me that after the show."

He opened the bag of chips and passed it to her. "Where's your sister? Doesn't she come to these things?"

Maggie shook her head. "I doubt it. It's too nice a day and she'll have figured a way to get out of it."

"Why would she want to do that?"

"I think you'll find out soon. Maybe it's because we've all heard them sing for so long years."

"Where's your helper today?"

"Working with his father. I don't have as much work for him as I thought. One more morning to size your rooms and that should be it for Ben. He'd rather be at the beach with his friends, anyway. I can't blame him."

"Do you sing?"

She almost choked while drinking the soda. "No. I'm strictly an appreciative audience."

"Me, too. Hopefully the girls have inherited their mother's musical talents, because I don't have any. Anne was preparing to be a concert pianist at one time."

Maggie thought of the photograph in the hall. "What happened?"

"I think it was Buffie's dream more than Anne's. She couldn't take the pressure. What about you? How long have you had your business?"

"Just a couple of years. I'd like to go back to college and get my teaching degree one of these days." Maggie couldn't believe she'd told him that. It wasn't something she'd shared with anyone before.

"You're good with kids. Why'd you leave college?"

He seemed genuinely interested, so she said, "I was halfway through my third year when I married Tony. We started a landscaping business, and I needed to get a job to support us until the business could."

"And did it?"

"The business survived longer than the marriage." She finished her lunch, while Sam idly munched corn chips.

Soon three husky men climbed up on the stage. Two dark-bearded ones held guitars and the third carried a silver whistle. A thin woman with a long braid trailing down her back adjusted the microphones and plugged wires into sound equipment.

"Looks like they're getting ready. Let me guess—the two with guitars are McGuires, right?"

"Right." Maggie looked around the park for her parents. They rarely missed one of the boys' performances. She finally spotted them sitting in striped beach chairs under a tree. She waved but couldn't get their attention.

Sam looked to see who she was waving at. "Your parents?"

"How'd you guess?"

"Your father resembles one of the Shanty Boys. Are we going to walk over and meet them?" Sam was curious about Maggie's parents. Would they look worn out after raising such a large family? Besides, they were sitting in the only patch of shade on the entire lawn and Sam figured he'd appreciate that right about now. He stood up, giving Maggie no choice but to agree.

"Okay, come on." Maggie shoved the trash into a bag and tossed it in the cooler before she let Sam help her to her feet. She was a little sorry when he dropped her hand. She would have liked to see her parents' surprise when she strolled across the park, holding hands with a handsome stranger.

Sam was happy to follow her. Trailing behind an enticing view of a rounded denim-covered derriere, he could have walked to Connecticut and not complained. All too soon Maggie was enveloped in a hug by the large, silver-haired man who'd jumped up from his chair to greet his daughter. Maggie's mother looked pleased when she saw Sam, and Maggie made the introductions.

Patrick McGuire was quick to shake Sam's hand. "So our Maggie has brought you to hear the boys sing!"

"That's right," said Sam. "Maggie talked so much about them I just had to hear them for myself." He shook Mrs. McGuire's hand. Now he knew where Maggie had inherited her height.

"Honey, that's wonderful," Lily McGuire said. "I didn't think this was your cup of tea, but it's nice to know you're proud of your brothers."

"Looks like they're getting ready to start," Mr. McGuire boomed. "Sit down, why don't you. We'd best be quiet and let the boys sing."

Sam would have liked to share the shade with the elder McGuires, but Maggie took his hand. "We have to finish our lunch," she said in a regretful voice. "And then I have to get right back to work."

"It was a pleasure meeting both of you," Sam said.

Mrs. McGuire wagged a warning finger. "Don't you let her overdo, Sam."

"I'll try," he promised before Maggie led him away to the other side of the lawn.

"Couldn't we move the towel and sit with them?"

"Not a chance. I intend to take a nap during this. With my sunglasses on, as though I'm caught up in the music. You're going to sit right there—" she pointed to the section of towel closest to her parents "—so they won't notice I'm not joining in the applause."

Sam laughed as he watched her lie down and make herself comfortable. The men onstage introduced themselves and launched into a rousing Irish folk song. The people in the audience, Sam guessed fifty or sixty, cheerfully clapped in time to the music. Sam sat down and leaned toward Maggie. "So far so good."

The man in the middle then played a haunting melody on the whistle, with the guitars accompanying him. "What's wrong with this?" he asked Maggie.

She adjusted her sunglasses. "Nothing. The whistle's great. The best is yet to come."

Sam soon understood what she meant. The trio began to sing a sea shanty about life aboard a whaling vessel. After the seventeenth chorus of "Row, row, ye mother on the ocean-o," Sam was ready to jump ship. There were other sea songs, and after thirty minutes they all sounded alike, especially the "ocean-o" part. Sam wanted to crawl over to the shade and beg Mrs. McGuire to put a stop to it.

But the crowd remained enthusiastic until the end. Shanty connoisseurs, Sam imagined. He'd liked the first two songs; it was the last ten or so that had ruined him. "Maggie?" he whispered.

She didn't move. He stretched out on his side and propped his head up on his hand, moving closer to her.

"Maggie," he tried again. But she still didn't budge. She was asleep, just as she'd said she would be. Her lips were relaxed, parted gently. Above her sunglasses the dark waves of her hair rioted against the bright beach towel. "Hey, sleeping beauty," he whispered in her ear.

She growled. "Don't even think it."

His lips grazed her earlobe. "I wasn't."

Maggie frowned. He was giving her chills on one of the hottest days of the summer. She sat up, pushed her glasses to the top of her head and blinked. "Is it over?"

Sam sat up, too. "I think I've heard the last chorus of 'row ye mother.'"

She smiled. "On the ocean-o?"

He lifted her chin, pretending to study her face, when he was actually deciding whether or not to kiss her. "You don't look like your brothers."

"How can you tell? They're wearing beards and strange caps."

"Well," he said, putting his arm around her shoulders. "You don't sound like them, either, which is comforting."

Maggie enjoyed the feel of his fingertips on her bare skin. "Let's go tell them how wonderful they were."

IT WAS TOO SHORT a trip back to the house, Maggie decided, pulling into the driveway.

"Back to reality," Sam said. "I wish you'd let me buy you an ice cream cone." A beat-up truck and trailer was parked off to one side of the pavement. "The gardeners have arrived."

"And the housecleaners," Maggie said, noting a pink van with Dust Devils stenciled on the back. Buffie must be delirious with joy. Maggie hoped no one had touched the drying paper in Julie's room or moved any of the tools. She'd put her equipment into Justine's room before lunch. Before she'd gone grocery shopping, Lou had piled the room's contents into the middle of the floor so Maggie would be able to manipulate the ladder against the walls. She hurried out of the car toward the house.

Sam opened the back door for her. "Thanks for the musical interlude."

"Anytime."

Buffie met them in the kitchen. "Oh, my dears, it's just going beautifully, now that all the extra help has arrived. I'm so glad I thought to come early."

"Good, Buffie." Sam looked past her to where two young women were polishing the wood floor. "Don't let anyone in my study, okay? And no one will disturb Maggie's work upstairs, will they?"

"Of course not." Buffie beamed. "We don't want to slow her down. I've told the ladies to do only the hallway, your bedroom and the master bath. I don't think we should bother with the girls' rooms until they're completely finished, do you?"

"That's fine," said Sam. He looked longingly at his study. "I have paperwork to catch up on. Where are the children?"

"Upstairs, with instructions to stay there for a while. And dear, before you disappear again, would you check with the workers outside? They need more directions. And don't you think the tennis court should be attended to? Franco and Elena so love to play."

"Excuse me," Maggie said. "Julianne's room is finished. You should be able to arrange furniture this afternoon."

"I'll have Lou see to it." Buffie dismissed her with a nod.

Maggie resisted the urge to curtsy; she didn't think Mrs. Vanderberg would see the humor in it. She went upstairs to begin work in Justine's room, and found both girls sitting slumped on the unmade bed in the middle of the room.

"What's up?"

Julie sighed. "We're s'posed to stay out of the way."

"Grams said."

Maggie tried not to smile. "So what are you going to do?"

They shrugged.

Justine said, "It's *impossible*." Clearly she liked the sound of the word. "We can't play outside because we might bother the workers and we can't go downstairs because we might bother the maids. We put away our new clothes and now there's nothing to do, cuz you're gonna kick us out."

Maggie laughed. She'd missed the two rascals and their conversations. "Do you like your room, Julie?"

The child nodded. "They let me peek in."

"Mine's a different color, isn't it?" Justine asked.

"Yep, but it's pretty, too." She held up a roll of paper. "Did you look?"

"Grams showed it to me this morning."

Maggie selected a tape measure and scissors from her pile of equipment on the floor. "Have either one of you seen my radio?"

Julianne held it up from behind her back. "Here," she said guiltily.

"Great. Plug it in and see if you can get a good country-western station. We'll sing about cowboys for a while, okay?"

"You mean we can stay here?"

"Can we play Barbies, too?"

"Sure," Maggie said. "Just stay away from the water bucket, don't step on the paper and we'll do just fine."

Later, almost hoarse from singing and with a good start on the bedroom, Maggie heard voices outside.

"I refuse. You must never, ever suggest such a thing again." Franco's voice boomed from the lawn below Justine's bedroom window.

"That's ridiculous. I'll suggest anything I want anytime I damn well want to," a woman said. Elena? Maggie wondered. Or had other guests arrived. She looked out to see what was going on. The conductor was yelling in Italian and gesturing wildly to someone out of sight near the house.

"They're fighting again." Justine sighed. She climbed across the mattress and turned the radio off.

"Who's fighting?"

"Prob'ly Franco and Miss March," Julie supplied. She brushed her doll's hair into a pile on top of its head and surveyed it critically.

"You mean Elena," her sister said.

"Grams said we had to call her 'Miss March' or learn better manners."

"*Must* you be so dramatic?" Elena's exasperated voice floated through the open window.

"What do they fight about?" Maggie asked. She knew she shouldn't be surprised about the girls' knowledge. The little scamps were probably aware of everything that went on in the house.

"Just 'bout lots of stuff."

Justine joined Maggie at the window as Elena interrupted the conductor's tirade with one of her own in Franco's mother tongue. "It's pretty funny."

Maggie looked down at the little blond head beside her. "It is? Why?"

The child shrugged. "I dunno. Don't you think his head gets shiny when he yells? I do."

"I think you're right, Justine." Maggie turned away from the window and climbed back on her ladder. "And I think we should be very glad we don't understand Italian."

7

A HEAT WAVE, the radio weatherman had called it this morning. Maggie stood on her ladder in Justine's bedroom and knew WPRO was right. The air was especially stifling near the ceiling and Maggie looked longingly at the open window. With luck and a new burst of energy, she'd be working in front of it in an hour and a half.

She smoothed the paper with careful strokes of the Styrofoam brush. Once again she was working with the tiny peach floral print, designed to coordinate with the pattern in Julianne's room and the bathroom. The decorator had done her job well. Maggie hadn't locked the door today, so Sam sat on the floor nearby. He seemed content to spend the afternoon in the midst of the mess.

"Just a little peace and quiet. Is that too much to ask?" he said.

"Of course it is. You don't deserve any sympathy." She frowned at the wall and gently stroked a bubble from the paper. "Besides, didn't you know it would be like this when you volunteered to host?"

"I don't remember volunteering. It was more like being railroaded," he grumbled. "You think this whole thing is fun, don't you?"

She grinned at him and pulled the knife from her back pocket. "Sure. And deep down you're really enjoying it." She trimmed the excess wallpaper and tossed the gooey strip onto Sam's sneaker. He didn't look as if he were enjoying anything. "You'll be a pretty grim-looking host at the party tomorrow night."

"Don't remind me." He plucked the paper from his shoe and threw it into the garbage bag.

"I don't know how you can ignore it. The lawn looks like a golf course, there are pots of flowers everywhere and the last time I looked out the window men were unloading pieces of a tent."

"I know," he said. "Buffie's in ecstasy making last-minute demands on the caterers, the phone rings constantly and Lou's threatening to retire when all this is over."

"Poor Lou." Maggie knew he was right. The housekeeper raced through the house every ten minutes, keeping track of the girls and the dog. Maggie could hear it all and was constantly entertained. The end of this job was coming closer, but she wasn't happy about it. Eight-unit condominiums were going to be very dull in comparison. Especially without Sam.

"Has Buffie given you any more trouble?"

"No."

"Good. I told her to leave you alone and let you do your job. You think you'll finish this room today?"

She climbed off the ladder to rinse out a sponge. "I hope so."

He looked around at the mess. "I should have had it cleaned out for you."

"Don't worry, Sam. I've worked in worse messes before, and I just move anything that's in the way." She stepped onto the ladder and began to scrub the wall. "I'll do the bathroom in the morning, but you still may not want to have people up here tomorrow night."

"No one will be, anyway."

Maggie raised her eyebrows. "Buffie won't be giving tours?"

He shook his head. "She can show off the living room, but everyone else should stay outside. Even Lassie's going to spend the night at the vet's boarding kennel."

"What about the girls?"

"They want to watch the party from their bedroom window. By the way," he said, pulling an envelope from his shirt pocket, "here's your official invitation."

"I don't know, Sam—"

He stood up and put the invitation beside Maggie's brush on the ladder's shelf. "Make my evening and attend?"

"Make your evening?" She laughed at him from her perch on the ladder and he stepped uncomfortably closer.

"Please?" He stood eye level with her breasts. "Wear something stodgy."

"I have an old flannel bathrobe you might approve of," she teased, resisting an inner tug of desire. Maggie was glad she'd worn a loose T-shirt. Sam looked up at her with an interesting gleam in his eyes. It made her want to lean over and brush her lips against his mouth. He drove her crazy with longing. Could she get even? The thought was intriguing.

He skimmed a hand along her hips and caught her waist. She froze, sponge forgotten in her hand. "You shouldn't look at a man that way, Maggie." His eyes were dark charcoal, his voice rough.

Maggie felt herself melting toward him as heat snaked through her insides. "I have work to do," she murmured, trying to remind herself.

"Sam!" Lou's voice bellowed up the stairs. "Telephone!"

He sighed, dropping his hand and stepping away. "Don't go anywhere," he said as he left the room.

Maybe I should. Maggie sat down on one of the ladder's steps. What was going on here? What were she and Sam doing? He couldn't lack for female companionship; money, good looks and charm were potent attractions. He obviously didn't need a mother for his children. He had Lou and Buffie and didn't seem at all dissatisfied with that arrangement. Maybe he just had the hots for women on ladders. She looked at the sponge and decided she'd better finish wiping glue.

But her mind continued to whirl. Maybe he was lonely...and she was convenient. *Or was it the other way around?* An uncomfortable thought, but possibly true. She was very attracted to Sam, but was that because he had two gorgeous little girls and she didn't have any?

Sam returned as Maggie was rinsing the sponge in the bucket. "There," he said. "Another important decision made on behalf of the symphony festival."

He picked the envelope off the ladder. "Don't forget this." "You will join us, won't you?"

"Oh, come on, Sam," Maggie said. She dried her hands. "I don't think I really belong there."

"What the hell kind of talk is that?"

She began to roll a length of paper inside out. "I won't know anyone there."

"I'm not sure I will, either." He smiled. "Buffie engineered the guest list from this season's symphony contributors."

"Sounds really exciting."

"Come for the food, then." He leaned against the ladder. "Do you drink champagne?"

"Oh, every night. By the gallon." She dunked the paper in the water box and held it under the water.

"Good. Then we can celebrate the house being finished."

"Except for your room," she corrected.

He shrugged. "That's the least of my worries. I won't let the photographers in there. I don't know why they'd be interested, anyway." He paused. "You haven't answered my question."

Maggie was busy handling the wallpaper as she pulled it from the water and folded it carefully. "What question?" She set the paper on a towel and wiped her dripping hands on her shorts.

"Come with me tomorrow night."

"You have to move."

"What?"

"I have to move the ladder and you're in the way." She didn't want to give him an answer about tomorrow night.

"Here. Let me do it." He pushed it over to where she pointed.

"Lunch!" Lou carried a tray into the room. She beamed at Maggie. "I see you have another helper. Where's Ben today?"

"At a Red Sox game." Maggie looked at the amount of food on the tray. "But I brought yogurt."

"Not enough," said Sam, taking the tray from Lou and setting it on the floor near the window. "You can eat in here or downstairs on the deck with the others, but I'm staying here. Those temperamental musicians are driving me crazy."

"They are loud, aren't they? You should have heard them yesterday."

Sam winced. "Were they arguing in French or Italian?"

"Italian."

"I think that was because Elena wanted to have pizza for lunch. Christofaro couldn't deal with the idea."

"They're not shy about their opinions, I'll say that for them," Lou added. "They were fighting about high tide last night until I gave 'em a chart." She eyed Maggie sternly. "Don't you start arguing with me, too."

Maggie leaned against the ladder. "Okay, Lou. I'll just eat here."

"You two have a nice lunch now. There's roast beef sandwiches, potato salad and brownies." She winked at Maggie and left.

Sam sat down on the floor in front of the food.

"Start without me," Maggie said unnecessarily. "I need to get this strip up before it dries out."

"Do you want some help?"

"Oh, no," she hurried to assure him. "Stay where you are."

He flashed her a charming grin. "That's what I wanted you to say."

JUSTINE'S PRIZE piece of driftwood was almost seven feet long and looked like an elephant's leg. Precariously propped against a chair, it fell when Maggie, ready to hang the decorative border, pushed Justine's desk away from the wall. She tried to jump out of the way, but the wood bounced on her big toe before rolling onto the floor.

Maggie swore and sat down to survey the damage, a suspicious numbness spreading through her toe. A ceramic Cinderella lay broken in half beside her.

"What the hell was that?" Sam rushed through the door. "Did you fall—"

He looked surprised to see the ladder standing upright in the middle of the room.

"It's okay, just my toe—"

He knelt in front of her. "Here," he said. "Let me help." He untied her shoelaces and eased her foot from the sneaker. "What happened?"

"The driftwood fell over and landed on my foot." She watched as he pulled off her sock. There was an odd-looking white mark across her toe and pain began to seep through the numbness. "Darn. I was so close to being finished. I just started the border." She looked at her watch. Almost four o'clock. She was going to lose at least three hours of work and she didn't like that one bit.

"I'll get some ice. I think it's starting to swell." Sam looked at her with concern. "Are you okay?"

"Sure, Sam."

"Don't try to move. I'll be right back."

As soon as he left she tried to wiggle the toe, but nothing happened. Maggie leaned back on her hands and silently cursed.

"Do you need a doctor again?" Julianne's expression was hopeful as she peeked in the doorway.

Maggie laughed. "Nope. At least I hope not."

The child came closer and studied the swelling toe. "Gross."

"My feelings exactly."

"Wait right here," she ordered unnecessarily. "I've gotta go get Justy. She'll love it."

"Just stay out of the way," said her father, carrying a dishpan of ice water. He knelt at Maggie's feet. "Stick your foot in here."

Obediently she dipped her toe in the pan, but pulled it out again. "Ow!" The water was freezing.

Sam grabbed her ankle and shoved her foot back into the pan, holding it there despite Maggie's pleas to stop. "This will help," he insisted.

"I'm turning blue." Her foot went numb from the cold.

"No, you're not." He smiled at her, his thumb absently caressing her ankle. "This will keep the swelling down."

"Good. I'd like to get back to work."

He shook his head. "I don't think so. You may need X rays to see if it's broken."

"Oh, come on. This is silly." Maggie hated to admit there was anything seriously wrong. She made a face. "There's nothing a doctor can do even if it is broken. You can't wear a cast on a toe."

"Oh, poor Cinderella," Justy cried as she and Julianne ran into the room.

"Who?" Sam was confused.

Maggie reached for the broken figurine and handed the headless body to Justine. "Sorry, honey. One of your big pieces of driftwood fell over. I hope nothing else around here is broken."

"That's okay, Maggie," the child said. "We'll find her head and Daddy can glue it back on."

"Would one of you get me a towel? I think I've soaked long enough. Let me go, Sam, please?"

"All right." Sam released Maggie's leg and she pulled her foot out of the water and rested her ankle against the edge of the pan.

She smiled at him. "It feels better."

"Good. Dry off and I'll take you home."

Darn. She wanted to finish the border so Justine

could have her room back tonight, but that wasn't going to happen now. "I can drive, Sam."

"You can't step on the gas pedal while holding your toe up in the air. Maybe I should take you to the emergency room at the hospital, just in case there is a broken bone."

"No, please." It would cost a fortune, and she didn't think anything was broken.

Sam took the towel from Julianne and gently dried Maggie's foot, being careful to avoid hurting her. "Can you stand?"

"Sure." She wasn't *really* sure, but she knew she couldn't sit on the floor for the rest of the afternoon. Sam stood up and held out his hand to help, and easily lifted Maggie to her feet.

Maggie liked the feeling of being able to lean on him, and hobbled out into the hall. She navigated the stairs slowly by putting her weight on her heel.

Anxious not to miss anything, the girls scrambled ahead of them.

"Where are you guys going?" Justine asked.

"I'm taking Maggie home."

"Can we go, too?"

"No." Their father's answer was final and the girls knew it.

Buffie met them in the kitchen. "What on earth…?"

Sam kept helping Maggie walk through the house. "A slight accident with driftwood, so I'm driving Maggie home. The girls will tell you all about it. Don't wait dinner—we may make a detour to the hospital."

"Maggie, dear, are you all right?" Buffie's voice was kind, her expression worried.

Maggie smiled through gritted teeth. The toe throbbed with every step. "I'm fine, but Sam's determined to worry. I think I just need to get off this foot for a while."

Lou hurried into the room. "Did the cold water help at all?"

Sam nodded. "Yes, but the foot may need more than that."

"Don't worry, really," Maggie told the two women. "I'll see you tomorrow."

The girls ran ahead to open the door and Maggie limped across the driveway to the Volvo. "Leave the Pontiac here," Sam said. "I'll pick you up tomorrow if you feel like working."

Maggie was relieved to sit in the car and too distracted to argue. There was gravel imbedded in her bare heel and she brushed it off as the girls said goodbye. "Good luck with Cinderella," she told them.

"Justine," Sam called as he shut the car door. "Get all that driftwood out of your room and into the garage. We don't want any more accidents."

As he drove out into the street Maggie saw the worry lines on his face. "Sam, it's only a toe."

He smiled over at her. "I know. I just don't like seeing you hurt." He reached over and took her hand, and Maggie thought wearily that she was closer to falling in love with Sam than ever before.

She didn't like it. The summer afternoon heat suddenly became stifling and she wanted to run away, sore toe or not. Just as long as she wasn't running directly into Sam Winslow's arms. The V between her breasts was wet with perspiration. She ran her fingers through her hair, pushing the heavy mass away from her face, feeling the dampness on her scalp. Her toe ached, and she tried to concentrate on her foot and forget how she felt having Sam so close to her and so damned available.

But maybe he wasn't thinking what she was thinking. About making love on a hot summer afternoon, about slippery bodies on cool sheets. She tried to remember what the first summer days of her marriage had been like. A new bride, anxious to please, ready to learn, and a young husband who hadn't yet tired of his eager wife. Maggie sighed. She could barely remember those days years ago when she'd felt desirable and wanted, before making love had become a sexual science experiment and she'd flunked the class.

Sam released Maggie's hand in order to steer the car along the twisting road and drove silently through Narragansett. He knew she must be hurting, but her face wasn't pale, so he doubted that she was in a great deal of pain. "Taking Maggie home." It sounded like a song title, Sam decided. Had a nice ring to it, too. He stopped the car at the busy Wakefield intersection and waited for the light to turn green.

"Sam?"

He looked over to her and smiled. "What?"

"Thanks for being so concerned."

"You're welcome." The light changed color and Sam automatically followed the traffic along Kingstown Road to Maggie's home.

"Just drop me off."

He ignored the suggestion and parked the car in the narrow driveway. "Not a chance. I'm going to make sure you get in the house."

I was afraid of that. She opened the door and swung her legs out onto the pavement. "No problem," she said.

"Stay put. I'll come around to help."

She enjoyed the feel of his arms under her fingers as she steadied herself against him. *This had better stop*, she thought, and she let go. Her balance shifted and she landed hard on the heel of her bare foot. "Ouch."

"What are you doing? Hang on, Maggie." He gripped her tightly around the waist and held her close to him until they'd negotiated the front steps.

Maggie realized her keys were still hanging in the ignition of the Pontiac. "There's a spare key under the plant. Could you get it?"

In a moment Sam had the door unlocked, and supporting herself against the wall, Maggie hobbled into the living room. She had drawn the shades before she left, so the interior was cool, its darkness intimate and private.

Maggie collapsed on the couch. "I'm a mess," she moaned, then realized she'd said that out loud.

Sam stood in front of her. "Go take a shower while I make something cold to drink."

"I can wait," she said.

"Don't be ridiculous. You look miserable."

There was nothing that would feel better, but Maggie was uncomfortable. Still, she was an adult and should be able to manage the situation. Sam certainly seemed at ease. With two young daughters he must be accustomed to handling females in distress. "Okay. Help yourself to anything in the fridge."

"Here," he said, giving her his hand so she could get to her feet. "Need help?"

He was standing too close. "No," she said, "I can hobble into the bathroom all by myself."

Mustering as much dignity as she could with her toe up in the air, Maggie thumped around the corner to the bathroom. When she was safely behind the bathroom door she sat down and self-consciously peeled off her clothes. It was odd knowing Sam was only a few yards away. She heard the crack of an ice-cube tray and thought she heard Sam whistling a sea shanty chorus. That made her smile and kept her smiling through the shower, even when the warm water hit her toe and made it throb. She soaped quickly, freshened her hair with a quick shampoo and rinsed with lukewarm water. After she dried off, she wrapped herself in the turquoise robe hanging from the hook on the door. Then she hobbled into the hall, hoping to head to her bedroom undisturbed.

"Here, Maggie." Sam intercepted her. She wondered if he'd heard the shower stop and had been waiting. He handed her a brandy glass. "Strawberry daiquiris."

"Thanks. You've been into the freezer." She took the icy glass and followed him back to the living room.

"You didn't have any gin or beer, so I made these. Are all those containers filled with strawberries?"

"Yep. Patsy and I pick them every summer. I save mine for drinks or on top of ice cream, and Patsy makes jam."

He led her over to the couch, noting her limp was less pronounced than before. "There must have been a dozen cans of daiquiri mix in there. I have this vision of you making pitchers of this stuff and drinking it all alone, night after night." He helped her sit down on the couch and made himself comfortable next to her.

She laughed. "I do have a social life, you know."

"No, I don't. Is there someone special?"

She hesitated. "No. But I have friends and I like to have them over when I'm not this busy with work."

"And I've kept you busy," he said, satisfaction in his voice.

"Yes." She sipped her drink. "But it will be worth it. There's a lot at stake."

"Like what?"

"I told you my partner, Fanny, ran off to Hawaii with a painter she met on one of the condo jobs we did last fall. It was a real blow to her husband and I was in for a surprise, too." She looked at Sam with a wry smile. This story sounded stupid each time she told it. "Fanny was the one who took care of the bills and the bookkeeping, and I found out after she left that a lot of bills hadn't been paid and I owed Paper-To-Go several thousand dollars."

"What did you do?"

"Worked my tail off ever since to pay off that bill."

"But what about Fanny? Could you contact her?"

"My family was wild. They thought I should go to Hawaii and sue. But it wouldn't have made any difference. She was gone, with all the business records, too. It would have cost me a small fortune in legal fees to straighten out the mess. It was easier just to let the thing go and chalk it up to experience." Maggie took a large swallow of her drink. "This tastes pretty good. I wouldn't have thought you'd know how to work a blender."

He relaxed against the back of the couch. "I read the words on the buttons. How's your toe?"

"Better." She held her leg out in front of her and tried to wiggle the toe but couldn't. "I think it's starting to stiffen up."

Looking at Maggie wrapped up in that robe was starting to make him feel the same way, Sam thought. "Maybe I should go," he said.

She tucked her legs underneath her and finished her drink. "Maybe you should."

He didn't move. "Maybe we should finish off the blender of daiquiris."

She held out her empty glass and smiled. "Maybe we should." He seemed to hesitate, so she added, "I can hold my liquor, if that's what you're worried about."

"Not really." He took the glass and slid off the couch. "I just don't want to see you fall over anything."

"I won't," she promised and he headed for the kitchen. She leaned forward and slid a hassock in front of the couch, then rested her outstretched legs on it and surveyed her right toe. It was growing bigger, but it didn't feel all that bad. "I'm going to live," she called out.

He carried two filled glasses into the living room. "Good. I'm not sure what I'd do without you."

"Hah!" She took the glass he handed her. "Thanks."

"Even though you're probably ruining my summer," he continued, sitting down beside her. Maggie had turned his house upside down, but just as easily put it back together, room by room, with a smile on her lovely face and a country song on the radio. Irresistible.

"How?" She couldn't take him seriously.

He toasted her with the glass. "I'm having too much fun."

"Is that some kind of sin?"

He frowned. "I'm not sure." He studied her with a serious expression. "I do know things are moving faster than I like. And I don't even care."

"Your house will be finished in a couple of days, Sam."

"Don't be dense, Maggie. I'm talking about you and me and whatever is going on between us."

"I'm not good at this," she said, sighing.

"Neither am I."

"Maybe you should go."

He didn't move. "Maybe I should."

She pulled her turquoise robe tighter across her legs. She was naked underneath and she knew Sam knew it. Lord, this was so complicated! Drops of water trickled from her wet hair, cooled her neck and soaked into the collar of the robe as she fiddled with the lapels.

"You can quit fussing with your robe, Maggie. I'm not going to jump on top of you."

She drained the drink in one large swallow and set the glass on the end table. "Good."

"It's been awhile," he explained in a matter-of-fact voice.

"Awhile?" she echoed. What did "awhile" mean to a man like Sam, Maggie wondered. A year? A month? Forty-five minutes?

"Yes." His voice was a caress. "I'd like to take my time."

She couldn't keep the challenge out of her voice as she turned to face him. "What makes you think you're going to take anything?"

"I've kissed you, Maggie." His voice grew husky. "And you've kissed me. We're unfinished business, you and I."

She couldn't tear her gaze from his. "Maybe it's best to leave it that way."

He set his drink on the floor and reached over to touch her cheek. "Kiss me, Maggie. Kiss me again and then tell me to leave it alone."

It was a dare, and Maggie could never resist a challenge. She turned to him, oblivious to the slight gaping of her robe and the revealing swell of skin exposed to Sam's gaze. She scooted closer, put her arms around his neck and gave him a quick peck on the lips. "There."

He touched the soft top of her breast.

"Leave it alone," she said.

"What?"

"You said I could say that after I kissed you." She smiled into his eyes.

"Tease," he whispered. He kissed her, his lips opening to claim the softness of her mouth. *Strawberries and rum*. It was a seductive taste, and he grew hard with wanting her. His tongue explored her mouth, while his hand cupped her neck and held her close.

Maggie wasn't going anywhere. She felt as if she were melting; the terry cloth brushing against her bare skin created more intense sensation than she thought she could stand.

Sam eased his hand inside the robe and along her shoulders. His thumbs caressed the small bones at the base of her throat before pulling off the robe to reveal her breasts.

"You are gorgeous," he murmured as he hands traced the roundness of her body.

Maggie could feel her body swelling against the touch of his hands. "Sam, I meant it when I said I'm not very good at this sort of—"

"Lovemaking?" he supplied.

"Yes. I mean, no. I just, well, I'm better at hanging wallpaper."

He tucked the folds of her robe neatly across her chest and leaned back into the couch cushion. "Better?" he asked, tilting up her chin with one finger and forcing her to look at him.

"No." Her body ached for him. Even her toe ached for him.

"Talk to me."

He held out his arm and she snuggled into his chest. Embarrassed, she didn't know what to say.

Sam's voice was a comforting rumble above her head. "How many years were you married?"

"Almost five."

"Were you happy?"

"For a while." She didn't want to tell him any more than that.

"Maggie, you're beautiful and warm. Passionate, too—Don't protest. You're generous and giving and loving and kind."

"I sound like a Girl Scout."

"You're not built like one."

"Thank you. But that's not the point."

"What are you worried about?"

"I don't know." That was a lie. "What if you're disappointed?"

"What if you are?" he countered. "I'm willing to take the chance. I'm willing to try to please you for as long as you want me to." With his free hand he untied the loose knot of fabric at her waist. "Eight minutes, eight hours, eight days," he murmured as he glided his hand along her smooth shoulder and then dipped lower. "You decide."

"Starting now?"

"Now," he answered.

Her stomach fluttered at his touch and she drew in her breath as his hand caressed her breasts and left a heated trail beneath his fingertips. She put her hand over his and stilled the motion. For a long moment she felt her own heartbeat under his hand, until he captured her hand and tugged it to his lips.

"Sam..." She wasn't sure if she should encourage

him or draw away. It was growing harder to make any kind of rational decision.

"Shh," he murmured into her palm, then tickled it with his tongue, tasting the rough work-worn skin. "I'm busy."

She turned to face him and stroked his jaw, willing him to look at her. "Sam," she began, but the expression in his eyes stopped her words. Desire, delicious long-forgotten desire, flamed between them. He wanted her. The realization was sweet. She slipped her hands behind his neck and gently tugged him to her.

"I guess you don't want to talk anymore?" he inquired unnecessarily.

He nuzzled her ear and his warm breath made her shiver as his hands clasped her shoulders. She knew he wouldn't let her go easily.

"Not for the next eight hours," she answered, shaking her head.

He claimed then, his tongue parting her waiting lips to stroke the sensitive folds of her mouth. Exquisite currents of sensation flooded her body, turning her bones to cream. It was a seemingly endless kiss, as their tongues flirted and entwined erotically and needy lips turned bruised and swollen.

He caressed the aching tips of her breasts with his thumbs, teasing the peaks until she moaned, wanting more. He understood, and dragged his lips along the soft span of her neck to nudge damp tendrils of hair from her shoulder. Dipping lower, he laved her swelling breasts with his tongue, while his searching hands explored the dips and curves of her body concealed by the terry cloth.

Maggie leaned back against the sofa cushion as spasms of longing shook her. She knew that any minute she could melt into a puddle of delight. She'd known Sam Winslow for only ten days, give or take an hour or two. And could have fallen in love with him in half the time. *Now or never, McGuire. Do you want this man or not?*

Before she could decide, he reclaimed her mouth with a deep, lengthy kiss. Then he stopped and smiled at her. "I've wanted to do this ever since I saw you that first day in the bathtub."

"And I thought you were all business."

"Business was the last thing on my mind." He tickled the soft hollow behind her ear with his lips.

She attempted to sit up, but her trembling body resisted.

"Are you going somewhere?" He sounded amused. "I'd offer to carry you into the bedroom, but my knees are weak." He pulled away and smiled at her. "We could start slowly, though, by standing up."

"Sam..."

He moved off the couch and stood, leaving Maggie to feel deserted. Gently he lifted her feet from the hassock and placed them on the floor before pushing the hassock away. "Now give me your hands," he ordered, holding out his.

She did, and he tugged her to her feet and pulled her against his hard body. There was no answering jolt of pain from her toe, only longing to trace the texture of Sam's lips with her own. She wondered briefly if she'd lost all common sense as she wrapped her arms around his neck and pulled him to her. But there was no more time to think while she kissed him, no will to protest as his hands slipped inside her untied robe and roamed freely over her heated skin. And there was no reason to stop as he led her, with long pauses to kiss and touch and caress, out of the living room and around the corner to her bedroom. The shades were drawn against the sun, giving the room an intimate feeling. Bookcases served as nightstands on each side of the bed and a small television set perched on an oak dresser on the opposite wall. The room was tidy except for the unmade bed, which was growing rapidly more appealing.

She turned around to see him unbuttoning his shirt. "Can I do that?" She needed to touch him. With firm fingers she opened his shirt, slipped it off his shoulders and down his arms. It fell to the carpet. He unbuckled his slacks and kicked off his loafers.

"No socks?"

"Isn't that the latest style? I'm no Don Johnson, but I was trying to impress you." He stepped out of his pants and threw them out of the way.

Maggie surprised herself by not becoming embarrassed. "Designer underwear?" she asked.

"Not anymore." He peeled off his shorts. "If there's a problem with birth control I can—"

"No," Maggie interrupted. "There's no problem with that." She watched him throw his underwear on top of his pants. The man wasn't shy. She looked at his body and knew what desire was.

"Are you going to take off that robe?" He didn't wait for an answer, but opened the robe to reveal her body and gently pressed himself against her. Burying his face in her damp hair he groaned, "Maggie, you feel so good." His hands rubbed her back and cupped her buttocks.

She had to stand on tiptoe to kiss him and the movement caused her bare flesh to brush along his hard length. She caressed his chest and down, to capture his heat in her hands. She was amazed at her boldness, but wanted to touch him, needing to know if he felt the desire she did.

He groaned. "I don't know how much more I can take. How far away is the damn bed?"

"Four—no, three steps," she whispered into his chest. She moved backward until the backs of her knees hit the edge of the bed and she fell on the mattress, her legs dangling to the floor. She wriggled out of the sleeves of her robe.

"Move over," Sam said, leaning over her, "or I'll take you like this."

She couldn't move. Her body felt heavy and hot as she looked into his eyes. She saw desire there. Passion and kindness—nothing to fear. She smiled up at him, knowing he wanted her, hoping she could give him pleasure.

Sam slid his body over hers and a moist welcoming heat touched him. He braced his arms on each side of her head and leaned forward. "Like this, then," he said as his body found hers, the entering deep and sure.

Maggie hid a gasp at the size of him filling her, as powerful waves of desire connected them to each other. His thrusts were strong, pushing her deeper into the mattress. He stopped and kissed her.

"I'm sorry, Maggie. I'll try to slow down." He winced. "But you feel so good around me."

She put a finger to his lips. "Love me the way you want to, Sam."

With that his eyes grew dark again. He stood over her, fully joined, and smoothed his hand over her flat stomach to tangle in the curls below. "So perfect," he murmured, and began a steady pounding rhythm until much later, as Maggie tightened and arched around him, he stilled her cries with kisses. Then, unable to hold back any longer, he exploded into her tight warmth. After the waves of passion peaked, he held her close and whispered words of love against her throat.

8

IN THE STILLNESS following, Maggie caught her breath and held on to Sam's waist. She felt wonderful, as if a gift long lost had been returned. "You're not disappointed." It was stated as fact.

"No." His voice was hoarse. "Oh, no."

"Would you like to get into bed now?" Her lips curved into an impish smile as she touched the beads of perspiration on his forehead where his brown hair drooped. She gently brushed it back with her fingers.

"I'm going to fall on the floor if I don't." He slid out of her. "But I hate to leave you."

She used the last of her energy to pull her legs up on the bed and move over for him. Suddenly shy, she grabbed a corner of the sheet and slipped underneath it, lifting it for him when he lay down next to her. She curled on her side, her pillow scrunched comfortably under her head, to study his profile.

He folded his arms behind his head and sighed. "Hell of a summer."

"It's only just started." They'd started something, too, Maggie knew. Maybe something that shouldn't have begun, but how could there be any turning back?

"You make me feel sixteen again and as nervous as a cat near water."

"What?" She laughed in surprise.

He turned his head toward her and smiled. "One of

Lou's expressions. Sorry." He moved to his side and caressed her cheek. "I just don't know, Maggie. There are no promises here. I'm not sure what to say."

She felt wonderfully warm as his hand slid over her shoulders and along her breasts. She closed her eyes and allowed herself only to feel. "We don't have to talk at all, Sam."

"Good." He sighed. "My lips have better things to do." Then he touched her mouth with his and pressed closer, pushing her gently on her back and kissing the tip of each full breast before dipping lower to skim along her abdomen.

"Sam..."

"Shh. No more talking, remember?"

She tensed, torn between wanting the passion to continue, but shy with his easy experience. His strong fingers worked magic on her skin, making her crave more. His mouth dropped lower and claimed her, his tongue, lips and fingers combining to whirl her into a sea of feeling. She was lost as waves of climax shook her. His body slid over her, filling a need she couldn't put into words, and she held him close until, both sated, they slipped slowly back into the world that was theirs alone.

MAGGIE AWOKE in the dark, the sheets a tangle around her. The house was silent; the emptiness had returned to its familiar pattern. *Probably best*, Maggie decided, kicking away the sheets. She smelled Sam's after-shave on the pillow near her head. Perhaps the passion had now burned itself out, like a forgotten holiday candle. But the tingle in her body when she remembered his lovemaking left doubts about that. On her part, anyway. He must have gone home to his family and guests. She tried to recall if anything special had been planned for this evening. Then she smiled. She knew he must be tired, wherever he was.

She stood up, painfully putting her weight on her forgotten toe before lifting her foot. She sat back down on the bed and switched on a lamp. The toe had a purple glow, but otherwise looked acceptable, although climbing ladders might not be possible tomorrow. She hobbled to the bathroom and turned on the faucets in the tub. There were a lot of places that needed soaking.

She didn't want to think about falling in love with Sam, she wanted to remember making love with him. There was a difference, she told herself. *That's what you think*, a voice inside replied with a chuckle. She eased herself into the steaming water, carefully keeping her right foot dry by propping her leg up on the side of the tub. She leaned back, content to be quiet and think about what the past hours would mean.

Maybe nothing? Maybe too much. The water continued to fill the tub, easing her aches. She didn't ever intend to be married again. As soon as she was financially able, she could be a mother. She would adopt an older child, maybe a girl. Again she wondered if she was attracted to Sam because she liked the family package. Maybe it wasn't the man himself at all. Who was she kidding? The entire family package hadn't been in her bed this evening.

Maggie leaned forward to shut off the water. Life was becoming too complicated. She studied her toe. It was a good excuse not to arrive at the Winslow house tomorrow, and she was worried that it would be awkward facing Sam. She would have to put in an extra-long day Friday, but that was manageable.

Later she reluctantly stripped the tangled sheets

from the bed and threw them in the hamper. After she remade the bed she climbed into it, a little disappointed that all traces of Sam Winslow were gone. But, she reminded herself, there was no use hoping for an encore.

WHERE WAS the lovely gypsy this morning? I did not see her car in the driveway."

Sam climbed the steps to the health club before he answered Franco. "Do you mean Maggie?"

The conductor bared his teeth in a giant smile. "Who else in your household would fit the description?"

"She hurt her toe yesterday." He opened the door to Riverbend and ushered Franco inside.

"Ah, yes. And you so gallantly drove her to her home, I heard."

Sam ignored him and walked across the carpeted lobby to the counter.

"'Morning, Sam. Haven't seen you in here for quite a while."

"Hi, Don," Sam greeted the smiling man behind the registration desk. "Still playing racquetball?"

"Sure. Just let me know when you want to play and I'll book a court." He handed Sam a locker key.

"Thanks. I'll need a guest pass today." He introduced Franco. "We're going to take advantage of the air-conditioning and work out."

Two young women dressed in bright yellow, skintight leotards strolled by and went into the lounge. Franco sighed. "There are other advantages here, I see, Sammy."

Don selected another key from the drawer and handed it to Franco. He was clearly astonished by the conductor's exotic appearance. "Here you are, sir. I hope you enjoy yourself." He turned to Sam. "Are you signed up for the big race Friday?"

He nodded. "I don't know if I have a shot at beating you, but I'm going to try."

Sam led Franco down the stairs to the locker room. He hoped he hadn't made a mistake spending the morning away from the house. Still, it seemed the best thing to do, what with Buffie and Lou engrossed in the party plans and Maggie at home nursing her foot. Elena wanted to sleep late, but Franco's energy had become overwhelming in the midst of the party preparations. With any luck, he would be engrossed in rehearsals all afternoon and would stay out of everyone's way until the party began.

Sam changed into gym shorts and showed Franco where the weight room was located. What was Maggie doing now? He'd reluctantly left her while she slept, her warm body curled around the white lace-tipped sheets. He ached just thinking about her.

"You are dreaming, Sammy, and there is a man calling to you."

Sam looked around the room and saw Patrick McGuire on an exercise bike. The older man wore a headband, and although his face was ruddy, he looked ready to pedal a hundred miles.

"Maggie's father," Sam said, hoping Franco wouldn't follow him as he walked over to say hello to the man.

"Hello, son," Patrick boomed, shaking Sam's hand. "How'd you like my boys' music the other day? They wring a man's heart, don't they?"

That was one way of putting it, Sam decided. "Yes, sir, they certainly do. I enjoyed the performance very much."

Still pedaling, Patrick asked, "Is Maggie still working at your house, Mr. Winslow?"

"Call me 'Sam.'" He decided not to mention the accident with the driftwood. "Yes, she is. And doing a great job."

"Do you play racquetball, Sam?"

"I have, but I'm not very good."

"Fine," the older man replied. "We'll have to play sometime. I'll let you get back to your workout." He wiped beads of sweat from his forehead. "Keep an eye on my daughter, Sam. She doesn't like those high ladders."

Sam tried not to laugh. "My ceilings aren't over eight feet, Mr. McGuire." He turned away. It was hard to picture Maggie afraid of anything. Except last night, and then she'd been more worried than afraid.

Last night. Sam tried to put it out of his mind, but it wasn't easy. It had been the first time he'd made love to a woman since Anne had died. The first time he'd wanted to. He'd had opportunities in the past few years, but without any kind of emotional involvement, it just hadn't seemed worth the physical effort. With Maggie it was different. It felt right.

Sam returned to the other side of the room to find Franco flirting with the woman in charge of the Nautilus equipment.

"I'll be right back," he told him, and went upstairs to the pay phone. He'd do his best to talk Maggie into coming to the party tonight.

"I'M SENDING the car for you at seven." It was the third message from Sam on her answering machine. She listened to the exasperated tone in his voice and pushed the button to reset the machine's tape. There was an hour left before the car arrived to take her to Sam's party and she wasn't even close to being ready. Looking drop-dead gorgeous took a lot of time.

The decision to go had been an easy one. It boiled down to simple vanity, Maggie realized, taking her lavender dress from the closet. The next time she saw Sam did she want to be wearing her scroungy work clothes or a beautiful strapless knit sheath?

She zipped herself into the dress, looked in the mirror and knew she'd made the right decision. Thirty-seven minutes left. She swept her hair into a soft knot on top of her head, allowing wisps of curls to escape to her neck. Crystal lavender earrings shaped like flowers tipped her earlobes.

It was nine minutes before seven when she'd finished putting on her makeup: sheer foundation, eye shadow in shades of lavender, shimmery lipstick and subtle layers of mascara. Wishing she could wear heels, she slipped on white sandals, instead, and hoped no one would notice one of her toes was a different color from the other nine. When the doorbell rang she was ready to follow the chauffeur to the limousine.

"Mr. Winslow sends his regrets for not being available to escort you personally, miss," said the uniformed driver as he opened the car door.

"Thank you." She climbed into the back seat, liking the idea of having a few minutes in air-conditioned luxury.

When they arrived at Sam's, Maggie saw the large crowd on the lawn and almost lost her courage. The scene looked like one from a movie as men in white tuxedos and beautifully dressed women mingled near a huge yellow striped tent. In the distance the ocean was calm and the blue sky showed no sign of darkening. From somewhere inside the tent a band played a popular song from the forties. She tried to spot Sam in the crowd, but it was futile.

"Miss?" The driver patiently held the door open for her.

Buffie stood nearby. Her expression was puzzled. "Maggie?"

"Hello, Mrs. Vanderberg. Your party looks like a success."

"Oh, my dear, I hope so." She absently smoothed the skirt of her white lace dress. "It's been such a great deal of work, but the results are worth it, I think. Sam didn't tell me you would be able to join us tonight."

Maggie didn't know what to say. Obviously the woman was surprised Sam would invite the wallpaper contractor to an elegant party in honor of the town's symphony festival. "Well, I—"

"I do hope you have recovered from the accident with the driftwood yesterday."

"Yes, it—"

Buffie took Maggie's elbow and guided her toward the crowd. "How lovely you look, too, dear," Buffie said. "I must introduce you to— Oh, here's Franco. Darling!"

Franco approached, his appreciative gaze roaming Maggie's curves. "Ah, the little gypsy is here to make the party a delight. You have made my evening perfect."

Maggie laughed at his outrageous flattery. "You're good for my ego, Franco."

"And you are good for certain parts—" He paused when Buffie's eyebrows raised. "I shall take Maggie under my wing and get her a drink. Her cheeks are quite flushed, don't you think?"

"Rascal," Buffie muttered, waving them away.

Franco led Maggie into the shady tent. "Champagne, of course?"

"Of course."

The conductor waved his hand and a waiter promptly supplied two glasses of champagne. Franco handed one to Maggie and raised his glass. "To you," he said. "We missed you at the house today. I shall be discreet and not stare at your foot." He led her away from the band to a private corner, successfully avoiding people who tried to start conversations. "But I shall be indiscreet and state that our host has been extremely moody all day, smiling at nothing, then barking orders and contradicting dear old Buff. He took me to his health club because Buffie wanted us out of her way. He sometimes whistles the strangest melody, but I suppose you are familiar with it."

Maggie just laughed. "You'll have to go elsewhere for gossip."

"Shall I change the subject?" At her nod he prattled on, while she sipped her drink. "I am happy to go to Italy soon. Elena is quarrelsome these days and a trip will soothe us both, although I fear Buffie has other plans for her."

"Such as?" Maggie looked around the tent, hoping Sam would appear.

"It galls me to suggest it, but don't you think Elena would make a lovely wife for Sam? Beautiful, musical, rich."

"I'm sure Elena is all those things." Maggie refused to be baited. "But it really isn't any of my business."

His black eyes glinted with humor. "No?"

"No," said Sam. He encircled Maggie's waist with his arm.

Franco was undisturbed. "You should not sneak up on people. You do not know what we were talking about."

"Saying no to you would always be a smart thing for Maggie to do. Now go mingle. You're the guest of honor."

Franco sighed dramatically. "I will mingle if I must. Then I shall go seduce your housekeeper."

"She'll appreciate that."

Franco bowed to Maggie and strolled from the tent. Sam dropped his hand from Maggie's waist and she turned to face him. He looked elegant and foreign in his white tuxedo jacket, and she suddenly felt shy. "Hello, Sam," she said.

"Speaking of seduction, Maggie...last night was incredible. I've thought about you all day."

Maggie willed herself not to blush, but she couldn't help smiling up at him. "Seduction, Sam? Who seduced whom?"

"You invited me into your bedroom."

"And you left me," she teased.

"I'm sorry," he said, suddenly serious. "You were sleeping."

"You promised me eight hours." Her blue eyes twinkled with mischief and longing.

"Next time."

"Oh?"

He leaned closer to whisper, "You look beautiful in that color, Maggie. Your hair swept up like that makes me want to touch this soft spot—" he brushed his fingers behind her ear and down her neck to her nape "—like this."

Answering shivers swept up her spine. "You shouldn't be doing this, Sam."

"No?"

She looked at the people standing near and was glad she was in a corner. "It's not the place."

He dropped his arm reluctantly and signaled a passing waiter. "I know." He lifted a glass of champagne from the waiter's tray. "How's your foot?"

"Much better. I'll be back to work tomorrow."

"As I said, I've been thinking about you all day. Why didn't you answer my calls?"

She searched his gaze, hoping something in his expression would give her a clue to what he was thinking. "The phone seemed too impersonal," she said. He merely looked surprised. "And I wasn't sure if I should come tonight," she added.

"Why not?" He frowned.

She set her almost-full glass on a small table near her. "I wondered if it would feel awkward being together." *After we made love last night.*

"And does it?"

"Yes, a little." *Because I'm falling in love with you in front of three hundred people.*

"We need to take care of that." He put his glass beside hers on the table and grasped her hand. "Come on. There are people I'd like you to meet, but first we need to take a walk." He led her out of the tent and stopped on the outskirts of the crowd. "I forgot, Maggie. *Can* you walk?"

"If you go slowly." She smiled, happy to be with him, and they strolled across the lawn until they reached the hedge that separated the grass from the rocky outcrop fronting the beach.

He led her through an opening in the hedge and out across the flat boulders until they were out of sight of the crowd. Then he put his arms around her and kissed her thoroughly.

"There," he said. "Still feel uncomfortable?"

"I'm not sure." She tightened her arms around his neck and pressed against the hard length of his body. "Maybe you'd better do that again."

Upstairs, on the top floor of the house, flickering lights from the television illumined Sam's bedroom. But no one was paying attention to *The Cosby Show* re-run.

"You're not gonna believe this!" Justine kept the binoculars close to her face although Julianne tried to pull them away. "Quit it! You're choking me."

"I won't let go till you let me see," her sister threatened.

"It's Dad," she said, reluctantly handing the binoculars to her sister.

Julianne squinted into the lenses. "And *Maggie*?"

Justine nodded, trying to peer through the bedroom window to see more of the two small figures on the beach.

"And they're kissing!"

"*Still*? I don't believe it." She tugged on the glasses. "Give those back."

"They're gone. I can't see 'em anymore." She gave Justine the glasses. "Phooey."

"Something's goin' on, Julie. This is *good news*."

"You really think so?"

Justy nodded. "They looked just like Barbie and Ken."

The two little girls bounced gently on the water bed, identical grins on their faces, the binoculars forgotten in Justine's lap.

HAVING NO IDEA they'd been spied upon, Sam took Maggie's hand and led her across the lawn toward the tent. "Stay close," he said.

Maggie wouldn't argue with that. Hundreds of people she'd never seen before were gathered in groups, eating and drinking and talking together. Some were dancing on the grass. "Do you do this sort of thing often?" she asked.

"This is Buffie's idea of a good time, remember? I just supplied the location. But there are some people, friends of mine, I'd like you to meet." He bent and whispered into her ear. "I can't wait to be alone with you later, though."

"Do you mean I don't get to ride in the limo again?" she teased, loving the feel of his lips close to her neck, the scrape of his jaw against her cheek.

He straightened and tugged on her hand, leading her closer to the dancers. "Behave, Margaret. You're about to waltz with me." He swung her into his arms. "And then," he warned, "you'll be fair game for every adult male here. I'll try to fend them off."

"What about my toe?"

"Does it hurt?"

"No." There wasn't anything in the world that could spoil the magic of tonight.

"Good, because I want you in my arms for the rest of the evening."

Maggie smoothed her left hand along Sam's tuxedoed shoulder while he held her other hand in a gentle clasp and began to move in time to the music, a song Maggie didn't recognize but knew she would never forget.

MUCH LATER Sam stood alone in the darkness and said good-night to one of the last of his guests. He watched

Buffie chatting with her friends and hoped she wasn't too tired. She had knocked herself out organizing the festival, a lot of work at any age. Still, she looked happy, especially when Elena, elegant in black, joined the conversation.

He wished Maggie would hurry back. She'd gone inside to say good-night to Julianne and Justine. Before the party he'd promised the girls that if Maggie came tonight he'd make certain she would visit with them. They'd been worried and guilty about her toe, but he knew seeing Maggie would cheer them. He lit a cigarette and enjoyed the brief respite from playing host as he fought the exhaustion that threatened to overwhelm him. Even though he'd tried to keep busy all day he couldn't put Maggie out of his mind.

He wanted Maggie McGuire more than he'd wanted any woman for a very long time, since Anne. Yet the two women weren't remotely alike in looks or personality. Anne had floated around the noisy family chaos without seeming to notice, while Maggie thrived on the constant activity and contributed with noise of her own. The result was the same, Sam decided: the inexplicable feeling he had that everything was right with the world.

So now what? Time. He needed more time with Maggie, more time to understand what was going on between them. The house was practically finished; the festival would be over in two days; the girls would soon be off to camp, and Buffie would begin her summer round of traveling. He would sit in his house and enjoy the quiet. Maybe.

He wanted Maggie and him to go on together just as they were now and see what happened. He took a final drag on his cigarette and tossed it on the grass. He could be falling in love, he realized. *Love?* The word made him frown. Maggie was a beautiful woman—sexy, desirable. But where did love fit into the picture? Anne's memory was still with him and always would be. He saw Maggie step out of the house. Anne's house. She smiled as she walked over to him, and his chest tightened.

"The party's over?" Maggie asked.

"That's it until next year," Sam said. "Unless the festival doesn't catch on."

Buffie came closer and heard Sam's remark. "The symphony will be a success, just as the party was. It was wonderful," she said. "And everyone adored the house."

"I'm glad you're pleased." Sam smiled down at the older woman. "Now life returns to normal."

"Not for a few more days, my dear, so chin up. I'm going to dinner with the Aldriches now. Wouldn't you—and Maggie, of course—like to join us?"

"Thank you, Buff, but I've made other plans."

She sighed and in a low voice said, "Perhaps you'll see that Franco and Elena have dinner. Are you sure you won't come along?"

Sam shook his head. "I'll pass. And don't worry about Franco. I'll take care of everything."

Buffie lifted her cheek for a farewell kiss. "I hope you enjoyed the party, Maggie. Will we see you tomorrow?"

"Yes, to finish."

"Wonderful. Well, good night, everyone," she said with a smile before she joined her friends in the waiting limousine.

"There goes your ride home in the limo," Sam said.

"I was only joking, Sam. But where's my car? I didn't see it in the driveway."

He tossed a casual arm around her shoulders and they walked toward the front of the house. "Safely in the garage. How were my daughters? Were they ready for bed?"

"Yes, but they certainly had a case of the giggles. They must have been thrilled with the party. Lou turned out their light and gave them strict orders to behave when I left."

They climbed the stairs to the front deck. "I'd better kiss them good-night. Wait for me here. It's probably the only place that's safe from the caterers and cleaning crew."

"I should go home, Sam."

"Nonsense." He opened one of the French doors and went into the living room, while she slumped into one of the wicker chairs.

Elena came up the stairs and sat down in the chair across from Maggie. "Do you and Sam want to have dinner with us? We're skipping the next big bash and going to find someplace more...intimate. Franco says he's discovered a lovely seafood place on the bay."

"Have you talked to Sam?"

Elena shrugged. "I mentioned it, but I don't think he was paying attention."

Franco came out of the living room and clapped his hands. "Ah, I've had fantasies like this."

"Like what?" Elena winked at Maggie.

"Two women," he supplied. "One fair, one dark—"

"Take me to dinner before I fall asleep, Franco." Elena yawned. "Don't we have an early rehearsal in the morning?"

Franco turned serious. "Of course. And another to-

morrow evening, just to make sure we are perfection!"
He leaned against the deck railing and gestured toward the sky. "Then we shall fly away for a holiday, just the two of us."

Maggie looked at them. "Where are you going?"

"Italy," said Franco.

"Montana," Elena corrected. "There's a music camp there, and I'm off to teach flute and give several performances, Maggie."

Franco added, "And then you'll meet me in Rome."

"Perhaps." Elena shrugged. "Here's Sam," she said as he stepped onto the deck. "Darling, would you like to join us for dinner?"

Sam shook his head. "We have other plans."

"Come, my dear," Franco said, pulling Elena from her chair. "We shall leave these two alone."

After they went into the house, Sam turned to Maggie. "There. I have you all to myself. Are you hungry? We can go out to dinner if you like."

"No," Maggie said. "Besides, I should go home. Tomorrow's a workday."

He took her hand as she rose from her seat. "Take a walk on the beach with me first."

Maggie smiled her consent, although she knew she shouldn't be alone with Sam. Her body longed to feel his again, and the kisses awhile ago had left them both wishing for privacy. "Then I'll have to leave. There will be two bathrooms to finish tomorrow. If I make the deadline, Sam," she teased, "you'll have to live up to your part of the bargain."

"You're one tough businesswoman," he said, his voice soft. He led her toward the tent and disappeared inside, then returned moments later with a bottle of champagne and two glasses. "Now we're all set," he said.

"I've always wanted to do this." Maggie looked up at the stars and sighed.

"Do what?"

"Drink champagne on the beach."

"You never have?"

Once again she followed him through the opening in the hedge. "We had a few beer parties in the dunes when I was a teenager, but we were so afraid the police would find us it was hard to have a good time. Most of the senior class could have been arrested."

"I forgot to bring a blanket," he said as they stepped across the rocks to the narrow strip of sandy beach.

"Let's just walk for a while."

"What about your foot?"

"I'll take off my sandals. I'll be fine as long as I can see where I'm going and don't bump against any-thing."

"All right," he said, standing the bottle and glasses upright in the sand, while Maggie perched on a rock and slipped off her sandals.

"What about you?" She looked pointedly at his feet. "It'll feel good."

He smiled. He knew what would feel good and it didn't have much to do with bare feet. "If you say so."

Maggie scooted over on the rock to make room for Sam. He threw his shoes and socks onto the sand and haphazardly rolled up his pant legs.

"C'mon." He grasped Maggie's hand and they walked along the hard-packed sand close to the water. "The moon's almost full. Did you know Buffie planned the symphony's performance to coincide with a full moon?"

"You're kidding. I thought it had to do with the Fourth of July."

"No. She said she wanted the romantic atmosphere."

Maggie watched the moonlight dance on the rolling water. "She's right. What happened to *Mr.* Vanderberg?"

"He drowned in a sailboat race off the coast of Block Island when Anne was a child. Buffie was totally devoted to Anne until the day Anne died. Now she keeps busy with charity work."

"And the girls," Maggie added.

"Yes. They're going to play the piano whether they want to or not."

"You don't mind?"

He shrugged. "For now it's good discipline. If the lessons become miserable for either one I'll put an end to them. But I hope they have Anne's talent. She would have loved that."

"You must have been very happy together."

He squeezed her hand. "They were good years that ended in a senseless accident."

Maggie thought of the pictures hanging in the upstairs hallway. "You must miss her very much."

"The worst part—" He hesitated for a second. "The worst part is knowing she's missed seeing the girls grow up. That hurts. And—" he sighed "—the girls have missed knowing their mother."

"But they have you," Maggie said. "And they're good kids. You should be proud."

He tightened his hand around hers. They walked together along the moonlit beach, the silence broken only by the crashing of waves on the shore. A lone sea gull looked content to sit on top of the Atlantic and ride the swells.

"This is as far as we go," Sam said, stopping.

"Why?" Maggie thought she could have walked for miles.

He pointed to a rocky outcrop ahead. "The remnants of a hurricane. We can't go past this old foundation."

They turned around to walk the short distance back. Sam's house sat off to the right on a slight incline. Light beamed from the middle level, but the upper windows were dark.

"Let's not go back yet," Sam said. "The caterers and the cleaning crew will be there for at least another hour." He motioned to the large flat boulder tucked into the shadows and almost buried in the sand. "Have a seat and I'll open the champagne."

She perched on top of the rock and took the glasses from the sand while Sam wrestled with the bottle's cork until it popped toward the water. The sea gull coasted closer to see if they would give him anything to eat. Maggie held out the glasses for him to fill and watched the liquid shimmer in the moonlight.

He sat down beside her on the rock and took his drink. "This is a perfect way to end an evening."

"To perfect endings," she said, clinking her glass against his. *To moonlit nights and deserted beaches and handsome men in white tuxedo jackets,* she added silently as she sipped her champagne. *Here's to the reality of tomorrow morning.*

"I'd much rather drink to beginnings, wouldn't you? This is starting out to be an incredible summer."

"Oh, come on, Sam." She tried to keep her voice light. "My...involvement in your life is ending, as of tomorrow afternoon. Let's agree to stay friends, and when we bump into each other in the supermarket we'll smile and chat about the weather." She downed her drink in one long gulp.

"Stay friends?" he echoed, his voice cheerful. "I haven't heard that line since high school." He refilled her glass. "Try again."

She frowned at the glass. "I've probably had enough of this for one evening. It tastes wonderful, but any more could be dangerous." *Am I talking about the champagne?*

"Have as much as you want. I'll drive you home," he offered, a twinkle in his eyes. "I remember enjoying that very much."

Her body warmed, remembering, and she smiled. "Me, too. I hadn't...felt like that in a long time."

Sam touched her shoulder and turned her to face him. "Neither had I, Maggie."

"I thought you were Rhode Island's Bachelor of the Year."

He grimaced. "I don't know who dreams up those titles. The newspaper's society editor gets carried away, I suppose."

"Patsy was impressed."

"And you?" His voice was low. "Were you impressed, Maggie?" He took her empty glass from her hand and placed it carefully beside his in the sand.

"Not impressed," she murmured. "Intimidated."

"A wild Irish girl intimidated? Not a chance." There was a determined slant to his lips that Maggie found hard to resist. When he wrapped his arms around her bare shoulders and touched his lips to hers, she knew she'd wanted to feel this way all evening. She trembled, not from the salty ocean spray that blew toward them, but from the taste of Sam against her mouth.

"Mmm..." She rested her head against his chest and wrapped her arms around his waist under his jacket. "Pretty impressive."

"Let's do that again," he said. "I can't seem to get enough of you."

Was she in love with him? she wondered. Possibly. Happy about it? Not at all. This wouldn't have a happy ending.

He tilted up her chin with his finger so she would have to look at him. "Come to the symphony with me Saturday night." He traced her bottom lip with his thumb.

Two more days to fall in love, she thought. Two more nights to be with Sam. "Why?"

"What do you mean, 'Why?'" He trailed a path of kisses along her jaw to her earlobe. "You're a music lover, aren't you? I'll bring dinner. We'll picnic on the beach and feed each other strawberries." He took a soft bite of skin and pulled, sending shafts of heat to Maggie's insides. "You tasted like strawberries when we made love last night."

Maggie closed her eyes and wished she were made of stronger material. She should stand up and run like hell for her car. But she didn't move, except to twine her arms around Sam's neck.

"All right" she heard herself whisper against his lips. "I'll keep you company at the symphony, Mr. Winslow. I just love...music."

"I'm glad we have that settled." He carefully unzipped the back of her dress and caressed her smooth back. "I've never made love on a boulder before. Have you?"

Shivers swept along her spine. "You're crazy," she whispered.

"It's all your fault, Maggie," he said. "I start touching you and I never want to stop."

And I don't want you to. She slid the palm of her hand along his shadowed jaw and knew she might as well have spoken the words out loud. Their gaze held for a long moment while she traced his lips with her fingertips, and realized there would be no turning away.

"Have you ever been made love to on a tuxedo?"

She shook her head, knowing she was lost. "No," she answered softly. "Will I regret this?" *Never in a million years*, a brave voice inside answered.

Sam stood up, pushed his jacket off his arms and spread it on the sand. "Neither have I," he said as he pulled Maggie to her feet and removed her strapless dress. He kissed each shoulder. "I think it's something reserved for millionaire playboys, though."

"Then you should be...quite good at it." She shivered, clad only in a tiny strip of white satin underpants, and watched Sam toss his shirt and cummerbund onto the sand. The rasping of his zipper was lost in a gull's cry, and moonlight highlighted rippling skin as he bent to remove his dark slacks and kick them aside.

"Come here," Maggie whispered.

"I'm not finished," he said, tucking his thumbs into the elastic waistband of his briefs.

The darkness made Maggie bold. She knelt on the slippery lining of the jacket and held out her hand. "I'll do it."

He came to her then, and knelt in front of her, cupping her face in his hands with loving tenderness. "I want you, Maggie. I want to feel your tight warmth around me as I move into you and I want to hear you cry my name when you come."

Maggie drew in her breath. Sam was seducing her

with his words, the sound of his voice covering her skin as no caress could. No man had ever talked this way to her before, and the accompanying surge of desire threatened to knock her off her knees.

"Will you call my name then, Maggie?"

She slid her hands along his sides and felt the taut muscles beneath his rib cage. "Yes," she whispered. "Over and over again."

"Good." He ran his tongue lightly against the seam of her lips. "And I'll whisper yours, Maggie. But not for a long while."

He kissed her, holding her head while he plundered her mouth with sleek thrusts of his tongue. She pulled him to her, delighting in the feel of her breasts as sensitive skin brushed the crinkly hair on his chest. Her hands skimmed to his waist; her anxious fingers probed past the elastic barrier to find him full and hard and welcoming her touch.

"Maggie," he moaned, releasing her from his kiss as she pushed the cotton fabric lower and freed him. "You don't know what you're doing to me."

She stroked his sleek length, gentle fingertips tracing a circle around the hard ridge, palming the smoothness with a tentative hand. She felt him expand under her touch. "Maybe I do."

He chuckled softly and captured her hand. There was a wry note in his voice. "We have to slow down." He stood up and pulled her to her feet. "Besides," he said, "it's my turn."

He thumbed her breasts, urging the peaks to harden against his touch. When he was satisfied, his hands swept lower to skim the satin panties that molded her buttocks. Maggie moaned softly as he brushed against her, hot and hard against her thigh.

"Not yet," he whispered, kneeling in front of her on the jacket. In a tantalizing movement, he slid his hands under the elastic and cupped the smooth skin of her behind, capturing and holding her to him.

She could feel his breath on her upper thighs and her knees turned to water. Trembling, she clasped his shoulders while his lips moved back and forth along the satin cloth. He slowly dampened the material with his teasing tongue, probing the swelling flesh until the cloth barrier seemed to disappear and pulsing skin and slick satin melted into one.

Maggie closed her eyes to the moon and clung to Sam, her fingers unwittingly digging into his skin. The intensity of the sensations he aroused deepened until, when he slipped her panties down and guided her onto the jacket, she wondered how much more she could feel before bursting into a million pieces.

He covered her with his warm body and entered slowly. "You are so beautiful," he murmured into her hair.

He filled her, then pulled away, coaxing her to arch to meet him as he thrust into her again. She gasped, wanting more, urging him deeper, until they moved as one. The coat molded itself against the sand beneath them, and Maggie's bare feet tangled with Sam's legs in the sand as a timeless rhythm took over. He worked his sweet magic on her body until she whispered against his throat as she felt herself shatter beneath him. He answered with a shuddering force of his own, his cries of love merging with the crashing waves.

She stroked the hot skin of his back and slowly opened her eyes to watch the moonlight dance across the water and bathe them in its brilliance.

9

"LEAVE BEN ALONE, girls. He has a lot of work to do this morning."

"We hafta talk to him about something important," Justine insisted.

Ben stood on the ladder, brushing glue close to the ceiling. He looked as if he wanted to disappear.

"Later, loves," Maggie said. "Go harass the maids, play with your grandmother's jewelry, ask your father for the car keys—do anything except bother Ben, okay?"

After a longing glance at the teenager in the corner, the children dragged themselves out of the room, leaving Maggie to finish measuring the final strip of border for Justine's room.

Maggie glanced at her watch. Eight-thirty, with two bathrooms left to do. She'd finish the Winslow house today, even though hanging paper in bathrooms was painstakingly slow work. She could do it as long as she kept her mind on her work. And after last night, that would be tough. She sighed as she picked up her scissors. Was she in love with Sam? "I don't want to think about that."

Ben looked down at her. "What?"

Maggie didn't know she'd spoken out loud. "Nothing. Just getting old and talking to myself."

"Mom does that all the time, too." He stepped down

and moved the ladder to the other end of the room. "She said to tell you to call her because she can't stand the suspense."

"Okay." Maggie knew her sister would be going crazy wanting to know the details of a ritzy party like Sam's. Maggie wouldn't tell her everything, but she'd bet Patsy would read between the lines and guess the rest. Maybe calling her wouldn't be such a good idea. She remembered how long it had taken to shampoo the sand from her hair this morning and blushed. "Have you seen Sam?"

"No," Ben said. "I don't think he's around. But those girls are driving me nuts. I think they're setting a trap out in the hall."

"You're free to go as soon as you finish sizing Sam's bathroom."

"Great. I have basketball camp in two weeks, but I'm ready to work again before that if you need me."

"You've been a big help, kid."

He grinned and took the wet paper from her so she could get on the ladder. "Thanks. And Mr. Winslow's really a neat guy. He said he'd teach me how to play tennis."

Maggie decided not to comment on that. "Keep the level handy, Ben. I may need it."

Later, after they'd finished washing off the extra paste, Maggie went downstairs to tell Lou the room was finished.

"Good," Lou said, and followed Maggie upstairs. "I can't wait to see it, and I'll try to have it all put back together before Sam gets home."

"Where'd he go?"

"To work, for a change. There was some big problem that needed his attention. He'll be back by lunchtime, because the photographers from that fancy magazine are coming this afternoon."

"I haven't seen Mrs. Vanderberg, either." Maggie thought the house seemed empty.

"The florists delivered the wrong flowers this morning so she's off to terrorize them. Most of the cleaning was done last night, thank heaven, so it's just finishing touches now. I'm worn out just trying to keep food on the table."

Justine and Julianne followed Ben out of their father's room and into the hall. He looked as if he wanted to escape.

"Ben, you can put the ladder in my car. I'll just use the small one in the bathrooms," said Maggie.

"The girls are leaving for piano lessons in a few minutes, Ben," the housekeeper told him. "So you'll be safe."

"Thanks."

The look of relief on his face made the women laugh. "If they were ten years older, you wouldn't mind so much," Maggie said.

"Go on, you two!" Lou scolded. "Your grandmother told you to practice your music." She shooed them downstairs and went into Justine's room. "It's beautiful. I wasn't sure I'd like the paper, but now that it's on the wall it really looks different."

"I'll be working in their bathroom, Lou. Thank goodness it's small and should only take the rest of the morning." Maggie began to move her tools into the bathroom, while Lou pushed furniture back into place.

"Is this your last day, hon?"

Maggie nodded. "As soon as Sam's bathroom is finished, I am, too."

"We'll miss you around here."

"I'll be back when Sam's bedroom paper arrives, don't worry."

Lou chuckled. "Oh, I'm not really worried. I just know we'll be seeing a lot of you around here."

Maggie didn't know what to say, so she went into the bathroom and began to measure for the level lines. She knew she had to get out of there today, away from the seductive charm of the house before she was lost to loving Sam. She hardened her heart and tore the plastic from a new roll of paper.

By the time Ben finished, Maggie had a good start on her work and was ready to take a break.

"I called Mom. She said I could go to the beach and she'd pick me up at five."

"The Pier?"

He nodded. "I brought a towel."

Maggie rummaged through her purse and handed Ben several bills. "Here's what I owe you for the week, plus a little extra for lunch today."

"Great! Thanks!"

"I'll meet you in the car in a minute." She washed her hands and went downstairs. Buffie and a cleaning woman were in the dining room.

"Maggie?" Buffie called. "May I speak to you? Privately?"

Maggie heard the tension in the older woman's voice. "Of course, Mrs. Vanderberg," she answered. What on earth could be wrong? The maid brushed past Maggie and rolled her eyes as if to say "heaven help us" and Maggie stepped into the dining alcove.

Buffie held up an intricate diamond necklace, its ends dangling from her wrinkled hand. "A family heirloom," she said.

"It's lovely," Maggie replied. "Was there something you wanted to talk to me about?"

"Did you tell the children to play with my jewelry?" Her voice shook.

"What?"

"Justine said you told her it was all right."

Maggie frowned. "Of course I didn't," she began, until the realization dawned. "Oh, no. I told them to play with your jewelry, get the keys to the car, anything but bother my nephew Ben. They've been driving him crazy this morning. I had no idea they would take me so literally."

"Well, they did." Buffie sighed, dropping the necklace into the pocket of her dress. "And I must take responsibility, too. I didn't have time to put it back in the safe." She sagged into a dining room chair.

"Are you ill, Mrs. Vanderberg?"

The woman shook her head. "Just tired. The children are too much for me today, I'm afraid." She smiled ruefully. "Do you think they'll attempt to drive one of the cars this afternoon?"

"I'll speak to them about it, if you like."

"Thank you. You do seem to have a way with them. Although I hate to admit it, I think they've finally gotten the best of me."

"Not a chance." Maggie resisted the urge to smile. It was almost comical to see Mrs. Vanderberg unsure of herself, but Maggie had to feel sorry for her, too. "The girls would try anyone's patience today."

Buffie shrugged. "Possibly. I must apologize for my bad temper. Please—" she waved her hand toward a chair "—sit down."

"I really don't have the time, Mrs. Vanderberg." But

she walked closer. "I'm on my way to the Pier. If you'll tell me where the children are, I'll—"

"Please call me 'Buffie.' And they're at piano lessons. Hopefully that will take the wind out of their sails." She pushed herself to her feet. "I understand you're finished with Justine's room."

"That's right. I'll be back in a few minutes to finish up the girls' bathroom."

She beamed at Maggie. "Fine, dear. Now I can have the rooms cleaned before the photographers arrive."

"I'll be in Sam's bathroom next. That won't be a problem, will it?"

"Oh, no, no. Sam's rooms will have to be off-limits this afternoon." She frowned. "I just wish he'd return soon. I never thought I'd say it, but I'll be so glad when this is over!"

That makes four of us, Maggie thought, leaving the house. Sam, Lou, Buffie and herself. But she also worried about what the rest of the summer was going to be like. At least she had jobs lined up.

Tomorrow she would measure and bid a family-room addition for a couple who'd called a few days ago, and she would check with Greg to see if the paper for the condominiums was in. She'd go over her supplies, verify her schedule and try to avoid brooding about what kind of summer it would be if she allowed herself to love Sam.

SAM'S BATHROOM COUNTERS had been emptied and the room cleaned by the time Maggie was ready to start work in there. Divided into thirds, the room had storage space opposite the sink, a toilet around the corner and a divided area that held an ivory-tiled *Jacuzzi*. Sam's navy bathrobe hung from the hook behind the door. Maggie touched it, holding a fold in her hand for a brief moment before moving her equipment into the bedroom.

His room was neat in a bare sort of way. The bed was made with a quilt in shades of beige and there wasn't a trace of dust on the wood floor. Clean enough for a Quaker, Maggie thought, and a perfect place to unroll and cut the paper. She was on her knees, enjoying the quiet, when she heard voices in the hall.

"Maggie?" Elena called.

"In here," she answered.

Elena and Franco stepped into the room, then stopped when they saw the paper blocking their path.

"Darling," Franco said, "you are working yourself to the bone. Our Sammy can't really meant to have you continue this way."

Maggie laughed. "It's my *job*, Franco. I get paid to do this."

"Leave her alone, Franco," Elena ordered. "We came to see if you wanted to go swimming with us. The photographers are coming this afternoon and we're going to disappear."

Maggie gestured toward the bathroom. "Thanks, but I can't. I have to finish this today."

"Why?" Franco's expression was nonchalant.

"Because I promised Sam this job would be done today, and it's going to be."

"Admirable." Franco sighed. "I hope you will take time off to attend the performance tomorrow night."

Maggie hesitated. Last night she'd agreed to go with Sam, but now she wondered if she should. "I was planning to," she said ambiguously.

He clapped his hands. "Bravo. Elena and I will do our best to see you enjoy the music, won't we, love?"

She rolled her eyes. "Especially after the rehearsal this morning. He was so wild!" She took Franco's hand. "Now let's let Maggie go back to work. And," she added, "let's be very quiet so the children don't follow us."

"They're back?" Maggie said.

"Unfortunately," said Franco as he and Elena left the room.

Maggie finished cutting and rolled the paper into tubes before grabbing one of her buckets and going downstairs.

"Can I have some dishwashing soap, Lou?"

Lou looked up from frosting a chocolate cake. "You shouldn't be cleaning anything, Maggie. There are all sorts of people around here who are paid to do that."

"I know. I have a project to keep the girls occupied for a few hours."

"That's sweet of you, honey, but aren't you trying to finish up today?"

"Well, let's just say I owe Buffie a few minutes of peace and quiet from Julie and Justine."

Lou chuckled. "Lately wherever there's trouble, those children are finding it. Right now they're outside with the dog. I picked up Lassie from the vet's on our way home and the kids are trying to keep her away from the tennis court." She pointed the chocolate-coated spatula at the sink. "The soap's under there. Help yourself."

"Thanks," said Maggie, bending over to open the cabinet. "I saw something when I was at the Pier that I thought would keep the kids from giving their grandmother a nervous fit."

"Sam should be back soon. That will help." She smiled at Maggie, waiting for a reaction.

Maggie kept her expression bland. "Oh?"

"You can't fool me, Maggie. There's something going on between you and Sam. I won't pry, but I hope you and Sam work things out. This place needs you."

Maggie poured half the soap into the bucket. "Nonsense. Sam doesn't need anything in his life besides what he has now."

"Who says?" Sam came out of the living room, holding a batch of papers in one hand.

Maggie kept her voice light. "Aren't you the man who has everything?"

He looked surprised. "I've never thought of myself that way."

Lou waved the spatula at him. "Well, right now you have two children who are driving everyone crazy. If I'd known you were home I'd have sent them to you."

"Why do you think I was hiding in my office?" Sam looked at Maggie. "Are you washing dishes?"

Maggie realized she was still holding the bottle. She put it under the sink and grabbed the handle of the bucket. "I had an idea to keep the girls busy outside."

He tossed the papers on the love seat. "Come on. I'll help."

"I thought you were working."

"Hiding," he corrected. "I'm to stay clean and presentable until the photographer arrives."

Lou called after them as they left the kitchen, "Try not to muss him up, Maggie."

"I wish you would," Sam murmured. He gave Maggie a quick kiss on the lips, just enough to jumble her thoughts, and pushed the door open for her. "Show me what you're up to."

The humidity was heavy and there was little breeze from the ocean. The children, oblivious to the heat of the July sun, ran around the house. Maggie filled the bucket from the outside water faucet and swished the mixture of soapy water with her hand.

The girls ran over. "Where's Ben?"

"Gone," Maggie said. "You drove him to it."

"Is he coming back?"

Maggie laughed. "Probably not in this lifetime."

"How about 'Hi, Dad'?" Sam said.

"Hi, Dad," they chorused.

Justine giggled. "We told Ben our secret, but he wouldn't believe us."

"And he told us to mind our own business," Julianne added.

"Smart guy," said their father.

Maggie was anxious to get back to work upstairs. "Justine, go over to my car and get the package that's on the back seat."

"Okay," the child said. She and Julie ran off toward the driveway.

"What's going on?"

"Your kids are threatening Buffie's mental health. I told her I'd try to help. They were into her diamonds this morning."

"Uh-oh."

Moments later the girls stood entranced as Maggie unwrapped two large wands with nets attached. "You have to promise to stay out of Grandma's jewelry first."

"We do," Justine said.

Julianne nodded, her eyes solemn.

"Okay. I saw these in a shop at the Pier today when I went to get lunch. Anybody want to guess what they are?"

"Kites?" Julianne ventured.

Maggie held a wand and dipped the net into the soapy water. She lifted it up and slowly pulled the net through the air, creating a giant bubble almost as big as a child. Lassie barked and tried to bite the bubble as it floated through the air.

"Holy mackerel!" Justine cried. "Thanks!"

Maggie handed the girls the wands. "Be gentle, and be careful not to get the nets twisted, okay?"

Sam threw his arm around Maggie's shoulder. "Thank you, Maggie. You didn't have to go to the expense. I'll pay you for them."

"No," she said. "It's a gift."

Before the adults could move away the girls blew two bubbles at them.

"Trapped," Sam said.

"But not for long," Maggie said, and popped the bubble that was in her way, while the girls groaned. "I have to go back to work." She ducked out of Sam's embrace.

"Ah," said Sam. "What a practical person you are."

"I'm anxious to finish up here." Maggie looked up at him, hoping she could divorce herself from her feelings long enough to get the job done.

He frowned at her. "I wish we could spend more time together."

"Me, too."

"Let's take the summer, Maggie, and spend it together."

"I can't." If she fell any deeper in love with the man she'd never be able to end the romance on Labor Day. It was hard enough to deal with now.

"Are you that busy working this summer?"

"I have a lot of work lined up, Sam. I can't just take the summer off to play."

"But you're going to the symphony with me."

"Yes, but—"

"No buts." He touched her shoulder so she couldn't walk away. "You promised," he said. "Lou is fixing a special picnic dinner for us and we'll eat on the beach before the performance."

She stalled. "We've been sharing a lot of picnics lately."

"I'm not complaining." He smiled. "Besides, it should be fun."

"It sounds like it." It sounded wonderful. *Too* wonderful. What on earth did she think she was doing?

"Then you'll come?"

"Yes." *I've been smelling wallpaper paste for too long.*

Sam let out a sigh of relief and let Maggie walk away. It was important that she be with him tomorrow night. He didn't want to question why too closely. Later, when his life was his own again, he could decide what he wanted to do about Maggie McGuire. Was this love or lust? A man needed time to think.

"Sam!"

He looked up to see Buffie waving from the back door.

"What?"

"The magazine people phoned. They're down at the Pier and they're lost. I told them you would meet them and lead them here."

"Fine. Where are they?"

"Parked in front of the movie theater."

"Okay." He called to Maggie. "Do you want to go for a drive with a wealthy playboy?"

"He can wait."

"No, he can't. He's not very patient." His smile faded. "It's been a fast two weeks."

"That was the deal."

"There's still my bedroom. You'll have to come back to finish that. And you'll still get the bonus I promised."

She nodded, but felt awkward about taking extra money from him now. *Purely business*, she reminded herself. *Think of it as just another job*.

Sam fished the car keys out of his pocket. "We'll talk when I get back. We haven't argued about tonight yet."

"Tonight?"

"Yeah." He waved and walked away.

Maggie walked back to the house, wishing she could join the girls. They looked as if they were having so much fun. She thought she could spend the rest of the afternoon creating giant bubbles and watching them sail across the lawn.

"Maggie, dear, I want to thank you," Buffie said.

"Do you think the bubble blowers will keep the kids busy for a while?" She slipped through the screen door Buffie held open for her.

"One can only hope so." The older woman let the door shut and followed Maggie into the kitchen. "Did you have lunch?"

Maggie nodded. "Yes. I bought a sandwich while I was out."

"Well," Buffie said uncomfortably, not sure what to think of the calm young woman in front of her, "let me know if there's anything else you need."

"Okay," Maggie promised, and went upstairs. From the opened windows she could hear the children giggling. Even Lassie sounded happy, her excited yips echoing the girls' laughter. Again she wished she could play with them.

Instead she would fight the logistics of hanging paper in a bathroom, her last room at Sam's. Was she crazy to go out with him again? Was she insane to make love to him, to continue this affair? She loved making love with him, loved being desired and adored. But the word "love" hadn't been mentioned between them. Should it be? It gave her something to think about while she worked.

For the next couple of hours she measured, cut, trimmed and leveled to the sounds of Huey Lewis and his rock and roll. It cheered her up.

Buffie peered into the bathroom. "Would you turn that down, dear? I'm giving a tour."

"Sure." Maggie stepped off the stool and twisted the dial on the radio. There were unfamiliar voices in the hall.

"I like it," said Sam. He stood in the bathroom door and looked at the walls around the sink. "No Canadian duck border, right?"

"Right. Just beige and navy diamonds."

"Good." He looked pleased with himself.

"Shouldn't you be having your picture taken?" She grabbed her sponge and stepped back on the stool.

"I think they're through with me. I've been posed on the deck, the tennis court, in the kitchen, the living room and my library."

She couldn't help teasing him. "Did you look handsome?"

He shrugged. "I faked it."

"I'll make sure to buy the copy of *New England Life* with your picture on the cover."

"Have dinner with me tonight. I have to attend a gathering after the race this evening, but it won't be late. Let me take you out for lobster somewhere."

"No, Sam." She bent to pick up another section of paper.

"Come to the race. Cheer me on."

"You're kidding."

"The old guys like it when the women scream for us."

She gave him a doubting look. "I'll think about it." She didn't tell him she would be there, anyway, cheering for Bobby.

"Good. Then I'll hose myself off and we'll go out to eat."

"No."

"Why not?"

"I'm tired and dirty and don't want another late night." She smiled at him. "But thanks for the offer."

"*Miami Vice.*"

"What?"

"The kids told me that's your favorite show. You don't want to miss Don Johnson."

She wiped her hands on the sides of her pants. "They're all reruns."

"It probably doesn't matter to you." He came closer. "Be honest."

"Well," she said, grinning. "I try not to moan out loud."

His voice was low. "I hadn't noticed."

Maggie felt her face grow warm. Sam looked as if he was going to kiss her. "Go away. Someone could hear you."

"I don't care." But he lowered his voice to a whisper as he stepped closer. "I took my tux to the cleaner's today. I went to work this morning because I couldn't wait to see you."

"That doesn't make sense."

"I was afraid I'd want to carry you off and make love to you on my jacket again and I wouldn't be able to control myself." He pulled her off the stool and into his arms. "I'm not sure I can now."

Maggie's objections melted as he kissed her. Warmth invaded her body and she wound her arms around his neck and held him to her as her lips teased his tongue.

He groaned. "I want you, Maggie. But there are four people out there who expect drinks on the deck before they leave."

"Duty calls?" she murmured against his mouth.

"Before I can play host I'll have to go stand in the bedroom and count to fifty." With a wry look he released her and left the bathroom.

In a few minutes Maggie heard his voice mingle with the others. Then there was silence, and she turned the radio back up.

The cuts behind the toilet required all her concentration, and she tried to push Sam to the back of her mind while she finished the wall. But thoughts of him kept intruding. He was certainly cheerful this afternoon, she noted. But, then, he was probably happy to see the end of the festival in sight. Two more days and his life would be back to normal. Two more days and she'd still be in love.

ELENA CROSSED her long legs in front of her and admired her feet. "What do you think of the new shoes Franco bought me today?"

"Black sandals?" Sam leaned against the deck railing, his back to the ocean, and looked at Elena's slim legs. There was an amazing amount of tanned skin showing from some kind of white dress that looked like a T-shirt.

"Why not? They're handmade. We found them in a little shop in Wakefield."

Sam began to relax, glad the magazine people were gone. He checked his watch. Only five o'clock. He would still be able to run in the race tonight and could hardly wait. Buffie was in her room, dressing for the rehearsal party she was planning to attend tonight. "Where's Franco?"

"In the kitchen helping Lou mix up another batch of drinks." She leaned forward and helped herself to a juicy pink shrimp from the tray in front of her. "Aren't you going to eat?"

He shook his head. "I'm running in a race in an hour, remember?" He crossed his arms over his chest. "Don't you have an early rehearsal?"

"Later. I can't believe Franco's so calm about this. He's usually a maniac the night before a performance."

Sam kept his thoughts about Franco's mental health to himself. He obviously had different opinions from Elena. He thought Franco was a maniac most of the time.

"The house is beautiful, Sam," Elena continued. "*Now* what are you going to do?"

"What do you mean?"

"Well," she drawled, "at first I thought Buffie had invited me up here to see what kind of wife material I'd make. She didn't seem to realize I was in love with Franco. Or maybe she thought it wasn't serious and I'd take one look at you and the Italian would pale in comparison."

"What?"

"Oh, I know you were oblivious to it." Her look showed she thought men were ridiculously ignorant of such things. "Especially when I saw you and Maggie together. Quite a couple you make."

"Thank you," he said when he found his voice.

"Usually when a man remodels his house it's for a purpose."

"Not because the old roof leaks?" He was half-serious.

She shook her head. "Not by a long shot. It goes deeper than that." She helped herself to another shrimp and wiped her fingers delicately on a cocktail napkin before continuing. "You're getting ready for a change."

"Don't give me that midlife crisis crap." What was taking Franco and Lou so long to return?

"No. The nest has been redone." She waved her hand toward the living room. "Nice new sticks and mud. Are we getting ready for a new mama bird?"

"I don't think that's what Buff had in mind."

"Guess again, sweetheart. It's *exactly* what she had in mind, only the bird she picked is flying off to Montana on Sunday."

"With Franco."

She shrugged. "With or without. I love him madly, but he's not too keen on nest building and I'm discovering I'd like to sit down and keep a few eggs warm."

He eyed her empty glass. "Why are you telling me this?"

"Because your mother-in-law can't be too thrilled that her plans haven't worked out, and I'll bet my last tail feather she tries to keep your nest empty a while longer. Until the right bird comes along, that is."

He laughed. "How many drinks have you had this afternoon, Elena?"

She smiled and toasted him with her empty glass. "Tweet, tweet."

He laughed, though he didn't want to encourage her. He wasn't too thrilled having anyone make such personal remarks about his life. Except Lou, who was easy to ignore. Then there was Maggie, who was harder to overlook. But what if Elena was right? Could Buffie be hoping to get him a wife? Why would she bother?

The question answered itself. Because she thought the girls needed a mother. Because she worried. Easy answers, Sam knew. But what of Maggie? Had she sensed something from Buffie that would make her want to back away?

Franco returned with a fresh pitcher of drinks, but Sam, lost in his own thoughts, didn't pay any attention. He didn't need a mama bird, he told himself. Just someone to fly around with. The truth was a little harder to swallow. Sam knew he was falling in love with Maggie McGuire and he couldn't ignore it any longer.

"Has anyone seen Maggie?" His voice shook slightly as the rest of the group appeared on the deck.

Lou answered. "She packed up the car a few minutes ago. I'm sure she's gone by now."

"What'd I tell you, Sam? She's flown the coop," Elena announced. "Someone pass me that pitcher."

IT WAS OVER. One final shove to close the tailgate of the station wagon and Maggie was finished and ready to be on her way. She looked back to the house before getting into the car, considering going back to say good-bye to Sam.

He'd only argue about tonight, she thought. And she

was dirty and tired. *He's seen you dirty and tired for two weeks*, said a little voice inside.

The yard was quiet, the children nowhere in sight. Maggie slid behind the wheel and slammed the door. Maybe she would see Sam at the race tonight. After all, he'd asked her to go. She turned the key in the ignition and backed the car out of the driveway. Tomorrow was their date for the symphony. And then what?

10

"C'MON, BOBBY!" Maggie cheered as her brother ran past her on the street, only fifteen feet away from the finish line. He looked over and waved, sweat dripping from his neck and down his bare back as he jogged with several of his friends toward the end. About thirty runners had finished the race; Maggie overheard someone in the crowd say there were two hundred left to arrive. She waited with the large group of spectators edging the sidewalk to cheer every runner who raced, limped or staggered the last few yards of the ten-mile competition.

Maggie kept looking down the roped-off street, waiting to see Sam appear around the corner. It had taken her about five minutes after she'd arrived home to decide to watch the end of the race. She had to laugh at herself. She'd been sad after finishing the job at his house. For a moment she'd felt as if she would never return. But two and a half hours later, here she was standing on a curb in Narragansett, cheering for a lot of half-naked, good-looking men as they ran past. The only trouble was that the man she most wanted to cheer for, alias Bachelor of the Year, hadn't yet arrived.

"Hey, Aunt Maggie!"

Maggie looked around to see Ben waving at her in the crowd across the street. She waved back and watched as he crossed the empty road and came over to stand beside her.

"Did you see Uncle Bob? He had a really good time."

"I sure did. He looked like he was in pretty good shape. Why aren't you running tonight?"

"Dad wanted me to run with him, but I didn't."

"Why not?"

He shrugged. "I dunno. Just didn't feel like it."

"Where's your mother?"

"On the other side of the finish line, buying everyone lemonade. You want me to get you some?"

"No, thanks. I'll just wait here and cheer."

Ben looked doubtful. "If you're waiting for Dad, it'll be awhile."

Maggie just smiled. "Sam's running in it, too."

"Oh." The teenager seemed uncomfortable. "Here's Mom," he said. "I'll bet she wants to talk to you."

Maggie silently agreed. She knew her sister wouldn't rest until she'd heard all about the party last night. "Hi, Pat."

"You rat. You didn't call me." Patsy, holding two cups of lemonade and dressed in a bathing suit and shorts, edged through the crowd to stand beside her sister.

"Nice to see you, too."

Pat grinned. "I didn't miss Joe's big finish, did I?"

Ben answered. "No, Mom. These are still college guys. The old guys won't be along for another twenty minutes."

"Here's your drink. I won't tell your father you called him an old guy if you'll go keep an eye on your sisters." She offered the other cup to Maggie as Ben disappeared into the crowd. "Want to share?"

"Sure."

"Are you waiting for Sam?"

"How'd you know that?"

"Just a lucky guess. You have an anxious look on your face and you keep peering down the road to see if the runners are coming."

Maggie smiled and handed the lemonade to her sister. "Am I that transparent?"

Pat didn't take her gaze from Maggie's face. "How serious is it?"

"I'm not sure." Maggie thought of the long hours of lovemaking she and Sam had shared. "It's been—" she searched for the right word "—*special*, not something I thought I'd ever have again, but—"

"But what?"

"Not now, okay?" She felt uncomfortable discussing it, even though their words were masked by the crowd's cheers as another group of runners rounded the corner.

Pat shaded her eyes with one hand. "None of them are ours," she said, sighing. "What'd you wear to the party?"

"The lavender."

"Good for you, Margaret Jean. That dress is almost x-rated."

"It's not that bad."

"Speaking of bad, I heard some news about your old partner."

Maggie took the lemonade back and took a sip. "Fanny?"

Patsy nodded. "I just ran into her husband a few minutes ago. He and the kids are here to cheer on his girlfriend. She's an aerobics teacher at one of the health clubs and they're getting married as soon as the divorce is final."

"Good for him. What'd he say about Fanny?" *Maybe she was eaten by sharks off the coast of a Hawaiian island.*

"The guy she left with from *here* dumped her for someone else and now she wants to come home, but nobody wants her back."

This was more satisfying than the shark fantasy. "So what is she going to do?"

"She's working in a gift shop. She sent the kids a picture and she looked like she'd gained about thirty pounds."

"Guess she spent our profits on food," Maggie said. "Revenge is sweet, although I shouldn't feel that way, I guess."

"Why not?" Pat demanded as the crowd started applauding several runners. "You have the right."

But Maggie's attention was focused on another runner jogging toward the finish line. "That's Sam!" He looked good, even after running ten miles on a hot July evening. He wore black nylon shorts and a gray sweat-dampened T-shirt. His hair was wet, as if somewhere alone the route he'd had a chance to pour water on himself. The crowd applauded.

"Yay, Winslow!" Maggie cheered, until he heard her voice and found her in the crowd. His face broke into a surprised smile and he waved.

He called something as he ran past.

Maggie turned to Patsy. "I couldn't hear. What did he say?"

"Little sister," Patsy said, taking Maggie by the shoulders and turning her away from the street. "This is the part where you go behind the finish line and tell a panting, sweaty, smelly man how wonderful he is to be in such great shape and then, before he tries to hug you, you pick up a hose and spray him with water."

"YOU'RE NOT SITTING with us?" Buffie watched Sam examine the contents of the picnic basket that rested on the kitchen counter.

"No. I'm going to have dinner with Maggie on the beach." He opened the refrigerator and removed a bottle of wine.

Buffie noted the label. "Pouilly-Fuissé? How nice."

"I thought so," he said mildly. Sam carefully tucked the bottle into the basket. "We're going early. Aren't you dining with the Aldriches and the Sears?"

"Yes, but—"

He didn't want to hear any objections. "Lou will be here with the girls, so everything's all set."

"I wish Franco and Elena had let us prepare a light supper for them," she complained, obviously displeased with the way the evening was starting.

He picked up the basket and the cooler beside it and bent to kiss Buffie's cheek. "They were both too nervous to eat, I think. Elena was biting her nails and Christofaro looked wild."

"My dear, have you minded the company too awfully much? I so wanted this week to be a success." Her face crinkled into worried lines.

"It's been *different*, Buff. And how could it not be successful? Tickets are sold out, the photographers seemed pleased with their pictures of the house and you and your friends have raised a lot of money for charity. What more could you ask?"

She followed him out of the kitchen. "As long as it wasn't at the expense of your happiness, dear," she said sweetly.

Too sweetly, Sam thought. "What are you up to? You're usually bossing me around, not apologizing."

She sniffed, insulted. "Are you sure you won't join us in the private seats?" He shook his head and she continued, "I just hope you know what you're doing."

Sam looked stern as he warned, "I can take care of my own nest, Buffie."

He saw her eyebrows lift in surprise before he went out the door. There were going to be more changes around his house than just the remodel, he knew. Sam drove away from his home toward the woman he had fallen in love with. He'd spent a sleepless night trying to decide how to keep Maggie in his life. And he'd found the answer.

THERE WAS SOMETHING in the air, and it wasn't music. Sam was nervous, Maggie thought. From the time he picked her up until they reached the beach he hadn't said more than three sentences. Two of them had been about the weather.

The other had been "You look great."

He'd said to dress casually, so she'd worn white, wide-legged slacks and a stylish rose-colored tunic that hung past her thighs. Rose loop earrings and her loose curls gave her a gypsyish air that rivaled Franco's. She'd put on more makeup than usual, too, hoping to look exotic. As she opened the car door and stepped onto the crumbling asphalt parking lot, she sighed. She'd hoped for more than "great."

She walked beside Sam to the gate, where he showed his tickets and she received a program, and then onto the sand. She refused to be nervous; after all, she had lots of practice sitting on the beach. People waved to Sam, and Maggie greeted several friends. Greg waved and Maggie felt cheerful knowing she could repay him next week.

"Do you go to the beach here?" Sam asked as they wound through the crowd.

Sentence number four. Sam was really on a roll now. "Not for years. This was my hangout when I was a teenager, remember? It looks different now."

She looked around with interest. Hundreds of people sat on blankets and in low beach chairs. They weren't facing the ocean, either, which looked odd, because the orchestra would perform on the wide covered porch on the new town pavilion. Many people were enjoying candlelit dinners, complete with lace tablecloths and crystal goblets. Maggie was enthralled watching one couple, obviously in a romantic mood, being served dinner by a tuxedoed waiter. Other people had buckets of take-out fried chicken or boxes of pizza and six-packs of wine coolers. They all looked as if they were having fun, and Maggie wished Sam would lighten up.

"Is this spot all right?"

"Sure."

She helped him lay the old bedspread neatly on the sand, then sat down Indian fashion and watched as he made himself comfortable and began to unpack the basket. He'd shoved the sleeves of his vanilla pullover up to his elbows and kicked off his tennis shoes.

"Sam?"

"Hmm?"

"Is something wrong?"

"Why?" He held the wine bottle in one hand and rummaged through the basket with the other until he pulled out a corkscrew.

"You're quiet tonight."

"Am I?" For a moment he was busy uncorking the wine. "I'm concentrating," he said. "Millionaire playboys aren't used to waiting on themselves."

"Let me help."

He shook his head and smiled. "Oh, no. You just sit there."

"I'm not used to being waited on, either."

"Well, let me spoil you."

Maggie felt spoiled enough already. It had been an incredible two weeks, but there was no way it could last forever. Tomorrow she could send Sam a bill and get on with her life. Her life alone, which she was used to. It was what she'd had up until now and it was what she'd walk away with, so what was the big deal? The big deal, she thought, looking at Sam longingly while he pried plastic wrap off a casserole dish, was that she'd fallen in love. And she shouldn't have let it happen.

Sam tossed a bright paper plate toward her. "Have some lobster. There's silverware in here somewhere, and cocktail sauce." He uncovered strawberries, French bread, a container of butter curls and a colorful pasta salad and put them in front of Maggie. Then he grabbed the wineglasses. "Plastic," he said. "Sorry."

"I'll try to forgive you," she promised, taking a glass.

He poured pale gold wine as she wished he'd smile again. She kept the conversation going during dinner. They joked with the people sitting around them, comparing meals and checking out other people's ideas for picnics. Later she and Sam put the leftover food away as the sun began to set and the musicians gathered on the pavilion. The beach filled with people joining the diners on the sand.

"How many tickets were sold?" Maggie asked.

"Fifteen hundred. Buffie's ecstatic," he said. "There's chocolate mousse for intermission and coffee in the thermos whenever you're ready."

"Thank you, Sam. This has been wonderful. Lou went to a lot of work."

"She wanted it to be special, and so did I."

"I'm glad you talked me into coming tonight." Maggie knew she would never forget this evening. When she was old and sitting around in a housedress in the nursing home, she would dream of the taste of white wine and lobster and she would see a handsome man in a pale yellow sweater and white shorts smile at her with desire in his eyes.

"Here we go," said Sam, motioning to the pavilion. Tiny silver lights outlined the building's roof and sides, while discreet spotlights lit the porch.

An elderly gentleman stood on the stage and introduced himself as the chairman of the festival, and thanked several people for their help. Buffie received loud applause for her contribution as a fund-raiser. Then, in a firmer voice, Franco was introduced. After giving a brief history of the conductor's noteworthy background, the chairman offered praise for the fine job Franco had done conducting the newly formed New England Symphony Orchestra.

Franco appeared onstage to enthusiastic applause. The darkness settled quietly around the crowd as he turned dramatically to the orchestra and raised his arms. Then the music began and Maggie felt its beauty tug at her heart.

The whole evening was magic, she decided during intermission. The classical music wove its spell with a mood-changing beauty. Sam sat beside her, sometimes leaning close so that their arms touched, and Maggie's spine would tingle. The darkness was muted by the full moon and the sparkle of stars, while at the far end of the beach, twinkling lights outlined the Towers, making it look like an enchanted castle.

During intermission Maggie was almost afraid to move for fear the magic would disappear. Sam took a flashlight from the picnic basket and poured coffee from the thermos for both of them. He didn't seem as uneasy, Maggie noted, as if the music had soothed away some of the rough edges.

"Are you enjoying yourself?" he asked.

"I love it, and I didn't expect to," Maggie admitted.

He caressed her back, rubbing her shoulder blades gently. "Are you cold? There's an extra sweatshirt in the basket."

"No, I'm fine." She sipped her coffee and rested her head on his shoulder until Franco took the stage once again.

The second half of the program was a surprise: a complex medley from Joplin, plus other ragtime favorites. The finale, an array of patriotic George M. Cohan songs, was accompanied by fireworks in the sky above the Towers. It was a dazzling spectacle that entranced the crowd. A cheering standing ovation greeted the orchestra as the fireworks faded and the last notes of "Yankee Doodle Dandy" dissolved into the air. As the musicians stood to acknowledge the crowd's approval, Maggie thought she caught a glimpse of Elena and hoped the orchestra realized how wonderful they had been.

"Let's go congratulate them," Sam said. As the crowds of people slipped off into the darkness, Maggie and Sam gathered up their belongings and carried them to the car. A chartered bus waited in the parking lot to take the musicians back to Providence. Then Sam led Maggie to the back of the pavilion through a set a double doors. The orchestra was gathered in a large room, packing instruments and chatting with small groups of people. Elena was standing with several colleagues when Sam and Maggie approached.

"You were wonderful," Maggie told her.

"The crowd loved it," Sam added, hugging the happy musician.

"Thanks, Maggie. They *did* enjoy the performance, didn't they?" Elena held out her hand and Maggie shook it. "I'll say goodbye now. I'm leaving tomorrow, but I hope we'll meet again someday."

Maggie agreed. "Me, too, Elena. I hope Montana is good to you."

"Thanks. Sam, I'll say goodbye in the morning."

"All right. We were going to congratulate Franco, but he looks as if he'll be busy for a while."

"I'll tell him you tried," Elena offered.

The conductor stood in a circle of admiring fans, Buffie among them. Champagne was being uncorked and glasses filled for toasts.

"Are we staying to celebrate?" Maggie hoped Sam would say no.

He took her hand. "If you like."

"No."

They walked back to the car hand in hand, and Sam opened the door for Maggie. "Did you work today?"

"No," she said as he got in. "I could have started a bedroom, but I thought it could wait until Monday."

He started the car and waited his turn in the traffic. "Where to?"

"Home." She unrolled the window. "Will there be another festival next year?"

"They'll probably make it for two nights, since sales went so well."

"I loved the fireworks. I didn't expect such a spectacular ending."

"That was my idea," he admitted, pulling onto the road. "I thought the symphony could use a little razzle-dazzle, especially so close to the Fourth of July."

In a few minutes they arrived at Maggie's house. Sam parked the car in front and turned off the engine.

"Come on in," Maggie said, knowing he wanted her to invite him, knowing how much she wanted to. How much more of this could she take? She was only human. By the time she unlocked the front door, she was trembling. She needed this, Maggie told herself. She needed the desire, the wanting, the incredible feeling of joyful response to this man's touch.

"Speaking of razzle-dazzle," Sam murmured against the back of her neck. "I have a few more ideas about how to end this evening." He shut the door behind him.

"Corny, Sam." Maggie moved away from him and turned on the lamp.

He smiled. "I thought it might interest you."

"Oh, yeah?"

"Yeah." He took her in his arms and kissed her lightly on the lips.

"No fireworks," she lied. "No razzle-dazzle."

His gray eyes crinkled at the corners. "Liar," he said affectionately.

She remained in his embrace and looped her arms around his neck. "Shouldn't we discuss your next fund-raising project?"

"That's true." He nibbled her earlobe. "I've been meaning to talk to you about that." He kissed her again, his lips warm and hard, and Maggie pressed her body against his. When he broke off the kiss he looked down at her and smiled. "I think we should take off all of our clothes first."

"Why?" She was so content. Her body felt relaxed and crazy at the same time.

"I talk better when I'm naked. I think it's something you should know about me."

She pretended to think it over. "In that case, maybe you'd better be quiet and let me do all the talking."

But his hands were under her shirt, busy caressing her bare back. His lips found her neck and left a tingling trail to her earlobe. "Still want to say something?" he whispered. She knew he could feel her tremble in response.

"Yes," she replied. She felt him stop, suddenly tense, as if he thought she would tell him goodbye. "Take me to bed."

He sighed, slipping his hands lower to cup her buttocks. "Sweetheart, you took the words right out of my mouth."

They took their time. Clothes dropped slowly, garment by garment to the floor. Fingertips traced erotic patterns on exposed skin, while lips met and paused and danced together in perfect timing. When Maggie slowly folded back the covers on her bed in a formal gesture, Sam enjoyed the beauty of the silent invitation.

They made love as if trying to learn a lifetime of sexual patterns in one night, as if by moving slowly the mating would mean more, would go deeper into the heart. As if it could. He claimed Maggie's body with thrusts that were slow and sure, as if he needed to ensure that every pore was filled. Maggie met him with her own strength, her insides stroking his hard length with every move he made. When the climax came it was in unison, a mutual explosion in perfect harmony.

SAM ROLLED onto his side, keeping Maggie with him. "That," Sam said on a sigh, "was incredible."

"Um," she agreed, her body at peace. She reached up with a loving hand to brush the hair off his forehead. A shaft of light from the living room outlined his face and she watched him smile. She longed to open the bedroom window and let the air cool her skin, but she didn't have the energy to move, and Sam still held her, so she wouldn't even try. Moments later he closed his eyes and fell asleep, and Maggie slipped out of his arms and into the bathroom. She scrubbed the makeup from her face and, returning to the bedroom, opened the window. But when she climbed into the bed, Sam awakened.

"We need to talk," he said sleepily.

"We do?" A sense of foreboding made goose bumps rise on her skin, but she kept her voice light. "You mean now that you have your clothes off?" She slid next to him under the sheet and hoped she was only imagining the serious tone in his voice.

"Exactly. I had to get my courage up first."

She laughed. "Is that what you call it?"

He didn't smile. "That's not what I meant." He touched her cheek. "Thanks for coming to the race last night."

"You're welcome."

"I didn't expect there would be anyone to cheer me across the finish line."

"Spraying you with the hose was fun, too. I should have brought my camera."

"Why? To prove I finished the race?"

She wriggled closer. "To take up where *New England Life* left off."

"They wanted my house, not me." He draped his arm around her and held her against him. "I didn't get much sleep last night."

Maggie couldn't resist brushing her lips across his collarbone. "Why don't you sleep here?"

"We need to talk, remember?" He kissed her lightly. "I was awake most of the night, trying to figure out how we could spend the summer together."

"Sam, you know I can't—"

"Marry me, Maggie."

She lay there in shock. "But...why?"

"What kind of a question is that?" He stared at her. "Because we love each other." Into the silence he added, "At least, I love you."

"I need to get dressed," Maggie said, and rolled out of Sam's arms. She grabbed her robe off the chair and wrapped herself in it at the foot of the bed. *I'm in love with this man. He's just asked me to marry him. Now what?*

"All right," Sam said. "Since you don't seem to have anything to say, I'll just continue with this." He sat up, propped the pillow against the headboard and looked as if he wanted to strangle her. "I'm not sure when it happened, but I've fallen in love with you. You've brought something very special into my life and I don't want it to end. Ever. The house will be empty without you, so *marry me*, Maggie."

It was a beautiful proposal and Maggie felt her eyes burn with unshed tears. She swallowed the hard lump in her throat and couldn't tear her gaze away from his face. "I can't, Sam. It just wouldn't work."

"Why not?"

"We're too different."

"Bull. The differences make life more interesting and you know it."

She took a deep breath. "We've only known each other a couple of weeks."

"Do you want more time? I'll give it to you, if it makes you happy. But the proposal still stands."

She shook her head and stared at her clenched fingers. "No, Sam. Look, I've tried from the beginning not to have to say this, but I couldn't." She tried to stop the tears from falling. "I can't have children, Sam."

"Oh, honey, I'm sorry." He eased over close to her and reached to take her hand, but she didn't see the gesture of comfort he offered.

"That's why we haven't had to worry about birth control, you see. And it's why my husband left me."

"I wouldn't leave you, Maggie," Sam said softly. Now it all made sense: the scene in the supermarket with the two children and the man she called Tony. No wonder Maggie had been upset.

"You don't think so now, but you'll want more children—you're such a good father—and you'll start to resent me." She slid off the bed and began to pace back and forth. Her voice was rough with unshed tears. "I can't go through that again, Sam."

"What do you mean, *again*?"

"I can't go through the rest of my life being reminded that I'm not a whole woman, Sam. I just can't." She couldn't control the tears that edged past her lower lashes. "As long as I'm alone it's okay."

Sam looked incredulous. "You put me in the same category as your ex-husband? Maggie, I *love* you."

"He said he loved me, too." It was a harsh reply, and as she heard herself, she winced.

"Maggie, how many women do you think I've proposed to?"

She didn't think he really wanted an answer, so she stayed silent.

"Two." His voice softened. "I don't go around doing this every day. These past weeks have been—" he stopped as if he'd run out of words. "I can't believe this."

"I'm sorry. It shouldn't have gone this far." She wiped her face with her hands. "I'm sorry I couldn't be what you wanted me to be."

Sam rolled out of bed and started gathering his clothes. "Well, Maggie, you've really done a number on me. There has to be something more to this than not being able to have children. Do you think I asked you to marry me to have more kids? No. I asked you to marry me because I love you. I didn't propose to a room full of unborn babies!"

"That's cruel, Sam."

"Fine," he snapped. "I'm cruel." He pulled on his underwear, then his shorts. "I'm also pretty stupid."

"Sam..."

"There's something else wrong here. I just haven't figured it out yet." He looked around until he found his sweater on the floor.

"There's nothing—"

"Save it, Maggie. You're great in bed." He tossed the sweater over his head. "Maybe I mistook lust for love, after all."

"I didn't want to hurt you," Maggie said as she followed him into the living room.

"You didn't." He found his shoes and put them on, shooting her a humorless grin before opening the front door. His voice was deliberately casual, as if he were talking to a grocery clerk. "Thanks again for the great job you did on the house. I'll be sure to recommend you to all my friends."

With that Sam was gone, and Maggie stood at the window and watched the car's headlights disappear down the street. She never dreamed he would ask her to marry him. The longing to say yes was so strong that she was tempted to run down the street and chase his car like a moon-crazed dog.

She wrapped her robe tighter around her and sank to the couch. There was more at stake than a simple "I do." It had taken a long time to get her pride back after the divorce. She would love to be Sam's wife, to be a mother to those girls, to belong to a family that included Buffie and Lou. But how long could it last? No matter what Sam said now, he would want a Sam, Jr. There were a lot of spare bedrooms in that house and plenty of space for a big family.

She remembered the painful night Tony had come home for dinner and told her he wanted a divorce. Years of trying to get pregnant had resulted in grim mating rituals according to temperature charts and doctor's instructions. But apparently Tony had found a woman who was warm and loving, and he'd announced that with some pride in his voice. When he told her why he wanted a quick divorce the shock made her stomach heave.

"She's pregnant?"

He nodded. "I'm sorry, Meg."

She would try not to throw up at the dinner table. "No. You're not."

"All right, all right. So I'm not," he said, his voice rising defensively. "Living with you these past few years has been pretty rough, you know? I feel I'm trotted out of the barn like some kind of stud horse—"

She exploded. She actually saw red dots in front of her eyes. "Oh, for heaven's sake!"

He continued as if he hadn't heard. "While you just lie there like you're not even in the bed. I think it was better when you tried to fake a little interest, remember? It's no wonder you can't get pregnant! It sure isn't my fault."

Maggie had felt the sting of shame on her burning cheeks and had tried to cover her face with her hands, as if he'd hit her and were going to do it again.

And here I am, hurting myself and hurting Sam. After having so much with Sam, how could she give it up? She curled up in a ball, hugged her knees to her chest and let the tears pour down her face. There was no forgiveness or trust left—she'd used up her lifetime allotment. How could she ever forgive Sam if he walked out on her, too?

SAM SAT in his driveway and looked at his house. There was still a light on in the kitchen—Lou must have left it for him—and the rest was in darkness. He could still smell Maggie's perfume in the car, so he fumbled through the glove compartment for an old pack of cigarettes he'd left weeks ago. He lit a cigarette and rolled down the window. As he stretched his legs along the front seat he thought he could spend the rest of the summer in the car. The idea was more cheerful than going into the house and not seeing Maggie.

Wisps of fog trailed over the grounds and the ocean roared in the distance. Sam felt insulated and alone. He'd been a fool. She couldn't have children, she said. There'd been real pain in her voice, he remembered.

There had been no problem with birth control, so maybe she was telling the truth. But that couldn't be all. There had to be something more than that. He already had two children and was content. Anne had had her tubes tied after giving birth to Julianne and he'd never thought about it again. Until now. Now he just wanted Maggie, but he'd been a fool to fall in love.

We've only known each other a couple of weeks. Those were Maggie's words. Surely he could get over her in the same amount of time and life would go on as before. He tossed the cigarette butt out of the window and took another from the pack. He just wanted to sit in the car awhile longer.

11

"YOU'RE NOT GOING to see him anymore? Are you crazy?" Patsy stood in the kitchen as Maggie poured herself a cup of coffee.

"No." Maggie set the glass pot back inside the coffee maker and leaned against the counter.

"You want to elaborate on that a little? Two nights ago you're cheering his name in the middle of Narragansett and now you're not going to see him anymore? This doesn't make sense." Patsy opened the refrigerator to see if there was anything that could be thrown in the cooler for lunch. "Three cans of diet cola, a carton of mushy strawberries and half a—" she paused to unwrap the wax paper "—moldy Italian grinder. We'll take the cola and pass on the rest." She shut the door and frowned at her sister. "Maybe we should grocery shop after we come back from the beach."

"Or maybe not," Maggie countered. "I'm not up to it."

"Are you up to telling me what's wrong?"

"I don't see what else there is to say, and you're acting too maternal. Any minute now you're going to turn into Mom." Maggie decided she needed plenty of caffeine to survive the morning and took several swallows of the hot coffee.

"I already have," Patsy replied, unperturbed. "Just ask my kids."

Maggie yawned and sat down at the old pine table. She traced the familiar gouge patterns with her index finger while Patsy prowled through the cupboards. She hadn't slept. She'd curled up in bed and turned on the television, letting the noise fill up the silence. Reading hadn't helped, either. Her favorite book, *Gone with the Wind*, was too depressing. Even the title made her cry.

"You look awful."

Patsy didn't know when to quit, Maggie decided. "I stayed up late reading," she fibbed.

"Must have been a sad story. Your eyes are a mess." She sat down across from Maggie and leaned forward. "Speaking of stories, I pried an interesting one out of Ben last night."

Maggie smelled trouble. "I think I'll get my bathing suit on."

"Just a minute. You have to hear this. Seems that Sam Winslow's two kids saw their father kissing you on the beach a few nights ago, at the party you've never told me about. They couldn't wait to tell Ben."

So that's why the two girls had been so excited Friday, Maggie thought. How embarrassing. "So?"

"So what on earth is going on with you and Sam?"

"Nothing anymore." Maggie drank the rest of her coffee and hoped she would feel better soon.

"The creep! Your luck with people is unbelievably crappy."

Maggie sighed. "It's not his fault, Pat."

Patsy's eyes narrowed. "Does that mean it's *your* fault? Are we back to that again?"

"I don't want to get into it."

"Precisely." Patsy wanted to shake her little sister.

"You never want to get into it. Are you going to avoid love and marriage for the rest of your life?"

Maggie stayed silent. Two confrontations in less than twelve hours was too much to bear.

Patsy took a deep breath and continued in a calmer voice. "I have a weird feeling about this. You're in love with Sam—it's been obvious, so don't try to pretend—and now it's over. And you said it's not his fault. My goodness, Maggie—" her voice rose "—that's what you said when Tony left you and married his girl-friend. Is *everything* your fault?"

Maggie rested her head on her arms and stared at her sister. "Some things are. Tony said—"

But Patsy interrupted her angrily. "Tony was *pond scum*. I'm glad you went back to your own name."

"It was part of the deal. He kept the business and his name, I got the house."

"And a neighbor who wanted to go into the paper-hanging business. Lucky you."

"I can't handle this. Maybe I shouldn't go with you today." She set her forehead on the table in an attitude of defeat.

Pat touched her arm in a gesture of apology. "Sweet-heart, that brain of yours deserves to bake in the sun for hours. It sure can't do it any harm."

"GRAMS SAID the music was stu-pen-dous last night. Was it, Daddy?"

At first Sam thought he was on board ship. The waves beneath him turned into his water bed as he awakened to the sound of Justine's voice.

Julianne bounced near his head. "We saw some of the fireworks last night."

The voices continued, but he kept his eyes closed.

"Mr. Christofaro's still asleep. Grandma's crabby. Are you?"

"Lou told us to tell you what time it is."

"Why?" he mumbled, trying to hold on to sleep. The symphony was over, his obligations fulfilled, so why couldn't he stay in bed like a normal miserable person on a Sunday morning? He groaned. He knew he should have stayed in the car.

"Nine-one-three," Justine read from the digital clock.

Sam tried again. "Go away and leave your poor father alone."

"Lou said not to. She has a 'nouncement to make."

Great. He needed to hear more women make announcements. If this trend continued he would go back to work out of self-defense. He got out of bed and threw on last night's clothes while the girls bounced on the bed, then the three of them went downstairs to the kitchen.

Lou grinned and handed Sam a cup of coffee. "You look awful."

"Thanks." He took the cup and sat across from Buffie and Elena at the dining-room table. His daughters wriggled into chairs next to him.

"Good morning, dear. Elena and I were wondering when you'd join us." Buffie, elegant in an peach robe, raised her eyebrows at Sam's appearance.

"Good morning," Sam answered, surprised to see Elena. It wasn't like her to be awake before eleven. "You're up early."

"I'm on my way, Sam," Elena said. "My plane leaves in two hours."

"Franco, too?"

He should have known it would be the wrong thing to say.

Elena shrugged casually, but Sam could see pain in her eyes.

"I think we're about to go our separate ways, at least for a while. Montana sounds better to me than Italy right now."

Buffie spoke, concern in her voice. "Perhaps you shouldn't rush off, dear. Stay through the holiday, at least. Maybe a rest would do you good."

Sam caught the worry in his mother-in-law's voice. She was fond of Elena, he realized.

Elena shook her head. "I may tour Yellowstone Park or perhaps see what Jackson Hole looks like in the summer," she said. "I have some extra time before my classes begin."

"Please feel welcome to visit us again," Sam said. He called to Lou. "The girls said you have an announcement to make?"

Lou turned from the stove and put a platter of bacon on the large island counter. "You can eat first. There's no hurry."

Sam sipped his coffee. "C'mon, Lou. What's going on?"

Lou looked at the girls, who were bursting with excitement, and said, "There's going to be a wedding!"

He choked, and coffee sprayed across the table, perilously close to Buffie's shocked face. Julianne hopped over to pound him on the back until he thought his shoulder blades would splinter. When he could breath again he said, "Thanks, honey. I'm fine now." Then he looked into Lou's beaming face. What the hell was she talking about? She couldn't know he'd asked Maggie to marry him, could she? "Who's getting married?"

"I am," she announced.

Calmer now, Sam sought answers. "Congratulations. Who's the lucky guy?" He waited, wondering in a perverse way if the groom would turn out to be a gardener, Buffie's chauffeur or even Franco.

She beamed. "Will Brent."

"The veterinarian?"

She nodded. "I've been taking Lassie to him for quite a while now, and we've been seeing each other for months—just as friends—until last night." She blushed. "He came over to play cards and keep me company and, well, he asked me to marry him."

Buffie and Elena offered their congratulations as Lou glowed with happiness.

"It's *so* romantic, Daddy," said Justine. "Just like you and Maggie."

"What?" He stared at his cheerful daughter.

"You and Maggie," she repeated patiently. "Julie and me saw you kissing. It looked neat."

Sam heard Buffie clear her throat and Elena choke back a laugh, but he didn't take his gaze from his daughter's face. "And where did you see this?"

"At the beach. When you had that big party. We love Maggie, Daddy."

Julianne couldn't keep quiet. "You can have a wedding, too. Just like Lou and Dr. Brent. He told us we could have a kitten, if you said it would be okay. He has lots and lots and they're free."

Sam sat stunned, trying to find his voice. The conversation had gone from weddings to kissing to kittens, and he was reluctant to discuss all of them. "The only wedding around here will be Lou's. Maggie doesn't work here anymore and that's final."

The girls looked heartbroken. Sam stood and went

over to Lou. He hugged her and said, "I think your news is terrific. And I'd love to give you the wedding here, if you like."

"Thanks, Sam. I'll talk to Will about it."

"What about the kitten?" Justine asked.

"I'll think about it. But only if it's a boy."

MAGGIE LAY on her towel and let the heat soak into her skin. *I should be worrying about skin cancer*, she thought, but she'd rubbed enough lotion on her skin to protect a newborn baby. It was also convenient to hide her swollen eyes behind her sunglasses, since most of her family, ready to celebrate the long holiday weekend, was gathered on the public beach around her. Her parents sat in umbrella-shaded chairs, watching the parade of people who walked along the shore. The Shanty Boys were trying to out bodysurf one another, and Patsy stayed busy passing out food to her daughters and watching Ben watch the girls on the beach.

"Ben, there's a cute one. On the left, in red." Maggie's father pointed.

"Too old, Grandpa."

"Not if you're my age, son."

Maggie listened to the exchange and smiled for the first time all day. She was glad she wasn't home alone, feeling miserable. She wondered if she should call Sam. Maybe they needed to talk. Maggie knew she needed to be thinking less about herself and more about the man she loved. He'd offered her everything she'd ever wanted, but she couldn't give him anything in return. Maggie felt tears burn her eyes. Thank goodness she'd never told Sam she loved him.

"DO YOU THINK there's a billion people here?" Justine looked up at her father as he led her across the street to

Old Mountain Field. She waved to the policeman who'd stopped the traffic so the crowd of people could cross.

"At least. Looks like the whole town's here."

"This is my very best night." Her father made no comment, so Justine kept talking. "I just love the fireworks. Can we sit up close?"

"I don't think it matters."

"I wish Julie wasn't sick. She's gonna miss all the fun. Why'd she hafta throw up? It was disgusting."

Sam tugged her up the slope to the softball field before answering. "She shouldn't have eaten the entire contents of a bag of cheese puffs for breakfast."

Justine recognized Daddy's "disgusted" voice. He'd been a real crab all day. Yesterday, too. What was the big deal? She held his hand tightly as they picked their way along the narrow paths of grass between blankets and chairs. It was almost dark and Justine didn't want to get lost in the middle of a billion people. "Where are we gonna sit? We didn't bring a blanket."

He pointed to the bleachers. "We are *going* to sit over there. Any objections?"

She shook her head, staring up at him. Her sweet daddy wasn't smiling anymore. "Are you sad about Lou?"

"What?"

Justine raised her voice. "Are you sad about Lou?"

"Why on earth would I be sad about Lou?" He grabbed Justine's waist and lifted her onto the third tier of the bleacher. "What's the matter with her?"

Justine waited until he climbed up beside her. "Nothing. I just thought you were sad because she's getting married."

"She'll still be around every day." Gently he asked, "Did you think she was leaving us?"

"No." Justine sighed. "Never mind." It wasn't dark enough yet for the fireworks to start, so Justine gazed at all the people spread out on the field. Sam started talking to somebody he knew sitting near him, but Justine didn't pay any attention. She wanted to see if one of her girlfriends from school was here. Then, if she was lucky, she might get invited to sit with her and maybe her mom and dad would have boxes of pizza or bags of hamburgers and would want to share. Justine sighed again. It was boring to sit in the bleachers instead of on a blanket and not even have anything good to eat the way most of the other people did.

"What's the matter?" her father asked.

"My new jeans are scratchy. They hurt my bottom." When he didn't answer, she added, "Last year was funner than this." Then she saw a familiar teenager walk by with three other boys. "Look, Daddy, there's Ben." She stood up and waved. "Hey, Ben!"

Sam put his arm around her shoulders. "He can't hear you, honey."

Justine watched helplessly as Ben walked past them and into the crowd. She continued to watch him until she saw him stop and bend down to talk to a group of people. One of them was familiar. She wriggled out of her father's grasp. "Maggie's down there. I want to go see her."

"No."

Justine whipped around to stare at Sam. "Why *not*?" Her father turned away, but not before Justine saw the sadness on his face. She looked back over the crowd to where Maggie sat with the group of laughing people.

"Sit down," Sam said softly. "Look." He pointed to the edge of the field. "The fireworks are starting."

Justine slowly did as she was told. A burst of silver stars showered from the sky. She gripped her father's hand in the darkness, hoping he'd feel better. Grown-ups were so weird.

BEEP. "This is Sam Winslow. The paper is coming off the walls in one of the girl's rooms. Your bill won't be paid until the situation is taken care of." *Beep.*

The message was on her answering machine Tuesday when she returned home from work. Sam's voice was sandwiched between the condo contractor saying he'd be ready for her next week and Mrs. Anderson announcing her paper was in. Maggie returned her other calls, set up a tentative schedule for the next two weeks and wondered how she could work in the Winslow house without running into Sam.

She'd spent the morning cleaning out the Pontiac, scrubbing her tools until they gleamed and trying to erase any reminders of the Winslows from her life. She'd inventoried her supplies and picked up five-gallon drums of paste for the condominium project. And she'd Xeroxed a copy of the Winslow contract and enclosed it with the bill she mailed to Sam.

Maggie rewound the tape and allowed Sam's voice to invade the kitchen once again.

IT WAS THE STRANGEST SIGHT, Maggie thought as she studied the wallpaper in Julianne's room. The paper had peeled away from the bottom edge and now stuck out in a haphazard roll.

Buffie and Lou stood next to Maggie, waiting for her reaction.

"Maybe it's the dampness from the ocean. Or the humidity." Maggie didn't know what else to say.

"You will be able to repair it?" Buffie asked.

She nodded. "Yes. If I can't glue the original pieces together I'll use whatever extra paper I can find." She turned to Lou. "You saved the extra rolls, right?"

"They're in the hall closet, honey. I'll go get them for you right now."

The children ran into the room as Lou left. "Maggie!" They raced over to hug her. "We missed you a whole bunch," said Justine.

"I missed you, too," Maggie said, enjoying the affectionate embrace.

"Can you fix my room?" Julie asked.

"I'll try."

"Can we help?"

"Not right now. I'm going to have to concentrate very hard to make this all better." They looked disappointed, so Maggie added, "Give me a little while and then I'll call you, okay?"

Buffie said, "You have your piano to practice, too. Who will go first?"

There was silence.

"Very well," their grandmother stated, "it will be my decision." She guided the reluctant musicians from the room, while Maggie and Lou, carrying rolls of paper, tried not to laugh.

"Those girls aren't the only ones around here who've missed you," Lou said.

"Oh?" Maggie knelt to examine the peeling wall.

"Sam's been an absolute bear to live with." She put a comforting hand on Maggie's shoulder. "And you don't look so good yourself. He's a proud man, Maggie. I don't know what's going on, but I hope you two can work it out."

"Thanks, Lou, but there's nothing to work out. What is it they say?" She smiled grimly as she stood to gather the tools she'd need. "It's 'just one of those things'?"

Lou looked dubious. "All right, if that's the way you want to leave it, but I was selfishly hoping the two of you would—" Maggie winced, and Lou changed the subject. "I have some good news—I'm getting married."

"Lou, that's wonderful. Who's the lucky guy?"

"Will Brent, the vet. We'll be married in September. I take my vacation this month when the girls are off at camp for a couple of weeks, but Will's too busy to get away in the summer."

"Lou, I'm so happy for you," Maggie said. "Will you still work here?"

"Oh, of course. But now that the girls go to school, they need me less and less. I'll try to always be here for Sam, though, until he...doesn't need me."

Until he marries again were the unspoken words Maggie heard. He would marry again, she realized with a jolt. He was a passionate man with a strong sense of family.

"Well," Lou continued, "I hope you'll come to the wedding."

"I'd love to."

"Now I'd better go clean up that kitchen—it'll be time for lunch soon and I still have a mess from breakfast." She started to leave.

Maggie had to know. "Where's Sam?"

"He left early this morning, said something about taking up golf. Either that or he's at work, driving everyone crazy. Do you need to talk to him?"

"Oh, no. Just wondered." *Just hoping to avoid an embarrassing scene.*

"Okay." Lou sighed as she left Maggie alone in the room.

Maggie opened a quart of heavy-duty adhesive and found a small brush in her tool carrier. She hoped she could solve this problem quickly, before Sam returned. She'd never had this happen to her before except once, when the glue had been faulty and several strips of vinyl had pulled loose from the ceiling. But this, Maggie decided as she picked up her bucket, was something unusual.

If this job was ever over it would be a miracle, she thought awhile later as she sponged the paper. She worked hard for her money, just as the song on the car radio this morning had said, and was ready for a break.

Justine slipped into the room and stood behind Maggie. "Hi."

Maggie looked up from the painstaking gluing process. "Hi, hon. Did you finish practicing the piano?"

The child nodded. "Now it's Julie's turn. Are you fixing the wall?"

"Yep. Just a little while longer and it should be as good as new." She felt perspiration trickle down her neck as the room grew warmer and decided she should stand up to see if the window was open.

"It will?"

"That's right. And Julie's room will be pretty again."

When Maggie looked, the child was gone. *Guess she didn't think I was very interesting today. I don't, either,* Maggie decided as she returned to the tedious work.

"WHAT ON EARTH are you two doing over there?"

Justine looked up to see her grandmother standing,

hands on hips, near the foot of the bed. "Uh-oh."

Buffie stepped closer to the corner by the window. "What are you two up to now?"

Justine pushed the wet washcloth behind Julianne's back and gulped with fear. "Don't worry," she whispered to her sister, "I can take care of this." Then, in a louder voice, she told Buffie, "Looking for carpenter ants, Grandma. We saw a big one and we're trying to kill it."

"Let me see."

"Oh, no," Julianne muttered.

Buffie knelt near them and peered into the yellow carpet. "Are you sure that's what you saw? It wasn't a tick, was it?"

"No, I'm sure." Justine hoped her grandmother wouldn't see the wall. This was starting to look like big trouble.

But Buffie was suspicious. "Move," she ordered.

"What?"

"Move away. You both have guilty faces."

Justine didn't think she looked guilty. She wanted to do what she was doing and she didn't feel bad about it at all. But she and Julie reluctantly obeyed their grandmother.

"So," Grams said, staring at the mutilated wall.

The girls stared at it, too. A few more minutes and they would have gotten away with it. Peeling paper without ripping it took a long time.

Julianne elbowed her sister. "I told you we should've waited till night."

Buffie looked as if she'd eaten thunderclouds. "Would either of you like to furnish a satisfactory explanation?"

Julianne looked confused, and Justine hurried to explain, "She wants us to 'fess up."

"Do we have to?"

Their grandmother nodded and sat back on the floor, one sandaled foot tapping impatiently.

"We want Maggie to stay here," Justine said, deciding the only way out was with the truth. "We figured she and Daddy would start kissing again and then they'd get married and we'd have her around all the time."

"Well, well," Buffie said to herself. She stared into space for a moment, then looked back at the girls. "I'm supposed to be getting you ready for camp. We need to finish our shopping, you know."

"Can we do it later?" Justine was hopeful. Grandma hadn't thrown a fit or started lecturing.

"I suppose," Buffie conceded, again staring at the peeling wallpaper. Maggie wasn't at all musically inclined, but still she was a cheerful girl. And good with the children. Loving, like Anne. Buffie looked at her trouble-making granddaughters. "You're going to need help, ladies. Move over."

MAGGIE WANTED to get out of this house. She fought against its comfortable charm, against the ease of slipping into the welcoming pattern of belonging. But she missed Sam's company while she worked, his easy ability to make her feel special. She would not come back to do his bedroom, she decided. She'd hire someone to do it for her if she had to. It wasn't included in the bill she'd sent him, anyway, and once he paid it she would be free. Free of her debt, free of Fanny once and for all.

Finally finished, she stood and took a few steps back.

Once the paper dried there would be no way to tell there had been a problem, but it hadn't been easy. She stretched, satisfied she'd accomplished what she'd set out to do. She tossed her tools into the carrier and was halfway down the stairs, when Buffie called to her.

"Maggie? There's a little problem with the wallpaper in Justine's room."

Maggie turned around and went back upstairs. How could both papers be faulty, she wondered. They were both from the same company, so perhaps it was possible there was a glue problem, after all.

When she examined the peeling paper she said, "I'll have to replace it. Luckily it's practically under the bed and won't show." She shook her head. "This is very odd."

Buffie stood wrapping a cord around the handle of a blow-dryer. Her voice was sweet. "Perhaps you should be using a different kind of paste, dear."

"That's an idea, but this paper is prepasted. I may have to use more glue on the edges if I ever hang this brand again."

After they'd left, Maggie sat on the floor and took a better look. If she had to guess she'd say the paper had been deliberately loosened. But why would the girls damage their beautiful new bedrooms? It remained a puzzle, and although Maggie didn't want to get the children in trouble, she debated whether or not to suggest the possibility of sabotage to Lou.

The girls gave her no opportunity. They couldn't seem to stay out of the room, changing their clothes over and over again, rearranging the furniture in Barbie's dream house, borrowing the tape measure a hundred times and reading stories to Maggie, making up the words they didn't know or hadn't memorized. At one point Maggie wondered if she should lock them out.

When she was through, Maggie was hungry, hot and overtired from several sleepless nights. She never wanted to see another peach flower again as long as she lived.

"We're going down to the beach. Wanna come?" Justine asked.

"Can't, honey. Sorry." *I'm going home to die in my lawn chair.*

Julianne gave Maggie a hug. "Daddy's taking us as soon as we get our suits on. Are you sure you can't come?"

"I'm sure." Maybe she could get out of there while Sam was busy swimming.

"Hey, Maggie, this looks neat!"

Maggie looked up to see Justine poke her finger into the section of repaired wallpaper. "Don't!" she yelled. An hour and a half of painstaking work could go down the drain in an instant. "Get away from there right now!"

"What's going on in here?" Sam stood in the doorway, dressed only in white cotton bathing trunks; a towel was looped around his neck. His voice was aggravated as he gazed down at Maggie. "Is there a problem?"

A sheepish Justine joined her wide-eyed sister on the bed and looked as if she would burst into tears.

"Scat," he said to them. "Wait outside for me."

They did as they were told, while Maggie knelt to examine the wall. A few minor touches and it was fixed. She could feel Sam's eyes on her back and wished she could leave the room as quickly as the children had.

His voice was cool. "You could have told me the truth."

She stood and faced him. "I thought I had."

"That's not what I meant."

"What?" She'd already peeled off private layers of her heart and showed him the scars. How much more truth did he expect?

"You didn't want to put up with a ready-made family."

"What are you talking about?"

"It's your right," he said stiffly. "And I don't blame you, but I would have appreciated the honesty. I won't let the girls annoy you again."

"Sam, that's not how I feel. I've wanted to tell you—"

"Maybe you were right, Maggie," he interrupted. "It was too soon for the two of us—we really didn't know each other at all, did we?"

Maggie stared at him. "You've had my honesty, Sam, from the very beginning. You were the one who wanted more. And you were the one who walked away. I tried to tell you how I felt, why I couldn't—" She stopped, realizing what she had to say wasn't going to make any difference to the man standing in front of her. "I'm sorry, Sam. I didn't want to hurt you and I didn't want to get hurt, either."

"Well, it didn't work out that way, did it?" He felt no anger, only sadness. He wanted to take her in his arms, but clutched the ends of the bath towel, instead.

"No, it didn't," she agreed. She looked away, gathering her equipment for what she hoped would be the last time. When she looked up again Sam was gone.

12

"THE HOUSE has been so quiet this week with Elena and Franco gone."

"You miss Franco?" Sam raised his eyebrows at his mother-in-law. "Are you crazy? He threw such a fit when he woke up and realized Elena had left I thought I'd have to drag him down to the beach and throw him into the surf." He stretched out on the living-room couch and unfolded the Friday evening paper. "How can you miss noise like that?"

"Well," Buffie sniffed, sorting various lengths of yarn. "I did so enjoy the excitement of having the house filled with people."

"I noticed. So did Lou," he added. "I hope she's enjoying her vacation."

"Maggie and that nice nephew of hers added an extra dimension, also, don't you think?"

A dimension I'd like to forget, he thought. "Do you have to talk while you do needlepoint?"

"It's the fog. It makes me nervous."

"I hate it, too." Sam looked out the window at the rolling mist that surrounded the house. "But it comes with the territory," he said, thinking of the ocean, only a few hundred yards away.

"Yes," she said with a sigh. "That's a problem around here."

He rested the paper on his chest and looked at Buffie. "That sounded cryptic. Obviously," he said dryly, "you have something on your mind."

She pushed the yarn off her lap and tossed the needlepoint canvas onto a nearby end table. "There are a lot of memories in this house, Sam. But it's time to move on."

He put down the paper and sat up, arms folded behind his head. "What are you trying to say, Buffie?"

"The pictures upstairs—the ones of Anne—they have to go."

"I thought you'd be pleased I'd had them rehung." He'd even hired a young woman from a local art gallery to arrange the photographs for him.

"Oh, my dear," she said, her voice husky, "I do appreciate it, but the idea of this whole remodeling project was to give you a fresh start—a new outlook, if you will. Certain photographs belong in the girls' rooms, others should be stored."

"Wait a minute." Sam frowned. "Get back to the part about my new outlook. What exactly are you talking about?"

"You've been in a rut, Sam, ever since Anne died. I didn't want you to make the same mistakes I did when Harry drowned. By being totally devoted to my child and my own little life I missed out on loving again." She took a deep breath. "It's too late for me now, dear, and I'd hate to see you wake up some morning and realize you are very much alone and likely to remain that way until you're laid in your coffin—" She put her hands over her face.

"Buffie, for heaven's sake, don't cry...." He went over to her and knelt in front of the chair, fumbling in his pocket for a clean handkerchief, which he pressed into her hands. "Here, Buff, calm down."

"Thank you." She wiped her face and looked embarrassed. "I'd hoped to avoid such a scene. I just don't want to see you end up alone."

"I don't intend to." He thought of those nights he'd spent making love to Maggie. "I haven't been alone all the time."

She patted his hand. "You're in love with Maggie. Why aren't you doing something about it?"

"Why aren't you minding your own business?"

"When have I, Sam?" she asked unperturbed. "Why don't you marry that nice girl and have some fun?"

He thought about whether or not to answer, decided it didn't make any difference now. Besides, it might make Buffie feel better to know he'd considered remarrying. "I've asked her. She said no."

"For heaven's sake, Sam, why not?" Her face clouded over. "It didn't have anything to do with me, did it?"

"No. She said it was because she can't have children."

"The poor dear. I suppose you told her Anne had a tubal ligation because neither of you wanted more than two children."

Sam shook his head. "I didn't even think about it. Maggie's infertility didn't seem to be the real reason she said no. I just didn't believe her." He stood up and looked out the window into the night.

"And you haven't tried again?" She was incredulous at his revealing silence. "My dear, luckily your children inherited their persistence from my side of the family."

He turned back to her. "What do the girls have to do with this?"

"Follow me." She hopped to her feet and waved her hand. "You're going to be impressed."

"I just kissed them good-night and put them to bed," Sam grumbled. They climbed the stairs and stood in the hall.

"Girls! Come out here, please!"

Two doors opened and two children hurried out of their rooms. "What's goin' on?" Justine asked.

"We must confess," their grandmother announced. "Who shall go first?"

"Confess what?" Sam looked from one guilty face to another.

"You go first, Grams," Julianne said.

Buffie chuckled. "All right, so I shall." She faced Sam proudly. "I'm afraid I've contributed to a small act of vandalism, purely for unselfish reasons. I helped the children peel the wallpaper from the walls in an attempt to keep Maggie here at this house."

"Yeah, Dad," Justine said. "We wanted her to come back so you could get married."

"Whose idea was this?" Sam almost wished he'd thought of it himself.

"So you see, Sam," Buffie explained later, back in her chair in the living room, "your children didn't give up after one defeat."

"And neither should I." He nodded to her. "That *is* what you're trying to tell me, isn't it?"

He dialed Maggie's phone number the next morning, after Buffie and his daughters drove away in the limousine to Camp Happy-in-the-Pines in New Hampshire. He hoped he could catch her at home before she left for work. When he heard her recorded voice asking the caller to "please leave your name and number," he hung up. Moments later he felt foolish and called back. "This is Sam. I need to talk to you," he said after the beep.

At four o'clock the phone rang and Sam jumped to answer it. A stranger's voice said, "Mr. Winslow? This is Paper-To-Go calling. You'll be happy to know the wallpaper you ordered arrived today."

Anything but happy, Sam replied, "Thank you. I'll be right down to pick it up." At least it would give him something to do, he decided.

When he returned half an hour later with sixteen rolls of a muted beige-and-white striped wallpaper, he called Maggie again. Maggie's answering machine was still on. But this time at the sound of the beep Sam didn't introduce himself. "Maggie, where the hell are you? We need to talk."

He dumped the rolls of paper in his bedroom and sent out for Chinese food. As he ate he thought about going over to her house and making her listen to him, but that seemed to be too boorish an approach. Later that evening he tried the telephone again. He began to feel quite comfortable with the recording. "Buffie and the kids vandalized the wallpaper to make you come back and marry me. The girls have been sentenced to three weeks in Camp Happy-in-the-Pines. If you ever—" *Beep.*

He dialed one more time. "—enter your house again and happen to turn on this damn machine at least you'll know I'm trying to apologize." He thought for a second. "The check is in the—" *Beep.*

"MAIL?" Maggie finished for Sam as she listened to the messages on the tape. It was about time, she thought.

She'd promised Greg his money four days ago and felt embarrassed every time she entered the store without the payment.

So Sam was trying to apologize, was he? But for what? Maggie wondered. For storming out of the house after she'd said she couldn't marry him, for the ridiculous assumption that she didn't want to marry him because he had children, or merely because he was late sending her the money he owed? She rewound the tape and listened to it again. Buffie had helped peel the paper? Maggie couldn't picture that without smiling. And she couldn't be too upset with the children; they'd had a reason that warmed Maggie's heart. To make you come back here and marry me, he'd said. As if it were that simple.

ASSININE, that's what this was. Whoever designed the interior for the condominiums deserved to be up on this contraption instead of her, Maggie thought. She'd wanted to work herself half to death so she wouldn't have time to think about Sam, but this was going too far. She stood shakily on the plywood-and-metal scaffolding she'd rented and wondered why she'd ever given up office work. It was a long way down to the newly tiled floor, the ceiling peak measured nineteen feet, six and three-quarter inches, and Maggie detested every single inch.

"What's the matter, Aunt Maggie?" Ben stood below her, holding a full bucket of water.

"I'm afraid of heights." While she and Ben waited for the sizing to dry Maggie decided it would be easier to stay up on her perch rather than climb down. She touched the wall. Still tacky, but almost ready.

The electrician stood below, patiently threading wiring into the circuit box inside what would be a closet. "How are you gonna do five more of these, McGuire?"

"With my eyes closed, of course." The heavy vinyl paper was ready to go. Ben would paste the bottom half of the wall and she'd do the top. Then he'd hand the paper up to her and she'd hang what she could until he could take over. She felt her queasy stomach flip. She'd have to climb on a ladder on top of the scaffolding platform in order to reach the peak.

"Pour me a cup of coffee, please, Ben? I left the thermos in the corner."

She watched the activity around her. The worksite was busy this morning. Maggie knew that most of the men had been on the job since seven. By three o'clock this afternoon one of the bare-chested carpenters would open a six-pack and they'd all call it quits for this Monday.

Ben climbed partway up the ladder and handed her the metal top to her thermos. "Careful, it's real hot."

"Thanks."

"Hey, Maggie!" Barry, the head contractor, waved to her from the deck opposite the living room wall where Maggie was leaning. He wore nothing but low-riding jeans, his tool belt dangling low on his hips, and he looked like Arnold Schwarzenegger. His grin was infectious. "Are you sittin' in Dunkin' Donuts or are you hangin' wallpaper?"

Maggie took a slow sip of her coffee while the men guffawed. Then she smiled. "You're all in trouble if this wall isn't straight."

"Aw, hell, Maggie, you're here to cover up our mistakes, aren't you?"

"Not at twenty feet in the air."

Barry flexed his muscles. "Sweetheart, if you fall I'll catch ya."

She finished her coffee and grinned at him. "That had better be a promise, Barry." She peered over the edge of the platform and called to Ben. "Hand me the paste and a roller, and we'll get this over with."

"You want me to paste the whole wall now?"

"Might as well," she said. "We'll do this as fast as we can, before I lose my nerve."

The gray leaves were as big as Ben's sneakers and had fuzzy outlines that made them easy to match. It was a dramatic print that highlighted the wall and added a focal point to the living room, but Maggie wished the decorator had left the wall plain. She knelt and watched as Ben lined up the seams.

"Good job," she said. "Now take the drywall blade and smooth it down. Don't worry about it too much. I'll check the whole thing and trim the bottom when I get down from here."

They worked quickly toward the peak. Thank goodness the paper was wide and hung easily, Maggie thought. Ben climbed up on the platform when it was time to do the peak.

One of the plumbers strolled through the room and stopped to watch as Maggie climbed on the ladder and bent to take the end of the paper from Ben's hand.

"You want a drumroll?"

"Very funny, Hal." She climbed to the top step of the ladder and stretched the paper up to the ceiling. "Okay! Slide it over and hold on to it. Don't let the rest of it go until I tell you."

Maggie nervously concentrated on matching the leaves and not losing her balance.

"Maggie? What the hell...!"

The voice was all too familiar. Maggie froze, her hands spread against the wall. She didn't want to look down. "Sam?"

She heard Ben. "Hi, Mr. Winslow."

"Be careful up there, Ben," Sam said, then added in a louder voice, "Maggie? Are you all right?"

"I'm fine. I'm just a little...busy right now." She finished smoothing the paper down and clipped to the point of the ceiling's peak with the scissors. "Okay, Ben, let it drop to the platform." Maggie carefully negotiated the steps of the ladder, smoothing the paper as she went along until she stood on the deck of the scaffolding and looked down at the man who haunted her answering machine.

Exasperated, she put her hands on her hips. "Sam, what are you doing here?"

"You haven't answered my calls," he explained. "I tracked you down with the help of Paper-To-Go."

"If I'd wanted to talk to you I'd have called you." She thought he looked wonderful, if a little tired, but she hardened her heart against her feelings.

"I apologized." He held up his hands in self-defense. His crisply ironed white shirt and dark slacks looked out of place in the construction area. His shoes were already covered with drywall dust.

"For what? You'll have to be more specific." Maggie noticed some of the carpenters had drifted closer to listen. "You'll have to make this fast," she said. "My paste is drying on the wall."

"Can you come down here? We're attracting a crowd."

"No, I can't." She looked away. "Ben, hop down underneath and finish this section, will you?"

"Right." He climbed down and moved past Sam. "Excuse me, Mr. Winslow."

Why wouldn't he leave? He looked as if someone had nailed him to the subfloor. "Sam, move out of the way!"

He stepped back a few feet and frowned at the scaffolding. "Maybe I should climb up there with you."

"Look, Sam, I'll call you tonight. It's about ninety degrees in here and I'm going to have to repaste the rest of this wall if you don't—"

"Got it," Ben called.

"Great. Let's get number five up."

Sam looked as though he were thinking about climbing the ladder to the platform, anyway. "Maggie, my bedroom paper finally arrived."

"That's nice."

"You need to come put it up."

That sounded suspiciously like an order. "I'll check my calendar and see if I can fit you in." She took the paper from Ben and glanced toward her visitor. An angry flush had crept up his neck and she could see tiny muscles tensing in his jaw.

"While you're thinking about that," he said in a low voice, "remember that you won't be paid until this job is finished."

Maggie's temper began to boil. "Whatever happened to 'the check is in the mail'?"

He shrugged. "I'm out of stamps. Pick it up in person."

She wished she'd memorized a few of her father's choice Irish curses. Then she noticed other workers in the building had found jobs to do within hearing range of the scaffolding. "Get out of here," she whispered. "I have work to do."

Satisfied he was getting his way, Sam backed off. He was also afraid she might throw something at him. "Just remember, Maggie," he said in a loud voice before he left the room, "I want you in my bedroom first thing tomorrow morning!"

Maggie was horrified into silence as the workers burst into laughter.

"Hey, McGuire," Barry called, "does that line work on you all the time?"

Maggie ignored the laughter and climbed on her ladder. Sam would pay for this.

THE THICK CREAM-COLORED envelope bore Buffie's engraved return address, but Maggie's name and address were printed by hand in large uncertain letters. She knew right away it had to be from Justine or Julianne. She ignored the other mail that had been dropped through the slot in the front door and sat cross-legged on the floor to open the envelope. Two letters were folded inside.

"Dear Maggie," she read, "I rekked the paper. I am very sorry. Camp is fun. I love you. Love, Julianne."

Justine's was identical, except she'd decorated the bottom left corner of the page with a rainbow, while Julie was partial to butterflies.

I love you, too. Maggie reread the letters and tucked them carefully into the envelope before wiping the tears from her cheeks. *I love you all.* She remembered the look on Sam's face when she'd told him she wouldn't marry him. What had her fears cost her?

HER ALARM RANG at five-thirty. By six, dressed in shorts and a denim shirt, Maggie was behind the wheel of her Pontiac, heading for Narragansett. Sam had made it clear he wanted her in his bedroom in the morning and Maggie, bent on revenge, figured morning couldn't come too soon.

By tucking the small stepladder under her arm, she was able to carry her toolbox, sponge-filled bucket and water box to the back door.

"Lou?"

After a moment she realized there was no one in the kitchen to answer her call. She had to set her stepladder down to open the door, which shut quietly behind her as she made her way through the hallway into the silent house.

She tried to tiptoe, but she felt like a pack mule as she lumbered upstairs. With any luck Sam would be sound asleep and she would have the satisfaction of disturbing his rest. She pushed open his bedroom door a few inches and peeked in. Good, she thought. Sam lay on his stomach, the pillow scrunched under his head, one long brown arm dangling over the side of the bed. A beige sheet covered the bottom half of his body, but his tanned back and shoulder blades were exposed to the warm morning air. He was snoring lightly.

Maggie shut the door and backed away. She would fill her bucket in the girls' bathroom so Sam wouldn't hear the sound and wake up. The surprise factor was essential to the next part of her plan. When she opened his door again she saw he hadn't moved, and she walked carefully to the bed without taking her gaze away from his closed eyelids. She would have to be ready for Plan B if he saw her.

She stood next to the bed, holding the bucket above the mattress. "Sam," she whispered, using her most sultry voice.

There was no answer.

"Sam," she crooned again. "Wake up, darling." She watched as his eyelids blinked and his breathing changed.

"Hmm." He began to roll over.

She stopped him with a hand on his shoulder. "Don't move, Sam. I mean it." She rested one knee on the mattress, forgetting it was a water bed. She almost lost her balance when she moved closer to him.

"What are you doing, Maggie?" he mumbled.

Her voice was sweet. "I'm dumping an entire bucket of ice-cold water on your head unless you agree to pay me *before* I start work in this room."

"Is this a nightmare?" He opened his eyes and lifted his head off the pillow. Seeing Maggie next to him answered his question. "Guess not," he said.

"I might start with the sponge down your back—" she gazed longingly at his spine "—and then the grand finale."

"Look around, Maggie," he said with a sigh. "Notice anything?"

She glanced around the room for the first time since she'd stepped inside. The walls were covered in beige striped paper. "Who did this?"

"I did."

"I don't believe it." She longed to examine the walls more closely, but couldn't let go of the bucket of water. "How?"

"Took me two days," he grumbled. "I'd watched you enough, so I thought I could figure it out. I had to buy two levels, though. I threw the first one out the window in disgust, and Lassie ran off with it."

Maggie fought the urge to laugh and tried to concentrate on her business. "What about my money?"

"If I can't move without being drowned, how am I

supposed to write you a check when I'm facedown in bed?"

"There's a wallet on your nightstand. You rich guys carry cash, don't you? Get it."

He looked suspicious. "What about the water?"

"I'm holding on to it," she continued to threaten. She watched as Sam stretched his free arm toward the nightstand, but she was knocked off her feet as his arm swung backward to toss her on the mattress.

They both yelled as the cold water splashed over them.

"What did you do that for?" Maggie hollered. She lay on her back in the bouncing water bed and flailed at Sam's chest. The empty bucket rolled off the bed and thunked onto the floor as she tried to roll over and crawl away.

But Sam quickly maneuvered himself on top of her and pinned her down. "Damn it, Maggie! I didn't think you really put water in that bucket."

"I'm soaked and so's this bed. Get off me." She looked into his gray eyes and saw amusement there. "This isn't funny," she said.

"I'm not moving, not until we've talked."

There was a determined slant to his mouth that Maggie recognized as meaning business. "So talk."

He settled an elbow on either side of her head and smiled. "The money I owe you for the wallpapering—including the bonus—is in an envelope on the kitchen counter. I didn't pay you right away because I wanted to talk to you and it was one way of staying in touch. If you'd answered my phone calls we could have avoided all this."

"Go on." She shivered as a puddle of cold water soaked into her back.

"I apologize for my marriage proposal."

Maggie felt a pang of disappointment. "I thought it was beautiful."

He kissed the tip of her nose and continued in a casual voice, "I rushed you. And I acted like a spoiled brat when you said no."

She smiled into his eyes. "This is true."

"I thought I could get over you, thought I could convince myself you were just a passing fancy, but it didn't work. It's taken me five years to fall in love again and it isn't easy to get over you."

She wriggled to get an arm free and brushed Sam's hair off his forehead, sliding her fingertips along the side of his face to his cheek. "I think I'm glad."

His lips touched hers briefly and he pulled away. "I missed you, Maggie. It's been a rough week. I told myself you wouldn't marry me because you didn't love me. Then I convinced myself it was because of the girls. I couldn't blame you if you didn't want to be a mother to someone else's children."

"Not someone else's, Sam. *Yours.* I'm crazy about those girls."

"They're yours if you want them. And what about me?"

She smiled and caressed the rough stubble on his jaw, enjoying the feel of him under her skin. "I'm crazy in love with you, too."

He closed his eyes for a brief moment. "You've never said so."

"I couldn't, Sam. Sometimes I feel so empty, so scared—there's still the fact that I can't have children."

His voice was rough. "I can accept that, Maggie. Can you?"

She was silent and Sam lifted himself away from her and moved to get off the bed.

Now or never. Maggie knew there wouldn't be another chance. If she let it end now Sam would never be part of her life again. She would live alone in her little dollhouse with a whole pile of regrets.

"Sam?" Her voice shook.

He stood beside the bed, pajama bottoms stuck to his skin, and turned toward her. "Yes?"

Maggie took a deep breath and held out her hand. "When's the wedding?"

Epilogue

"Do you think this is wise, dear?" Buffie stood on the deck with an empty champagne glass in her hand and surveyed the crowd of people chattering below. "Two weddings in one week?"

Sam winked at his mother-in-law. "I got a good deal on the tent."

"Oh, Sam." She laughed, causing the purple bugle beads on her dress to quiver. "You shouldn't joke on your wedding day."

"How much champagne have you had to drink, Buff?"

"Enough," she admitted. "I must say I quite feel like celebrating."

Sam watched Maggie cross the lawn and speak for a moment with her parents. The old-fashioned ivory dress she wore seemed to match the style of the house and he felt a light-headed happiness that made him weak. Maggie then joined Patsy, the matron of honor, and Lou at the champagne fountain.

"I have a gift for your bride," Buffie said. "I'd like to give it to her now, if you don't mind."

Sam turned back to Buffie. "Of course not. But you already gave us a wedding gift."

"This is something more personal, dear, and just for Maggie." She handed Sam her empty glass. "Fill this for me, would you? It seems all the waiters are busy."

Sam took the glass. "Okay. Just don't topple over until I bring Maggie back, all right?" He quickly left the deck and went down the stairs to the lawn to join his bride.

He heard Maggie's happy laugh as he slid his arm around her waist. "What's so funny, Mrs. Winslow?"

Lou answered. "The four flower girls have demanded their own table inside the tent, plus a pitcher of root beer with champagne glasses."

"And," Maggie said, snuggling into her husband's embrace, "they have a cassette player and they're listening to their own music."

"Blasting their own music, you mean. Should we stop them?" Patsy asked.

"No," said Sam, remembering Lou's comments a few months ago. "It's happy noise. Let them have fun." He held Maggie to his side while he spoke to his red-haired housekeeper. "I hope you're ready to do this next week, Lou."

"Don't you worry about me. You two just go on up to Maine and let me handle my own wedding plans." She looked over to the tent, where the wedding ceremony had been conducted and which now held brightly colored tables and trays of finger food. "Long as that thing doesn't blow down I'll be just fine."

"Buffie's in charge of the caterers again," Maggie added.

Patsy laughed and Lou rolled her eyes. "Heaven help us all!"

"We'll be back on Thursday," Sam said. "In plenty of time for me to give away the bride." Lou blushed, and Sam added, "Will you excuse us? I need Maggie for a moment."

"By the way, Sam," Pat said, "thanks for including Ben as an usher."

"He's an important member of the family." Sam stopped. "I almost forgot the champagne." He refilled the glass from the fountain, then took Maggie's hand and led her away. "Have I told you how beautiful you look?"

"Many times, but who's counting?" She touched the ivory sprays of tiny pearls and flowers that wound through her upswept hair, trying to tidy the dark tendrils of escaping curls. "I only hope I can stay presentable for a few more hours."

They went up the stairs and joined Buffie on the deck. She took the glass Sam offered. "I know I've told you once before, dears, but I must say it again. The ceremony was lovely."

"Thank you, Buffie. I'm happy you were here to share it with us," Maggie said.

"I wouldn't have missed it," she snorted. "Now over there on the table is a little gift for you, Maggie."

Maggie hesitated and looked at Sam. He shrugged, not knowing what his mother-in-law was up to. Maggie walked over to the table and picked up a rectangular velvet box. She lifted the lid to reveal a sparkling diamond necklace nestled against a satin background. With trembling fingers she removed it. "Buffie, it's beautiful, but I can't accept something like this."

"Nonsense! Don't you recognize it?"

Maggie smiled at the older woman. "The one the children were playing with?"

Buffie nodded. "It's yours now. A symbol of... mutual respect."

Maggie's voice was soft. "And friendship." She stepped forward and kissed Buffie's cheek.

"That, too." The older woman cleared her throat. "You two have neglected your guests. There's a wedding cake to be cut, you know. I'd better see if it's ready." She went quickly into the house.

Sam took the necklace from Maggie's shaking hand. "Should I put that in my pocket for now?"

"Yes," she said, watching him tuck it safely away. "What a lovely thing for her to do."

"She wants us to be happy." He caressed Maggie's cheek. "Are you sure you want to keep working?"

She put her arm around his waist. "Just until I've finished the jobs I'm committed to do."

"And then?"

"And then I'll take some time to get used to being a wife and a mother, maybe take some courses and finish my degree in a couple of years."

They walked arm and arm down the stairs and across the lawn until Sam abruptly spoke. "We can afford the very best doctors, Maggie." His voice was gentle against her hair. "We can try anything you want."

Maggie stopped and looked up at her new husband. "You're trying to tell me there's hope, aren't you?"

He nodded. "We can find out, but only if you want to."

She wrapped loving arms around his neck and stood on tiptoe to kiss him. "I want to."

They kissed for a long moment, until the cheers from their family and friends mingled with the tuning of guitars. The sound finally grew loud enough to make Maggie pull away from Sam's embrace. "I love you, Sam," she said, "but—"

He frowned. "But?"

She took his hand and tugged him toward the tent. "The Shanty Boys are about to sing."

It was supposed to be harmless make-believe,
but things got all too real...

MAKE-BELIEVE HONEYMOON

1

"YOU'RE PACKING an awful lot of black clothes." Anne frowned at the contents of the suitcase. "Are they some sort of symbol of your mood these days?"

Kate tossed another package of black panty hose into her new Pullman suitcase, bought on sale at JC Penney's the previous week. She'd packed and repacked her suitcase three times, caught between trying to be prepared for any weather and refusing to drag a suitcase that weighed more than she did. "The shoe salesman at Jordan Marsh told me that everyone in London wears black. If you wear sneakers and jeans and a windbreaker, you look like an American."

"So? You *are* an American."

"I want to look like I fit in," Kate explained. "I want to look sophisticated and worldly when I'm in England."

Her older sister snorted. "You're crazy. You could take the money and go someplace warm. Who goes to London in March?"

"I do. Especially now."

"Well, maybe it's a good idea that you get away from here," Anne conceded. "Who would have thought he'd find someone else and get married so fast?"

Both of them knew who "he" was. "I'm not angry." Kate considered a yellow sweater, then tossed it back onto the bed. "Breaking our engagement was very brave of him."

"*Brave?* He's a rat."

Kate winced. She was to have married Jeffrey Lannigan next week, then he'd announced at the last minute that he'd reconsidered. "I guess I don't have very good luck with men."

Anne nodded her agreement. "You're entirely too trusting. Remember that football player in high school? The one who dated three other girls while you thought you were going steady? And then in college, the chemistry major, wasn't it? Ray something? Didn't you pay for all your dates because he told you—"

"He had discovered the cure for cancer and needed all his money for research equipment," Kate said. "I'm going to change," she promised. She didn't want to be reminded of her past...misunderstandings. Having three older sisters meant she had three people in her life who remembered every little mistake she'd ever made and weren't shy about pointing them out.

Anne smiled. "Not too much, I hope. We might not recognize you."

"I'm going to be very sophisticated and cool from now on. I'm through with men. When I get back from England, I'm going to buy a dog." She looked at her watch. "I have to hurry up and get out of here."

"A dog? What kind of dog?"

"Something small and friendly."

"I'll look into it for you," her sister said. "Carol might have some suggestions, too. You wouldn't want to buy the wrong—" She stopped as Kate tossed black tights into the suitcase. "More black? You'll look like you're going to a royal funeral."

"Hey, I'm feeling a little grim around the edges

lately." Kate tossed in a pair of black flats and tried to divert Anne's attention from her wardrobe. "Maybe I'll get lucky and see the queen."

"Yeah, right." Anne shook her head. "And Di, too. Tell them both I said hello."

Kate folded a cream cardigan and placed it carefully in the suitcase. "You never know, Annie. You're joking, but I could see them somewhere. I'm going to have my camera ready all the time, especially when I go to Kensington Palace."

"A trip will take your mind off things, I suppose. You can look for a new job when you get back." Anne picked up a pair of black pants from the bed. "I thought you had your colors done and weren't supposed to wear black anymore."

"I did. I'm an 'autumn.' I'm supposed to wear browns and golds and cream colors. But so much of my stuff is black I have to bring a mix." Kate held up a pair of brown stretch pants. "Black and brown go together, right?"

"Very sophisticated," Anne agreed. "What about earrings?"

"I bought gold dangles with black and brown beads. And now I can wear Aunt Laurabelle's old pin. I always thought it had too much yellow in it." Kate took a large oval brooch from her dresser and tossed it to her sister. "I think it will look great on my coat, don't you?"

Anne held it up to the light. "It's quite, uh, big. I'm glad you ended up with it and not me."

"It was one of Aunt Belle's favorite pieces. She wore it on special occasions, don't you remember? She gave it to me before she died, said it would bring my heart's desire." Anne placed the pin in the V of Kate's new chestnut knit dress and nodded her approval. The large yellow rectangular stone in the center was surrounded by smaller white and green stones, in an interesting geometric design. "It looks good with the brown, too, doesn't it?" Kate asked.

"Yes, it does. Heart's desire, huh? Maybe you should have it appraised. What if it's valuable? You may need to have it insured."

Kate laughed. "The stones are too big to be anything but glass. But it supposedly came from England, so I'll wear it. For a good-luck charm."

"Why don't you wait until school gets out and I can go with you?"

"I've told you before. I have the reservations and I won't have any trouble. London's supposed to be a very safe city." She smiled at Anne's worried expression. Her other sisters had said the same thing. None of them believed she could exist without their help, which was ridiculous. They'd bossed her around for twenty-five years, but this time she wasn't listening. This time she was getting on a plane and doing something she wanted to do, without their advice and without their interference. "And everyone speaks English. Don't worry about me. I'll be fine by myself."

"I wish you were taking one of those organized tours instead of exploring all alone."

"I didn't want someone telling me how long I could take doing this or doing that. There are things I want to see that aren't offered on a tour. I want to walk around and explore and daydream about what it must have been like two hundred years ago. I'm going to eat fish and chips and drink beer."

"Well, be careful. Maybe you'll meet a sexy Englishman in one of those pubs."

"I doubt it." Kate folded a black sweater and put it on the bed to consider. "I've heard they're very cold and reserved. And I'm not in the mood for flirting." Anne didn't really understand. How could she? She'd been married for four years and had an adorable two-year-old who wore pink bunny pajamas and kissed dolls. Kate winced. She'd dreamed of chubby babies and an adoring husband until Jeff had said, "I don't feel anything anymore." So much for the "adoring husband" fantasy.

"Dukes and lords and princes sound pretty interesting."

"I'll let you know when I get back." Kate smiled and picked up her aunt's brooch. *Heart's desire* was a little hard to believe. If she had what she wanted most, she'd be getting married next weekend. "I'd better put this on my coat now so I don't forget it."

Anne rolled her eyes. "I doubt if anyone could forget something that big and that gaudy."

Kate hesitated. "Do you think it's too much?"

"Not on black. Besides, it relieves that funereal look."

"All right." She pinned the brooch on the lapel of her wool coat and stood back to admire the affect. "I feel glamorous already."

"You look great," her sister agreed. "Especially with your hair that way. I'm glad you took Terri's advice and had it highlighted."

"Thanks." Kate's brown hair usually fell in a natural curl past her shoulders, but if she used the blow-dryer she could straighten it to look sleek and sophisticated. It all depended on how much time she had in the morning, and today she'd taken her time. She wanted to look her best when she landed in England, even if it would be seven-thirty in the morning. After all, she still had her pride, or what was left of it after calling two hundred people to cancel her wedding. She zipped the suitcase shut.

Anne hopped off the bed. "Are you ready?"

Kate slung her coat over her arm and picked up the suitcase, which was still heavier than she would have liked. "Ready," she agreed. "From now on I'm an 'international babe.'"

Anne looked doubtful. "A 'babe,' huh?"

"Definitely." Kate grinned. "At least for the next ten days. I have it all figured out so I don't miss anything. Carol gave me a lot of brochures." She picked up three typed pages of activities and tucked them into her guidebook. She couldn't wait to leave Rhode Island. She couldn't bear to be around when Jeff married a woman he'd fallen in love with while buying socks at the mall, a woman he was marrying three weeks later.

Men were crazy, Kate decided. Men were crazy and unpredictable and bizarre. They told you one thing and did something else. They told you they loved you, then changed their minds. She'd buy that dog, Kate decided. A little fluffy dog that would curl up beside her on the couch and never, ever lie about love.

IT WASN'T RAINING, which made the afternoon quite comfortable, William Landry, the ninth Duke of Thornecrest observed. He looked upward, past the stone buildings and chimneys to the clouds scattered across the pale blue sky. Some of his friends were skiing in Gstaad; he could join them if the mood took him. Afterward he'd return to Thorne Hall in time for the spring planting.

There were always important things to do at home,

he mused. Unlike London. He'd ordered new clothes at Turnbull & Asser, then he'd inspected a replacement chair for the dining room and, at Christie's, he'd listened to Gaylord rattle on about paintings and armoires for over an hour. He'd been in town for over a week, and tomorrow he could leave. He would have left already if Pitty hadn't kept coming up with excuses to keep him with her. For some reason she thought he'd find a wife in town this year. For some reason she thought he wanted one.

She couldn't be more mistaken.

He would now check in with his grandmother, describe every piece of Georgian furniture Gaylord had gushed over, change into appropriate clothes, then head to Wilton's for a long lunch with Lady Jessica Wilton, a tall silvery blonde who'd accepted the fact that he would never marry—at least not in this century.

William slowed down as he entered Essex Court, an exclusive London cul-de-sac. The bustling sounds of the city disappeared, left behind on St. James Street. On either side of Thorne House stood smaller town houses with the shining brass nameplates on immaculate white-painted doors their only introduction to the passerby.

A young woman stood on the front steps of Thorne House. An American, he guessed, noting the camera bag around her shoulder and the bright red *Guide to London* tucked under her arm. A tourist, of course, although they weren't as plentiful in March as they were in July, thank goodness. He'd been against showing the house, against making a deal with the Victoria and Albert Museum to allow tourists to traipse through the lower floors of the family's town house. But Pitty had insisted, and he'd acquiesced. As usual.

He stepped closer, unable to avoid the woman since she blocked his way to the front door. "Excuse me," he said, trying to be as polite as possible. "Is there something you need at Thorne House?"

"It's closed." She turned amazingly green eyes on him. Brown hair with gold-and-red highlights hung past the shoulders of her black coat. She swept her hair from her cheek, revealing a bright pin on the lapel of her coat. The yellow center stone winked and glowed in the weak sunlight. "I can't believe Thorne House is really closed," she repeated.

"You can't?" He lifted his gaze to her extremely pretty face and gave her a long look. She didn't come up to his chin. William backed up a step. He had no time for short American tourists, however attractive.

She shot another disappointed look at the brass plaque with Closed engraved upon it. "No. It's one of the places I most wanted to see. My great-aunt told me—"

"It's closed in the winter," he interrupted. "For refurbishment."

"That's a shame. I came all the way from Rhode Island—that's in America—to see this house." She turned back to the door, as if willing it to open by itself and allow her entrance.

He knew Rhode Island was in America. He'd even been there one summer, but he didn't particularly want to start a conversation with a stranger about his travels in the States. "It happens every year."

"What?"

"Refurbishment." He stuck his hands in the pockets

of his worn leather jacket. "From January through March, you see."

"It didn't say anything about that in the guidebook."

"I'm awfully sorry." He waited for her to move away. It would seem cruel to pull out the key and step inside, leaving the young woman to stare up at the house, so he waited. She'd probably expect a private tour if she knew he lived in the house she'd come "all the way from Rhode Island" to visit. He wouldn't want to be rude; he merely wanted to go inside and change his clothes.

"Yes, so am I." She sighed and finally moved away from the door. "Are you touring London, too?"

William hid his amusement at being mistaken for a tourist. He knew he looked scruffy; he usually didn't wear blue jeans in the city. "In a way." She seemed to be waiting for him to explain. "I work in London occasionally," he said, which was not exactly a lie. He'd been working his ass off since he'd arrived last week. "And I particularly enjoy English history."

"Oh. You should understand, then."

"Yes," he agreed. "But there are other houses to see," he added, hoping to alleviate her obvious disappointment. "Somerset House is an art museum now, but the building is quite impressive, and so are the Impressionist collections. And Marlborough House is often open by appointment. It's around the corner."

The little American held up her guidebook and smiled. "Yes, I know."

"Have that book memorized, do you?"

"A little." She backed up a step, as if finally realizing she was standing in a foreign city talking to a strange man. "Well, thanks a lot for the information."

"My pleasure." He inclined his head in a small bow.

"I hope you enjoy your vacation, despite this, er, disappointment."

"I will." She chuckled. "Unless you tell me that the Tower of London is closed for refurbishment, too."

"I wouldn't think of disappointing you."

She smiled a bit ruefully and turned to walk out of the courtyard. He waited for her to disappear onto St. James Street before he unlocked the entrance. The great hall was draped in white sheets, and the smell of paint hung thick in the air. He took the elevator to the third floor, where Pitty stood in the window, her binoculars around her neck. Her large face was flushed, her over-size bosom heaving with excitement.

"William! This is absolutely incredible! Who is she? Why didn't you ask her in?"

"Who are you spying on now?" He began to unbutton his jacket, anticipating a hot shower and a pleasant lunch.

"You, dear boy. Who was that woman?"

"A tourist."

"A *tourist*? Well, bring her back. I thought you knew her! Didn't you see me waving?"

"I wasn't looking at the windows. And how would I know an American tourist?" He joined her at the window and looked down at the empty court. "Good, she's gone. She was disappointed that she couldn't see inside the house. I thought for a moment she would refuse to leave."

She pointed to him and ordered, "Bring her back!"

"Pitty, your blood pressure—"

"Did you *see* it? Did you *see* what she *wore*?"

He frowned, trying to remember. "A coat, Pitty. A black coat, like every other woman in London." William began to worry. He could call her physician and have him here within minutes. Pitty was at least eighty, though she wouldn't reveal her age to anyone, not even the queen.

She pointed a finger at him. "The brooch. Didn't you notice the brooch?" Her hands fluttered over her chest. "The Thorne Diamond has returned at last! I never thought I'd live to see the day, but it has returned. Just in time, too, for I'm growing older, you know."

The Thorne Diamond, a six-carat canary-colored stone from the Kappur mine of India, was one of Pitty's favorite topics, usually discussed at the same time Pitty brought the subject of marriage to his attention. Although the diamond had disappeared two hundred years ago, he'd been forced to believe the jewel existed. After all, a painting in his home showed a Thornecrest duchess wearing the pin, but he couldn't imagine that it was the same jewel that twinkled from the shoulder of a stranger's coat, no matter what his grandmother thought. William went to the phone. "I'm going to call Dr. Halston and have him come over and pay a little visit...."

Pitty quivered with indignation. "You'll do no such thing. You'll find that woman and bring her back here, and she will tell me how the stone came into her possession! Go!"

He hesitated before picking up the receiver. "Why would a tourist possess such a priceless gem? And why would she wear it on her coat, as if it was a trinket?"

"That's exactly what I want you to discover, my boy. Now, go! Before she disappears."

William figured the attractive little American had had plenty of time to disappear, but he didn't want to add to his grandmother's anxiety. "I will if you promise to lie down while I'm gone. You shouldn't become so upset."

Pitty took him by the shoulders and pushed him toward the entry. "Go, Willie, please. I know I'm not mistaken. Bring her back her so I can purchase it."

"I shall do my best," William promised, heading toward the elevator. "If Jessica rings before I return, explain to her I'll be late, will you?"

Pitty clapped her hands. "Of course. This is perfect! Such a *lovely* girl, isn't she?"

William didn't bother answering; he'd become inured to his grandmother's attempts at matchmaking. To please her he would try to find the young woman, but the oddness of the situation struck him as humorous. The Duke of Thornecrest trailing a tourist...

He would do anything for his grandmother—he even allowed her to call him Willie—but he drew the line at kidnapping Americans. He walked quickly outside, through Essex Court to St. James. Pitty would be watching with her binoculars, he was certain. But as he'd anticipated, there was no trace of the American in the black coat. She could have gone in search of Marlborough House, he realized as he tried to reconstruct their brief conversation. A brisk walk took him to the entrance of Marlborough House, but no pretty tourist stood entranced at its door, and the mansion was obviously closed. William turned and surveyed the area, just in case she was wandering nearby taking pictures.

There was no help for it. William crooked his finger, and a gleaming black cab pulled to the curb. There was another place the tourist had mentioned, unfortunately for him. He could return to the house and tell Pitty he couldn't find the woman with the pin, but he'd promised to do his best. "The Tower of London, thank you."

"Right, guv."

He leaned back in the cab and sighed. Pitty had insisted he come to London this month. There had been decisions to make about Thorne House, decisions that only he could make. "As the Duke of Thornecrest," preceded her every order. He was thirty-six, had been the ninth Duke of Thornecrest since the tender age of ten, when his father had fallen from the balcony of Kittredge Manor. His mother, always frail, hadn't lived to see her son's eleventh birthday. And his grandmother, with the authority only a dowager duchess could command, had taken over raising him.

He'd inherited his father's hearty constitution, his mother's dark coloring and his grandmother's common sense. The title had come with six estates, Thorne House, a massive bank account, the family jewels and a responsibility to carry on family tradition.

Which meant marriage and a son to be the tenth Duke of Thornecrest. Except the ninth duke had no intention of marrying.

No one he knew was happy being married. No one in his family had ever been happy. Landrys were accustomed to marrying the wrong people and being miserable for the rest of their lives and, possibly, right through eternity. Generations of once-bickering Landrys lay buried in the family tomb at Leicestershire. How they had ever managed to produce children he never knew, but for the past five generations there had been one child born to each Duke of Thornecrest, a son named William, the son to carry on the title.

Traditionally the duke and duchess parted ways after the birth of the child, to separate houses and separate sex lives. There was nothing about this family tradition that appealed to the present duke, however. If he must do his duty and produce the next duke, he would wait for a long time. A *very* long time. He doubted there would ever be a shortage of women in England who were willing to be a duchess and live an independent life.

Not everyone required love, William reminded himself. But he would like to live a life without bitterness and rancor, bickering and unhappiness. Was that too much too ask?

"THAT LOOKS like the stone in your pin," the middle-aged woman next to Kate said. She pointed to the yellow diamond in the middle of a crown labeled The 1820 Diadem. "But yours is bigger."

"Yes, I guess so." Kate tried not to smile too broadly. She didn't want to hurt the woman's feelings. She leaned closer to the glass, noting that the yellow diamond really did resemble the center stone of Aunt Laurabelle's pin. She'd never seen jewels so beautiful or so large as the ones in the royal crowns.

The woman shot Kate's pin another admiring glance. "Did you get it at the tower gift shop?"

"No. It belonged to my aunt."

"She's not the queen of England, is she?" the woman teased.

"No. Too bad, though." Kate moved slowly down the aisle as the woman beside her chuckled. She didn't want to miss seeing a single treasure in one of the most famous collections of jewels in the world. She'd read about it in the guidebook: "Dazzling and brilliant, the most precious stones in the world are one of London's most popular attractions."

She could see why, and she was glad she was wearing Aunt Belle's pin. In the Tower of London Jewel House, the gaudy brooch fitted right in.

This was fun. She liked having only herself to worry about, even though her family thought she was crazy to come here alone after she'd lost her job and her fiancé in the same month. She could enjoy ten days without anyone giving her advice, or trying to give her advice. She was free. While she toured London, she could forget about Jeff and the wedding that wasn't going to take place.

"It's a sign," Anne had announced when Kate had told her about the breakup. "And I never thought he was right for you." It was a sign, all right. A sign that she should take the trip she'd been saving for. Kate had taken her severance pay and put it into traveler's checks. She had the *Guide to London* in her black tote bag. Things could be worse. She could be in Rhode Island, standing in line to collect unemployment and reading the classified ads. Instead, she was one of many fascinated tourists filing through the collection of crown jewels.

She lingered at the display, soaking up the atmosphere and trying to absorb the history involved. When she stepped outside, the sky had darkened and a chilly breeze blew from the nearby Thames. The famous ravens were nowhere to be seen, but the White Tower loomed in the distance. Kate glanced at her watch. She'd spent longer in the Jewel House than she'd realized. She could make a quick tour of the famous landmark, then hit the gift shop before the tower closed for the evening. A hot cup of tea, a sandwich and an early bedtime would round off the day.

"Excuse me," a male voice said behind her.

Kate turned and saw the man who had talked to her

in front of Thorne House. Tall and handsome, with piercing dark eyes and ruffled brown hair, he was easy to recognize. His skin was tanned, too, she noticed, as if he worked outside each day. Although his leather jacket looked about fifty years old and the jeans were worn, he didn't look like a thief or a rapist.

"You were able to see the jewels?" His gaze dropped to her pin, then returned to her face.

"Yes. They're wonderful, aren't they?" She took a step toward the White Tower, wondering why he was speaking to her. After all, her skills as a temptress were practically nonexistent. He fell in step beside her.

"Yes," he agreed, then hesitated as they walked together. "Do you mind if I join you? I, uh, particularly enjoy the collection of medieval armor displayed there."

Kate didn't know if she minded or not. She was pleased to be talking to this good-looking man with a British accent, but she didn't want to be accosted in London, especially not in her first hours in the city. "Oh, well, I don't think..."

"I'm sorry. I'm being quite rude." He stopped, blocking her path. "I'm William, er, Will Landry. Duke of Thornecrest."

Her pretty mouth dropped open. "Did you say Duke of Thornecrest?"

He bowed slightly. "At your service. I apologize for frightening you. I certainly didn't have any intention of doing so. It's just that..." He hesitated.

Kate knew she was gullible, but could he expect her to believe that she was talking to a duke? She wondered how far he'd go with his story. "Just that what?"

He gazed down at her with serious dark eyes. "My grandmother felt terrible that someone who wanted to see Thorne House so badly should be denied the opportunity."

"Your grandmother," she repeated.

"You don't believe me." He didn't look too pleased that she wouldn't take his word for it.

"Not exactly. Doesn't it seem a little odd to you?"

His stunned expression almost made her laugh. Then he pulled his wallet out of his pocket and showed her identification. "Satisfied?" His voice was haughty.

"Yes." Someone should have warned her that dukes were dangerously handsome, with charm oozing out of every aristocratic pore. Maybe if she'd been prepared, she wouldn't be acting like an idiot. Maybe she'd be able to think of something intelligent to say. "You *live* in Thorne House?"

William stuck his hands in his pockets. "I live north of here, actually. In the country. I'm here in London on business. Would you like a tour? I'd, er, hate to have you miss seeing the house. Even in its present state."

"You followed me all the way here to tell me your grandmother wanted to show me the house?" Dukes were kind, too, she added to her mental list of lordly characteristics.

"You did say you were coming to the tower. Are you enjoying yourself?"

"Very much."

"Well? Would you like a tour?"

"Yes, thank you." She would have to call Anne, no matter how expensive it was. She had to tell someone she'd met a duke the first day she was in London.

He looked at his watch. "We don't want to miss tea."

Tea. Very British, and on her list of things to experience. Still Kate hesitated. She'd never been the kind of woman who was pursued by handsome men. Not like

Anne, who, with her long legs and golden blond hair, could attract the attention of every male within sight. Or Carol, a voluptuous redhead with a degree in philosophy and three charming children. Or Terri, sleek and trendy, who owned her own beauty salon and had twins with genius IQs. Being short and ordinary looking didn't attract the kind of men who looked like William Landry.

He might be a duke, all right, but that didn't mean she was getting in a car with him. "I'll meet you there. I'd like to get a picture of the White Tower."

The duke gave her a thoughtful look. "I'll walk with you instead," he replied. "That is, if you don't mind the company. I haven't seen the armor display since I was nine."

They walked in silence for a few minutes, until Kate stopped to take a picture of the tower. "Would you mind?" she said.

He frowned. "Mind what?"

"Taking a picture of me by this sign?"

"Oh, I suppose not." He didn't look enthused, but he held out his hand for the camera. Kate stood quietly for a moment until the duke finished taking the picture and handed the camera back to her.

"Thanks. What do I call you? Sir? Your Grace? Lord?"

He winced. "'William' is fine."

Kate turned and held out her hand. "I'm Katherine Stewart. From—"

"Rhode Island," he supplied. "I remember." He took her elbow and guided her toward the white-washed stone building.

Much later, after examining every display of armor from each period in the history of Great Britain, Kate conceded it was time to leave. "You don't want to have to hurry your visit to Thorne House," William advised. "And my grandmother will be expecting us."

"That was incredible. All that armor was so old. And the jewels—" Kate's delight overcame her shyness. "I can't believe what I've seen in just one day. I could go home tomorrow and be happy."

"Tomorrow?" His voice sharpened. "You're leaving tomorrow?"

"No." She dared another look at him. Yes, he really was handsome. She wasn't hallucinating from lack of sleep. "I just arrived this morning. Everything they tell you about jet lag is true," she confided. "It's not easy staying awake, but I don't want to waste any time sleeping when I could be seeing things."

"How long are you staying?"

"Ten days. I booked the British Airways London Showcase special."

"What on earth is the Showcase special?"

"You get airfare and six nights in a hotel, but I added three extra nights. It includes a full English breakfast every day and one free dinner. Plus tickets to two shows, a seven-day card for the subway and a free afternoon bus tour of London."

"That sounds like quite an ambitious week for you."

"It's a dream come true to be here, so I don't want to waste a minute."

Americans, he thought, were all alike. Awestruck by England's history and royalty, they stayed in perpetual motion. He hurried her past the tower gift shop and into a cab. He'd played tourist long enough.

In a few minutes Pitty would see the brooch, realize it wasn't what she thought it was and send the American on her way. With her guidebook, her maps, her schedule and the oddest bit of jewelry he'd ever seen.

2

THORNE HOUSE SAT near the end of Essex Street. As the taxi came to a halt in the elegant street, Kate pulled her camera from her bag to record the moment. She stepped out the of cab and framed the doorway, with its graceful columns on either side of the polished mahogany door.

The duke climbed out of the taxi that had come to a stop behind her, so she turned and took a picture of him, too. She wanted to make certain she had pictures of everything so when she returned to Rhode Island a complete record of her London vacation would exist in four-by-six-inch color glossies.

The frowning duke paid for both taxis, despite Kate's objections, and waved her toward the door, which he unlocked and opened.

"I apologize for the state in which you find my home," he said, following her into the wide hall. The marble floors were partially covered by a plastic runner, and the paintings on the walls were draped with fabric to protect them from the dust. The duke led her from room to room, and Kate was amazed at the opulence of the interior of the London mansion. Even with much of the furniture draped with white sheeting, Kate could see that the rooms were beautiful. He took her into one of the completed areas, the museum, with its displays of Meissen and Berlin porcelain, a gold-plated silver dinner service and various swords used by Thornecrest dukes in a confusing number of wars; then on to the drawing room, its tall windows overlooking Green Park and the gallery, which ran the length of the house and held an impressive display of priceless paintings.

Kate listened to the duke's entertaining comments about the history of the family. He was an accomplished tour guide, yet he didn't sound bored reciting what must be familiar stories about his ancestors.

"Are you ready for tea?" He finally stopped in front of a discreet elevator door.

"Yes," she gulped, and followed him into the elevator, which took them to the private apartments on the third floor. The large living room, done in green and ivory, was only slightly less opulent than the downstairs rooms.

A large elderly woman rose from the emerald-striped sofa. Her gray hair was piled on top of her head in a bun, and her bright pink suit was classic and, Kate guessed, very expensive. Large pearls gleamed at her ears and throat and draped over a massive bosom. She held out her hand and Kate hurried to take it. She wondered if she was supposed to curtsey and resisted the impulse.

"Katherine, I'd like you to meet my grandmother, Patricia Landry, Duchess of Thornecrest and family tyrant. Pitty, this is Katherine Stewart, from Rhode Island."

"Thank you for inviting me to your home," Kate said, wondering why the elderly woman gave her such an assessing look. "I've enjoyed seeing it so much."

"It is my pleasure, of course," the dowager replied. She gestured to Kate to sit in an ivory wing chair as she settled herself back on the sofa. "I'm sure my grandson told you—"

"I've asked Kate for tea," William interjected. "I told her you were distressed that someone who wanted to see it so badly be denied a tour of Thorne House." He turned to Kate and smiled. "May I take your coat?"

Feeling out of place, Kate stood once again and removed her coat with William's assistance. She wished she'd worn her knit dress. The black stretch pants and matching fuzzy sweater certainly weren't dressy enough for tea, but at least her suede boots were acceptable. It helped, she told herself, that knits didn't wrinkle, so no one would know she'd been in the same clothes since yesterday.

"What an interesting pin," the duchess declared as William handed the coat to the tiny maid who had appeared like magic. "It's very unusual. Where on earth did you find it? In London?"

"You're the second person today who has asked me that. It was a gift from my great-aunt."

The dowager turned her gaze back to Kate. "Then it's a family heirloom?"

"Yes."

"It's much too valuable to be worn on the streets of London," the old woman declared. "You should deposit the brooch in a vault."

"Oh, don't worry. It's not valuable." Kate smiled, hoping the intimidating dowager's expression would soften.

"Except to you," William pointed out.

"Yes," she said, watching the satisfied smile he gave his grandmother.

The dowager sniffed, then looked past Kate's shoulder. "Mary, we'll have our tea now. Miss, er, Stewart will be joining us."

William poured something into a glass on the mahogany sideboard, then settled himself in a low chair and crossed his feet on the matching striped hassock. "We toured the tower, Pitty. It was just as I remembered."

"Was it?" She ignored him and turned back to Kate. "Tell me about yourself, my dear. Where do you come from?"

"Rhode Island."

"And what brings you to London?"

"I'm on vacation."

"By yourself?"

"Yes." The dowager looked at her as if waiting for her to explain.

"I just lost my job," Kate added reluctantly, "so I took the severance pay and my savings and came to London."

"How interesting," Pitty declared, seeming to mean it. "And why did you come to Thorne House?"

Kate felt a little silly explaining she might be distantly related to these regal-looking people. "There's a family story that says my grandmother's family came from here."

Pitty raised her eyebrows. "Do go on, dear."

"An Englishwoman, supposedly related to one of the dukes of Thornecrest, married a cattle rancher. Have you ever heard of a relative like that?"

"No, I don't think I have. Perhaps you're mistaken."

"Maybe. You know how family stories get exaggerated." Kate hoped she wasn't mistaken at all. She rather liked the romance of it all.

Pitty wasn't through with her questions. "Tell me, my dear, what are you going to do while you're here?"

Kate smiled. "As many things as possible, I hope. I've planned all sorts of tours."

The maid entered the room and placed the tea tray on the low table in front of the elderly woman. Besides an ornate silver service, there were three delicate cups and saucers, and several plates piled high with tiny sandwiches and little cakes. Pitty poured and William jumped up to help serve a cup of tea to Kate.

Tea with a duchess. Imagine. Odd that people still had tea in the afternoon, just like in books. Kate felt herself begin to relax as she sipped the hot tea. That tiny bed at the St. Giles was going to feel wonderful. She wondered how many hours she'd been awake without sleep. Twenty? Twenty-three?

"Katherine?"

She looked up, realizing she hadn't heard what had been said. She smiled at William. "Sorry. I just realized how tired I am. What did you say?"

"I told Pitty that you enjoyed the Tower of London."

Kate looked back to the duchess. "Yes. Very much."

The old woman selected a dainty sandwich and put it on her plate. "And the Jewel House? What did you think of that?"

"I've never seen anything like it."

"No?"

The duke hurried to join the conversation. "I remember that Father took me to see the display of armor. I don't think it's changed in the least."

"William must show you the rest of London, Katherine. There are so many things you must see."

"I believe," the duke drawled, "Miss Stewart has her trip completely organized."

"That's true," Kate said. She set the teacup on the lace-covered table to her left and then pulled the sheaf of papers from her bag. "Tomorrow is Buckingham Palace, Hyde Park and the rest of the Covent Garden area. And I especially want to see Carlton Terrace."

The duchess held out one hand. "May I?"

Kate handed her the papers. The old woman perused them, then handed them to William, who also read them.

Kate waited for him to look up. "What do you think? Have I missed anything?"

He handed them back to her, a stunned expression on his face. "I think," he said slowly, "you must be a very energetic young woman."

"I don't want to leave anything out." She tucked her itinerary safely inside her tote and reached for her teacup. She felt a little wobbly; maybe it was time to leave before she did something to embarrass herself. Still, this was her one and only chance to have tea in an English mansion, so she really shouldn't hurry off, and the luxurious room was oddly comfortable.

"I don't think you should worry about that," Pitty replied, giving Kate another assessing look. "Would you like a watercress sandwich?"

"Thank you." Kate took the fragile china plate offered her. "You've been so nice. When I came here this afternoon, I didn't expect anything like this."

William raised his eyebrows and turned to glance at his grandmother before smiling blandly at Kate. "Neither did I."

"IT'S THE PERFECT solution." Pitty stood at the windows that faced Essex Court and watched their American guest step into the black taxi. The jewel twinkled briefly before Katherine disappeared inside the cab. "I'm sure it's the same piece of jewelry the third duchess wore to the coronation. The painting is in the Long Gallery at the Hall."

"I doubt that it's the same brooch." William stepped away from the window, poured himself another brandy and took a swallow. Pitty must be growing senile after all. It was a shame, too. The old girl used to be sharp as a tack, and now she was obviously slipping.

His grandmother sank back onto the couch, looking quite determined. "But the diamond..."

William turned to glare at her. "You don't know whether or not that stone is the diamond, or if that brooch is the original Thorne piece. It could be a very good copy. It takes a jeweler to distinguish between real and fake now."

"Which is precisely my point," Pitty agreed. "We have to find out, and what better way than to take Katherine into Longmire's and have them look at the pin? Discreetly, of course. I will prepare them ahead of time."

"And how do I explain a trip to an exclusive jewelry store, Pitty?"

"She'll believe anything you say, of course." Pitty sniffed. "You're a duke and she's...an American."

An American with a tempting smile and a body that would stop London traffic. When she'd removed her coat, he'd almost dropped it on the carpet. "I've followed her, brought her home, given her a tour of the house and served her tea, for heaven's sake. And now you want me to play tour guide?"

"Yes. Just until we find out if the stone is real or not."

The stone couldn't be real. Nothing so priceless could exist for over one hundred and fifty years without being discovered. "I'd planned on leaving tomorrow, you remember. The refurbishment is almost finished, and I've made every decision there is to make about furnishings and wallpaper. Gaylord has selected several pieces you'll find interesting and can aid you with any other problems that come along."

Pitty didn't flinch. "I want the brooch. I want the Thorne Diamond returned to the family once and for all."

He could feel his plans to escape London slipping away. "And if this American brooch is not the real one? What then?"

"If it's not the Thorne brooch, I'll promise to stay out of your affairs for the rest of my life. Which isn't for long," she reminded him. "I'm—" She stopped, making William chuckle.

"You almost slipped. Someday I'm going to find out how old you really are."

Pitty gave him an arch look. "On the death certificate, I presume."

He ignored the comment, knowing she wanted him to feel guilty enough to agree to her plan. "I'm going to change. I've already missed lunch with Jessica. I should ring—"

"I already did that," Pitty informed him, pouring herself another cup of tea. "I told her you would be in touch with her later and apologized for the inconvenience. She was most understanding."

"I'm sure she was." Pitty wanted him to marry, and she would not want him to alienate a very eligible candidate for the position.

"Jessica's a lovely girl. She'd make a wonderful duchess." Pitty sighed. "Naturally you have to own the brooch first. It guarantees your marital and lifetime happiness, and that, of course, is what I wish for more than anything else."

William didn't want to talk about the damn brooch for one more minute. "I'm going to change."

"The Smithfields are joining us for dinner at eight," she reminded him. "You remember them, don't you?"

"Yes. I suppose they are bringing their niece with them."

"She's a sweet girl."

"I am not interested in 'sweet girls,'" he snapped before leaving the room. It was almost archaic, William decided as he headed down the hall to his rooms in the east wing. His grandmother would have been at home in another century, where men spent their days buying horses and gambling, and women's only purpose was to produce male children. But this was the twentieth century. There was no butler, no calling cards and no valet to care for the closet full of expensive clothes he only wore in London. He entered his enormous bedroom and considered his situation.

Jessica could wait, and so could Thorne Hall. He didn't want to remain in London, but here he was. And there were Pitty's feelings to consider. If owning that ugly brooch would make her feel better, then he would have to do his best to acquire it. After he found out its authenticity and value, it shouldn't be difficult to convince the green-eyed American to sell.

Katherine Stewart should wear emeralds anyway, he thought, stripping off his clothes. Or tourmalines, to match those eyes. And nothing else, he decided, remembering the fit of her sweater and the way her pants clung to slim legs. Perhaps spending a couple of hours with her wouldn't be such a hardship after all. He'd go along with Pitty's scheme, up to a point. Just to humor the old girl.

After all, what were the chances that the Thorne Diamond would turn up on his doorstep after two hundred years? All he had to do was prove the stone was glass and he could return to the hall, blessedly alone and confident he'd done his best to make an old woman happy.

And, just to be cautious, he'd call Pitty's physician in the morning.

THE BOXY BLACK TAXI stopped in front of the St. Giles, and the driver waited patiently as Kate sorted through her British money. The array of coins was confusing. Embarrassed, she held out a palmful of coins and let the driver take what he needed.

"And the tip," she reminded him.

"Thanks, luv," he said, nodding his head.

Kate stumbled out of the cab and headed toward the door of the hotel. She managed to collect her luggage, check in at the desk and stumble to the elevator that took her to her sixth-floor room. She didn't bother to unpack. Her mind, foggy from lack of sleep, swam with images of London. In twenty-four hours she'd flown from Boston to England, walked through the streets of St. James and Piccadilly, toured the Tower of London and met a duke and a duchess. Thorne House was as she'd imagined, splendid and elegant.

Tea with a duchess. A walk with a duke. Would anyone believe it? Kate rummaged through her suitcase and found her flannel nightgown and her cosmetics bag. She brushed her teeth in the tiny bathroom, then undressed quickly and snuggled under the covers of the single bed. The room was small, so small that it would be difficult to get out of bed if the chair wasn't pushed in place under the desk. A television hung from the ceiling, and a small window stood in the corner by a simple armoire.

Kate pulled the covers up to her chin and took a deep breath. The queasy feeling that had plagued her since Jeff broke their engagement had eased a little, and her heart didn't ache as much as it had before. She'd been right—the change of scenery had been good for her already. Despite everything that had happened in the past two months, she'd survived. Kate smiled as she closed her eyes; she was no glamour girl, no sexy twenty-one-year-old with long legs and masses of hair. Jeff had made his choice; now it was up to her to get over it. She'd lost her boyfriend and she'd lost her job, but she'd plan the rest of her life the same way she'd planned this trip to London: she'd cram as much as she could into every day and not worry about what anyone else thought.

KATE HESITATED at the entrance to the large breakfast room and handed her room card to the maître d'. After the complimentary buffet breakfast, she planned to wander down Charing Cross Road, see Carlton House Terrace and walk around Covent Garden. She'd read there was an antique market there on Mondays. Then there was the free bus tour this afternoon, something else included in the package from British Airways she didn't want to miss.

The man nodded and handed it back to her. "The Duke of Thornecrest is waiting for you, miss."

She hadn't expected to be told the duke was in the St. Giles dining room. "The Duke of Thornecrest?"

The maître d' pointed to a table for two against the

far wall where William Landry sat reading a newspaper. Kate walked carefully around a table full of rolls and cold cereal to join the duke. He stood when she approached, an apologetic smile on his handsome face.

"I hope you'll forgive me," he said, waiting for her to be seated before he joined her. "I was told this was the best way to catch up with you this morning."

"But how did you know when I'd be here?" *And why are you waiting for me?*

The waiter approached, asked her if she wanted coffee and poured a foaming liquid into her cup. It looked hot and strong, but why was it foaming? She eyed it with suspicion and took a cautious sip. Not bad, she decided, just a little different.

"Your schedule." He folded his paper and set it aside. He wore dark slacks and a charcoal sweater over a gray-striped shirt. No jeans and scruffy jacket today, she noted. Today he looked as if he was indeed an English aristocrat. "You showed it to me yesterday afternoon."

Kate placed her napkin in her lap and took another fortifying sip of coffee. "Okay, you read about my travel plans. Why—"

"Why am I here?" he finished for her, his smile charming. "I expected you to ask."

"Consider yourself asked, then."

He leaned back in his chair. "Pitty insisted you required a tour guide. She says, um, she says you, er, have the look of a Landry, so you must be a member of the family through some connection."

"Then Aunt Laurabelle was right."

He frowned. "Aunt Laurabelle?"

"She gave me the brooch. She never had any children, and I was the niece closest to her."

"Aunt, er, Laurabelle is the person who told you the story about the relative who may or may not have come from London and may or may not be related to the Landry family?"

"Yes."

"I see." He eyed her with a thoughtful expression. "Pitty could be correct after all."

"It's nice of her to worry about me, but I don't think I'll have any trouble finding my way around London. I bought several maps and—"

"You're refusing me, then?" He looked disappointed.

"I'm sure a duke has better things to do than act like a tourist." This was one of the strangest conversations she'd ever had. How could she tell a duke she didn't want to spend the day with him?

"Actually I don't," the duke was saying. "I've been dragged to town for the refurbishment. Pitty pretends she needs my advice, when actually she just wants company. She thinks I spend too much time in the country."

"Do you?"

He smiled, showing a perfect set of white teeth. "Yes, thank goodness. Why don't we have breakfast and discuss the day ahead?" He looked at his watch. "It's only eight o'clock. There's plenty of time for you to decide whether or not you'll let me tag along."

"All right." She hated to eat alone. Besides, she and William were related...maybe. And she didn't want to be rude to someone who had gone out of his way to be nice to a total stranger. "I didn't mean to be rude."

William looked surprised. "You're not the one to apologize, Katherine. I'm forcing my company upon you because my grandmother thinks you need a guide.'' He gave her another charming smile, one that warmed a little corner of her frozen heart. ''Now you're forced to converse with a stranger over breakfast, which must also tax your patience.''

''I don't...''

He slowly stood up. ''I'll tell Pitty I couldn't find you,'' he offered, tossing his napkin on the table. She noted his rough hands, the callus on his right thumb. A duke who preferred farming, he'd said. A man who would rather be working outdoors than sight-seeing in London. Kate knew she couldn't send him away even if she wanted to, which she didn't. The idea of touring alone had seemed better in Rhode Island than the reality of being in London with no one to talk to. ''Please, sit down.''

He paused, one eyebrow raised, waiting for an explanation.

''I hate to eat alone.''

''So do I.'' He gestured toward the buffet. ''Shall we?''

''Sure.'' Kate crossed the crowded room and eyed the selection of food. Aside from the stack of yogurt cups, everything in the heated bins looked as if it contained at least one hundred grams of fat. She didn't have to diet anymore, she reminded herself as she took a plate from the stack at the end of the table. She didn't have to squeeze her size-9 body into a size-7 wedding dress in order to look good in the photographs.

She could let herself go, at least for a week. Kate speared a thick sausage and dropped it on her plate. She was on vacation, so she might as well enjoy herself.

''Ever had bangers before?'' William said from behind her.

''Bangers?'' She glanced up at him. Was the duke

turning kinky now that she'd invited him to stay for breakfast?

His eyes twinkled. "Sausages." He nodded toward her plate. "Take two. I think you'll like them."

She did as he suggested and watched as he helped himself to four of the sausages. She skipped the eggs, selected a bagel, a small helping of fried potatoes and a bowl of canned apricots. Tomorrow she would be sensible and eat yogurt, but today she'd laugh in the face of cholesterol and eat "bangers" for breakfast. After all, she was in England, alone. She could do anything she wanted.

HE WAS INSANE, Will told himself. He'd let Pitty talk him into this, and now he had talked Katherine out of dismissing him. He could have left, he *should* have left when he'd had the opportunity. Pitty would have had no choice but to accept the fact that the Thorne Diamond hadn't returned to London after all. And pigs would fly, he thought, spearing his final portion of sausage.

"We'll walk down Charing Cross Road and then through Covent Garden before heading to Buckingham Palace," Kate said as she reached inside her purse. "I've looked at the map, and it doesn't look too far away."

"It's not." But Longmire's and Pitty's expectant jeweler were in the opposite direction. "What about a tour of St. James Square?"

"I did that yesterday, on my way to Thorne House." She studied her list, her chestnut hair brushing the paper.

"Oh." He should be able to think of some way to convince her to walk through that area again.

"It was very nice," she assured him.

"If you like jewelry, there's a store there you might—"

"I don't think I'd be able to afford anything in there." Katherine turned her green-eyed gaze on him, and all thoughts of Longmire's flew out of his head. He'd always preferred pale blondes with long legs and a certain level of sophistication. How could he explain his fascination with a luscious little redhead—or was it more brunette?—who wolfed down four bangers for breakfast and admitted she didn't have eight generations of her family's money to spend on baubles. "I read that Covent Garden has an antique market today."

"Antiques," he repeated. "You like antiques?"

She shrugged. "I like old costume jewelry and little things like that. You never know what you'll find, you know."

"Oh, I know." William stood and picked up his coat. "I'm quite aware of that, you see."

Katherine smiled at him as she stood up and hooked her purse straps over her shoulder. "Then maybe you'll find something at the market, too."

"Perhaps," he conceded, still wondering why the sudden attraction to green eyes. Of course, the luscious little body didn't hurt, either.

He waited downstairs in the lobby while she went to her room for her coat and the indispensable guidebook. When she returned, the brooch was pinned to her coat lapel, as it had been yesterday. William didn't know whether to be relieved the pin was still available or annoyed at the sparkling reminder of his grandmother's failing mental capacities.

"Is something wrong?"

William realized he was frowning at her. He made an effort to tear his gaze from the pin and force his lips into a smile. Or at least what he hoped looked like a pleasant expression. "No. I was thinking about our morning. You don't mind walking? It's a bit cloudy, but I doubt we'll get wet."

"I'd rather walk," she agreed, so he led her out to the sidewalk and turned toward Oxford Street and Charing Cross Road. Somehow he'd have to figure out how to stroll by Longmire's. He could invent an errand, he supposed. With a few turns they could be in St. James instead of Covent Garden, and she'd never suspect him of deliberately confusing the directions.

He hadn't counted on the damn map. Katherine pulled it out and examined it at regular intervals, despite his assurances that he knew the way to the Covent Garden Market.

As they headed down Garrick Street, Katherine was clearly enjoying herself, he realized. She studied the buildings and the assortment of people around them with undisguised interest as they negotiated the narrow sidewalks. They passed the theater where *Miss Saigon* played, then spotted the open square of the marketplace. Off to the left was a covered area crammed full of tables and people.

"That must be it," Katherine said, and increased her pace toward the flea market.

"Stay with me," William warned, conscious of pickpockets. Under the roof were crowded paths between tables laden with silver, jewelry and the oddest assortment of things he'd ever seen. It looked as if everyone there had dumped the contents of their cellars and attics on their tables.

Katherine was thrilled. "Look," she said, pointing to a pile of silver spoons. "Do you think they're old?"

"Yes." And ugly. He hurried after her to the next table, where she glanced at an assortment of cracked teapots and ceramic figures.

"You don't have to stay in here," she said. "I could meet you outside in an hour or so."

"I'll stay." He wandered the aisles beside her, watching as she peered into glass cases of jewelry and eyed little boxes of Roman coins. At a corner table he picked up a silver candlestick with a distinctive pattern on its base.

Katherine turned. "What did you find?"

"I'm not sure." The markings were right, but would it match the one at the Hall?

"Thirty pounds will take it home," the ruddy-faced owner said, nodding toward William.

"I'll think about it," he replied, setting the candlestick back on the table. Katherine peered into a glass case filled with rings, and William saw the man's eyes widen as he spotted the brooch.

"How much is that one?" Katherine asked. The man blinked and turned his attention to the display case.

"Which one, dearie?"

"The tiny one with the pearls and...emeralds?"

"Victorian," he announced, putting it into her palm. "Late Victorian, and those are emeralds. Very delicate," he added. "It suits you."

"How much?" She slipped it on her middle finger and admired the effect.

"For you, forty pounds."

"Twenty," William interjected.

"Thirty." The owner grinned. "Final offer, guv."

"I'll think about it," Katherine said, handing the man the ring.

"Come back soon if you want it," he cautioned as he replaced it in the case. "Rings like this don't last long, especially at that price."

"Thank you anyway," she said, and crossed the aisle to the next row of tables.

The red-faced man turned to William. "So, you must be Thornecrest."

"How—"

He shook his head and continued in an awed voice. "I didn't think the Thorne Diamond existed. Just read about it, y'know. Lost in 1814, wasn't it?" He looked over at Katherine, in conversation with a lady selling lace. "But not lost after all. Plain as day, staring at me. Couldn't believe my eyes, I couldn't."

He had to mean the brooch. "It's a copy," William explained.

"No." The man shook his head again. "That's the real thing, it is." He handed William one of his cards. "Give this to your lady, in case she changes her mind about the ring. I'm here every Monday."

William took the card, but he didn't want to discuss the odd brooch any longer. "It's not what you think."

The man winked. "She must be the future duchess. No wedding ring yet, I see, but it's only a matter of time, according to the legend." He winked once again, and William turned away. He hurried to catch up with Katherine, who had moved on to another display of costume jewelry. So Pitty wasn't the only one who recognized the brooch. He eyed it curiously as Katherine chatted with a lady who had necklaces for sale. The central yellow stone winked and sparkled, even in the dim building. White diamonds and emeralds surrounded the large stone, with rays of yellow topaz shooting to the corner in an ornate metal setting that looked to be painted.

"What do you think?" Katherine asked.

He glanced up. She held up an amber necklace, a simple strand of beads that matched the highlights of her hair. "Lovely," he murmured, picturing the beads on naked skin.

"Ten pounds?" She looked uncertain.

"A bargain," he assured her.

"It *would* be a perfect souvenir from Covent Garden."

"What about the emerald ring?"

"I can't have both, and this is cheaper."

"Then you should buy it," he insisted. "It suits you."

She handed the woman the money and then fastened the necklace around her neck as William watched. The heavy beads fell above her breasts and gleamed against the black sweater.

William gulped. He'd broken a major rule today. Shopping with a woman was something he'd avoided up until now, although Covent Garden wasn't exactly Regent Street and Kate didn't appear to expect him to pay for the amber beads. Still, he wasn't acting like himself at all. Since yesterday, since that damn pin had appeared, his life had been turned upside down.

It was time to take control.

3

"WE'LL HAVE a light lunch at Green's Oyster Bar, near St. James Street," William announced as he turned from the gates of Buckingham Palace. "They serve a delicious selection of seafood, especially oysters. I'm sure you'll enjoy it. Then we could do some shopping in the area."

Kate's heart sank. She hated to refuse him, but she had all the oysters she wanted in Rhode Island and she was certain she couldn't afford to buy anything in the exclusive neighborhood of Thorne House. "Oh, I'm sorry. I booked an afternoon tour and I have to be at Russell Square by two-thirty."

He frowned at his watch, then at her. "What sort of tour?"

"A bus tour of London. It came with the package, so I'd hate to miss it." Kate didn't believe that he was disappointed she couldn't have lunch with him. She knew the duchess had coerced him into spending the day with her, which only embarrassed her a little. Her ego had been so badly trampled that a little bit of pity from a duchess couldn't make much difference. Kate rummaged through her bag and found a map. "There's a tube stop at Russell Square, so getting there should be easy."

"Where are you supposed to meet this tour?"

She glanced through her papers hurriedly. His

frown made her nervous. "At the Royal National. I think it's right around the corner from the tube."

He took her elbow. "I'll go with you."

"On the bus? I think they're booked ahead—"

"Not on the bus," he said. "To the hotel."

"You don't have to do that, William." She liked calling him by his first name once in a while. It made her feel that he was almost...friendly. Which, she concluded, glancing at his stern expression, was probably just an illusion. Although he could be charming when he wanted to. It was easy enough to like him when he was trying to be likable. He had the kind of lean strength that made her long to curl up against him.

She reminded herself he was a duke.

"Yes," he replied, taking her elbow and turning her around. "I know."

William seemed familiar with London's subway system and got them to Russell Square easily. When they emerged from the stairway, Kate stopped on the sidewalk and tried to get her bearings.

"This way." He pointed to a street on their right. "We can get a bite to eat at the hotel."

"Just a minute," she said, and started off toward a grassy park where people were lounging on benches and eating out of cardboard containers. "There must be a place over here."

They rounded the corner and saw a line in front of a low building. The smell of fish and french fries wafted through the air. "Fish and chips!" She grinned happily. "Let's get some."

He stopped. "Here?"

"Sure. Why not?"

William looked as if he could have given her a few hundred reasons, but she turned away before he could say anything. He followed her along the paved path to the building. Tables and chairs dotted the concrete patio in front of the restaurant. "You get a table," Kate told him. "I'll get lunch."

William opened his mouth to protest.

"No, really." Kate stopped him. "It's my treat. You've been so nice, it's the least I can do." The line was moving quickly, and she was soon able to order two plates of fish and chips and two soft drinks. The young man behind the cash register took her money and handed her two large cups of soda, then told her she'd have to wait a bit for the food. The line for lunch had lengthened, and the cooks looked harried.

Kate crossed the patio to where William sat. She set the drinks in front of him. "The fish will be here in a minute. I think they're pretty busy."

"We could still go to the hotel. They're sure to have a restaurant—"

"And eat inside? No way." She went back to the building to wait for their lunch. When she returned with two cardboard plates piled high with fish and french fries, William eyed it hungrily.

"Here," she said, dropping plastic forks and paper napkins on the table. "Help yourself."

"Thank you." He arranged his napkin in his lap and picked up the fork. "I appreciate the lunch."

"You're welcome. I know this morning wasn't your idea of a good time."

"Why would you say that?"

"I'm sure dukes have better things to do than play tour guide to distant American cousins." She speared a piece of fish and sampled it. "Mmm, good," she murmured. "This is something I've always wanted to do."

"Dine in Russell Square?"

"Eat fish and chips in England."

"Does this live up to your expectations?"

"Yes." An outdoor English lunch with a handsome duke? She couldn't hide her smile. What a story she'd have to tell when she got home.

"I see you're wearing your pin again today. It matches the color of the daffodils."

Kate reached to touch it. "Yes. I think it brings me luck."

"Why?"

"I'm not sure. Back home things kept going wrong, and since I've been in England *nice* things have happened. If I were a superstitious person, I'd think Aunt Belle's pin had something to do with it."

To her surprise, he didn't smile, just regarded the pin with a serious expression. "Some people might believe so."

She turned her attention to her lunch. "What brings you luck?"

He shrugged. "I have no idea."

"Maybe because you're a duke you don't need any."

"I've never thought about it," he admitted, pushing his empty plate away a few inches. "I suppose most people would consider me fortunate."

"What about your parents?"

"Both dead. Pitty—my grandmother—raised me."

"I'm sorry."

"It's not as tragic as it sounds."

She didn't believe him. "Do you have any brothers or sisters?"

"No. I come from a long line of only children." A bitter smile accompanied the casual words, and Kate's heart twisted in sympathy. "And you? I suppose you come from an enormous family."

"Three sisters, all married, all living in Rhode Island. My parents died four years ago." He waited for her to continue. "Everyone thought I was crazy to come to England instead of job hunting."

"Did you need to 'get away' from something in particular?"

"My fiancé called off our wedding last month, which was bad enough, but I worked as a computer programmer for his father, so I lost my job, too."

His perfect eyebrows rose over his brown eyes. "A bit of bad luck," he agreed. "You enjoyed computers?"

"No, not really." She took one more bite of french fry and wiped her lips with her napkin. "I was looking forward to being married and having children and making pot roast and apple pies." She made a face. "I know you're not supposed to admit to something so old-fashioned, but I really was excited about having babies and pushing strollers and all that."

"I'm sure you'll find someone else," he assured her.

"What about you?"

"Me?"

"Don't dukes get married?"

"Not this one."

"Maybe I've read too many romances, but don't dukes have to get married and have a son to carry on the family name and all that? Like Prince Charles and his two sons. Don't they call them the 'heir and the spare'?"

"I've heard that," he drawled. "But I have no desire to marry. The dukes of Thornecrest have had marriages more turbulent than Prince Charles's and Princess Diana's. I have no desire to carry on that particular family tradition." He looked at his watch and stood. "You're going to miss your tour unless we leave now."

Together they gathered up the garbage, deposited it in a nearby trash can and walked along the path to the street corner. It was an odd place to say goodbye, but Kate held out her hand and he shook it briefly.

"Thanks for everything," she said, meaning the words. "You didn't have to be so kind, and I appreciate your taking the time to show me around."

"It was nothing," he said, looking down at her.

"It was quite a bit," she countered. "I'll be sure to tell my family that I met a real-life duke and he was very nice."

He smiled, a very charming smile that made Kate's breath catch in her throat. "And I'll be sure to tell my grandmother you enjoyed yourself," he promised.

"Thank you." She forced herself to turn away and cross the street as the light conveniently turned green. The mild spring breeze blew her hair across her face as she adjusted her purse straps on her shoulder and headed for the hotel. She fought the urge to turn back and wave, knowing that the Duke of Thornecrest was certain to be heaving a sigh of relief now that he was finished fulfilling his grandmother's idea of family duty. She'd write the duchess a note next week and thank her for being so thoughtful.

"YOU LET HER GO? You let her walk away? What on earth were you thinking?"

The Duke of Thornecrest tossed his coat to the maid, then loosened his tie. He went to the sideboard and poured himself a drink. Scotch, he decided. He was definitely in the mood for Scotch. "Should I have tackled her in the middle of Bloomsbury and dragged her to Longmire's?"

Pitty sniffed her disapproval. "You should have

kept her with you. What if something happens to the pin?"

He took a grateful swallow of whiskey. "On a bus tour?"

"I'll have one of those," she said, nodding toward the glass of whiskey. "With a little ice."

William fixed her a drink and crossed the living room to hand it to her. She wore a lime green sweater-and-skirt set today. The color made his head ache. "Here," he said. "You can drown your sorrows with this."

"I don't have any sorrow. Except one." She took a sip, then studied her grandson. "You smell like fish."

He ignored her. He wasn't going to tell her that he'd had a very pleasant lunch at a dingy metal table in Russell Square, or that he hadn't been able to take Katherine to a restaurant around the corner from the jeweler's. He wasn't going to tell her he was disappointed that Katherine's wonderful figure stayed hidden under her black coat, or that when she smiled at him and shook his hand he'd felt a jolt of lust that nearly knocked him to the sidewalk.

"You're going out tonight?"

"I'd planned to, yes." Actually he'd made no plans, thinking he would be home at the Hall tonight. And Pitty knew it, too.

Pitty's fingers drummed on the sofa. "And the diamond? Where will that be? Do you remember?"

Unfortunately he did. "I imagine Miss Stewart will be wearing her brooch to the theater tonight. *Miss Saigon*, I believe."

"Then you will escort our little cousin to the theater."

"It would be impossible to get another ticket to *Miss Saigon* this late in the day, Pitty."

Even as he said the words, he knew he was wrong. She had that familiar determined look on her face, the look he'd first seen when he was ten years old and a solicitor had told her she was too old to raise a child. She'd stared at the man, with her "queen face," as he'd called it, until the solicitor stammered an apology and hurried from the library. Pitty had remained his guardian until he'd no longer needed one.

"Nonsense." She reached for the phone and began to dial. "I'll take care of everything."

"She's going to think I'm a stalker," he grumbled. "A lunatic. A lust-crazed aristocrat out to shadow her every move."

"Quiet," Pitty ordered, then turned her attention to the voice on the other end of the phone.

William stood in front of one of the long east windows and finished his drink during Pitty's conversation with one of her cronies. He should never have come to London. He was accustomed to having his own way, of being in charge of his own life, until Pitty decided to interfere. She used his affection for her shamelessly, knowing full well he could deny her nothing. Now she'd involved him in a wild-goose chase over the ugliest brooch in Britain...with one of the most appealing women.

"You now have box seats for tonight's performance," Pitty declared, replacing the receiver. "Miss Stewart will be enchanted."

"She's not my type."

"Of course she isn't." Pitty chuckled. "What an outrageous thought! This has nothing to do with matchmaking, my dear. We're restoring a family heirloom to its rightful owner."

"You?"

Pitty shook her head. "You. There have been no happy marriages since the gem disappeared generations ago. It was a wedding gift from the mother of the first duchess, you know. And rumored to have been part of Edward the Confessor's coronation crown."

"*If* it is real, Pitty."

Her expression was wistful as she looked up at him. "I pray it is, Willie. Then you can settle down and have sons. I've made a list of eligible women for you, so take your time—"

"Do not continue, Pitty. A dozen brooches wouldn't make me marry Jessica or anyone else, for that matter. Landrys have a poor history for that sort of thing, as well you know."

Pitty shrugged and finished her drink with one long swallow. "Once we own the brooch, the rest will take care of itself." She glared at him. "I thought you promised to help me."

"Up to a point," he agreed. "And then I call your physician."

"There is nothing wrong with my mind, William. I'm as sharp as a tack, and you know it." He noticed her hand shook as she set her empty glass on the table.

"Perhaps," he teased, knowing she expected it. He didn't want to embarrass her by letting on he'd seen her trembling hand. "You'll need your wits to convince Katherine to allow me to accompany her to the theater tonight."

"Ten pounds says I can do it."

"Ten pounds it is," he agreed.

"And will you take her to dinner afterward?"

"Don't push your luck. I'll see her safely to her hotel, nothing more."

"That's enough," his grandmother declared. "I'm perfectly satisfied with that."

"Why don't I believe you?"

Pitty didn't answer. Instead, she stretched out on the couch and closed her eyes.

He went to his room and found the list of names propped against his pillow. Twelve women Pitty thought suitable for the position of Duchess of Thornecrest. Jessica's name was at the top; the Smithfields' youngest granddaughter was next. The others were no more than acquaintances, although three bore the surnames of Pitty's oldest friends. William didn't know whether to laugh or curse. It was obvious he must prove the pin was a fake or fend off prospective brides for the rest of his life.

"HAVE YOU EVER SEEN *Miss Saigon?*"

"No. I've always wanted to." This was going too far, Kate decided. The duke and his grandmother didn't have to make sure she had good seats to the theater. He didn't have to escort her. He didn't have to look so handsome as he strolled beside her across the St. Giles's utilitarian lobby.

"You're upset," William declared, opening the door onto the street. "I told Pitty not to call you."

"You did?" So he hadn't wanted to take her to the theater after all. Which was no surprise, she realized, ignoring her disappointment.

"Yes." He took her elbow and guided her across bustling Oxford Street. At seven it was dark, but the city was alive with people. Kate shivered, noting the dampness that had come with the night. "I thought you would find the suggestion an invasion of privacy."

"She told me it would be a favor to her to keep you company."

"I assumed it would be something like that." When they were safely on the sidewalk on Charing Cross, he looked down at her, a worried expression in his eyes. "I thought we'd walk, but if you're cold we can hail a taxi."

"I'd like to walk. I get to see more of the city that way."

"You're not tired?"

"I took a nap after the bus tour," she confessed. "I think I'm still fighting the time difference."

She'd slept until Pitty had called, asking her help with her "stubborn grandson." She worried about him, the elderly woman had confided. Worried that he was lonely in London, that he would grow so bored he would return to the country ahead of schedule, leaving Pitty with no one. Kate didn't believe that story for a minute. William's grandmother had something else on her mind, or maybe she was simply eccentric. Whatever the reason, Kate had decided she'd be crazy to turn down an escort to the theater.

"What about you?" she asked. "What does a duke do in London in the afternoon?"

"A duke takes care of business," he replied.

"Farm business?"

"Yes."

"There must be quite a bit of it."

"Yes. And Pitty requires help with the redecoration of Thorne House."

"She must value your opinion."

"That's what she'd like me to believe. Tell me what

you saw today," he suggested, easily changing the subject.

"I think we saw everything." She smiled in the darkness. "We spent a lot of time admiring the bridges."

"Were you suitably impressed?"

"Of course." She liked him when he relaxed. When he teased her she forgot he was a duke and enjoyed him as a man. A man, she realized, feeling the warmth of his hand on her arm, who was definitely attractive. One of the most handsome men she'd ever seen. He was also rich, polite and kind—perhaps they were requirements for an aristocrat. Well, maybe not kind. William Landry might be an exception. Or maybe she'd read too many historical novels.

They wound through the streets of the Covent Garden area until the Drury Lane Theatre was in sight. The ornate lobby was thick with people, but Will led her through the crowd and up a red-carpeted staircase and down a narrow corridor to a curtained box. The usher checked their tickets, sold William a program, wished them a good evening and left them to their seats. Kate thought she'd died and gone to heaven.

"May I take your coat?"

"Thank you." She forced her attention away from the crowds pouring into the theater. Another first for Kate Stewart: an evening of London theater. She unbuttoned her coat and stood. William helped her slide it from her arms and placed it carefully on a nearby chair.

"I notice you're not wearing your brooch—" He stopped in midsentence as he turned back to her, his gaze focused briefly on her chest. "It's quite lovely where it is now, of course," he murmured, lifting his gaze to her face.

She felt her cheeks grow warm, the curse of pale skin and hair with a touch of red to it. She'd worn her new chestnut knit dress, a simple design with a V neck, long sleeves and a hem just above her knees. She'd pinned the brooch to the point of the V, and that, along with gold earrings, was her only jewelry. Jeff had always said her eyes were her best feature, stating her breasts were a "little too obvious." He'd also said he wished she was taller, that she lighten her hair and wear more makeup.

To hell with him.

"Thank you." She lifted her chin, hoping William wouldn't realize he'd flustered her.

He gestured toward her seat, and she took it, anxious for the show to begin. She didn't want to feel attracted to him. It was too embarrassing, too much a cliché.

William removed his own coat, revealing a perfectly tailored charcoal suit and striped white shirt. The tie was a conservative paisley in shades of gray and maroon. "Two kings were shot in this theater. George II and George III. Are you familiar with English history?"

"A little. The guidebook said this is where William IV first saw Mrs. Jordan."

"So you're a romantic." He sat down and leaned back in his seat to look at her. "Love at first sight, happily ever after."

He made it sound like something horrible. "Of course. I'm the person who wants children and pot roasts, remember?"

"Yes." His gaze dropped to the brooch, then moved back to her eyes. "What would you do with a great deal of money, Katherine?"

"Travel," she replied easily. "Buy a house, maybe. Help my nieces with college, things like that."

"You've given it some thought."

"Rhode Island has a lottery. I play it sometimes."

"When you feel lucky." He nodded toward the brooch. "Maybe that will bring you luck, as you said."

Kate touched the middle stone with her index finger. "I think it already has."

"And if it was valuable?"

"If it was valuable, I'd have to make sure I took very good care of it."

He opened his mouth to reply, but the theater darkened. Kate settled back in her seat and prepared to enjoy her first taste of London theater. She couldn't believe this was only her second day in England. She didn't know how it could get any better than this.

William leaned toward her. "Is something the matter?"

She realized she'd sighed too loudly. "I was just thinking, I could go home tomorrow and be happy."

He gave her an odd look, then smiled. "I'm glad you're enjoying yourself so much."

"Thank you for tonight," she whispered as the curtains rose. "I'm sure your grandmother put you up to it, but it was nice of you to go along with it."

William turned startled brown eyes in her direction. "Nice?"

"Yes, you *are* nice," she stated, turning her attention to the stage. "Whether you like it or not," she added softly.

HE LIKED IT. Too much. He liked the way her hair glinted red in the sunlight and darkened in the dim light of the theater. He liked the way she smiled at him and the way her green eyes lit up when she teased. He liked that damn brown dress and the soft, enticing cleavage above the sparkling pin. He didn't care for her choice of restaurants or her ambitious tourist plans. He didn't think she'd forego a tour of Hampton Court for three days in a suite at the Ritz.

She might believe in romance, but he believed in lust.

Kate cried at the end of the show. He handed her a handkerchief and waited for the tears to subside. He'd seen this particular show with three other women, and all of them had wept a little, careful not to smear their eye makeup. Kate couldn't be worried about eye makeup, he decided, not with the flood of tears pouring down her cheeks.

He cleared his throat. "Are you all right?"

She took a deep, shuddering breath. "It's been a rough month."

"I can see that." He waited, pretending a patience he didn't feel. He hoped she would get herself under control soon, before people began to stare.

"It's just that I thought it was all planned." She sniffed. "My life, I mean. Oh, the wedding was all planned, too, but that was just going to be one day out of a whole lifetime of wonderful things."

"Like children and pot roast," he added, longing to put his arms around her. He drummed his fingers on his thighs. "Would you like some air?"

She nodded but she didn't move. "He said I didn't interest him anymore, that he was bored already."

Bored? William's gaze was incredulous. The man must have been an idiot. "Do you still love him?" For some reason it was important to know.

"No." Katherine winced. "I'm too angry."

"What's wrong with being angry?"

"It hurts."

"Oh." He waited as she wiped her tears and took another deep breath. "Would you like some dinner? Londoners dine after the theater," he explained, hoping to distract her. "Or we could have coffee and dessert somewhere, if you prefer."

"I'd like that."

He stood and helped her with her coat. He patted her shoulders in what he hoped was a reassuring gesture. She didn't appear to mind. They discovered a shop nearby, with tempting pastries displayed in the window. They drank coffee topped with whipped cream. She offered him a bite of her chocolate truffle cake; he shared his éclair and told scandalous stories of royal affairs, pleased with himself when the sparkle returned to her eyes. He hailed a cab, bundled her inside and saw her safely to the front door of the St. Giles.

"Wait here, please," he told the driver, then escorted Katherine inside, through the empty lobby and around the corner to the elevator. Kate hesitated before pushing the sixth-floor button.

"Thank you again," she told him, her lips curved into an appealing smile. "I enjoyed the day."

"So did I." He meant it, too. He put his hands on her shoulders and stepped closer, lowering his head. Surprise flickered across her face, but then his lips touched hers and he closed his eyes. What began as a simple good-night kiss turned into something more, something he didn't want to stop. He'd expected warmth and sweetness; he hadn't expected heat and passion. He felt her lean closer, and he moved so their bodies touched. Despite the layers of wool coats between them, he could sense the heat from her skin and feel her tremble when his tongue parted her lips.

He stopped, blinked, released her. He managed to say good-night; she said something equally polite in response, but he didn't bother to listen. He turned and walked out of the hotel before he could change his mind.

He arrived at Thorne House in minutes, not long enough to forget the feel of Katherine's body against his. Not long enough for the aching tension in his body to ease.

Not long enough to decide what he was going to do about her. William Landry didn't seduce American tourists, especially not vulnerable "cousins" recovering from broken hearts and canceled weddings.

He should run; he should hide. He should return to the manor and bury himself in spring-planting preparations. He should go skiing and have sex with Jessica or someone else equally sophisticated, someone who wouldn't expect anything more than discretion and the good sense to leave the bedroom before dawn. Katherine would expect sweet words and promises and happily-ever-after.

He didn't know why he was thinking this way about a woman he'd only met yesterday. A woman who wore a pin that drove his grandmother insane with curiosity and longing. He didn't care about the pin. The damn piece of jewelry was what had gotten him into this mess in the first place.

"Well?" Pitty peered out from behind her bedroom door. He could see a strip of crimson chiffon from her neck to her toes.

He stopped in the wide corridor, knowing he was trapped. He unbuttoned his coat and reached up to loosen his tie. "Don't put any more lists on my bed, Pitty."

"I just thought—"

He cut her off. He was not about to discuss her crazy marriage plots. "Did you have a pleasant evening?"

"Very nice, thank you." Her tone was hurt. "Did you?"

"Yes."

"Will she sell the brooch?"

"I don't know. And you're not buying it unless you know it's authentic."

"Tomorrow," Pitty declared. "Tomorrow you will drag her into Longmire's and have the pin appraised. I don't care how you do it. This foolishness can't continue."

He'd like to drag Katherine somewhere, but it wouldn't be to a jeweler. But he did agree that this couldn't continue. He had to get control of himself. "I believe she's taking a tour tomorrow."

Pitty looked at him with her queen face. "Have her postpone it," she ordered. "This has gone far enough. I will call her in the morning and explain everything."

"No," he replied, looking her right in the eye. "You won't. I will take care of this from now on, without your interference. I will determine whether or not the diamond is real, and if so, I will purchase it. From now on you are no longer involved."

"But—"

"Good night." He watched her eyes widen, then her mouth closed in a thin line and she shut the door. William didn't linger in the dark hallway. He wanted to get to his rooms and a cold shower. He heard Pitty's door open again and he stopped, bracing himself for another argument.

"Willie!"

He didn't turn around. "What is it now, Pitty?"

Her voice was triumphant. "You owe me ten pounds."

KATE EYED the telephone and tried to remember the time difference between London and Rhode Island. Five or six hours? Forward or backward? What a day it had been: buying an antique necklace in Covent Garden, eating fish and chips in a park and watching *Miss Saigon* with a handsome bachelor who just happened to be a duke. She'd never met anyone like William Landry before, and she wasn't sure how she would describe him. Self-contained, naturally. Cynical? Sometimes. Polite to a fault and dangerously charming, definitely.

Kate climbed into the narrow bed and turned off the bedside lamp. She pulled the covers over her shoulders and snuggled into the pillows. William Landry was also an experienced kisser and a very passionate man. He kissed her as if he found her irresistible, which made her smile into the darkness. His suit probably cost more than she made in a month, and yet he'd treated her like a princess. Correction, he'd treated her like a desirable woman. And that's what made him so very interesting. Apart from all the other things, that is.

It was over. She'd toured Thorne House as she'd intended. She'd had the unexpected bonus of William's company while sight-seeing and at the theater this evening. She'd thanked him; he'd kissed her. She'd said goodbye, not good-night. There was no reason to think she'd ever see him again.

All the same, it had been quite an adventure.

4

KATE WOKE EARLY, before the alarm buzzed at six o'clock. She wrote postcards, took a quick shower and put on her black stretch pants, suede boots, brown turtleneck and ivory cardigan. The amber beads added just the right touch, she decided, hooking them around her neck. After all, she was going to a castle and a palace today. She wanted to be comfortable, but she didn't want to look like a frump. She'd enjoyed dressing up last night, enjoyed the flattering expression on William's face when he saw her.

Jeff had looked at her like that in the beginning. Then he had stopped being charming, and his criticisms had begun. Maybe a lot of men were like that. She put on her makeup, fixed her hair and checked to make sure she had enough money. After a hearty breakfast of bangers and bagels, Kate hurried to the lobby. The tour bus stopped at the St. Giles at eight-fifteen, but the concierge had advised being early. A familiar figure stood by the fern in the corner, tall and lean in jeans and a patterned sweater, a raincoat folded over one arm. He smiled a little sheepishly as she walked over to him.

"What are you doing here?"

"Spending the day with you," William replied. "If you'll allow me."

"Did your grandmother put you up to this again?"

She refused to be the object of the dowager's pity any longer.

He shook his head. "She was still in bed when I left. Supervising the refurbishment has worn her out, I suppose."

"I'm heading to Hampton Court and Windsor Castle. The tour bus should be here any minute."

"Could I possibly talk you into postponing that until tomorrow? I thought you might like to see Kensington Palace, where Princess Di lives. I'll even take you to some of the stores where she shops." He gave her a charming smile and waited for her answer.

"I can't. I'm sorry." She certainly was, she thought. "But I already paid for this tour, thirty-eight pounds, and it's only offered twice a week in the winter. This is my only chance. We also have lunch in a real pub, so I wouldn't want to miss it."

"And what about Kensington? You shouldn't miss it."

"It's on my schedule for Saturday." There. He could go home to his mansion and tell the dowager that he had done his best, but their American cousin already had plans for the day. She was a little tired of people feeling sorry for her.

"Too bad," he said, and looked as if he meant it. His disappointed expression shocked her. "I thought you'd enjoy tea at Browns. It's one of the best teas in London."

"Really?" Kate almost wavered, but caught herself in time. Even a duke couldn't change her plans at the last minute. And shouldn't. "I'll have to remember to go there before I head home."

"You would enjoy it." He looked at his watch. "Excuse me for a moment," he said, and moved through the crowd toward the concierge.

Kate felt sorry for him. He looked a little lonely. It mustn't be easy living with his grandmother and having his house torn up, and he obviously missed his farm.

He returned within minutes, a satisfied expression on his face. "There. I've booked a seat on the tour, too."

"You booked a seat on this tour? How?"

"With a credit card, Katherine. It took no great skill." He lowered his voice. "Should I apologize for kissing you last night?"

"No, of course not."

"Good." He smiled with satisfaction. "I didn't intend to. Actually I intend to do it more often."

A warm feeling snaked through her chest. It was foolish to believe him, but it was fun to pretend. "Are you flirting with me?"

"Definitely." His gaze flickered to her coat. "You'll be glad you brought that. It's a bit chilly out this morning."

"So we're discussing the weather now."

"To kill time," he explained. "To distract you until the bus arrives so you won't have the opportunity to send me away."

"Look," she began, trying to resist his teasing smile, "you don't have to look out for me. I'm twenty-five, old enough to tour England by myself. You and your grandmother don't have to worry about me, you don't have to spend your day on a bus, you don't have to—"

"But I have tickets for *Phantom of the Opera* tonight," he protested. "I thought you would enjoy it, since you like romantic shows."

"*Phantom*? In London?" She stared up at him. How was she supposed to resist that?

He looked surprised at the question. "Why, yes. At Her Majesty's theater, on Haymarket. Do you already have a ticket?"

"No. I tried but I couldn't get one."

William looked very pleased with himself. "Then—"

"Tour bus to Hampton Court and Windsor Castle!" a man announced from the doorway. "Anyone here for the Evan-Evans tour?"

Kate raised her hand. "We are."

"Come on, then," the gray-haired man said. "We've many stops to make before we're out of London."

William followed her onto the huge tour bus and sat beside her near the front. She folded her coat over her lap and turned to him. "Why are you doing this, William?"

"Call me Will."

"Tell me the truth." She waited, and the bus roared to life and lurched into first gear.

"The truth," he repeated. He looked over her shoulder toward the window for a long moment before turning back to her. "How about this? My grandmother is matchmaking again, and I am avoiding her *and* the women she's proposing as candidates for duchess. It sounds archaic, and it is. She's like that, though. Immersed in another century."

"And you don't want a duchess?"

"Not in a million years." He grimaced. "I am the last man in England anyone would want to marry."

She didn't believe that for a second. Gorgeous and charming William Landry would have trouble keeping women away from him even if he wasn't a wealthy aristocrat. She tried not to laugh. "I would think a lot of women would want to marry you."

"Oh, for the money. And the estates." His eyes twinkled. "I know you're teasing me, but really, I have no intention of marrying anyone. Pitty continues to try, and I continue to, ah, stick to my guns."

"Until you have to resort to hiding out on a tour bus." Kate couldn't help but laugh. "You expect me to believe this?"

"Yes, I do." He didn't seem to mind her laughter. In fact, he leaned closer. "If you will help me." She waited for him to continue. "Let me take you to Kensington tomorrow and to the theater tonight. The less time I spend in Thorne House the better. I would prefer to play tour guide for another day."

"I have a lot of things to see," she warned him.

"I know. I saw your list, remember?" William relaxed against the seat as the bus stopped to pick up more people. So far, the only men on the bus were the driver, William and the tour guide, who'd announced he was Richard and "anxious for everyone to have a jolly day."

"Think about it," William said. "You'd have your own private tour guide."

Tempting, but Kate didn't believe he was telling the whole truth. "And what do you get?"

"The company of a beautiful woman."

"Stop it," Kate said, embarrassed. "Don't make fun of me."

"Who's making fun?" He touched her chin with his index finger and lifted it slightly. "The man who broke your heart is a fool," he declared. "He didn't deserve your apple pies or your children."

Fortunately, the tour guide began to point out London landmarks, and Kate didn't have to reply. She pretended to look out the window as they passed Westminster Abbey, but her thoughts were centered on the man next to her. He had asked to spend the rest of the week with her. She was going home Tuesday, one week from today. For a few days she would see London with a duke, an Englishman who obviously knew his way around. Knew enough to get theater tickets to sold-out shows, at least.

Knew how to kiss.

He'd made her feel sexy and pretty and lighthearted. He'd made her forget about Jeff. She didn't even miss him anymore, which was a relief.

Kate turned away from the window to find William's gaze upon her.

"Still thinking?" he asked.

"Yes."

"That's not very flattering. I thought you'd feel sorry for me and agree immediately." There was a light in his dark eyes that showed he was still teasing her.

Again she wanted to laugh. "You're not an easy person to feel sorry for."

He sighed. "Would bribery work?"

"No!"

"I thought not." He pointed out the window. "That's the Victoria and Albert Museum. Have you been inside yet?"

Kate peered at the enormous stone building as the bus whizzed by. "Not yet. I suppose your family donated some of the artifacts?"

"A few."

She shook her head. "We lead different lives, William."

"'Will,'" he corrected. "My friends call me Will."

Kate looked at him and nodded. "Call me Kate, then."

"I didn't think you were a 'Katherine.' It's much too formal a name for you."

"I've always been Kate, or Katie," she admitted. "How long have you been a duke?"

"Since I was ten."

"*Ten?* Can a child be a duke?"

"Of course. When my father died I inherited the title."

"No wonder."

His raised eyebrows were a question.

"No wonder you're the way you are," she said. "Very duke-ish."

Will's shoulder touched hers. "Be quiet, Kate, and enjoy the scenery."

She quit teasing him and concentrated on looking out the window as they passed through the same suburbs she'd seen coming from Heathrow Airport. Soon the houses disappeared, replaced by rolling green hills dotted with trees. Richard pointed out different sights, including the island where historians agreed the Magna Carta was signed. When the bus rolled down the straight road to Windsor, Kate took her camera from her bag and took a picture. The bus pulled into the parking lot, and everyone on the tour followed Richard up the hill to Windsor Castle.

"Unbelievable." Kate framed the castle in her lens and took another picture.

"Come on," Will said, putting his arm around her. "Richard said to meet him at King Henry's Gate in two hours." He handed her a map. "Here's another souvenir for you."

"You've been here before, haven't you?"

"Yes. Not informally, though. I feel as if I'm on vacation."

"Stand over there," she ordered. "I'll take a picture of you with the tower in the background. Then you'll *really* feel like you're on vacation."

He did as he was told.

"Cute couple," an elderly lady told her companion. "I always like to see the young people enjoy themselves."

Will winked at Kate and took her hand. "Now we're a couple."

"If only she knew that I was just doing you a favor."

He chuckled, then tugged her along the path to the main building of the enormous, sprawling castle. It was too big, too impressive to seem real, and Kate hadn't expected to walk through what had been a walled fortress. They toured the State Apartments, but the paintings were gone from the walls. Stored since the fire, they would be rehung when the renovations were complete.

Will declined to join her in the gift shop, preferring to wait outside on the bench and watch the guards parade in the grassy quadrangle that separated the public area from the private wings.

"What on earth could you find to purchase in there?" he asked when she stepped out of the small stone building.

"Lavender bath gel, grown from the queen's garden, for my sisters." She pulled one of the boxes from the paper bag to show him. "It smells wonderful," she explained.

"Did you buy one for yourself?"

"Yes. And wait till you see this." She held up a small tin replica of the castle. "It's filled with candy."

"How...interesting."

"Come on." She tugged him from the bench. "Let's go to the chapel. Kings are buried there."

"Something to look forward to," Will muttered, but his smile was good-natured as he stood beside her. "You love this, don't you?"

"I'm having a *great* time. What about you?"

He draped his arm over her shoulder as they walked around the building. "I'm finding this highly educational."

Kate didn't believe him, but it wasn't her business if the man wanted to spend his day acting like a tourist. She'd heard the English could be eccentric, and William Landry proved it.

HE LOST HER in the Clock Courtyard, named for the large timepiece towering above the grassy square. He knew where she was, or at least, he knew where she'd eventually end up. Nothing in the Hampton Court gift shops would escape her notice. So he wandered around the brick walkways of the enormous palace built by the powerful Cardinal Wolsey and eventually given to Henry VIII. He remembered visiting Hampton Court long ago, with his father. It had been a bright summer day, unlike today with its overcast sky and bitter March wind. There had been a ceremony of some kind; his father was an honored guest and hadn't seemed to mind the crowds or the long speeches.

Now family duty brought him once again to Hampton Court. If Kate Stewart owned the Thorne Diamond, then it was his duty to protect it. It was his responsibility to see that it was returned to the family where it belonged. Tomorrow he would discover once and for all if the brooch was real, *if* he could continue to convince

Kate that he needed her company. The odd thing about all of this was that he actually enjoyed showing her around London.

His friends would think he'd lost his mind. He could be skiing. He could be in the Bahamas, where the Westons stayed every March. He'd joined them last year for a week for a house party that revolved around tanning one's body and drinking as much rum as one could hold.

Somehow it paled against purchasing lavender bath gel and tin castles. Besides, it was the least he could do for Pitty. She'd have spent too much money purchasing a questionable heirloom if he hadn't stepped in to prevent her.

Now Kate would be shopping again, and he would wait outside the building for her to find him. She hadn't stopped smiling all day, except once, when she'd studied the portion of boiled cabbage on her plate at the pub. He'd teased her into sampling a bite, but she hadn't liked the taste.

"Will?" Kate came up behind him. "I lost you. Sorry. There was a gift shop off the Tudor Kitchens, and I couldn't resist—"

"More bath gel?"

"A poster," she informed him. "And I bought myself a coffee cup." She attempted to balance the bag under her arm until he reached out to hold it for her. She unwrapped a white cup with gold lettering and the palace seal. "Pretty, isn't it?"

"Very." He peered into the bag. "What else?"

"Books, postcards and cute little pencil erasers for my nieces." She wrapped the cup in its tissue paper and placed it carefully in the paper bag. He insisted on carrying the bag, then took her hand and led her toward the gate.

"Have you seen everything you wanted to? We have to be back at the bus in about fifteen minutes."

"I've seen a lot," she told him. "I'll bet you could spend days here and not see everything."

"Yes, I'm sure that's true. If it was warmer, we could walk to the maze."

"I'll have to come back here someday."

It was natural to hold her hand and stroll through the courtyards like vacationing lovers. He really didn't know what had come over him. Tomorrow, he promised himself. Tomorrow, no matter what, he would find out the truth about the stone. After that he would make his excuses, say goodbye and return home. Nothing Pitty could say would stop him.

THE YOUNG WORKMAN with the mustache and the large shoulders finally found the box she wanted, the one marked Personal, 1800s. He carried it into the elevator and rode with Pitty to the third floor, then set it on the floor of her sitting room. The family correspondence had been packed away for safekeeping several years ago, and the box was covered with a thick layer of dust. Pitty eyed the dirty carton with distaste, then braved the dust to slit the cord with her embroidery scissors. Something the American girl had said about a Landry woman going to America kept nagging her.

There had been boys in each generation, not girls. It seemed Thornecrest dukes were incapable of siring daughters, thank the Lord, since they were not at all prolific. Her husband had spent his enthusiasm and energy on polo instead of in the bedroom. Their own son had had too many women to bother his wife once he'd gotten her pregnant. Marion had given birth to Willie and kicked her husband across the county to Kittredge Manor.

Pitty peered inside the box at the stacks of ledgers. Willie needed someone to love him. After all, she wasn't going to live forever, and then what would he do? He'd need someone in his life, someone to warm his bed and his heart. Someone who would give him a son. If the legend was true, then he needed the brooch to guarantee wedded bliss.

Nothing else would do. And the foolish boy refused to believe her. Well, she'd just have to prove it to him. It was time to take matters into her own hands.

Pitty reached into the box and set the ledgers on the floor. Estate journals wouldn't tell her what she needed to know, but the old duke's journals might. If she could prove there was a daughter who left Britain, she might be able to convince William of the brooch's authenticity. He didn't seem to be making progress on the appraisal. She couldn't imagine why such a simple task had become so difficult. Well, William had always been a stubborn child.

She took one of the wide black books from the box and opened it to the first page. The date in the corner, January 1, 1809, was scrawled in a firm, masculine hand. She wiped her dusty fingers on a dainty handkerchief and began to read.

WILL FOUND HER there hours later. Her faded purple sweatsuit meant she hadn't left the house or received visitors, both of which were unusual. He entered the room and stepped around the piles of books near the door. "Pitty? Mary said you've been in here all afternoon. What are you up to?"

She looked up at him and cocked her head. "Where on earth have you been? You're rather windblown and ruddy."

"Never mind me." He cleared a spot near her, sat down and stretched his long legs in front of him. "I asked you first."

"I'm pursuing family history, obviously." Pitty pushed a pile of old ledgers toward him. "Your great-great-great-great-grandfather, the third duke, kept journals, of course."

"Why the sudden interest in—" he opened one of the ledgers and read the date "—1810?"

Pitty tried to struggle to her feet. "I'll tell Mary we'd like our tea now."

Will put his hand on her arm and tugged her gently back down. "I already did. You look as if you could use some refreshment."

"Very true, dear." She yawned. "I've been reading for hours. Your ancestor was rather wordy."

Will didn't try to hide his smile. "And what are you attempting to learn through all this...research?"

She shot him a despairing look. "About the brooch, of course. Our supposed American cousin mentioned a Landry woman who emigrated to America, but I could find no record of a daughter in the family bible, so I've been searching through some of the old papers."

Intrigued, Will flipped through the pages. "And what have you discovered?"

"I'm not sure." Mary's polite knock distracted her. "Just set the tray down here, dear. It's easier for me to stay on the floor, I suppose."

Will waited while his grandmother fixed her tea and consumed three sandwiches. He never knew what she was going to do next, but he doubted she'd learned anything that would link Kate to the family jewels. He fixed himself a cup of tea and wondered what Kate was doing now. Writing postcards? Admiring today's crop of royal souvenirs?

Pitty patted the book beside her. "The journal mentions a young woman who seems to be under the duke's care. I can't seem to discover who she is, exactly."

"Some poor relation, perhaps?"

Pitty shook her head. "I don't think so. He speaks of her fondly, though she appears to be quite a handful."

"Where does the missing brooch fit in?" He leaned his head back against the couch and closed his eyes. He'd probably walked fifteen miles today, which was not unusual for a typical day in Leicestershire. Maybe the gift shops were what had worn him out.

"She could have stolen it and run away to America. Or sold it to a woman who passed herself off as a Landry."

He yawned. "There were two sons. Did they both marry?"

"Yes." Pitty sighed. "Both unhappily, of course. The brooch had disappeared by then."

Will debated whether or not to tell her about the antique dealer in Covent Garden, and then decided she would only worry that the pin had been recognized. "Have you read all of these?"

"Only two. Help me up, Willie. I'm dining with the Beauchamps tonight and need to rest for a while. They have a lovely granddaughter, you know."

Will stood and obediently hauled his grandmother to her feet. "I think she was on the list."

"She'll be at dinner tonight. I told Phyllis that you might join us."

He kept his hand on her arm until she steadied herself. "I already made plans."

Her eyebrows rose. "With Jessica Wilton?"

They slowly made their way to the door. "No."

"One of the Weston girls? I prefer the tall one. She has..."

Will gave her his haughtiest look. "I'm not going to discuss this any further."

"Don't play the duke with me, young man," she warned as he guided her down the hall to her bedroom. "Neither your father nor your grandfather dared try, and I won't put up with it from you."

He helped her onto her bed and tucked an ancient wool throw around her until she was satisfied her feet would be warm. He went to the door and turned back to see her eyes closed already. Probably dreaming of old journals and young brides, he decided. This business about the pin had gone on for too long. Pitty would soon work herself into a state of nervous exhaustion, and she was too old for this kind of excitement.

It wasn't doing him much good, either. He was a little old for cold showers. Tonight he would see that Kate enjoyed Webber's show. Tomorrow he would have the pin appraised. He would explain everything to Kate and hoped she understood how important it was to prove to his grandmother the brooch wasn't really the Thorne Diamond.

He was tempted to purchase it anyway, since it brought Pitty such happiness. There would be nothing wrong in letting an old woman believe she'd found the answer to her prayers. When that was settled, he would wish Kate well and wave goodbye. She could tell her sisters she'd met a duke; he would smile whenever he thought of her.

He knew that would be often.

SHE WOULD HAVE PAID five pounds for a bath. Kate eyed the shower stall and knew it wouldn't soothe her aching feet. She wanted to soak in a hot tub for an hour or two and warm the chill that had settled deep in her bones. No wonder the English consumed such large quantities of tea. A cup of Earl Grey had to be the next best thing to central heating.

Kate settled for a shower, letting the water run as hot as she could stand. She didn't have a lot of time, just enough to put her souvenirs away in the armoire and dress for the show. She'd have to wear the brown dress again; she didn't have anything else suitable. Will would return in an hour and a half. She'd offered to meet him at the theater, but the suggestion had seemed to offend him.

He was so proper. So very reserved and self-contained, except when he'd kissed her last night, and even then she sensed his surprise at making the gesture. She'd been a little shocked herself. She hadn't expected an Englishman to be quite so...passionate.

She decided to wear the amber beads tonight and left the brooch pinned to her coat. William seemed to admire it; she'd caught him staring at it more than once. He'd probably just never seen anything like it before.

Kate chuckled at the thought of his grandmother's matchmaking. The handsome duke wouldn't be able to avoid marriage for long. He'd be walking down the aisle with some suitably aristocratic bride before he was much older. The elderly woman had had a very determined look in her eye, Kate remembered.

She wouldn't want to be in the way of something the dowager wanted.

5

"MORE WINE?"

"Please." Kate watched William wave the waiter to their table, and in minutes her glass was refilled. This evening was too good to be true. She eyed William over the rim of her glass. "You're not going to turn into a pumpkin soon, are you?"

"Excuse me?"

She sipped carefully, knowing it was the most-expensive wine she'd ever tasted in her entire life, in the most expensive restaurant and with a man who wore a Rolex on his wrist. "You know, like Cinderella. Turn into something else at midnight?"

"You're enjoying the wine, aren't you?"

She set the glass on the linen-covered table. A candle, surrounded by crystal and fresh flowers, lit the center of the small round table. "Very much."

"I'm glad."

Kate looked at him thoughtfully. "You've been very kind. I still don't understand why. And I don't believe it's all your grandmother's doing."

"She's a large part of it," he replied, meeting her gaze squarely. "But I've enjoyed our two days together, I confess, even though I didn't actually expect to do so."

"Honesty at last," Kate murmured, reaching once again for her wine.

"You don't think I've been honest with you?"

"No." She couldn't help teasing him a little. "You're not much of a tourist, no matter how hard you pretend. I thought the gift shops would do you in."

He shook his head. "I didn't mind, although I can't imagine why you find them so fascinating. Actually visiting Hampton Court again was quite a treat. My father took me there when I was six or seven, so it brought back pleasant memories."

"What was he like?"

William stared at his glass and didn't answer immediately. "A bit stern but kind. It's difficult to remember after so many years. He fell off a balcony in Kittredge Manor, his home at the time. He didn't believe in spending money on restoration, and the railing was rotten."

Kate swallowed, trying not to picture the outcome. "I'm sorry," she whispered. "That must have been terrible for you and your mother."

"They were separated at the time—another Landry tradition. She didn't live a year after that. I like to think she loved him, despite their differences."

"She married him. She must have felt something, at least in the beginning."

He shrugged. "Perhaps. My grandparents were no different. Pitty and her husband lived apart for thirty years, until he died of heart failure. She has always blamed—"

Kate waited, but he didn't continue. "Blamed what?"

"Nothing," he said. The waiter delivered their soup and made certain everything was to the duke's liking before leaving them to the first course.

"This is lovely," Kate said, picking up her spoon.

"When you talked about dinner after the show, I never expected anything like this."

"I come here often when I'm in town. The food at Lorenzo's is always excellent. How is your soup?"

"Delicious." She looked past his shoulder to a crowd of people. A tall woman was staring at William. She spoke to the waiter and, when the man nodded, she tried to catch William's attention. "There's a woman waving to you," Kate said. "By the door."

William turned to see, then tried not to groan out loud. Jessica was smiling and making her way through the tables toward him. He had no choice but to toss his napkin on the table and stand.

"Darling," she cried, kissing him on both cheeks. "Where have you been? Have you been avoiding me on purpose? Leaving messages with Pitty is becoming a bit tiresome." Before he could answer, Jessica turned her wide smile on Kate and held out her hand. "How do you do," she crooned as Kate shook the offered hand.

"Kate, I'd like you to meet a friend of mine, Jessica Wilton. Jessica, this is Katherine Stewart, a, er, cousin from the States."

"It's nice to meet you," Kate replied, amused at the suspicious expression that crossed the blonde's face.

"My pleasure," Jessica murmured, then turned back to William and tossed her long hair over her shoulders before leaning closer to him. "We really must get together sometime soon. When you're not so committed to family obligations."

"I'll look forward to it," he said. Kate didn't think he sounded too enthusiastic, which was interesting.

Jessica waggled her fingers toward Kate. Diamonds sparkled on her right wrist. "Ta-ta!"

"Goodbye," Kate replied. She'd never said *ta-ta* in her life, and she wasn't going to start now. William sat down and resumed eating his soup.

Kate watched the tall woman join a group of young people at a corner table. The men were in expensive suits, similar to Will's. The women wore simple, sleek dresses and had simple, sleek hairstyles. One of the couples separated from the crowd and started toward their table. The woman was tall and athletic, the man short and stocky, with sandy hair and a beard.

"Kate? Are you looking at something in particular?"

Kate turned her attention back to Will. "I think you're going to get more company."

"This is a popular place after the theater." He shouldn't have brought her here. He'd wanted to impress her, not embarrass her. Damn Jessica.

He felt a strong hand clap him on the shoulder, and a familiar voice said, "Will! I thought you would have returned to the country by now."

Will stood, surprised and pleased. "Sam! I thought you were skiing. Hi, Paula." He shook Sam's hand and kissed Sam's wife on the cheek, then turned to Kate.

"And who is this beautiful woman?" Sam turned to Kate and grinned.

"Let me introduce you to some old friends, Kate." Sam didn't have to look so interested, Will thought. He made the introductions, noticing Paula's curiosity and Sam's unspoken approval, and once again explained that Kate was a distant American cousin. "Sit down," he offered, gesturing toward the empty chairs.

Paula hesitated. "We don't want to interrupt—"

"Just for a minute," Sam interjected, guiding her toward a chair. "The others won't miss us."

Paula shot Kate an apologetic smile and shrugged. "Do you come to London often?"

"This is my first time," Kate explained. "And I've really enjoyed myself."

"How wonderful! You must have Will bring you to Leicestershire. It's beautiful country, and we live nearby."

Sam agreed, his eyes twinkling. "Yes, Will. You must do that. We'll be staying close to home for the next seven months," he announced proudly.

"Congratulations," Will said, shaking his friend's large hand once again. He turned to Paula. "Congratulations. That's wonderful news."

"You're going to have a baby?" Kate asked.

"Yes. We're celebrating tonight, then heading home tomorrow."

"Now we'll leave you to yourselves." Sam stood, took Paula's hand and winked at Will. "Sorry to have interrupted your supper," he said, but he didn't look the least bit apologetic.

"I hope you enjoy your visit, Kate," Paula said. "Come to the country," she called as Sam led her away.

"Nice couple," Kate said. "Good friends of yours?"

"And neighbors, too." He couldn't believe Sam was going to be a father. He'd known the burly Scot since their days at Eton. It was difficult to picture him wearing one of those baby backpacks. Will shuddered.

The waiter cleared their dishes and informed them their entrées would be ready shortly. William leaned forward, unwilling to allow the evening to be spoiled by so many interruptions. "Did you enjoy the show? Wasn't the music beautiful?"

He was pleased when her green eyes lit up. "The

music, the costumes, the voices, everything. It was more beautiful than I could have imagined."

"I never tire of it, either," he admitted. "It's one of my favorites."

"When I tell my family I saw *Phantom* in London, from box seats, they won't believe me."

"You have the program to prove it."

"Yes. Thank you for that, too."

He didn't want her thanks. He simply wanted her to continue to enjoy herself. He'd never met anyone with such enthusiasm for new places. Most of his friends enjoyed traveling, but they also expected luxury, entertainment and friends to amuse them. Kate's only expectation was to see everything she possibly could see.

Kate's attention had wandered back to the corner table. "Is your grandmother hoping Jessica Wilton will be the next duchess?"

"I believe her name is on the list."

She stared at him. "The list?"

"Yes. My grandmother left a list on my pillow. It contained the names of twelve women of which she approved." He couldn't help chuckling, forgetting that it hadn't been at all amusing at the time he'd discovered it.

"It's a good thing you have a sense of humor."

"I told her never to do it again."

"Yes, you did," a quavering female voice replied near him. The familiar voice grew louder. "In no uncertain terms, too, for all the good it did you."

He didn't want to look. He'd been so intent on Kate he hadn't noticed his own grandmother. It was hard to notice anything when Kate wore that dress with the low neck.

"Good evening," Kate said. "How nice to see you again."

She sounded as if she meant it, William realized. He came to his feet and greeted his grandmother. "Your nap revived you, I see."

Pitty frowned. She didn't like to be reminded of her need to take naps, and William knew it. She turned to Kate and inclined her head in a regal nod. "Katherine. How nice."

Will remembered his manners. "Would you care to join us?"

"No, dear. My friends have reserved a table. We saw *Grease* tonight."

"What did you think?"

"It was quite loud and quite energetic," Pitty declared. "Very American, of course."

"Of course," William echoed, trying to keep a straight face.

Pitty waved him back to his seat. "Do sit down, for heaven's sake. I wanted to ask Katherine something about her family history. How lucky I am that she is here tonight!"

She must have heard him make the reservations, William figured. This was no coincidence.

"I'd be glad to," Kate said.

"Do you happen to know the name of the woman— the Landry—who emigrated to America? Or the date, perhaps?"

"I might be able to find out. I'd be happy to send you any information I can."

"Thank you, dear. I would appreciate that."

"It's the least I can do."

"And where is your lovely brooch tonight?"

"On her lovely coat," William replied. "And here comes our lovely dinner."

"So nice to have seen you again," Pitty murmured to Kate.

William sat down and waited for their plates to be set in front of them. "I didn't know it would be like this," he apologized. "I thought we would have a peaceful supper."

"You didn't have to hurry her away."

"Yes, I did," he muttered. Next time he would select a more private, less popular restaurant. Next time?

"She must be lonely when you leave London."

"Not really. We spend part of February together in London each year, and she comes to Thorne Hall when she wants a taste of the country. She has a lot of friends around England. Her social life is quite extraordinary."

"But you are her only grandchild?"

"Yes."

"Then you should be nicer to her," Kate declared, picking up her fork.

He couldn't get any nicer, William fumed. He'd delayed his return to the Hall, he'd ridden a tour bus and eaten greasy fish and chips, he'd bought two theater programs, he'd kept his eye on the brooch throughout most of London's tourist attractions. He was the nicest grandson in Great Britain.

And he should be appreciated.

Kate distracted him with stories of growing up on a farm with acres of apple orchards. She made him laugh, made him want to take her in his arms. She made him want to hold her hand and whisper nonsense until the rest of the world disappeared. Instead, he ate dessert and paid the check and helped her climb inside a taxi when the evening was over.

He wasn't sure why, but it seemed natural to put his arm around her. When she turned to him to say something, he stopped her words with a kiss. It appeared to surprise her, but it seemed inevitable to William. Her lips were soft and warm. He held her closer; she twined her arms around his neck. He ran his tongue along her lower lip; she parted her lips to allow him entry. She tasted of chocolate, sweet and mysterious.

"All day," he breathed, lifting his mouth a fraction from hers, "all day I've wanted to do this." The interior of the cab was dark and intimate, and William's free hand swept through Kate's hair and along her cheek.

"We shouldn't—"

"I know." His lips found hers again, and the long kiss continued. Once again they parted and drew ragged breaths.

"Thank goodness the St. Giles is on the other side of town," he said.

Kate laughed, so he kissed her briefly once more. "Do you know where we are?"

"No. But I know I've never made a fool of myself in a taxi before." He grimaced. He didn't know what had gotten into him. He was usually more of a gentleman, more restrained.

"Well, neither have I." She attempted to straighten her dress. "Another international experience no one will believe."

"Why not?"

"I'm not exactly the type who makes men crazy with lust."

"You're not?" She could have fooled *him*.

Kate smiled. She thought he was joking, he realized.

"It's the dress, then," he declared, keeping his voice light. Her coat was open to reveal the amber beads draped over that tempting cleavage. Kate shifted and the yellow stone on her lapel blinked and winked at him. He closed his eyes briefly, trying to remember what he was supposed to be doing. The brooch. The legend. His grandmother.

He sighed, muttered an apology and released Kate. The taxi slowed, crossed Oxford Street and turned the corner to the hotel. "I'll come by for you at nine," he said. He helped her out of the cab and watched her cross the sidewalk and step into the brightly lit lobby.

"Essex Court, please," he told the driver. That cold shower was going to be a relief.

PITTY WATCHED Will hurry through the rain and into a taxi. She frowned. It was ridiculous to depend on taxis. She didn't know why he wouldn't spend the money on a car and driver. A perfectly nice Jaguar sat in a garage, too. Perhaps it was time for her to learn to drive, she mused. Wouldn't *that* drive poor Willie to the asylum? She dropped her binoculars and rang for Mary.

"Find that nice young man with the mustache," she said. "I need his help again."

Mary muttered something under her breath, but Pitty paid no attention. Katherine had looked quite at home at San Lorenzo's last night, and William had not been pleased when she'd interrupted them. Poor Jessica had looked daggers at both Will and the American. Yes, it had been quite a show.

This marriage scheme was not progressing the way she'd planned. William should have owned the brooch by now. Then he could have met the nice English women on the list she'd prepared, and been guaranteed marital bliss.

Unlike the rest of the Landrys, she mused. Her own

William had been as worthless a husband as ever stepped over the Thorne Hall threshold, but he'd known how to turn one pound into five and had tripled the family fortune before he died.

Pitty lowered herself onto the couch and waited for the young workman. There were boxes to remove and boxes to fetch. She planned to find the answer to this family mystery soon, before William could make a fool of himself over the little American.

She didn't want her grandson to marry a mysterious American. Besides, Katherine was much too short to be a duchess.

KATE ROAMED around the crowded palace gift shop. The Duke of Wellington teapot was tempting, but it might be hard to get back to Rhode Island in one piece. This would be her last day with the handsome duke, Kate resolved. It was bad enough to have been a fool in Rhode Island, but to go international with her stupidity was even worse. Of course, she found him attractive. Who wouldn't? And charming. Who could be immune to his charm?

She could, Kate told herself. She had to. She was much too attracted to him.

Of course, that could be a rebound kind of thing. After all, her ex-fiancé was getting married in three days. She'd be expected to do something strange and reactionary. Like kiss a duke in a taxi.

Thank God her sisters knew nothing about this. She'd never hear the end of it. She selected three packets of floral bath salts for them. She could tell them this was what Di used, and they might believe her.

No more dukes, she promised herself. He'd been pleasant and polite when he'd escorted her through the dark rooms of Kensington Palace. She thought he might be a little embarrassed about last night, too. And regretting it, of course. The display of coronation robes had been interesting, but the real attraction would have been Di's wedding dress, no longer in the display. Being refurbished, no doubt.

She bought a postcard of the wedding dress anyway. Thank goodness she had been able to return hers before it had been altered. She'd lost her deposit, of course, but that was better than getting stuck with sixty yards of satin and lace that she didn't need. She'd tried to repay her sisters for their black off-the-shoulder gowns, but they wouldn't hear of it. They'd selected them, after all, with an eye to wear them again on special occasions.

She paid for her purchases and met William in the foyer. The rain continued to pour, so he opened a black umbrella and held it over her head as they stepped outside onto the paved walkway.

"Typical English weather," he said above her head. "You'll get used to it."

"I don't mind," she fibbed, feeling the cold seep through her damp boots. They weren't waterproof, but she'd worn two pairs of socks. "Where are we going next?"

"We're going to find a taxi. We'll head up Sloane Street and King's Road so you can see where Princess Diana shops. Then on to Harrods, if you would like to see the world's most famous department store. Wasn't that also on your itinerary?" He looked at his watch. "If you're not too hungry, we can skip lunch and have tea a bit later."

"You know, you don't have to do this," she said, looking up at him. A curl of damp hair hung over his forehead. He was just as attractive in the rain, she thought. "I'm perfectly capable of finding my own way."

"I wouldn't hear of it. Come on." He took her elbow and, avoiding puddles of water, hurried her to the side of the busy street.

Well, she'd tried, Kate mused. She scrambled into the boxy black taxi as if she'd done it all her life. Will climbed in after her, and they exchanged sheepish glances. It was a little too easy to remember what had happened the last time they were in a taxi.

"We're going to Antiquarius, 135 King's Road," Will told the driver, then settled back in his seat.

To break the silence, Kate asked, "Is your grandmother still matchmaking?"

"Yes. She offered to arrange a lunch date with someone today, as a matter of fact."

"And you refused."

He smiled. "I claimed a previous engagement."

"So you're really glad to be out in the rain?"

"Absolutely. I had an errand to do anyway. I have to stop at an antique market for a few minutes. Something I have to check on. Would you mind?"

"Of course not. It sounds like something I'd enjoy. Is it like the Covent Garden Market?"

"No," he replied. "But you might find it amusing."

Kate found it overwhelming. The bright interior of the building was sliced into individual jewelry stores, or "stalls," as William called them. More than one hundred and twenty, he said, guiding her through the middle aisle. Everywhere she looked there were exquisite gems displayed in glass cases. No, it was not like Covent Garden.

William stopped in front of one of the corner stalls

and shook hands with a small elderly man whose expression was serious and respectful. He glanced over at Kate and nodded hello. Kate didn't hear what William said. She was distracted by the rows of sparkling jewels: diamond rings, sapphire earrings, emerald bracelets and ruby necklaces. Diamonds and gold, diamonds and platinum, diamonds combined with other gems and displayed to advantage on black velvet sparkled under the lights.

"Let me take your coat," William offered, sliding it from her shoulders. "It's very warm in here."

"Thank you."

He handed it to the elderly man. "Mind if we leave this with you for a few minutes, Eric?"

"Not at all." The man shot her a questioning look. "May I show you anything, madam?"

"I wish you could." She turned to Will, who looked pleased that she was so impressed. "I've never seen anything like this," she breathed. "Is the whole building full of jewelry?"

"And antique books."

"Good heavens."

"Would you like to look around?"

Look around? She'd like to live here forever. "What about your errand?"

"Eric is taking care of it for me," he assured her. "What period do you like best? Georgian, Victorian or art deco?"

"You explain the difference and I'll decide," she replied, wandering to the next stall. "I never cared for old jewelry until Aunt Belle gave me that brooch."

"GENUINE," the old man whispered reverently. "Absolutely real and of the highest quality. Two of the smaller diamonds are chipped, but that is of no consequence. It needs cleaning, but the large stone is intact. Flawless," he breathed. "Absolutely flawless."

William realized his mouth had dropped open. "You're quite certain?"

Eric looked offended. "I've been studying jewels for forty years, Your Grace. Have you taken it to Longmire's yet? Sheldon will *die* when he sees it. He'll absolutely *die*."

"I feel a little shaky myself," Will said, picking up the coat. "If it was for sale, Eric, what would you expect for it?"

The jeweler turned pale. "I couldn't calculate a value, not until I'd had time to examine all of the stones in the piece. The historical value of such a piece must also be taken into account. The setting is silver gilt, popular in Henry VII's time."

"Not even a guess?" Will urged.

"I wouldn't presume," the little man insisted. "And the young lady? Whatever will she do, walking around with a king's ransom on her lapel?" He lowered his voice to a whisper. "I hope you intend to store it in a vault, Your Grace."

"I intend to take very good care of it," William assured him. "Thank you for your help. And for your discretion."

"I was happy to be able to help such a good customer," Eric said.

William tossed the coat over his arm, then checked to make sure the brooch was still attached to the lapel. The stones were real, which didn't necessarily mean this was the Thorne Diamond, but it certainly meant that Pitty could be on the right track. He would have to tell her she could be right. And he would have to decide how to buy a very expensive piece of family sentiment.

"All set?" Kate approached him and reached for her coat.

"Yes," he said, holding the coat for her. "I suppose I am."

She turned and pulled her hair from the collar. "Is something wrong? You look a little upset."

"Upset?" he echoed. He looked at the pin and tried not to wince. Then he took Kate's hand and moved toward the door. "I'm sure it's nothing a good cup of tea can't cure."

"Before Harrods or after?"

"After," he assured her. He glanced at her shoulder one more time, and the "absolutely real" yellow diamond twinkled at him. What was it worth? A hundred thousand pounds? One million?

Pitty would swoon when she heard the news. Already planning a wedding that would never take place, she'd most likely begin furnishing the nursery for the next Duke.

"Are you sure nothing's wrong?" Kate asked once again.

"Positive," he assured her. They stepped outside into the rainy afternoon, and William fumbled with his umbrella. A feeling of dread settled in his stomach like a lump of cold porridge. Nothing, absolutely nothing and no one could force him into marriage, he promised himself, but the tension in his stomach didn't ease.

"I THINK I'll have to start saving for a silver tea service," Kate declared. She and William sat facing each other in matching wing chairs in front of a cheery fireplace. Between them was a low, polished table filled with a three-tiered serving dish, individual teapots, plates, clotted cream, strawberry jam, sugar, milk and a dish of sliced lemon. "I can't believe how elegant this is."

"I'm glad you're enjoying yourself," the duke replied.

The first tier of the serving dish contained delicate sandwiches. Kate studied the selection, then chose a tiny roll filled with egg salad. "I'm starving. Aren't you?"

"I seem to have lost my appetite today." He selected a watercress sandwich, put it on his plate and poured himself another cup of tea.

A small blob of egg salad landed on the toe of Kate's suede boot. So much for sophistication, she mused, tucking her feet under the table and hoping William hadn't noticed. She wiped her mouth on a pink napkin and looked around the room. Shades of rose and green were in the upholstered furniture and the elaborate printed carpet. They had been seated in a room directly off the lobby, but there were others beyond this one. Couches and chairs were arranged in cozy settings, as if in someone's living room. Every seat was filled. Everyone was drinking tea. It was such a wonderfully *English* setting.

She turned back to William and helped herself to another sandwich. The other tiers contained little cakes and thick scones. She'd take her time and taste everything. "This is a lovely way to end the day."

"Yes." He half smiled. "Very British. Very civilized."

"I'm going to take my time and make this last."

"There is no hurry," he agreed. "No one is waiting for your chair."

"They can't have it." She patted the rose-striped brocade fabric. "I'm going to have to start redoing my apartment."

"When do you return to the States?"

"Tuesday afternoon." She spoke without thinking. "The wedding is Saturday, so by Tuesday Jeff and his new bride will be on their honeymoon. On Wednesday I'll start hunting for a new job."

He frowned. "The wedding?"

"One of the reasons I left the country," she said, picking up her teacup to take a sip. "I couldn't bear to be in town. Saturday was supposed to have been my wedding day, but Jeff is marrying someone else on that day."

"From what you've told me, you're better off without him."

"And you're right." She decided to try a scone. "I realize that now." She thought of her beautiful wedding dress and the four-tiered cake decorated with white roses. Then she thought of Jeff, and the tempting vision of perfect love vanished. "But I'm a slow learner."

"No one can be right all the time. We all make mistakes," he said.

"Even dukes?" she teased, waiting for his answering smile. He didn't disappoint her.

"Oh, *never* dukes." He chuckled. "We're infallible. I'm talking about the common folk."

"Of course you are. You're perfect in every way. Isn't that what your grandmother always told you?"

"As a matter of fact," he drawled, helping himself to a fat scone, "that's precisely what she told me."

"Too bad," Kate replied. "A perfect life doesn't sound very interesting."

"Oh, I don't know. It has its moments." He opened

the scone and lathered it with a liberal amount of clotted cream and jam.

Kate copied him and hoped she would like clotted cream. It didn't sound very appetizing, but it looked like whipped butter. She tried a bite, then proceeded to eat the rest. She'd never tasted anything so delicious. "Have you ever been in love?"

He answered without hesitation. "No."

"Never?" She couldn't believe it. "You've never had your heart broken?"

"No."

"You've never written love letters or gotten goose bumps when the phone rang or mooned around listening to romantic music?"

"No."

"That's very strange."

William shrugged. "I don't know why. I've never felt that...silly. And I've never felt the need to 'moon around,' as you call it, over Barry Manilow songs. I come from a long line of very unromantic men."

"That's too bad." William Landry would be more interesting if he had a few more flaws.

"Kate, there's something—"

The waiter interrupted by bringing hot water to refresh their tea. "Is everything satisfactory?"

"It was wonderful," Kate assured him.

The duke nodded his approval and asked for the check. When the young man moved to the next table, William set his cup and empty plate on the table. "Kate, there's something you should know—"

"You're really married, with twins?" she joked, trying to forestall what she was afraid might be an embarrassing disclosure. She didn't want to hear an apology for last night's kisses. She didn't want to know that the past days had been some kind of farce. She wanted to return home with only good memories of her trip. She wanted to pretend she'd experienced a little bit of romance with a handsome stranger.

"Very funny."

"Well, I don't think you're gay."

"No." His eyes twinkled as his gaze dropped to her lips. "I don't think so, either."

"You're saying goodbye," she realized, and felt a pang of regret. She would miss him. Which was crazy, because she'd only met him four days ago. She tried to hide her disappointment. "Are you going back to the country now?"

"Shortly," he said, relief evident in his voice. The waiter returned and set the bill, tucked in a leather folder, on the table. Kate made an attempt to take it, but William stopped her. "What are you doing?"

"I wanted to pay this time," she said. "It doesn't seem fair that you are paying for everything. I don't care if you *are* a duke, it's still not fair."

"It is not an issue," he declared, putting a credit card inside the folder. "I am not going to discuss it."

Very haughty, very sweet. "Are you sure?"

He looked at her as if he thought she was insane. "Yes, Kate. I'm positive."

"Then thank you," she said. She bent over and discreetly wiped the egg salad off her boot before she stood up. They collected their coats from the cloakroom, then stepped outside into the misty afternoon.

"Shall we walk?"

"I'd like that." She buttoned her coat and lifted the collar to protect her neck from the chilly wind.

"I wanted—" He stopped, no sound coming out of his mouth.

"Will?"

"The brooch..."

Her hand went to her right lapel but didn't find the familiar stone. She looked down. "It's gone! William, it's gone."

He pulled her under an awning, next to the building. "You had it when we went to Browns. I remember seeing it on your coat when I handed it to the coat-check woman."

"It must have fallen off. It's nothing anyone would want to steal." She felt an embarrassing sting of tears against her eyes. "I'd hate to lose it after all these years."

"Come on. We're not that far away." They hurried back down the sidewalk to the hotel and rushed into the lobby. "Wait here," William ordered.

Kate took a tissue out of her tote bag and wiped her eyes. Will went over to the coat closet and talked to the woman behind the small wooden counter. She let him inside, and they disappeared. Long minutes later he returned, a relieved expression on his face.

"All set," he said when he drew closer. "I have it."

"Thank goodness." Kate held out her hand, and William dropped the brooch into her palm.

"It must have been caught on something, then dropped to the floor when we collected our coats. There doesn't seem to be anything wrong with the clasp, but you should be careful. Perhaps have it checked by a jeweler? I know a good one nearby..."

"I'll have to wait until I get home," she said, placing it carefully in the bottom of her tote.

"Perhaps the hotel safe..."

"I'd rather keep it with me," she told him as they stepped outside once again. She didn't know why, but having the brooch made her feel optimistic. It had brought her luck, in the shape of William Landry. Four days in London had been heaven, and even if she never saw him again, she'd remember.

He walked her into the St. Giles's lobby and took her hand.

"Thank you. For everything," she said.

He looked surprised. "It was my pleasure."

That was that. He smiled, the charming-duke smile she'd grown to expect, then left the hotel. Kate watched him leave, watched his black coat disappear around the corner. He would walk to Essex Court, no doubt. It wasn't that far. Kate swallowed the lump in her throat and tried not to cry. Even the silliest romantic fool wouldn't hope for a kiss goodbye.

6

"I KNEW IT! I knew it all along," Pitty declared, clapping her chubby hands together in delight. "My dear, I cannot tell you how happy I am."

"Don't bother. I can guess," William said, pouring himself a generous helping of unblended Scotch. He took a healthy swallow and allowed himself a satisfied sigh. He didn't know when he'd experienced a day as nerve-racking as this one.

"Well, where is it?"

"I don't have it." He took his drink and sat down in his favorite overstuffed chair. "Do you have the heat on?"

"Yes, but the chill seems to be hanging on." Pitty pushed his feet aside so she could sit on the hassock and face him. Her hot pink sweater made him blink. "Tell me everything," she demanded. "How did you do it?"

"First we toured Kensington Palace." He grimaced. "Kate bought a Duke of Wellington teapot."

"How odd. Were there matching cups?"

"I have no idea." He took another drink and felt his insides begin to warm. "I took her over to Antiquarius. I know one of the dealers and I thought it might be a little less obvious than parading into Longmire's."

"And?"

"Eric said it's the real thing but Sheldon would be the best person to estimate its value."

"Did you make an offer?"

"No. I tried to tell Kate it was valuable, but there were a few, ah, interruptions." Such as losing the damn thing. He could still feel the wave of relief he'd experienced when he'd spotted the pin on the floor behind a fallen coat hanger. He'd held it in his hand, long enough to resist putting it in his pocket. Even though it had been stolen years before, he could not justify its return to the family by illegal means. The stone had been surprisingly warm in his palm.

Pitty gasped. "She doesn't know?" She heaved herself off the hassock and went to the phone. "We must ring her. She can't possibly walk around London wearing something so valuable. What if she loses it before we are able to purchase it?"

"She's not there, Pitty. And she won't lose it," he replied sharply. "It means a great deal to her, too."

"Where is she? We have dinner plans, but perhaps—"

"She's away this evening, Pitty. Something called the Jack the Ripper Tour. And what do you mean, we have 'plans'?"

"Lady Benton, Viscount Lindley and the Smithfields are dining with us tonight."

"Let me guess. Lady Benton is on the list."

"Just a coincidence. I'm feeling particularly social these days, and now Thorne House is almost finished I'm not so tired in the evening."

He leaned back and closed his eyes. There was no way to avoid it. He could no longer use Kate as an excuse to avoid Pitty's social plans. Besides, it would do him good to be with other people for a change. He'd spent the past two evenings with Kate, after all. He thought of the feel of her in his arms and wished she wasn't going on her macabre tour.

"What are you smiling about?"

"Was I smiling?" He opened his eyes to see Pitty close by, peering at him suspiciously.

"You looked positively dreamy," she snapped, frowning. "Not like yourself at all, Willie. Should I worry about you?"

"Of course not."

"What about the brooch?"

"Tomorrow I'll meet with Kate and explain how valuable the brooch is, both monetarily and to our family. We'll go to Longmire's and settle on a price. I'm sure she'll be quite pleased with the amount I'll offer."

"Good, good."

"After that I'm returning to the country. You're welcome to join me if you like. The lambing will be starting soon." He finished his drink and climbed to his feet. It was time to see other women, and it wouldn't hurt to dine with Pitty one more time before he left for the Hall. "I'd better dress for dinner. Is Lady Benton a blonde or brunette?"

KATE REALIZED she'd had too much beer when she had trouble inserting the card in the slot and couldn't open the door to her room. She tried it three more times before the knob finally turned. As she entered her room, she stepped on an envelope that had been slipped under the door.

She opened it and drew out a fax from her sisters. Actually Carol was the one with access to a fax machine, so it must have been her idea. Kate read it quickly. Carol hoped the London tours were working out and she was seeing everything she'd planned; Terri wanted to know if she'd met any interesting men and if she'd packed enough clothes for the English weather; Anne told her not to do anything risky and not go out after dark unless she took a taxi. They wanted her to call them so they would know that she was all right.

Kate decided to put them out of their misery and call. It was five or six hours earlier in Rhode Island, so she tried Anne's number, since she was the one most concerned about safety. The phone only rang twice before Anne's voice said, "Hello?"

"Hi. It's Kate."

"Kate! How are you?"

"I'm fine," she assured her, "but I'm going to keep this really short. I don't want a big hotel bill."

"That's okay. Did you get Carol's fax? Are you having fun?"

"Yes. I just got back from a tour." She didn't specify that it was a spooky tour of Jack the Ripper murder spots that included drinks at three pubs. "How is everyone there?"

"Just fine. We think about you a lot."

Meaning they were worrying. "I'm twenty-five, not seventeen."

"I know. Sometimes it's hard to remember," Anne sighed. "Tell me, have you seen the queen or any royalty yet?"

"Not yet, but there's still hope. I met a duke, though. At Thorne House. Remember I told you I thought we were related to people who once came from Thorne House?"

"Those were just family stories. I think Aunt Belle exaggerated a little. And what do you mean, you met a duke? A *real* duke?"

"The Duke of Thornecrest." Anne clearly didn't believe her.

"Look, sweetie, I bet they *all* say they're dukes. Be careful."

"I will. Don't worry, he's gone to his country estate."

"Sure he has. Don't fall for anything he says. You're vulnerable right now."

For a second Kate didn't know what her sister was talking about. Then she remembered. Jeff's wedding. Her former wedding day. "Anyway, I'm having a great time."

"How old is this supposed duke?"

"In his thirties," Kate fibbed. "And quite handsome. A bachelor, too. I've just left a pub where I was drinking beer with three handsome Germans."

"I should have known you were teasing me," Anne said.

Of course Anne wouldn't believe her. "I'd better go before this costs a fortune. Tell Terri and Carol that I called and that I'm fine. And don't worry. London is beautiful and very safe."

"Take good care," Anne repeated. "And call collect next time."

Kate hung up the phone and kicked off her boots, then hooked her coat behind the door and removed the pin from her black sweater. She'd almost lost it today, but William had found it. It was sweet of him to act as if it was a valuable antique and not a sentimental trinket. She'd miss him. And she'd never forget him—of that she was sure. Even if no one believed her, she'd have photographs to prove he existed. She wished he'd kissed her goodbye, instead of informing her he'd had a "very pleasant day."

Kate hurried to put on her nightgown and get ready for bed. Those mugs of ale had made her tired and maybe even a little bit sad. The Germans had been fun, though. As college students, they'd added a boisterous element to the tour, which had been missing on the trip to Windsor. Two of them had asked her to join them in the hotel's own pub for a nightcap, and she'd thrown caution to the wind and accepted.

She looked at the bags on her bed. She hadn't had time to put today's purchases away before meeting the evening tour group. What on earth was she going to do with a Duke of Wellington teapot?

Remember a duke, of course.

"GO OVER THERE and sit in the lobby," Pitty pleaded. "Katherine has to return to the hotel eventually."

William ignored her. Mary poured him another cup of coffee, and he continued to read the newspaper while his grandmother paced back and forth alongside the dining room table. The IRA had threatened to bomb Heathrow again, and the scandal involving Lord Westley continued. He turned the page, ignored the latest comment on Princess Di's whereabouts and the little princes' school marks.

"You've let her escape," Pitty muttered. "I shall have a stroke before this day is over."

"No, you won't," he said just before his eye was caught by an item in the social column.

Who is the petite redhead dating the D. of T. this week? They've been spotted at the theatre twice, dining cozily at Lorenzo's and snuggling in a taxi. Are L.'s bachelor days numbered?

"Damn," he exclaimed.

Pitty stopped and looked over his shoulder at the newspaper. "Oh. You've finally noticed, have you?"

"What is this rubbish?"

"You can't run about town and not have someone notice."

"Katie's not a redhead," he muttered, tossing the paper on the table.

"Katie?" Pitty sniffed. "Are we using *nicknames* now? How cozy."

"Can't a man have a peaceful breakfast without being badgered?"

"Not necessarily," Pitty replied, unruffled by her nephew's temper. She sat down at the table and waved to Mary for more tea. "I think we may have more of a problem than I thought."

"What now, Pitty? I can't imagine what else you want. Aside from my obtaining a priceless brooch, a pin so ugly it boggles the mind. And will shatter my bank account, too."

"I shall buy it myself."

He arched an eyebrow. "And bankrupt yourself?"

"If that's what needs to be done, of course. I can always sell the Monet."

She actually looked sad. William felt guilty. "I apologize," he said, lowering his voice. "I know how important this is to you, but I hope the thing is worth it. It seems a lot of trouble for a—"

"You enjoyed last night?" Pitty interrupted.

"Yes," he lied. He'd have had a better time dining on an airplane.

"Cornelia is lovely."

"Yes." That much was true. She was a little serious for his tastes, but she appeared to be sincere and polite. A little too polite. Boring, almost.

"Will you see her again? I understand her uncle has an estate fifty miles north of the Hall."

"What a coincidence." Kate hadn't told him she was going on a tour today. He wished he could remember the rest of her schedule. There was something about Bath and another day at the museums. He would be very, very careful about explaining why he wanted to buy the brooch. He didn't want her to think he had only been nice to her because he wanted her ugly old pin.

"William!"

He looked over at his grandmother. She was wearing that awful purple robe again. He must remember to purchase a new one for Christmas. Something in white or pale pink. Anything that didn't hurt his eyes in the morning. "What is it now, Pitty?"

"You were daydreaming again." She eyed him curiously. "I'm going into my study. The workmen will be done before noon, and Gregory wants us to accompany him through the renovations to make certain we are pleased."

"Fine. I'll leave a note for Kat-Katherine."

"I can accompany you to her hotel this afternoon."

William nodded. He hadn't committed himself to anything, she noticed. He probably thought he was being sneaky.

Pitty left the room and hurried to her study. There were still ledgers to read, still a mystery to be solved. There had been no mention of Alicia after June of 1814. In fact, there had been few entries in the summer of 1814. Perhaps the duke had been ill during that season, Pitty mused. She took the ledger and sat at her desk, but she didn't open the book.

The third Duke of Thornecrest was the least of her

worries. The ninth was giving her fits. Daydreaming, smiling at nothing, following that little American from palace to palace and not complaining. And box seats for *Phantom!* He thought she wouldn't notice such an extravagance? She drummed her fingers on the blotter and looked out the window. The birds would be nesting soon. She would watch their babies hatch and learn to fly.

And Willie, where would he be? Was the brooch already working its magic? If so, she had to get hold of it before her unsuspecting grandson fell in love with the American. He'd been exposed to the yellow diamond for only four days, but she had no idea how long it took to weave its spell. The damage could have been done already, she worried.

After all, the Thorne Diamond was pinned to a totally unsuitable bosom.

"A MESSAGE?"

The woman behind the desk nodded. "If you'll wait a moment, I'll fetch it."

"Thank you," Kate said, wondering who it could be from. William was most likely back "on the farm," and she knew no one else in London. Unless the Germans wanted to party tonight. The serious young woman handed her an envelope, and Kate took it and headed toward the elevator. She'd open it upstairs, after she'd removed her boots.

It had been a wonderful day. Bath was the most romantic place she'd ever seen, Kate decided. She'd spent a lovely hour in the costume rooms, eaten lunch in the famous Pump Room and toured the excavated Roman baths. She'd shopped and walked up hills and down hills. She'd ridden the two-tiered bus from one end of the city to the other. She'd taken a lot of photographs.

She could live there, she decided. Take a "flat" in one of the famous crescents and find a computer job in London. After all, she had a degree in math and four years' experience. And she'd passed a lot of corporate skyscrapers near the airport. The train ride was only seventy minutes from London, but expensive. Maybe she'd be better off living in London and visiting Bath when she felt the need to see rolling hills and Georgian buildings.

The note was brief: "Call me when you return. Yours, William."

Kate sat on the bed and stared at the hotel stationery. It wasn't much of a message, but it made her smile. He hadn't returned to the country after all. He hadn't said goodbye...yet. She reached for the telephone and dialed the numbers printed at the bottom of the page.

The maid answered on the first ring. "Thorne House," she said.

"This is Katherine Stewart, returning William's call," Kate announced, slipping into her "office" voice.

"I'm very sorry, Miss Stewart, but His Grace is not available at the moment. I suggest you call again in the morning."

"Thank you," Kate said, more disappointed than she cared to admit. Maybe he had called to say goodbye after all. Perhaps he had already left for the country. It was after eight. He was most likely at San Lorenzo's, dining with Jessica Somebody and the rest of his aristocratic friends. Kate eased her boots back on and slung her purse over her shoulder. She'd buy a sandwich in the pub downstairs and maybe even have a beer. She would not call him in the morning. It was time to admit they were from two different worlds. It was time to admit there was no reason for a duke to be interested in an unemployed, jilted and slightly depressed computer programmer.

"ARE YOU feeling better, dear?" Pitty looked up from her breakfast as William entered the dining room.

"I'm still a little green around the edges," William answered, "but I'm going to live." He'd been sick most of the night, but he hoped he was over the worst of it.

"Do you think it was something you ate?"

He sat down at the table and poured himself a cup of tea. "I doubt it. I'm afraid it was probably one of the twelve-hour flu bugs."

"I hope so, Willie. You don't look too well."

Since he'd spent half the night hanging over the toilet bowl, the observation didn't surprise him. "I'm feeling much better," he assured her. After several swallows of sweetened tea, he realized the words were true. He was over the worst.

"Good. You'll contact Katherine after breakfast? Or would you prefer I do it?"

William didn't prefer any such thing. "I will take care of it."

"Oh, good. I'm sure Katherine will be quite pleased with her good fortune. She'll be able to buy all the teapots she wants, won't she?"

He didn't pay close attention to what Pitty was chattering about. She wore a silk suit this morning, a bright aqua silk suit with a yellow scarf and pink-and-yellow earrings. She looked like an Easter egg. "You look quite, er, festive this morning. Do you have plans?"

"I'm going to the Fabergé exhibit with Penelope Farley this morning. There's a special showing, then we're off to lunch and a little shopping. Now that the brooch is off my mind, I can concentrate on finding new linens for my bedroom."

"Something bright, I suppose."

"How you do know me," she chirped. "You must tell me Sheldon's reaction when he sees our diamond." She frowned at his paisley robe. "You really shouldn't lounge around any longer, Willie. Once you wash up, you'll feel so much better."

"I think I'll have some toast first," he said. "Or I shall have a relapse and have to spend the rest of the day in bed."

"Don't tease me," she ordered, pushing back her chair. "I'm off!"

William waited until Pitty left before calling Kate. It was almost nine, which was a little late for her, but there was no help for it. He'd overslept. She answered immediately, her voice sounding cautious.

"It's William," he said. "Did you get my message?"

"Yes. I called you last night, but the maid said you were 'unavailable.' I figured you went out."

"No. I was in bed early and didn't want to be disturbed."

"Oh."

He stalled. He didn't want to discuss the brooch over the phone. He wanted to see her again. It could take all day to make the arrangements, but after that he'd be free to leave London and she'd be quite a bit richer for her last days in England. "Where were you off to yesterday?"

"I took the train to Bath."

"Did you enjoy it?" He knew what her answer would be. She'd probably read all of Jane Austen's book and thought the Georgian city was extremely romantic.

"I loved it."

"Meet me in Green Park and tell me all about it. There's something I'd like to show you." He heard the rustle of papers. "What were you planning to see today?"

"Museums."

"The weather is too nice for that. The sun is shining, which means you must walk in the parks. We're quite proud of them, you know." He waited while she considered.

"What time?"

"You decide. I'm still in the middle of breakfast."

She chuckled, her voice sounding sweet and sleepy. "I'm not out of bed, but I'll hurry as fast as I can."

William pictured her curled up in a soft gown, her skin warm and her body waiting for him to slide next to it under the sheets. Now he knew he'd recovered. "Name the time," he managed to say.

"In an hour? I'll get dressed and grab a quick cup of coffee."

"Don't eat too much. We'll go out to lunch. Shall I come to the hotel?"

"Heavens, no. I can find my way around."

"Meet me in front of the Ritz, on Piccadilly. There's a tube station on the corner, if you don't feel like walking."

"Okay. Ten o'clock. The Ritz."

William hung up the telephone and realized he hadn't told her to wear the brooch. In fact, he'd forgotten all about it.

That was not a good sign.

IT WAS FOOLISH to be so happy to see him again. He looked a little pale, and there were shadows under his eyes, as if he hadn't slept well. But he smiled when he saw her, and Kate smiled in return. She didn't like thinking that she'd missed his company yesterday, but it was true.

"I see you still have the brooch," he said.

"I'm taking good care of it," she assured him. The brooch was securely fastened to her black sweater. She'd left her coat in her room and figured she'd be warm enough without it. "I felt awful when I lost it the other day."

"So did I," he said, and she had the strange feeling he meant it. "Let's walk through here." He led her along a path toward Buckingham Palace. "Look," he said, pointing to their left. "The tan roof is Thorne House."

"I didn't know it was this close to Green Park."

"Yes. That's the view from the rooms in the back, in the museum."

"How is the refurbishment coming along?"

"It's almost done. The dust covers will come off, and the house will be cleaned for the tourist season. Pitty is pleased."

"I can imagine." Kate felt at home as they strolled through the park, then watched the Queen's Guards ride their horses along the horse path in Hyde Park. They stopped to catch the Changing of the Guard at Buckingham Palace, then walked back toward Piccadilly and the bustling sidewalks.

"How about lunch at the Ritz?"

"Really? Am I dressed for it?" She frowned at her calf-length brown skirt and matching suede boots. "Is this appropriate for a place like the Ritz?"

"You're perfect." He meant it. He thought he was crazy for meaning it. He took her elbow and led her into the elegant hotel. "Don't worry. You'll be treated like a queen. And if you're lucky, we may even find a gift shop."

He requested a table overlooking the park. The majordomo recognized him and gave William what he wanted. They treated her like...a duchess, Kate decided. And she liked it. She hoped the afternoon would last a long time. It wasn't every day she was bowed to every time someone refilled her wineglass.

"There is a favor I need to ask you," William began when they had finished their lunch. "It's rather strange, but I hope you won't mind."

"Ask me anything."

"It's about the brooch," he said. "It's quite valuable, Kate. In fact, it's a priceless example of medieval jewelry. It used to belong in my family, and I'd like to purchase it."

She touched the yellow stone. "You're talking about *this* brooch?"

"The center stone is a six-carat canary diamond. It's really quite rare."

"*This* brooch?"

He nodded. "Pitty recognized it immediately as a piece that had belonged to the first Duchess of Thornecrest. It, ah, disappeared in the early 1800s. Presumed stolen, you see."

"But it's been in my family for years. How could it be—" She stopped. "You think someone in my family stole it from someone in your family?"

"I have no idea."

"Maybe there are two. Yours and mine."

"Not with a stone like that. You have to admit, the brooch is really quite, ah, original."

"Meaning gaudy."

"I'm not debating the quality of the design, Kate." He really didn't want to debate anything. He wanted to get this whole thing over with so he could return to the country where it was quiet and sane.

"I don't believe this." She finished her wine in one large gulp. "I know I've believed a lot of weird things in my life, but this isn't going to be one of them. Thank you for lunch."

"Kate." He put his hand on her arm. She looked as if she was getting ready to bolt. "I can prove it."

"How?"

"We will go to a jeweler near here. Very reliable, of course. They deal in only the finest gems and are also experts in antique jewelry. They will be able to tell if the brooch is authentic and how much I should pay for it."

"Could I have some more wine?" she asked in a small voice. "I don't usually drink, but this is a special occasion."

He smiled, satisfied that the afternoon was going so well. "You're about to become a very wealthy woman, I fear."

Kate looked at him, her eyes wide. The waiter refilled her glass and, sensing drama, quickly left. "Oh, I have no intention of selling it."

William's smile faded. He couldn't believe what he thought she'd said. "Pardon?"

"I'm not going to sell a family heirloom. It wouldn't be right."

"Why not? You can buy something else."

"I'm to hand it down to my daughters. Someday I'll get married and have children."

It was time to change tactics. "It's going to cost you a small fortune to insure it. You're going to have to keep it in a vault."

"That's if I believed you. I get the feeling that there's more to this than you've told me. Maybe you're a jewel thief or a smuggler."

"I'm a *farmer*," he sputtered. "I make cheese."

"Cheese?"

"Cheese." William motioned the waiter for the check and quickly paid the bill. "Jewel thieves don't own dairy farms."

Kate felt a little dizzy. She wondered if she should leave the elegant dining room and disappear into the bustling city. This is when her sisters would say, "Get out. You don't really believe all this, do you?"

She touched the sparkling stone, remembering the way the waiter's eyes had widened when he saw it. And the curious expression on the antique dealer's face yesterday. She turned to William as they walked across the crowded dining room. "You took me to Antiquarius on purpose, didn't you? You took my coat and handed it to that little man and let me wander off while he examined it, didn't you?"

He sighed. "Yes."

She shook her head in disbelief. "This is amazing, absolutely amazing."

"My sentiments exactly," William muttered, following her through the door. "Shall we?" He motioned toward the crosswalk. "Longmire's is in this direction. Don't you want to know what that pin is worth? Aren't you the least bit curious?"

Kate took a deep breath of fresh air and slipped on

her sunglasses. "I'm a *lot* curious, but that doesn't mean I'm going to sell it to you."

"Let's discuss that after the appraisal."

She walked beside him in silence, but her mind was churning with questions. The first day in London his grandmother had stared at the brooch and had asked her about its origins. And ever since, her grandson had escorted an American tourist around the city. He'd wanted to buy it; he'd wanted it appraised.

7

"NOW WHAT?"

"Tea." He took her elbow and guided her toward St. James Street. "You look a little pale."

"I'm wearing a quarter of a million pounds on my chest," Kate said. She could still see the look of shock on the jeweler's face when she'd handed him the brooch. "I guess that could be making me a little shaky. Where are we going?"

"Home," he answered, and began to hurry her across the street when the signal turned green. "We'll get some tea into you and go on from there."

Kate stayed close to him but didn't reply. This was no time to tell him there would be no "going on." The handsome duke thought all he had to do was write a check and she'd hand over her one and only family heirloom. She had no fiancé and no job, but she sure as hell had Aunt Laurabelle's prized possession, and no one was going to take it from her. Besides, Aunt Belle had promised that the brooch would bring her heart's desire. Kate was determined to keep it, at least until her "heart's desire" arrived.

They were inside Thorne House in a matter of minutes, and Kate barely had time to admire the hall before Will swept her past the cleaning crew, into the elevator and up to the third floor.

"Mary!" he called as he led Kate through the foyer

and into the living room. When the maid appeared in the doorway, William ordered tea, then turned to Kate. "Are you feeling faint?"

"No," she lied. Actually she was feeling a little woozy, but she didn't want William to know. She sank into one of the wing chairs and touched the brooch to make sure it was still there. She'd insisted on wearing it when they left the store, despite disapproving looks from the jeweler and his young assistant. She'd wanted to walk out of that fancy store the same way she'd come in—wearing her twelve-dollar dangle earrings and her worth-a-fortune diamond brooch.

Mary appeared holding a heavy tray piled with all the necessary ingredients for tea and placed it on a low table by Kate's knees. William thanked her and shooed her out of the room. Kate didn't know if she could say a word. She leaned back and closed her eyes while William fiddled with the teapot.

"Drink this," he said, and she opened her eyes and took the delicate cup and saucer from his hand.

"Thanks," she said, and took a sip. "You're right. Tea was just what I needed."

"You're becoming quite an Englishwoman."

"It's the black clothes."

"What?"

"Never mind." She watched him sit down. He seemed to have forgotten to pour himself anything.

He leaned forward and clasped his hands together. "When are you leaving London?"

Leaving London was not what she wanted to discuss. "Tuesday afternoon."

"That gives me time."

"For what?"

He didn't answer. Instead, he stood and walked over

to the sideboard and poured himself a drink. "I have to return to Leicestershire, but I can arrange with the bank to pay the sum you require for the brooch. By Monday that should be accomplished."

"But I'm not going to sell it."

His eyebrows rose. "Do you think that's wise?"

"I'm not famous for making smart decisions," she said, "but I don't think *anyone* would believe this particular story, do you?" She might never tell her sisters about this, she decided. They'd lock her up.

"You still don't believe the stone is genuine?"

"I've seen enough movies to make me wonder if I'm in the middle of a sting."

He choked back a laugh. "A sting," he repeated. "You think I could be trying to con you?" She nodded, and he couldn't help chuckling. "And you don't believe I'm a duke, either, I assume."

She studied him as he crossed the room and sat in the chair near her. Expensive haircut, expensive clothes and accessibility to Thorne House. William Landry had a sophisticated presence that broadcast an aristocratic upbringing. All signs pointed to the fact that he was who he said he was. "No," she replied. "I guess I believe you're a duke."

"Who else would he be, my dear?" Pitty, elegant and cheerful in a bright aqua suit, swept into the room and patted William's cheek before she sat down on the couch. "Tea! Perfect." Mary brought another cup and saucer and set them in front of the duchess.

"Thank you," the dowager said, obviously pleased with something. She smiled at Kate and William. "What have you two been up to this afternoon?"

William answered. "We've been to Longmire's, Pitty. Sheldon wished for more time to appraise the stones, but he evaluated the piece at a quarter of a million pounds."

"Oh, my," Pitty breathed, forgetting to pour herself any tea. "So, he thought it was the Thorne Diamond?"

"Yes."

She turned to Kate. "What a lovely surprise for you!"

Kate wasn't sure if that statement required an answer. Being told the brooch was valuable was one thing; believing it was another. "Yes, I guess you could say that."

Pitty's gaze dropped to the pin. "Magnificent." She looked at Kate and smiled. "It's been lost for five generations. I suppose William told you it, ah, disappeared in the early 1800s."

Kate set her empty cup on the table. "He also told me that means one of my ancestors stole it."

Pitty nodded. "Yes, that's highly probable. More tea?"

"No, thank you." She wanted to leave this mansion and its crazy rich inhabitants and go back to her tiny hotel room and collapse. She wanted to put her brooch in the little safe at the bottom of the armoire and then she wanted to take a nap. "My great-great-whatever-aunt or grandmother did not steal anything."

"How else would it have appeared in America?" Pitty asked as she poured herself a cup of tea. "I've been reading through the family journals. No mention is made of a relative emigrating to America in that particular century. There are no records of Landry daughters, not since 1653. William, go through the books in the Hall library and see if there are any more journals there. We should be able to find something that solves this mystery."

Kate touched the brooch again, just to remind herself it was still there. She had a feeling she'd be doing that a lot from now on. "My ancestors aren't jewel thieves."

Pitty's three chins quivered. "My dear, I mean no offense, but one cannot rewrite history."

William shot Kate an unexpectedly sympathetic smile. "You don't have to decide anything right away," he said. "There is no rush."

"No rush?" Pitty yelped. Drops of tea spattered from her cup and spotted her wide aqua bosom. "After one-hundred and eighty years there's *no rush*? Willie, for heaven's sake!"

"A few days aren't going to make any difference either way, Pitty. I'm leaving for the country this evening, as planned. I'll be happy to make all the arrangements with the bank—"

Pitty's teacup clattered to the table. "No!" She took a deep breath and fanned herself with her hand before turning to Kate. "You will go to Thorne Hall with William and see the picture of the first duchess wearing *that* brooch. Then you will believe me when I say you are wearing the Thorne Diamond, the diamond that belongs in my family, where it should have been all these years."

Kate protested. Spend the night under the same roof with a man who made her heart pound when he looked at her? A man who kissed with amazing passion and left her breathless? She struggled to come up with an excuse. "I can't leave London. I'm staying at the St. Giles. I'm supposed to be going to Westminster Abbey tomorrow afternoon. In the morning I'd planned to do a gravestone rubbing at St. Martin's—"

"There are graves at Thorne Hall," Pitty interrupted.

"Plenty of them. Rub all the stones you want, but first—"

"That's enough, Pitty," William said, a thread of steel running through his voice.

His grandmother stopped in midsentence. "William?"

"You are not going to bully Kate any longer." He turned to Kate and lowered his voice. "Would you like me to escort you to the St. Giles now?"

"Yes. Just call a cab." The long days of touring had finally caught up with her, she realized. She needed some quiet time to absorb everything that had happened.

He turned back to his grandmother. "I'm going to send for my car. I packed this morning, so I'll drop Kate at her hotel and head north."

"William..."

Will ignored her, moved to the phone in the corner of the room and spoke a few words into the receiver. When he was finished he excused himself. "I'm going to fetch my things. Not one more word to Kate about the brooch," he warned, giving Pitty a sharp look. "She's been through quite enough for one day, and so have I."

Pitty hesitated, but William didn't move until he had her consent. When he'd left the room, the elderly woman leaned back against the couch cushions and sighed loudly. "I'm too old for this kind of excitement," she said.

"I know what you mean," Kate agreed. They sat in silence for a long moment until Pitty sighed again.

"I only want what's best for him," she muttered. She turned faded blue eyes toward Kate. "He's all I have."

Kate wasn't sure what to say, but the duchess didn't seem to expect a response.

"His grandfather was completely worthless. I don't know why I ever married him. His father—my son—was a sweet boy, but married a woman totally wrong for him. I told him, but would he listen to me? Of course not. Willie is a fine boy, smart and sensitive, but much too stubborn." She studied Kate with an assessing eye. "Have you ever been married?"

"No. I was supposed to have been married tomorrow," Kate replied.

"Tomorrow? What happened?"

"He said I wasn't—" she didn't want to say *desirable* to the Duchess "—interesting enough. He found someone else and is marrying her tomorrow instead."

"How very fascinating," the duchess said, leaning forward. "And were you quite devastated?"

"At first," Kate admitted. "And then I realized he probably wasn't the right man for me after all. I wanted to be married and have children. More than I wanted to marry Jeff, I think."

"Having children is very important," the duchess agreed, her expression thoughtful. She struggled to rise from the couch, then perched on the chair next to Kate's and patted her hand. "My dear, I am going to give you some advice and I'd like you to listen very carefully."

Kate waited, wondering what on earth was coming next. For some odd reason, despite the fact that the old woman thought one of her ancestors had stolen jewelry for a living, she liked William's grandmother. The mischievous light in the faded blue eyes reminded her of Aunt Belle. Kate found herself willing to hear the dowager's words. "All right," she agreed.

"Go to the Hall with him. Just for two days. You'll have a lovely time seeing the Midlands. It's a large house, with a small staff. You would be quite comfortable."

"It sounds lovely," Kate said. "But—"

"The painting is above the fireplace in the formal dining room," Pitty explained. "The first duchess was a beautiful woman, very much in love with her husband."

"I'm sure she—"

Pitty continued as if she didn't hear her. "You shouldn't be alone on the day you were to be married, do you think?"

"I don't—"

Pitty tugged on her hand. "Is it such a difficult decision? A day in the country with a handsome devil like my William?"

The handsome devil himself stepped into the room and dropped his bags in the wide doorway. "We're ready," he announced. He looked like a man ready to flee prison. "Kate?"

She stood, and the dowager did also. Kate held out her hand, and the old woman took it, but didn't let it go. "I enjoyed meeting you," Kate said, meaning the words. "I don't intend to sell the brooch, so I don't think we'll see each other again."

"One never knows," Pitty murmured. She looked at Will, standing stubbornly in the door, and raised her voice. "I have done my best to convince Kate to see the portrait at the Hall."

William stared at his grandmother. "What's going on?"

"Kate shouldn't be alone tomorrow." She patted Kate's arm. "Right, my dear?"

Kate took a deep breath. She'd come to England to see things she'd never seen before, to have an adventure and forget about her nonexistent career and her canceled wedding. She told herself that her acceptance of Pitty's invitation wasn't because going to Thorne Hall meant she would have another day with William. "I'd like to see the portrait, if you don't mind my tagging along."

"We'll stop at the hotel for your things. You'll be spending the night." No "how wonderful," no smile of pleasure or sigh of relief. Kate felt like an idiot for expecting a reaction from him.

"Thank you," the dowager whispered, squeezing Kate's hand. "Wear the brooch all the time so you don't lose it," she advised. "We'll discuss its future ownership on Monday."

"But—"

"Go," Pitty said. "Have a lovely weekend, children."

William kissed her on the cheek and picked up his bags. Kate followed him into the brass-trimmed elevator. Five days ago she wouldn't get into a cab with him. Now she was heading off to the country in his car. It boiled down to one thing, she realized, following the silent man outside to the waiting Jaguar sedan.

She wasn't ready to say goodbye.

PITTY HAD SOMETHING up her sleeve. He could tell by the innocent expression in her eyes when she'd said goodbye. William nearly groaned out loud as he waited in his car for Kate to reappear with her luggage. This was insane. He could barely keep his hands off her in taxicabs and now he was taking her to his home.

He wanted to spend the weekend making love to

her. He wanted those soft breasts in his palms and that sweet little body pressed against his. He wanted to bury himself inside her and watch her eyes darken with passion.

And he couldn't. A weekend affair would only be messy. One night, he promised himself. One night and a tour of the manor house. The dairies, too, if she wanted to photograph British cows. She could gaze up at a hundred paintings of dead Landrys for as many hours as she liked, then he would bring her back to London and say goodbye. He would turn right around and go back to Leicestershire. To mud, cows, dogs, sheep and all the rest, and he would heave a sigh of relief to have escaped yet another romantic entanglement.

William drummed his fingers on the steering wheel and wondered why the prospect of saying goodbye to Katie Stewart made his stomach knot up. Making love to her held much more appeal. He hardened his heart as Kate hurried from the hotel and crossed the sidewalk, a carry-on bag slung over her shoulder and the familiar tote bag in her hand. She opened the back door and tossed her bags in as William leaned over to open the passenger's door.

Once she was inside, seat belt fastened and sunglasses in place, Kate gave him a big smile. "I wasn't sure this was the right thing to do," she said, "but I couldn't resist seeing more of England."

He drove carefully into the late-afternoon traffic. "Why wasn't it the right thing to do?"

"You didn't invite me. Your grandmother did. You were forced into going along with it."

William glanced at her when he stopped the car for a red light. "I rarely allow myself to be forced into anything." *Except following a tourist to the Tower of London and playing tour guide for a week.*

"Really?"

He'd always been a sucker for green eyes. "Really." He put the car in gear and headed north. Keeping his mind off sex wasn't going to be easy.

KATE DIDN'T INTEND to fall asleep. Leicestershire was one hundred miles north of London, William had explained, punching the radio buttons until he found classical music. One hundred miles was a long time to listen to Beethoven and struggle to keep her eyes open, so she curled up on the soft ivory leather and rested her head against the back of the seat. When she woke, it was dark and the car had slowed down.

She opened her eyes and straightened up. "Where are we?"

"Northeast of Leicestershire, near Rutland."

The directions meant nothing. "Are we close?"

"Very. We've been driving through Thornecrest land for over a mile." He pointed to a road leading through green pastures to a prosperous-looking farmstead. "One of my dairies."

"One? How many are there?"

"Five," he said, pride tingeing his voice. "We're one of the biggest dairy operations in the Midlands."

"That must be a lot of milk."

"We use it," William said. He pointed ahead. "There. See the stone pillars?"

She could barely make out the markers through the dark. "Yes. What are they?"

"The entrance to Thorne Hall." He turned the car left and swung onto a wide paved road. Kate expected to see a house, but the surrounding fields were dark. Trees lined the road and low hills rolled to the horizon.

"Where's the Hall?"

"You should be able to see it soon." They crested a small hill, and in the distance, lights spilled out of the windows of an immense stone building. "There." Will stepped on the gas pedal and hurried along the road, which eventually curved in front of the stone mansion.

Kate couldn't think of anything to say. Grander and more impressive than she'd ever imagined, Thorne Hall faced acres of manicured lawns. Trees rose from either side of the three-story building, an arched entrance protected the door and ivy occupied much of the space between the mullioned windows.

"It was built in 1695," William explained. "But two-thirds of the house was destroyed in the early 1800s. It's a manageable size now."

"It's beautiful." Kate tried to picture a structure three times its size, but couldn't. William parked the car in front of the entrance and stepped out of the car, as did Kate. A round-faced older gentleman scurried from the front door and down the steps.

"Welcome home, sir!"

"Thank you, Harry. It's good to be home." William turned to Kate. "I'd like you to meet my guest, Katherine Stewart. Kate, this is Harry Goodfellow. He and his wife run Thorne Hall."

"Welcome to Thorne Hall, Miss Stewart." Harry hurried past them to the car.

"Thank you." She was in heaven, all right. Kate let William lead her up the wide stone steps to a massive door. He opened it and ushered her into the hall. The "great hall," William called it and led the way, explaining a bit about the architecture. Kate tried not to let her mouth hang open as she walked across a black-and-white marble floor. Pale stone walls rose for two stories, and a wide stone staircase swept to an upper balcony. Portraits hung everywhere, and over the doors and the fireplace were ornate carvings of fruit and cherubs.

"On the right is the formal dining room and, beyond that, the morning room." William waved toward a double door opened to reveal yellow walls. "Straight ahead is the main salon and Long Gallery. To the left are the library and offices." He looked down and smiled at her. "Don't look so worried. You won't get lost. The house was redesigned in 1949, after World War II, so it would be economical and efficient."

"I feel as if I'm back in another century." Rhode Island was very far away, another lifetime even. An unemployed computer programmer didn't expect to be standing beside a duke beneath carved cupids.

The feeling of unreality continued as William led her up the stone staircase, past pictures of his ancestors painted with their horses, dogs or armor. A few looked pleasant enough, but most appeared as if they took their titles seriously. The upper floor was split into east and west wings. William led her to the west, explaining the east-wing rooms were only used when Pitty visited or there was a large house party over the holidays.

"How many rooms are there up here?"

"Ten." He led her down a long hall, its wall painted soft ivory. A pale green-and-yellow floral carpet softened their footsteps. "My rooms are at the end of the hall." He opened the first door on the right. "This is the largest guest room, Kate, so you should be comfortable enough." He flicked the light switch, and a tiny bedside lamp lit the room.

"I think it's perfect," she managed to say as she stepped inside the room. Ivory walls and yellow carpet gave the large room a sunbathed glow. Lace curtains hung from the tall windows at either side of the double bed, and a matching lace coverlet decorated the bed. It was an exquisitely furnished room, fit for a queen, Kate thought. Harry arrived with her bags and set them down on the floor by a chintz-covered chaise lounge.

"If you need anything, just ring for Mrs. Goodfellow." William pointed to a set of buttons in the wall beside the bed. He looked at his watch. "It's almost eight. I'll check with her to find out about dinner, but I suspect it's ready when we are. Are you starving or would you like a chance to freshen up?"

"Give me ten minutes," Kate said. Ten minutes to convince herself she wasn't dreaming. Trite but highly necessary. Especially when she looked at the Manet hanging over the cherry bed.

"I'll knock," he promised, and followed Henry out of the room. William paused in the doorway and looked back at Kate. "You're not afraid of dogs, are you?"

"Not usually."

"Good." He shut the door behind him and left her alone in the elegant yellow room. Along one wall were three doors: one was the entrance to a large white-and-gold bathroom, the others, on either side of the bathroom, opened on empty closets. Kate's clothes did little to fill the closet on the right. She splashed cold water on her face, redid her makeup and willed her queasy stomach to behave. It was nerves, she decided. She'd been on edge since the visit to Longmire's.

This morning she'd awakened planning to visit the Victoria and Albert Museum. Tonight she wore a priceless diamond and would sleep in Thorne Hall under a Manet. Kate took several deep breaths. No wonder she was a little unsettled.

She sat on the edge of the bed and rubbed her forehead. Her real problem wasn't owning a brooch worth almost four hundred thousand dollars, or being a guest in a mansion three hundred years old. Her real problem was being perilously close to falling in love with William Landry. If she wasn't already. She could leave here tomorrow with her pride intact. He would never have to guess an awestruck American tourist had fallen for him if she was very, very careful. She would be cool and sophisticated. She would enjoy her tour of the country and admire the portrait of that duchess with the brooch. She would return to London tomorrow, maybe by train.

No one would ever have to know she'd spent her London vacation falling in love with a duke.

It was so ridiculous that no one would believe it anyway.

MRS. GOODFELLOW LIKED HER. William could tell by the way the plump woman bustled around Kate's chair and served her healthy portions of roast beef and Yorkshire pudding. Harry had winked at him in the hallway, showing his silent approval of the surprise house guest. The pair of springer spaniels tried to lick her hand and whined for attention, while the tiny mutt Mrs. Goodfellow had rescued last summer wagged its tail and put its tiny brown paws on the seat of Kate's chair until Henry called the dogs from the dining room.

Kate didn't appear to mind the dog's attention, William thought. In fact, she seemed oblivious to the commotion her presence at Thorne Hall had caused. Mrs. Goodfellow had dragged out the finest plates and had filled a silver vase with daffodils as if the queen herself was to eat in the dining room Henry Holland had designed in 1788. In fact, silver gleamed everywhere. Kate was seated to his left, beyond a trio of candles in an arrangement of silver candlestick holders.

The platter of beef almost crashed to the floor when Mrs. Goodfellow spotted the brooch on Kate's sweater.

William hurried to lend a hand and avoid giving the dogs the meal of a lifetime. "There," he said, steadying the gleaming silver platter.

"Thank you," Mrs. Goodfellow murmured. As she met Will's gaze, her eyebrows rose as if to say "What on earth is going on here, Willie?"

He pretended he didn't notice. "Everything looks wonderful. You've outdone yourself."

"Your grandmother called. Said you were bringing a special guest." She moved away from the table. She smiled once more at Kate. "Wanted everything to be lovely."

"It is," Kate assured her, and moved her fork around on her plate as if to prove her words. When Mrs. Goodfellow had left them alone in the room, she glanced up at the portrait above the fireplace. "I guess that proves it, doesn't it?"

"Proves what?"

"The brooch belonged to your family."

"Hard to imagine there would be two pieces of jewelry that looked like that, isn't it?" The first duchess wore a flowing white gown, with the ornate brooch pinned to her ample bosom. A crown of flowers topped her dark curls, and her smile was kind. William had never minded having her in the dining room.

"Yes. Are you sure there wasn't a Landry woman who went to the United States? Maybe she owned the brooch and it was hers to take with her."

William shrugged. "I doubt it. Pitty wondered the same thing and has been going through old journals from the nineteenth century. Have you forgiven me yet?"

"For which offense?"

He couldn't tell if she was teasing him or not. "How many are there?"

"Deceiving me at the tower, hiding the fact that the brooch was valuable, pretending you were taking me out because you wanted to and—"

"I apologize. I was speaking of today. I know it's been a shock for you."

Kate nodded toward the portrait. "You're forgiven. I'm starting to understand why your grandmother wanted me to see that. The brooch belongs to a duchess obviously."

"Aren't you hungry?"

"Not very." She put down her fork and dabbed her lips with her napkin. "I don't want to hurt Mrs. Good-fellow's feelings."

"You won't. I'll eat enough for both of us tonight."

"All right." Kate looked at him gratefully. "It was kind of you to bring me here. I'll take the train back to London tomorrow. There is a train station in Leicester-shire, isn't there?"

William deliberately looked at his plate and cut a piece of beef. "Yes, but you're welcome to stay the weekend."

"I don't think so. There's still a lot I want to—"

"Of course," he agreed a little too quickly. "I'll show you the dairies in the morning if you like."

"I'd like that." Her eyes sparkled in the candlelight, but her skin was pale, making her look fragile and vulnerable.

"Was tomorrow really to have been your wedding day?"

"Yes. Up until three weeks ago." She smiled at him. "Don't look so sorry for me. I'm not."

"No?" He put down his fork and reached for her hand. He told himself it was a friendly and sympathetic gesture that meant nothing. Heat snaked through his fingers and up his arm and knocked him in the groin.

She squeezed his fingers gently, then pulled her hand away.

"Don't go," he whispered.

"I have to." She gulped, scooting her chair away from the table. "Excuse me."

"Don't go." He stood and reached for her, but she shook her head. Her face was very white. "Stay and—"

"I can't," she insisted. "I'm not feeling—"

Too late he realized every bit of color had drained from her face. He reached for her and caught her in his arms before she crumpled to the floor.

8

"I'M SO EMBARRASSED," Kate moaned. "Go away."

"No." William held a cold cloth to her forehead. "This is all my fault."

"How? Did you poison me?" Kate kept her eyes closed and tried to ignore the queasy feeling that rolled in waves throughout her body. Vomiting was bad enough. Vomiting all over the Duke of Thornecrest was a disaster.

He chuckled softly. "No. But I had this flu yesterday. I was sick as a dog, too, for about twelve hours. I must have given it to you."

"I'm never kissing you again," she moaned.

"You're breaking my heart," he whispered. "Lie still and try to relax."

"What time is it?"

"Almost three. You should be able to sleep soon."

Sleep or kill herself, Kate decided. Will had helped her back and forth to the bathroom, and when she was too weak to get out of bed, he'd held a basin and rubbed her back. Will stroked the damp cloth across her forehead and down the side of her face. "Mmm," she said. "Feels good."

"Go to sleep."

"You, too."

"When you're better," he said, his voice low and soothing.

"I'm better," she whispered, but she kept her eyes closed. She'd moved past embarrassment, she realized. Past embarrassment and into total humiliation. Tomorrow she'd crawl out of here and hitch a ride to the train station. She wouldn't have to face him and she would never tell anyone what had occurred during her visit to a country estate.

"Go to sleep," he repeated. "I'll leave when I'm sure you're going to be all right. I don't want you fainting on my marble floors and breaking any bones."

"You'd be stuck with me forever," she sighed. "Not good."

There was a brief silence. "That's a matter of opinion, isn't it?"

Kate didn't answer. She turned onto her side and slipped into a welcome sleep. William watched her for a while until he was satisfied that the worst was over. He left a light burning in the bathroom and made sure Kate was covered with a blanket before he tiptoed out of the room. He'd never been good at taking care of anyone. In fact, he couldn't remember ever having done it before tonight. There were no younger brothers and sisters, no cousins or nieces and nephews. But he thought he'd done pretty well. After all, what choice had he had after she collapsed?

If he hadn't been through the same thing the night before, he would have panicked and called a physician. He still would, William promised himself, if Kate hadn't improved by morning. He went through his sitting room and on to his bathroom. He'd take a shower and go to bed, but he'd leave his door open in case Katie needed him.

SUNLIGHT WAS POURING in through the lace when Kate opened her eyes. She was going to live. The queasiness was gone; the wanting-to-die feeling was gone, too. Kate tried to sit up and was glad when no dizziness interrupted the motion. She saw her reflection in the mirror over the antique makeup table: tangled hair, pale skin and dark circles under her eyes that made her look as if she'd escaped from a mental institution. She'd vomited in front of a duke. She'd vomited *on* a duke. She'd been sick all over someone she was half in love with. Talk about killing passion.

And, even worse, today was to have been her wedding day. Kate put her head in her hands and groaned.

"Miss?" Mrs. Goodfellow paused in the doorway. "I brought you some tea. His Grace thought you might be needin' some nourishment."

"He's not around, is he?"

"No. He's outside, but he'll be back in a while." She set the tray on a little glass-topped table in the corner. "You'll have time to freshen up."

"Thank goodness."

She poured a cup of tea. "What do you take in your tea?"

"Just a little sugar, but you don't have to wait on me."

"No." Mrs. Goodfellow stopped her with one chubby hand. "You stay right where you are. It's not often we have guests. Are you feeling better? I hear you had a nasty case of flu."

Kate took the teacup and sipped. The hot, sweet liquid was just what she needed. "I'm fine. A little shaky, but nothing worse."

"Good, good. There's some toast and a few biscuits, too. And my own strawberry jam."

"Thank you very much, for everything. I'm not used to being waited on."

"We've our orders to give you the royal treatment." Mrs. Goodfellow winked at her. "Wouldn't do to have Will, er, His Grace, think we didn't do what we were told."

"Have you worked here long?"

"All my life. My husband, too. And my mother before that."

"Then you've known Will all his life."

"A fine boy." Mrs. Goodfellow nodded. She handed Kate a plate of toast. "Take a bite of that and see how you go along."

"All right." Kate tasted the fresh-baked toasted bread and smiled. "Heaven," she declared. "I must be better if I'm hungry."

"Yes," the plump housekeeper declared, "that's the truth of it, all right. You'll need to build your strength up if you're going to see Thorne Hall and all that it entails. The dairies alone will take hours."

"Are there that many cows?"

"Oh, yes, but the cheese is the most interestin', I think, though not like they made it in my grandmother's day. You'll be getting a real treat. Finish your toast so you can pop into the bath before he returns."

"Good idea."

"Don't worry about the tray," Mrs. Goodfellow said. "I'll send one of the girls for it later." She closed the door behind her, leaving Kate to wonder how long it was going to take to look halfway decent. She was determined to succeed or die trying.

"HOW ARE YOU FEELING?" William crossed the stone floor and stopped at the bottom of the staircase. He watched Kate hesitate for a second, then continue down the stairs toward him. She looked fragile in a black sweater and brown leggings. The brooch peeked out from beneath the collar of a white shirt and the rounded neck of the sweater. He was getting accustomed to having the damn thing in his face all the time.

"Much better, thank you."

She still looked embarrassed. He wanted to put his arms around her to reassure her, the way he had last night. He'd sat on the mattress next to her, and she'd melted into his arms and he'd felt very strong and protective. "You look fine."

Kate joined him at the base of the stairs. "I'm feeling much better." Her smile was rueful. "Thanks for taking care of me last night. I didn't mean to fall into your arms quite so dramatically."

"That was the best part. I'm sure my ancestors saw a lot of swooning women, but I never have."

"You knew what to do."

"Genetic memory." There, he'd managed to make her smile, a real smile, which made him feel ten feet tall. "Are you ready for a tour or would you prefer to relax in the library?"

"A tour, I think. Fresh air would feel good."

"All right. It's a bit breezy and damp, but the sun is trying to come out. Maybe we'll be lucky." He led her to a narrow hall behind the dining room that took them past an enormous kitchen and into a warren of smaller rooms.

"You'll need this." William tossed her a heavy leather jacket lined in shearling. "You're going to need some protection from the wind." He rummaged through the collection of boots lined up under the coat rack until he found a small pair of waterproof boots.

"These, too," he said, and handed them to her. "Do you want to see the gardens or something muddier?"

"Both, as long as I'm outside." She kicked her shoes off and stuck her feet in the boots. "Hey, that's a pretty good fit."

"Good."

She pulled a pair of old work gloves from the pocket of the coat. "Mind if I wear these, too?"

"Go ahead." He smiled. She looked cute in the oversize coat. "You look a lot better than you did last night."

She shuddered. "Don't remind me."

"Come on." He held out his gloved hand and she took it. "You might as well see how a duke spends his time."

Kate grinned up at him, her eyes twinkling. "You mean you *work*?"

He tugged her closer and gave her a quick, hard kiss on those inviting lips. He purposely didn't linger, or he knew he'd be making love to her in spite of mud-caked boots and old jackets. He lifted his head and tugged her toward the door. There was a new intimacy between them this morning. After all, he'd held her in his arms half the night.

William took a deep breath of fresh air and promised himself he could make it through the morning, get Kate on a train, and ignore the aching in his gut.

THE BRIEF KISS CAUGHT Kate by surprise. His lips were cool, his skin still chilled from the outdoors. It was over before she could think about enjoying it, and then she was out the door and standing beside him in what looked like a garden. Paved walks, flower or vegetable beds separated by stone and neatly trimmed shrubs sprawled along the east side of the house.

"Where are we?"

"We just left the old servants' entrance," he explained. "Around the corner is the kitchen and the herb garden, but we're going to walk over that hill to one of the dairies."

The three dogs raced around the corner of the house and greeted them with eager, wagging tails. Kate petted each one, which seemed to satisfy them. "How many cows do you have?"

"I couldn't say. I have over a dozen farms, leased, of course, in this part of Leicestershire. Come along." He took her hand. "I'll show you how we make Stilton cheese."

Kate hated to sound ignorant, but she had to know. "What exactly is Stilton cheese?"

"The most famous cheese in England," he declared. "It's only made in the shires of Leicester, Derby and Nottingham. It's a wonderful ending to a meal, with fruit especially. Do you like blue cheese or Roquefort cheese?"

"I like blue-cheese salad dressing."

"Ah," he said, sounding pleased. "Then there's hope."

The next hours sped by as Kate followed William and the excited dogs over the countryside and eventually back to the stables, where the dogs were left behind. She climbed into a battered old truck, and William drove her to the buildings where the cheese was made. He proudly explained the complicated process, starting with the formation of curds from the pasteurized milk and ending with the large rounds of cheese being tested for ripeness and texture by a skilled cheese grader. The white-coated workers were too polite to stare, but Kate saw the curious looks that were cast her way. Will introduced her to several people as his "American cousin" and behaved as if there was nothing unusual in escorting someone through the refrigerated rooms stacked with cylinders of cheese.

"Where do you sell them when they're done?"

"We have distributors for markets, both in Britain and overseas."

"I could buy one in Rhode Island?"

"I would imagine. Maybe not one of mine, but I can't imagine that it would be hard to find Stilton anywhere."

They shared a lunch packed by Mrs. Goodfellow: small thermoses of chicken soup, crusty bread and fruit salad. William made tea in his small office, then drove her through several small towns, past Rutland Water, a huge reservoir, and past countless acres of pastureland.

"Hawthorn," Will explained, pointing to the hedges that bordered much of the land. "May Blossom, we call it."

"This is beautiful country. I'm glad I was able to see this part of England." She looked at her watch. It was after three and past time to find a train back to London. "Do you have a train schedule somewhere? I should get back to London before dark."

"Are you certain?"

"I think it's probably a good idea." Kate didn't look over at him. Instead, she watched the stone house appear in the distance. Of course, she'd like to stay, but she was tired of knowing he was with her because of his loyalty to his grandmother. Everything he'd done for her, he'd done because his grandmother had insisted or begged or coerced, which included taking her along to Thorne Hall and entertaining her today. Naturally she'd like to believe it was because he found her irresistible, but Kate knew better.

William didn't answer. He drove the truck into the stable and parked it beside the Jaguar. He turned off the engine and ignored the dogs who had followed them inside and whined for attention. He looked serious as he turned to her and spread his arm over the back of the seat. His fingers grazed her shoulder. "Is there some reason in particular you want to leave so soon?"

Kate faced him reluctantly. He was the kind of man she'd dreamed of loving: strong and kind, sexy and quiet; nice to old ladies and pesky dogs. He looked good with a little mud on his left cheek and a faded old jacket that had one of the pockets half ripped off. She liked him better today than she had that evening at San Lorenzo's. She liked the man who had kissed her in the dim hall and had found boots for her to wear. She was more than a little bit in love with him, and it was her wedding day. Her ex-wedding day.

"No answer?" He gave her a half smile. "Or no reason?"

"No idea what to say."

"Then say you'll stay. At least until tomorrow. I'm sure Mrs. Goodfellow has planned to serve tea now, and she's probably been working all day on something special for supper. You'll hurt her feelings if you leave."

"I don't believe Mrs. Goodfellow cares one way or the other."

He leaned closer to her. His fingers brushed the shoulder of her jacket and touched the ends of her hair.

"Oh, that's where you're wrong, Katie Stewart." His voice was soft. "She and Harry are chattering now, wondering who you are and why I brought you here. Beth has recognized the brooch, you see. Naturally she's curious as to why you wear it."

His wonderful lips moved closer. If she wanted to, which she did, she could put her hands on either side of his face and pull him to her. "Your grandmother told me not to take it off. I think she's afraid I'll lose it."

"She has her reasons." He tilted his head closer. "We both do."

Kate forgot to take the bulky gloves off before she touched his face. He held her against him as they kissed, and Kate wrapped her arms around his neck to draw him close. It was as if she'd been waiting all day for him to hold her again. She parted her lips slightly, at the gentle insistence of his tongue, and soon his mouth slanted over hers in a kiss that burned through her body until she no longer remembered her frozen toes. She forgot she had toes. William tossed his gloves aside, unzipped her coat and slid his bare hands along her waist. Kate turned, to kiss him better. Their tongues tangled, and her heart expanded in her chest until she thought she could no longer breathe.

He slid his warm palms under her sweater and cupped her breasts. A gasp of startled pleasure escaped her as his roughened skin moved above her bra and unfastened the center hook. She realized she'd been waiting for him to touch her, waiting for this breathless, aching feeling that swept across her skin. She managed to take off her gloves, then slid her fingers along the soft skin at the back of his neck and wound them through the thick waves of dark hair. She couldn't help pulling him closer, couldn't help wanting his hands on her breasts and his thumbs teasing her nipples to hard peaks. She couldn't help wanting him, couldn't help wishing they were anywhere but sprawled on the seat of an old truck in a dark garage that smelled faintly of horses and old leather.

She wished they were in a bed.

"Come on, boys! We'll go—" Mr. Goodfellow's booming voice reverberated through the large stable, along with the dogs' excited barks.

Kate pulled away from William's arms and hoped her brain would kick in and restore her to the sensible woman she knew she was. Or she used to be, she thought, gazing with regret at William's lips.

"Sorry, lad!" Harry called as he backed out of the building. "I didn't know anyone was in here. I thought you forgot to close the door."

"You're a dangerous woman, Kate," William said. He hooked her bra with experienced fingers, tugged her sweater over her hips and swept a lock of hair from her flushed cheek and tucked it behind her ear.

"That's a compliment, isn't it?" She liked the idea of being dangerous.

"Yes. I suppose."

"You're not exactly white bread yourself, you know." She discreetly adjusted her sweater. Her bra felt two sizes too small.

"It's not always easy to be around you," he muttered, reaching for the handle on the door. "I forget where I am."

"You do?"

Will got out of the truck and shut the door. "Yes, I do. In lifts, taxicabs, trucks." He shook his head in mock disgust as he walked around to Kate's side of the truck and opened the door. "I'll have to listen to

Harry's apologies for the rest of the weekend. Now you have to stay. Otherwise, he'll think he scared you off."

Kate chuckled. "I can't."

"Can't or won't?"

"Shouldn't."

"I'll have Mrs. Goodfellow move you to the east wing, if you like." He lowered his voice to a whisper. "And there are locks on all the doors. You're not required or expected to sleep with your host."

Oh, she was definitely in love with him, Kate decided. Which was exactly why she shouldn't stay. She was lonely and vulnerable and on the rebound. And tonight should have been her wedding night. Her first night as Jeff's wife, and now she felt nothing but relief at the thought of escaping that particular fate. "Unlike other guests of past dukes?"

"Most likely," he agreed. "I'm sure they all had mistresses. House parties at Thorne Hall were probably excuses for illicit sex with someone else's willing wife." He took her hand. "Come on. Let's see if Beth baked scones for us. I'll tell her you're staying the night."

"I guess I could," Kate conceded. Being in love with William Landry didn't mean she had to run out the front door like a frightened virgin. Because she wasn't, either frightened or virginal. She was twenty-five and free to enjoy the company of a handsome man. She wasn't the first woman to fall in love with the Duke of Thornecrest and she wouldn't be the last. He'd kissed her as if he'd thought she was the most desirable woman in the world. He'd taken care of her when she was sick and had smiled at her jokes. He didn't seem to mind when she teased him, either. He was kind and thoughtful and very, very sexy.

And as dangerous as a runaway train.

"You should be in the morning room or the library," Mrs. Goodfellow muttered. "I would've fixed you a proper tea, using the old duchess's porcelain."

William stretched his legs beside the worn oak table. "That's ridiculous and you know it. I always have my tea in the kitchen, with you."

"You have company." She sniffed. "I could've done it up right, with the silver and all." Mrs. Goodfellow shot Kate an apologetic look. "You would've liked something a little fancier, I know you would, though you're too polite to say so."

"I like your kitchen," Kate assured her. William wanted to laugh at her expression. Kate didn't want to hurt the housekeeper's feelings, but he could tell she meant her words. She looked more relaxed in the midst of the oak-beamed kitchen than she had drinking tea at Browns. "It's very comfortable," she added after helping herself to another scone.

Mrs. Goodfellow wiped her hands on a red-checked cloth. "You're feeling better, I hope?"

"Yes."

"Neither one of you must have had much sleep last night. I'm planning a late dinner, so there's time for a nap."

He watched in fascination as Kate's cheeks turned pink. Obviously the fact that he'd cared for her still embarrassed her. She and his plump housekeeper discussed the unpredictability of the stomach flu, then moved on to a discussion of the evening's dinner menu. Mrs. Goodfellow launched into the virtues of cooking with a gas stove, and Kate appeared to be enthralled. William poured himself another cup of tea and lathered another scone with clotted cream. He never took company in the kitchen. He entertained rarely, usually only during the fox-hunting season. He didn't hunt himself, but some of his friends waited each year for nearby Melton Mowbray's famous hunts. He hadn't known it would be so enjoyable to sit in a warm kitchen and listen to the women chatter.

The women now moved on to Mrs. Goodfellow's favorite subject: her grandchildren. Her daughter lived in nearby Oatley, she explained, and the three children, two boys and a girl, visited Thorne Hall often. Kate thought that was wonderful. Her mother had died only a few years ago, she confided to the housekeeper, shortly after her father's death. Mrs. Goodfellow clucked sympathetically. Kate told her of her three older sisters, adding that as the youngest she'd always been considered the black sheep of the family. She'd never known her grandmother, but she'd been very close to her great-aunt, she told the older woman. In fact, Kate continued, her aunt had given her this brooch. Mrs. Goodfellow admired it and gave William a curious look.

"Yes, it's real," he said, answering her unspoken question. He wiped his mouth with a napkin and tossed it on the table.

"But that means—"

"It's been in Kate's family for years," he interrupted, unwilling to discuss the legend behind the brooch. He could see the pleased sparkle in Mrs. Goodfellow's eyes from across the room. Kate hid a yawn, which gave him the perfect opportunity to excuse them both from the kitchen. "Go take a nap," he told her. "I have several hours of paperwork waiting in my study." He looked at the clock over the hood of the massive black stove. "It's almost five-thirty. Come down at seven-thirty, and we'll have a drink before dinner, all right?"

"It sounds perfect." She took her empty mug and plate to the sink, then hid another yawn and smiled. "Sorry. I guess it's all this fresh country air."

He wanted to kiss her, but he settled for holding open the kitchen door and watching to make certain she turned left at the end of the hall.

"She's a lovely girl," the housekeeper said from behind him.

Will turned around and leaned against the wall. "Yes," he agreed. "She is."

The housekeeper nodded toward the black sweater hanging on the back of Kate's empty chair. "I never thought I'd see the day."

"The brooch, you mean?"

"That, and your bringing a young lady to sit in the kitchen like the mistress of the Hall. None of those city airs about her, y'know."

"Kate's here for the weekend. Nothing more." Somehow the thought wasn't pleasant. William frowned and crossed his arms in front of his chest. "Pitty wanted her to see the portrait in the dining room."

"And what do *you* want?"

"Peace and quiet," he declared. "I want that damn brooch out of my life once and for all."

"And what about that nice young lady? She looks at you as if you hung the moon."

"The stars, too," Harry added, entering the kitchen through a side door. "You've a smitten look yourself, lad. Best be careful, or you'll find yourself tied to a noisy female till your dyin' day." He dodged the red dish towel his wife attempted to swat him with and gave her a swift hug.

"I'll be careful," William promised. He picked up Kate's sweater and threw it over one arm before leaving the room. "I'll be *very* careful," he repeated to himself as he went down the hall. He would keep his hands off her for the rest of the weekend, he promised himself. He would not kiss her. He would not make love to her hour after hour in the dark, quiet hours of the night.

He could, however, deliver her sweater and her troublesome pin to her. He would smile and be polite and then he would turn away, go into his study and concentrate on cheese.

IF ANYONE ASKED what she had done in England, she'd have to say she'd drunk a lot of tea, Kate mused, tugging her turtleneck over her head. She'd tell her sisters about the tea; she wouldn't tell them about the Englishman or this visit to a stranger's country estate or about having the stomach flu. She kicked off her shoes and her socks, hung her jeans in the closet, and turned down the lace coverlet. None of this "resting on the bed" stuff. She was going to treat herself to a real nap between crisp cotton sheets, with the thick covers pulled up to her ears and the shades drawn shut against the fading afternoon light.

Yes, her trip to England would be highly censored, much of it her own little secret. Memories she would not share. She was about to climb into bed when a knock came at her door.

"Yes?"

"May I come in?" William asked.

"No. I mean, not yet." She looked about for something to put around her. She couldn't answer the door wearing nothing but panties and a bra, even though he was slightly familiar with the bra. She hurried into the bathroom and grabbed one of the large yellow bath towels to wrap around her. Then she twisted the doorknob and opened the door a few inches. "Sorry," she said, peeking out, "I, um, was just—"

"I didn't mean to intrude," he said, avoiding her eyes. "You left your sweater in the kitchen. I didn't want you to think you'd misplaced the brooch."

He held out the sweater to her, and Kate opened the door wider in order to take it. She smiled. "I'm sorry. I feel a little silly hiding behind a door but I was just about to get into..." She stopped, feeling even more ridiculous.

"Bed," he finished for her, and let go of the sweater as if it were on fire.

She could see half his face, half of his rueful smile. "Yes," she said. She heard him sigh.

"Close the door," he said. "Now."

She kept it open, about eight inches from its frame, and asked, "Why?"

"Because I'm a weak man," he explained. "I look at your shoulders and your soft skin above that towel and I remember the way you felt under my hands a while ago. I'm remembering the taste of your mouth and the scent of your hair and how your fingers touched the back of my neck when you reached up to kiss me."

Kate's knees weakened.

"Shut the bloody door, Katie," he ordered.

"All right," she whispered. She put her hand on the door and gave it a push. It closed with a miserable finality. But William was right, she reminded herself.

They couldn't, shouldn't make love to each other. She wasn't the kind of person who had one-night affairs, who slept casually with anyone who attracted her. She leaned against the door and waited to hear his footsteps move down the hall. He had lots of women. Scores of them, probably. She remembered how Jessica and her friends had stared at her from their exclusive corner table at San Lorenzo's. She was only one in a long line of the duke's conquests.

"I apologize," he said from the other side of the door. "I was out of line."

"No. I've been kissing you right back," she admitted. *And I've fallen in love with you, too. How about that for a laugh?* What was she afraid of? Getting hurt? She'd already been dumped once, by one of the most boring men in New England. He'd said they didn't have anything in common, that she wasn't exciting enough. Now a duke was apologizing to her for wanting to make love to her, for finding her desirable. "Thank you," she said.

"What on earth for?"

"For wanting to," she told him. "I know you must have lots of women—"

He swore, turned the knob and pushed the door open. "What on earth gave you that idea?"

She gripped her towel, making certain it was securely fastened. She wished her arms weren't so pale. "Well, don't you?"

William glared down at her. "I've never brought anyone here, alone, until now. You are absolutely driving me insane, too. What the hell are you thanking me for, anyway?"

"Y-you look at me as if I'm beautiful," she stammered. "I appreciate it."

He stared at her as if she'd surprised him. "You are beautiful," he replied. "Why wouldn't I look at you? Of course, there are times when I wish you were a little less stubborn and a little more willing to follow directions—"

"Like, 'Shut the damn door'?" Kate grinned. "Very fierce, very duke-ish."

He shut the bedroom door and turned back to her. "I don't think 'duke-ish' is a word."

"It fits you."

He bent his head and kissed her lightly. "You should have kept the door closed," he said when he lifted his lips from hers.

She reached for him, standing on tiptoe to put her hands around his neck. "It's more fun talking to you in person."

"But I'm not going to talk anymore," he said, lifting her into his arms. He carried her over to the bed and set her gently on the mattress.

"Even better," Kate murmured, looking into his dark eyes. There was nothing to fear, except making a fool of herself. He would never have to know that a foolish American tourist had lost her heart to a very eligible duke. He would never realize she wanted to believe in fairy-tale endings.

She could hide how she felt, she promised herself. He bent down and kissed the pulse in the hollow of her neck, and she shivered at the sensation.

He stopped, lifting his head to look deep into her eyes. "Are you cold?"

"No. I'm not cold." She reached for him, smoothing her hands over his wide shoulders. He would never have to know she'd fallen in love.

9

WILL DRAGGED HIS LIPS lower, to the tempting cleavage above the towel, and unfolded the towel to reveal the woman underneath. She was beautiful, in scraps of lace and nothing else. Will unhooked her bra and slid it from her shoulders. He felt as if he was unwrapping a special package, a gift he had been waiting to open for a very long time.

"You are very beautiful," he said, hoping to convince her.

His lips found hers, seeking her warmth with his tongue. She responded to him with a longing of her own, and her hands wound around his neck to hold him against her. When he finally released her, it was only to remove his clothes and toss them onto the rug. Kate turned on her side and watched him, entranced by his hard male body. His shoulders were more powerful than she'd imagined, his legs muscular and long. He didn't seem to mind that she looked at him. He was comfortable with the way he looked, of course. He was used to being admired and treated like royalty.

Dark hair covered his chest and tapered to an intriguing path down his abdomen. His arousal was obvious, yet he seemed not to notice her surprise at the size of him. She wanted to reach out and touch him, wanted to feel that odd combination of steel and satin under her fingertips, but Kate stopped herself. Her experience was limited; he might not like it.

"You're beautiful, too," she said, then couldn't believe she'd spoken aloud. The dim light from the window shades gave the room a cozy, shadowed feeling, where everything seemed muted and unreal. She felt disoriented and yet she didn't want William to leave. She wanted him with her, wanted to feel his skin against hers. She wondered what he would feel like inside her, what it would be like to make love with him.

Kate started to bring the sheet over her shoulder, but he stopped her. One large hand reached out and grasped the sheet. "Don't cover yourself," he said, his voice gruff. "You needn't be shy with me."

"It's hard not to be," she admitted. "You keep looking at me."

He sighed. "Of course I do, Kate. I want to look at you and touch you and make love to you all at the same time. I've wanted you since the first time I saw you," he said, surprising himself by admitting the truth.

"You wanted the brooch."

"No," he said, approaching the bed. "The brooch would have been a favor to my grandmother. I wanted you." He traced a finger along her cheek to her lips and brushed them with tantalizing softness. "I didn't understand it myself."

"Neither do I."

"Do we have to understand it?" He slid into the bed beside her, brushing skin like warm satin.

Kate shook her head.

"I'm going to make love to you now." Will leaned over her, and his mouth touched hers with exquisite softness. Ever so slowly he deepened the kiss as Kate parted her lips to allow him entry. They kissed for long moments. His hands moved to her breasts and cupped their weight in his palms. His thumbs teased her nipples, sending pangs of desire through her. He kissed the corner of her mouth and her throat. His lips sought the column of her neck, the hollow near her shoulder. Kate felt herself melting, as if every inch of muscle and bone was dissolving under his touch.

She was still on her side, her breasts brushing his furred chest and her nipples sensitive and aching from the friction. He seemed to know what she needed, and he bent down and began to caress one breast, then another, with his lips. Finally, after long minutes when Kate thought she would melt into the mattress, he took one peaked bud into his mouth. The exquisite pressure was almost her undoing. Shafts of pleasure lunged downward as his lips tugged and teased. His free hand smoothed her hip and lowered her panties.

She moaned and moved closer to him, and felt his hard arousal touch her thigh. He lifted his head and pushed her gently onto her back, smoothing his hand over her abdomen as he kissed her mouth. His hand moved lower, and he dragged the lace past her ankles and tossed it aside. He urged her thighs apart and touched her where she was warm and wet. His tongue moved deep into her mouth as he slipped one finger inside her. Kate trembled with the pleasure he gave her as his hand moved over her and his palm cupped her flesh.

He was taking his time, she realized, but she wanted him inside her. She didn't want to wait any longer to know how he would feel sunk deep within her. He withdrew his finger and stroked her flesh, centering the spiraling heat in one throbbing place.

"Do you like my touching you?" he whispered. She looked into his eyes, eyes dark with passion.

"Yes," she managed to say, and gasped as he slid two fingers into her. She closed her eyes and let the sensations sweep over her as he moved his hand for long moments before gently withdrawing his fingers.

He nudged her legs wider apart and slipped a condom over his hard length before entering her. He took her slowly, to prolong her pleasure at his entrance. She gripped his hips and arched against him, and Will knew he was lost.

She was liquid and slick and panting, and Will forced himself to slow his thrusts. He wanted to pound into her, needed to bury himself over and over again in her tight, welcoming warmth. He stopped, buried fully within her. She stilled, and his mouth found hers. He moved his tongue deep into her mouth, stifling her soft whimpers. Her hands smoothed the sides of his face and tried to draw him closer, even though it was impossible.

Sweet Kate, he thought, the fine thread of control snapping as his arousal swelled even larger. He withdrew slightly, then moved his hips forward, gliding and withdrawing for long, breathtaking minutes until he felt Kate tighten around him. He lost all sense of time and space. He forgot who he was. All he knew was Kate, her sweet breath and her satin skin and the sleek, tight warmth that surrounded him. She pulled him closer, so when shudders shook her body he still had possession of her mouth and heard her passionate whimper as she climaxed. A few more thrusts and he joined her, burying himself into her over and over again as spasms shook him.

KATE FLOATED back to reality very slowly. He had moved from her, but his arms were around her and her face was buried in his chest. She felt sated and spent. She felt as if she'd just learned what lovemaking really was. She hadn't felt awkward or shy. She'd only known him for a week, but he was achingly familiar, as if she'd known him all her life. As if they'd been making love all their lives. She inhaled, trying to memorize his scent, and the hair on his chest tickled her nose.

"What are you doing?" His voice was sleepy.

"Trying not to sneeze." She wasn't going to tell him that she was trying to remember the way he smelled of lime and leather and English rain.

William lifted his head and looked down at her, his expression amused. "Sneezing's allowed, Katie."

"I thought you were asleep."

"No. Yes. Almost." He turned on his side to face her. "Do you want me to leave?"

"No." She nuzzled his chest, and he reached past her to pull the covers over her bare shoulders. "Sleep here."

Will hesitated. "All right. For a while."

"You don't have to," she said, lifting her chin to look up at him.

"I'll make love to you again," he warned. "I don't want to hurt you."

"You won't hurt me."

He ran a large hand along her waist and smoothed her hip. "You're so soft. And so small. And I want to make love to you all over again." He nuzzled her neck and tucked her firmly into his shoulder.

Kate closed her eyes and murmured an agreement as the warmth of his body wrapped around her and lulled her into sleep.

SHE DREAMED of butterfly kisses on her knees, of gentle fingertips moving across her thighs and higher, releasing heat and causing a heavy, familiar throbbing between her legs. She dreamed a gentle pressure spread her legs apart, and she heard a voice whisper, "Wake up."

She didn't want to. She didn't want the dream to end, didn't want to wake up alone and cold in the hotel bed. She wanted to pretend that William's warm breath fanned her thigh, that his lips sought to release the aching pressure building inside her, that his tongue slipped—but it wasn't a dream, she realized, slowly coming awake. She was naked and aroused, and William was touching her with his fingers and his lips and his tongue. She arched, whimpering with bliss and awe, but he splayed one hand across her abdomen to hold her still while he pleasured her. Kate yielded as the familiar throbbing echoed through her body. He held her against his mouth and brought her to exquisite release, and only then did he move above her.

William entered her swiftly, and she arched to meet him as he filled her with long, smooth strokes. He made love to her as if he couldn't get enough of her, as if he needed to prolong the time together as much as was humanly possible. He held himself hard against her and groaned as he climaxed. His lips found her throat, and he traced the rapid pulse until his own heartbeat eased and he knew he wasn't going to die from sheer pleasure.

"Not a dream," she murmured.

"No." He lifted his head so he could look into her eyes. They were a deep forest green now, and sleepy. "No. Just a man who couldn't wait any longer for you to waken."

"I'm glad," she said, closing her eyes. He lifted himself from her, and she turned on her side toward him but she didn't open her eyes. He fixed the covers and propped his head on his hand to study her. Her cheeks were flushed, her lips slightly swollen and pink. Her hair lay wavy and tangled against the white pillowcase. He should be embarrassed for taking her twice. He should be appalled that he'd made love to her while she slept, but he hadn't been able to resist tasting her.

And if he didn't get out of this bed, he'd be more than willing to do so again, he realized. She would awaken thinking the Duke of Thornecrest was a lust-crazed animal. He didn't know what had come over him, but a hot shower and a couple of hours of bookkeeping should help. He slid out of bed and picked up his clothes. Next to his boots, so close he was lucky he hadn't stepped on it, lay the brooch. William resisted the urge to kick it under the bed. Still pinned to the sweater, the brooch shone with an ominous glitter.

KATE AWOKE in the dark and realized she was alone. She moved her hand across the mattress and felt the cool sheets. He'd been gone awhile. She knew she should get up and take a shower and dress for dinner, although how she was supposed to sit across from the table from him after his mouth had... Well, Kate decided, she didn't regret the experience. He'd made her feel sexy and desirable and beautiful. He'd looked down at her as if he'd loved touching her, loved being inside her.

She just wished she was more experienced at country weekends and sex-filled afternoons. Was she supposed to stroll downstairs as if nothing had happened?

Well, Kate decided, she'd have to try. She didn't really have any other choice.

"KATE?" William knocked on the door when she was brushing her hair. Kate looked at her watch and realized it was seven-thirty already. She'd soaked in the tub for a long time, wondering how jilted and jobless Kate Stewart from Rhode Island had managed to be in an English mansion surrounded by luxury and having great sex with a duke. Kate put her brush on the makeup table and reluctantly went to the door.

"I'm ready," she called. Bracing herself, she opened the door. She pasted a casual smile on her face and lifted her gaze to his face. He swallowed hard, then smiled a small, tight smile that showed he was a bit ill at ease, too, and Kate realized everything was going to be all right.

Will lifted a bottle of wine. "Have a drink with me in the study."

"That would be nice." She stepped out of her room and turned left. He caught her arm.

"No, I meant my personal study," he said, turning right. "Follow me."

"Okay," she agreed, intrigued. She hadn't seen this part of the house before. He led her down the wide corridor, past several closed doors, until he reached the wide double doors at the end of the hall. He twisted the knob and pushed the door open to reveal a wide living room lined with tall windows, dark green drapes and cherry bookcases. A massive desk sat at an angle in the corner, a leather chair behind it. A fire burned in the fireplace in the center of the wall that faced them, and a small round table was set for dinner in front of it.

"I told Mrs. Goodfellow we'd eat here. I thought it would be less formal. Do you mind?"

"Of course not." She thought it was very romantic.

Will led her over to a forest green sofa, its faded velvet surface covered with needlepoint pillows. "Mrs. Goodfellow gives me a pillow every year for Christmas," he explained. "Toss them aside and make yourself comfortable." Wineglasses on a tray perched on the marble table, along with a selection of cheeses and crackers on a gold-edged plate. Mrs. Goodfellow had outdone herself.

"This is a nice surprise." She sank into the couch and tucked her legs underneath her. The room was warm, the fire crackling and snapping, and she was glad he'd chosen to show her his study. "This must be the room you really live in. It's like your own apartment within the house."

"Yes." He uncorked the wine and filled the two glasses with golden liquid. "I thought you might like it. And the salon downstairs is a little overwhelming for two people."

"You must have wonderful parties, though."

He handed her a glass and joined her on the couch. "No. Not really. I save my social life for London."

She gave him an odd look, as if she didn't believe him. He knew she hadn't been convinced when he'd told her she was the first woman he'd brought here alone. She probably thought he did this every weekend. "It's true," he insisted. "I don't bring women here."

"Never?"

"A house party or two during hunting season, perhaps." William wanted her to know she was special, but he was afraid to let her know she was special. "Up until now this was—is—a private place. I've had guests, of course, but I don't sleep with them here. I've kept those parts of my life separate, you see." He didn't stop to question why today was different, why Kate was the only woman he'd ever wanted at the Hall. He touched her glass with his. "Until now."

Kate took a sip of the wine. "You've gone to a lot of trouble for a diamond pin."

"I don't make love in order to buy jewelry." His gaze dropped to her sweater, a brown turtleneck that blended with her hair. "You're not wearing it tonight."

"I forgot."

"Good."

"But it's my good-luck charm. My aunt promised it would bring my heart's desire," she said, taking another sip of the wine.

"And has it?"

"I'm in England. That's a start."

"If your heart's desire is a great deal of money, then I would say you have more than a start."

She changed the subject. "Your grandmother told me to wear it all the time."

He frowned. "My grandmother has odd ideas."

"It's not odd to want to regain something that once belonged to you. I just don't think that it was stolen. So it's not really out of the family. Didn't she ask you to find some old books or diaries?"

He refilled their glasses and moved the cheese tray within reach. "She did. She's attempting to discover if one of my ancestors actually went to America with the brooch."

"Then she believes me, at least a little." Kate helped herself to a cracker and a piece of cheese. "I'd like to know that myself. Have you found anything?"

"No. Not yet." He smiled. "I suppose you'd like to help me locate them."

Kate forgot the food in her hand. She'd love to see more of the house, especially if she had a chance to find something as wonderful as old diaries. "Are they in the library, or do we get to go up in the attic?"

"The attic, I think. I've already searched the library."

She leaned forward, her eyes shining. "When?"

"Tomorrow."

"Why wait? We have time tonight," she argued. "It's still early."

He should have known that an English attic would fascinate her, although exploring dusty boxes of books wasn't exactly what he had in mind for tonight. But he couldn't refuse her something so simple when she looked so eager. "All right, if that's what you want."

"I do."

He leaned forward and kissed her. Her lips were pliant and sweet and tasted of chardonnay. "Are we pretending this afternoon didn't happen?"

"I don't think I could," she admitted with her usual frankness. She put her glass on the table and turned to face him. "Is that what you want, to pretend it didn't happen?"

"No." His voice was rough as desire surged through him again. He wanted to make love to her on the couch right now, wanted to feel her tight around him and hear her little gasps of pleasure. "No," he repeated, clearing his throat. "I couldn't pretend and I couldn't forget." He touched her cheek. "I don't want to."

"Neither do I."

He kissed her again, telling himself that he could stop whenever he wanted. After all, he still had some control left. Not much, but enough to keep his hands off her before dinner. "Don't leave tomorrow," he whispered against her mouth. "Stay one more day, and I'll take you back to town Monday or Tuesday or whenever you like."

She twined her arms around his neck. "I have a flight home on Tuesday."

"Monday, then." She was leaving already? The thought bothered him. He hadn't stopped to consider that he would not see her again and he would want to.

"All right. That will give us time to find the books."

The heaviness in his chest eased. "I don't give a damn about the books." He kissed the little spot beneath her ear and felt her shiver, then attempted to regain control of himself before he made an idiot of himself. "I'd better ring for dinner before we start taking our clothes off."

"I think you're right." Kate released him and gave him an embarrassed smile. "I'm afraid I have that reaction when you kiss me."

Her honesty overwhelmed him. That's what he liked best about her, William decided. Or one of the things he liked best. "I'll be more careful in public places," he teased. He would have to be careful in every way, he decided, crossing the room to the call panel. He was in danger, serious danger, of falling in love with her.

And that was the last thing he intended to do. He was a bachelor, a happy bachelor. Or, he amended, a *contented* bachelor. Marriage might start out with soul-shattering sex and sweet words and promises of love, but there would be no happily-ever-after if you were the Duke of Thornecrest.

"HAVING FUN?" he drawled.

Kate took her head out of a large trunk and sneezed.

"Excuse me." He handed her a handkerchief, and she sneezed again.

"We've found no boxes of books," he informed her. "Isn't it time to give up?"

"No." She'd never had so much fun in her life. She'd left the search for books to William after discovering the trunks in a corner of the enormous attic. They were stuffed with antique clothing of all colors and sizes. Pastel dresses of silk and muslin, with lace trims and velvet edging and pearl beads, were packed carefully in layers. Kate held a pink gown in front of her and pictured waltzing around a ballroom. "Your ancestors were very well dressed. Somebody went to a lot of trouble to preserve these clothes."

"A Landry throws nothing out. I believe that's why we can barely move up here."

She put the pink gown aside and unfolded an ivory one. A wide band of lace dipped low across the bodice, and the long, puffed sleeves were trimmed to match. "I think duchesses were quite thin."

"Take it downstairs and try it on," he said. "If you like, I'll have Harry put the trunk in your room. Better yet," he added, eying the low neckline of the dress, "I'll have the trunks put in my room."

"Every girl loves to play dress-up, you know."

"I'm beginning to realize that." He shoved his hands in his pockets while she dove into the trunk, anxious to see if there were shoes to match.

"You should have daughters," she said. "They'd love it up here."

"We breed only boys. That and bad husbands."

"That's why these clothes are still up here." She lifted out stacks of underwear, or what she guessed was underwear. She'd have to figure out what went where later. "Little girls would have found them ages ago."

"I suppose. Have you reached the bottom yet?"

"Almost." Her fingers touched something hard, but she was afraid she'd topple into the trunk if she tried to get her hands around it. "Come here, Will, and help me. There's a box or something."

"After this we're leaving," he said, coming over to stand next to her. "I'll tell Pitty I couldn't find a thing."

"Right down here, on the side. Can you feel anything?"

"Got it." He hauled up a packet of leather-bound books tied with velvet cord. "Must have belonged to one of the duchesses."

Kate reached for the books. "Let's see."

"Downstairs," he said, looking down at her with a hungry expression. "You can read later. After you put on that white dress and after I remove it."

Kate's heart flipped over in her chest. "You are such a romantic man."

William looked appalled. "You don't know me very well."

"Maybe not," she said, wishing she could say what was in her heart. She wished she could tell him that she'd fallen in love with him. She wished she could tell him what this week had meant to her. Instead, Kate turned away and scooped up the dress and a pile of undergarments and hugged them to her chest. "Come on, then," she said, keeping her voice light. "Let's hope the duchess was a size 9."

"WAIT," she said. He heard the rustle of silk. "Okay, now open your eyes. You can't see all of me until after you button me up."

Will opened his eyes and touched the creamy fabric that hugged her skin. He held his breath and hooked the tiny buttons along Kate's spine. She'd piled her hair on top of her head, and when he remembered to breathe, he planted a tiny kiss on the nape of her neck and held her waist between his hands. "Will you turn around now?" he asked.

"It fits," she said, and swirled to face him. "I can't believe it fits."

"It's quite beautiful," he agreed. He didn't point out that the duchess who had worn the dress must have been at least six inches taller and not as well endowed as Kate. Creamy skin swelled above the lace in a dress meant to tantalize. "The dress is quite old, early to mid-1800s, I'd guess. Those are the dates written inside the books."

"What kind of books are they?" He watched, fascinated, as Kate attempted to tug her bodice higher, but the fabric didn't budge.

His hands tightened at her waist. "The packet contained four novels and two diaries. Pitty will be beside herself with joy. I'm going to kiss you now."

He bent closer, and she tilted her head back. "Be careful."

He stopped. "Why?"

"The dress," she murmured a scant inch from his lips. "It's very old."

"I'm not concerned with the dress." He pulled her closer and heard the oddly erotic rustle of silk as he held her against him and took her mouth. She was soft and pliant, and William thought he could kiss her for hours and never tire of touching her. He moved lower, touching his lips to the tops of her breasts. Lace tickled his chin, and he felt Kate's trembling hands tangle in his hair. He kept hold of her waist and backed her against the paneled wall. Then he braced both arms on the wall and looked down. Her lips glistened, and she looked up at him with her heart in her eyes.

Damn. He should have known a woman like Kate would fall in love. He should have realized that she wouldn't have given herself to him so freely unless her heart had been involved. He should be upset, but all he could think was to make love to her again, as soon as possible. "Lift your skirts," he said.

"Why, sir!" Her eyes twinkled. "Whatever do you have in mind?"

"Lift your skirts and I'll show you," he whispered, kissing the corner of her mouth. "You like that dress so much you may as well keep it on."

"The undergarments are, um, open down there." She grabbed hold of the fabric at her hips and lifted it. "Do you think this is the reason?"

"I don't care." He unzipped his fly and readied himself, then helped Kate with her petticoats. He found the opening in the silk underclothes and paused to make her ready for him before taking her. "Open your legs," he commanded softly. He felt her legs tremble. "And put your arms around my neck."

She did, and he slid inside her, then cupped her buttocks in his palms and pulled her tight against him. Kate moaned.

Will stopped. "Am I hurting you?"

"No," she said. "You feel so good—"

He stopped her words with another thrust and made love to her with slow strokes until she tightened around him and cried out. As he moved still deeper, sensation overwhelmed him, making him forget everything but Kate around him, Kate's breath on his throat and her pliant body under his hands. He felt himself shatter inside her, and knew he wanted only this, only Kate, forever.

"WHO'S ALICIA?"

"I haven't the foggiest idea," he drawled, looking at her. "Now that you're naked and in my bed, I think I've lost the capacity to think."

Kate blushed and pulled the sheets up higher. She'd taken most of the pillows and propped them behind her so she could study the diaries. "Her name is written in the inside covers of the diaries. I don't think she was a duchess. She talks about making her 'come out' and meeting suitable young men. Her father is mentioned often, and her governess, too." Kate looked down at William. He had one pillow tucked behind his head and he turned to face her. There was a gleam in his eye she was beginning to recognize. "I've only looked at a few pages, but doesn't she sound like a young woman to you?"

"Yes. A debutante, if she's talking about her 'come out.'"

"How can we find out who she was?"

He sighed. "We can read the diaries. Tomorrow."

"I meant besides that." She glanced over at the chair beside the bed where the gown lay in a tangle of silk and lace. "Don't you have family records?"

"Oh, most definitely. Kilos of them." His hand slid under the white sheet and caressed her thigh. "Turn off the lamp."

"I think I like these country weekends," Kate sighed, setting the book on the table. She turned off the bedside light and waited for a few seconds for her eyes to adjust to the darkness.

"Come here."

"This was much more fun than getting married."

His hand stopped its tantalizing journey up her thigh. "What are you talking about?"

"I was supposed to get married today, remember?" Kate rearranged the pillows and lay down on her side to face Will.

"He was a fool, but considering the circumstances, I'm glad you're in England instead."

She kissed his chest. "You're absolutely right. I'm quite content with the way things have turned out today. After all, I wore an ivory dress and have been made love to three times."

"Four," William murmured, reaching for her in the darkness.

10

"THE YOUNG LADY is still sleeping?"

"I assume so." Kate was asleep, all right. Snuggled in the middle of his bed with the covers pulled up to her chin and her dark hair spread over the pillows, she'd looked content, as if she were sleeping in her own bed. Now *that* was a frightening thought. And a strangely appealing one.

Will had no desire for Mrs. Goodfellow to discover where his house guest had spent the night. She was as enthusiastic a matchmaker as his grandmother. He selected a mug from the cupboard and poured himself a cup of coffee. His housekeeper stood at the stove frying strips of bacon. The smell made his mouth water, and his empty stomach growled.

"Should I bring up a tray for her when breakfast is ready?"

"No," he said quickly, too quickly. Mrs. Goodfellow's eyebrows rose as she stared at him. "I'm sure Kate would like to sleep late."

"I see." She turned her attention back to her cooking and poked the bacon with a spatula. "Your grandmother called this morning. I told her you weren't awake, and she seemed quite put out."

"She'll survive." Will took his coffee to the kitchen table. He sat down, and Harry shoved part of the Sunday newspaper over to him.

"She told me three times to tell you to ring her as soon as you woke. She wanted to know if you'd found any other journals, she said. And she *also* wanted to know if Miss Stewart was still here. How many eggs do you want?"

"Three. No, four. Did you tell her?"

"Yes," Mrs. Goodfellow answered. "I said she was here and nothing more. It's none of my business, either, I told her."

Harry eyed William over the edge of his newspaper. "Hungry this morning, are you?"

William frowned and didn't answer.

"It's pouring today. You're lucky you did your tourin' yesterday," the older man continued. "The little miss wouldn't like getting wet."

"She probably wouldn't mind," Will said. "A little rain wouldn't bother Katie."

"Mebbee you're right." Harry nodded. "She's the first one you've brought home, and I'm mighty glad to see she doesn't walk around with her nose up in the air."

Mrs. Goodfellow placed a plate piled high with fried eggs and bacon in front of Will, then returned with silverware and napkins for both men. "She's a lovely young lady. You could do worse."

"I don't intend to 'do' at all," Will declared. "I'm taking her back to London tomorrow, and then she returns to the States."

Beth handed her husband a plate identical to Will's. "Why don't you go with her, then? Have a little vacation and then bring her back here? It's time there were children—"

"Children? I'm not cut out for fatherhood," Will drawled, though suddenly the vision of little girls playing dress-up in the attic pleased him. He shook his head as if to clear it. Landry men had sons. One and only one son. There would be no giggling daughters and no teasing older brothers. There would be no children because there would be no marriage. "Or wedded bliss, either," he added. "Despite what you or Pitty wish to believe, I am not interested in marriage, no matter how many women visit the Hall."

Mrs. Goodfellow brought her coffee to the table and sat down. "Nonsense! She's the first one you've brought home all by herself. And you'd make a lovely husband, you would, even if you are impatient and bossy."

"I have lots of patience," he argued, thinking of the days spent touring London with Kate. "More than you know."

The housekeeper sniffed. "Oh, there's lots I know," she said, unimpressed. "I know you're nothing like your father or your grandfather. Silly men, with a taste for women who didn't suit them at all. Not like you. Now, finish your eggs so you can take Kate's breakfast to her. I made some apricot scones I think she'll like."

William looked around hungrily. "Where are they?"

"You can have one each," she told the men. "The rest are for the young lady."

William started to protest, but Harry caught his eye and winked. "You may as well give up, lad. If she says the scones are for Miss Katie, then that's where they'll go."

"Miss Katie isn't the duke around here," he grumbled, picking up the last piece of bacon on his plate.

"And you're not smart enough to make her a duchess, either," Mrs. Goodfellow retorted. "I wash my hands of you, I really do."

Kate a duchess? She'd looked like a queen in that ivory dress. William pushed his plate aside and finished his coffee in one swallow. "I'm going for a walk," he said. "The fresh air might clear my head."

"You do that," Mrs. Goodfellow said. "But I don't expect that the cure for what ails you lies in the east pasture."

Will ignored her and left the kitchen, grabbed his oldest coat and hat from the hall and slipped out the back door. The dogs wagged their tails and jumped around him, begging for attention, so Will petted them before he set out for a long, wet walk. He would let Kate sleep, he decided. Alone. And he would spend some time away from her and try like hell not to hurry back to the house to wake her and watch her smile.

KATE KEPT her eyes closed. She lay snuggled under the warm blankets, afraid that if she opened her eyes she might discover that yesterday had been a dream. Making love with Will and falling asleep in his arms were definitely the stuff of an overactive imagination, or the result of eating chocolate-chip ice cream before bed. If she opened her eyes, Kate reasoned, she would see the bathroom door of her plain St. Giles hotel room.

She didn't want to see the bathroom door of her hotel room. She wanted to see an ivory gown sprawled across a spindly-legged chair and the rich velvet drapes hiding the morning sun, but most of all she wanted to open her eyes and look into William Landry's familiar and handsome face.

"Kate? Are you awake?"

An intriguing male voice, she thought, and one she recognized. Kate risked opening her eyes slowly, hoping she was really in the master bedroom at Thorne

Hall. Will came closer to the bed. He held a large silver tray, and Kate smelled coffee. "Hi," she whispered. "I'm awake. I think."

"Maybe this will help." He set the tray on a delicate round-topped table and poured coffee into a porcelain cup. Kate struggled to sit up, keeping the blankets covering her naked body, and Will waited for her to prop two pillows behind her before handing her the cup of coffee.

"Thanks," she said. "Is it very late?"

"After eleven."

Kate grimaced and took a sip of the coffee. "It isn't like me to sleep so late." She glanced at his amused expression. "*None* of this is like me, but I guess you wouldn't believe that."

He walked over to the window, shoved his hands in his pockets and stared out the window. "You don't have any idea what I believe, so drink your coffee and get dressed. The rain has stopped for now, but it doesn't look as if it's going to stay clear for long. We could take a walk through the gardens or drive over to Hallaton. It's the sort of picturesque English village you would enjoy, I think."

It wasn't fair that he looked so darn handsome in the morning. He wore dark slacks and a soft blue cotton shirt and he looked as if he'd slept for twelve hours. "Can we do both?"

"Of course. The day is yours." He turned to face her, but he didn't come closer. She'd foolishly hoped he'd kiss her good-morning, so she hid her disappointment by drinking the coffee as quickly as possible and burned the inside of her mouth.

"Mrs. Goodfellow baked scones for you," Will said,

turning away from the window. "There are some here on the tray, and more in the kitchen."

"They look delicious! Give me twenty minutes to finish this coffee and get dressed," she said.

"There's no rush." He looked nervous, as if he regretted last night and wanted her out of his bed and his room as quickly as possible.

Kate tucked the sheet higher above her breasts. "May I borrow a robe?"

"Certainly." Will perched on the side of the bed and looked down at her. "I'll fetch you one of mine."

"Thanks." She smiled, and to her relief he smiled back at her.

"I've been wondering about your plans," he began, reaching out to tuck a strand of her hair behind her ear. "Must you leave tomorrow, Kate?"

"I really think I'd better get back to London."

"That's not what I meant, Kate. Do you have to leave England right away?"

Kate set her empty cup on the nightstand before answering. "Yep. I have to find a new job."

"You could live a long time from the sale of the brooch." He stood up, crossed the room and disappeared through a door.

"I can't do that. If there was some kind of family emergency, I would sell it in a minute, but I can't just get rid of an heirloom because I don't want to start job hunting." She wished he understood. "It wouldn't be right. Besides, I like the brooch. Somehow I feel that it's brought me luck." There was no "somehow" about it. She'd met William because of the brooch. She'd experienced a trip to England that she would never have believed possible.

"You could stay in England for a while longer," he

suggested, as he came across the room with a navy silk robe slung across his arm. "There is so much you haven't seen."

"I'll save my money and come back," she said, keeping her voice light.

"Can you postpone leaving for a few more days?" He sat down on the bed and handed her the robe.

"I can't change the tickets without a big penalty."

"I'd be happy to take care of that," he offered. "If you'll allow me."

"I can't. That wouldn't be right, either."

He sighed. "I thought that would be your answer, but I had to try. Are you certain you won't stay? Just for a few more days, of course. We could drive north, to Scotland. There are plenty of gift shops there, too. In castles, no less."

He was teasing her again, Kate realized. He'd lost his solemn expression and was once again the lighthearted man from yesterday. She would have given every souvenir in her hotel room to stay, to journey on to Scotland, to stay here at the Hall, to wake in the morning and talk with William about the plans for the day.

"It's time I got on with my life," she said, trying to convince herself. "I'll start by sneaking back to my room."

"You don't have to sneak at all. There's no one else around."

"I keep thinking your grandmother will appear and scare us both to death."

"She called this morning, actually." He reached over to the table and refilled her coffee cup. "She wants to know if we've found anything."

"We don't know if we did or not." Kate couldn't believe she'd forgotten about the books. "That's what we should do today."

William grimaced. "Later," he declared. "Much later." He looked down at her and sighed. "Have I kissed you good-morning yet?"

"No." Her heart lightened. "I was wondering if you'd forgotten."

"No." He set her cup back on the silver tray and leaned closer. "That's all I've thought about since I woke up." His lips brushed hers in a sweet reminder of last night's passion before he slowly lifted his mouth from hers. "There," he whispered. "I feel better."

"Me, too." She reached for his shoulders, and the sheet dropped. William's gaze lowered to her breasts. "Why don't you come back to bed?"

He kissed her neck. "That is an excellent idea. I think I will."

Kate unbuttoned his shirt and smoothed her palms across his bare chest.

He stood to remove his pants, then climbed into bed beside her. "Come here," he said, pulling her close.

She was beginning to be familiar with his body, to know what touches made him shiver and what kind of caresses made him moan. He pulled her on top of him and wound his arms around her back while he kissed her, but she wriggled from his arms and dragged her lips across his chest and lower, to his abdomen and the rigid flesh below. She took him in her hand and into her mouth while he gasped with pleasure and surprise. After long moments he pulled her above him and, tumbling her onto her back, took her with swift strokes.

Kate wanted it hard and fast. She wanted to remember everything about making love to him: his touch on her breasts, the feel of him filling her, the taste of him on her lips.

Kate lay in bed long after Will rose and retrieved his clothes.

"Are you certain you have to leave tomorrow?" He grinned at her and poured another cup of coffee.

"Yes. I'm sure." Kate avoided his eyes and took the coffee. She didn't want him to see the truth. She didn't want him to realize that a silly tourist had fallen in love with a charming duke and dreamed of happily-ever-after in a cheese factory.

IF ANYONE HAD TOLD HIM that he would spend a perfect weekend with a woman he barely knew, William knew he would have smiled. If anyone had warned him that he would fall in love with her and want to keep her with him always, he would have been quite overcome with mirth. And if anyone had told him that he would feel sharp pains in the vicinity of his heart as he drove this particular woman through the gates of Thorne Hall and out of his life, he would have wiped the tears of laughter from his eyes and choked back a rude reply of disbelief.

William's hands tightened on the steering wheel as he guided the car down the winding driveway. He didn't feel at all like laughing. He didn't want Kate to leave and he didn't know how to persuade her to stay. He dared a glance toward her, but her face was turned to the side window.

"We should be in London by three o'clock," he said, trying to erase the memory of making love to Kate this morning. They'd stayed in bed long after they should have risen. They'd made love one more time in the murky morning light while a light rain drizzled

against the windows. There hadn't seemed to be any
reason to hurry out of bed.

Kate turned away from the window and looked at
William. "That's fine. What about Pitty?"

"I'll tell her you won't sell the brooch," he said. He
wished he'd never laid eyes on the thing. Even now it
sparkled on the lapel of Kate's coat, reminding him of
how he'd met her. Was Pitty right? Was the legend of
the Thorne Diamond true after all? He'd fallen in love
with the woman wearing it. He'd acted like a lovesick
fool for days. What on earth was the matter with him?
An early midlife crisis or a simple case of infatuation?

He didn't know. And wasn't about to find out.

"I can tell her myself," Kate offered, "if you don't
mind stopping at your house first. Besides, I think I
owe her that much."

"All right, if you like." He drove in silence for a few
minutes longer, negotiated the turn onto the main road
and headed toward the highway. His heart felt heavier
by the minute. "Pitty won't accept your decision easily,
you know. She wants the brooch back in the family."

"I know. I wish we could have found something in
the diaries that would prove my ancestors didn't steal
it."

"We didn't exactly have time to read diaries."
They'd spent their time in other, more interesting
ways. They'd made love, taken walks yesterday and
had visited with Paula and Sam when they'd dropped
in to say hello. Sam had winked at him, and Paula had
taken him aside and whispered how pleased she was
that he had finally found someone special. He'd agreed
with her; he hadn't told her of Kate's plans to leave.

Then they'd eaten an enormous dinner of pheasant
and wild rice, walked in the gardens in the rain and, af-

:er warming each other in his wide bed, made love again.

William took a deep breath and attempted to keep his thoughts focused on the conversation. "Besides, Pitty will spend weeks poring over every word. You've challenged her, you see. She must prove there was no Landry in America after all."

"Will you let me know what she finds?"

"Yes."

"No matter what?"

"Of course," he promised. "I'll tell her about the clothes, too. They should probably be in a museum." He would package the ivory one and send it to Kate as a souvenir. She'd looked beautiful in the gown. She'd looked beautiful without the gown.

"Save one or two for some little girls to discover someday." She smiled a bit ruefully. "That's what attics are for."

"I'll remember that," he promised. "Unless you'd prefer to stay in England and remind me?" He pictured little auburn-haired girls parading around the Hall in lace flounces and satin slippers, and dark-haired boys running with the dogs, and laughter and chaos echoing through the once-quiet rooms of a home that once was too big for one lonely man. He reached for her hand and held it within his own. "There is no reason why you can't stay...a while longer."

"So Pitty can convince me to sell my pin?"

"So I can convince you to stay in England."

She didn't answer immediately. Finally she spoke into the silence. "For how long, William?"

He shrugged. There was no way he could answer that question. He could promise nothing, after all. This weekend, this past week had been wonderful, but intimate relationships had a way of disintegrating. It was just a matter of time. "Until you want to return home, I suppose. Nine days in England is not a long time. You've lots more to see."

"As much as I'd like to stay, I think it's time I go back to the real world," she said. "This has been wonderful, of course. Thorne House and Thorne Hall and Stilton cheese and priceless jewels and a duchess serving tea have all been very exciting. Especially when I didn't expect to experience any of it. But it's time for a dose of reality."

"That sounds quite ominous."

She smiled. "I didn't mean it to be."

"I'm not certain I can let you go," he said, staring at the road. Kate looked at him. He could feel her gaze on his face. "It doesn't seem at all right," he muttered, mostly to himself.

Kate didn't reply.

William took his hand from Kate's and turned the car onto the highway and headed south, to London. She was the kind of woman who wanted promises of love and lots of children. She'd told him she'd dreamed of making apple pies and pot roast. Kate would settle for nothing less, he knew. And she was right to do so.

He was the wrong man for her.

SOMETHING INTERESTING had happened in Leicestershire. Pitty could tell by the proprietary way William removed Katherine's coat and handed it to Mary. His hands had lingered on the American's shoulders in a most loving way. It wasn't her imagination, either, Pitty decided. She nodded when Mary asked if she wanted tea and settled herself in the wing chair. She wondered if the young people would sit on the sofa together.

They did, to her great delight, although they were quite discreet about sitting apart. Mrs. Goodfellow had revealed nothing, but Pitty could read between the lines. You didn't reach the age of eighty-nine without learning a few tricks. She smoothed her chartreuse skirt as if she had all the time in the world. "Did you enjoy the country, Katherine?"

"Very much."

"Kate had a touch of the flu," William interjected. "But she's feeling much better now."

"Good." She turned back to Kate. "And the painting? Did you see the brooch?"

"Yes, but—"

Pitty held up her hand to silence the girl. She wasn't in the mood for unhappy news right now. She'd rather wait for a bit, she thought. At least until she'd watched the lovesick expression on her grandson's face a little longer. "Tell me what you found," she ordered, noting the packet of books William had dropped on the table.

"Diaries," he said. "We haven't figured out whose diaries, precisely, but from what we've read we assume it is a young girl about to make her debut into society in 1812."

He'd said "we" three times. How encouraging. The brooch had worked its magic after all. Pitty resisted the urge to clap her hands and order champagne. "And there were no names?"

"She used initials to indicate the people in her life. I didn't read every page, of course."

"Neither did I," Katherine admitted. "We found several trunks in the attic. One of them was filled with beautiful gowns, and the diaries were at the bottom."

"Clothing, too? How very fascinating!"

William leaned forward. "You've never gone through the attic, Pitty?"

She shook her head. "I only lived in Leicestershire for a few years. Long enough to give birth to your father and realize what an idiot your grandfather was. I moved to London after your father entered school. And after your parents died, I hadn't the time or energy to begin rummaging through the family attic."

"You should see the gowns," Katherine said. "They're beautiful."

"I made arrangements with Mrs. Goodfellow to hang them and air them out. We can decide what to do with them after you've had a look," William explained.

"Good." Mary brought the tea tray into the living room and set it on the table. "We'll have some tea and discuss what to do about the brooch," she declared. "Thank you, Mary."

"There really isn't anything to discuss, Pitty. Kate isn't going to sell it."

Pitty ignored him and looked at the young woman instead. "Are you quite sure, my dear? The Thorne Diamond has been missing for a very long time, and I would be willing to pay a great deal to have it back."

Kate's voice was soft. "I don't want to sell it."

"If you ever change your mind, you have only to contact either William or me, of course."

"I will."

Pitty smiled. "Let's have our tea now, shall we? William, will you pour or shall I?"

"I THINK SHE TOOK IT quite well, don't you?" Kate whispered after Pitty left the living room.

William frowned, wondering what the old girl was

up to now. She'd excused herself after she'd finished her tea, said her goodbyes to Kate and had taken the books with her when she'd left the room. "Perhaps," he said. "I didn't think she'd give up so easily."

"Easily?" Kate chuckled. "She's been trying for more than a week to buy the pin. Maybe she finally accepted the fact that she can't have it."

"You don't know her. She's the most stubborn and persistent person I've ever known."

"I'm sorry, Will. I hope this doesn't make things difficult for you."

He looked at her, obviously surprised. "I never wanted the damn thing, Kate."

"You didn't?"

"Well," he amended, "only at first. To placate Pitty so I could return to the Hall. She had her heart set on it, and I hate to refuse her, you know. She's all I have." He reached for Kate, and she went willingly into his arms. "Stay, Katie. Stay with me."

Kate waited for him to say the words, to say something about love and forever, but they never came. "We've been over this before."

He took a deep breath. "Cancel your flight home and live with me at the Hall. We'll travel." He kissed her. "We'll walk the dogs and make love and explore the attic. You haven't seen Paris or Switzerland, either, and Florence is perfect in the spring."

"You make it hard to say no."

"Then don't. Say yes and we'll pick up the rest of your things at the hotel and return to Leicestershire in the morning."

"You're asking me to live with you," she stated. She was definitely in love with him, with a power and depth she'd never experienced before, but how did she fit into his life? "Why?"

The question stymied him. He frowned. "Why?" he echoed.

"Why do you want to live together? Great sex? Companionship? You want someone to eat scones with in bed?"

"Yes. I don't know," he said quietly. "I only know I don't want you to leave."

"I could only stay *if* I was very much in love with you, and maybe not even then."

"We've only had a week."

He'd smoothly ignored the "I" word, she noted. Kate smiled, but it wasn't easy. "It was one hell of a week."

Will touched her face with gentle fingers. "Don't say no yet, Katie. Give me a chance to change your mind. I'll take you to the airport tomorrow. When does your plane leave?"

"Maybe that's not such a great idea." She'd cry all over his fancy car and embarrass herself.

He ignored her comment. "When does your plane leave?"

"Three-ten. I should be there around one-thirty, though."

"I'll pick you up at twelve forty-five. We'll have lunch together at the airport after you check in." He smiled. "*If* you check in."

She would not fall into his arms, she told herself. She would not blubber about how much she loved him and how much she wanted to stay in England. She would not tell him she wanted marriage and his babies and a fiftieth wedding anniversary party with their children and grandchildren. She took a deep breath and hoped she wouldn't make a fool of herself. "And what if I stayed, Will? What if I fell in love with you? What then?"

"I don't know, Katie. I've never been in love before and I'm not sure I want to be."

"At least you're honest."

He grimaced. "Not always, but I'm trying to improve." He stood up and took her hand to lift her to her feet. "Come on. I'll take you back to the hotel."

"Thank you." She couldn't believe her vacation would end tomorrow. Tomorrow night she would be on a bus heading to Rhode Island, and Anne would meet her at the bus station and take her home. But home to what?

"I'll ring you later," he promised, sliding the coat onto her shoulders. "I'm not going to give up."

"Falling in love isn't so terrible, you know." Kate turned in his arms and lifted her face for his kiss. Mary scurried out of the room and left them alone.

His lips brushed hers. "It's the very worst thing that could happen," he whispered.

"WHAT IN BLOODY HELL have you done?"

"Don't swear at me, Willie." Pitty patted his cheek as she passed by him and plopped onto the sofa. "I did it for your own good."

William made an effort to control his temper. A Ming vase hitting the wall would make a most satisfying sound. He took a deep breath and willed himself to stay calm. "How could stealing the Thorne Diamond be for my own good? Except, of course, if you were caught and locked up. *That* might be in my own best interest."

"Don't be sarcastic. Have you asked the American to marry you?"

"Of course not. Where is it?"

"That's what I thought." She sighed and patted the couch cushion beside her until he reluctantly sat down. "Have you told her you love her?"

"Where is it, Pitty?" His grandmother eyed him silently, waiting. Was it that simple, he wondered? Was falling in love as easy as admitting he didn't want to live another day if Kate wasn't part of his life? "No," he admitted. "I haven't."

"Idiot," she murmured, and patted his face affectionately. "You still don't believe in the diamond's power, do you?"

"Tell me where it is and I'll return it to Kate with your apologies. I can tell her it fell off her coat and we found it in the closet."

"Or maybe you believe after all," she mused. "You're in love with her, of course. Any fool can see that. Are you going to ignore your chance for happiness?"

"I will call the police. I will tell them you have become a kleptomaniac in your senior years and I will have you shipped to a sanatorium in Wales. You can spend the rest of your days looking at the sea and counting gulls."

"I would have preferred an Englishwoman, naturally. So I've decided to give this one more chance. The brooch has gone to Jessica's flat. With a note from me requesting she wear it to the theater tonight, as part of an experiment. You'll accompany her, of course."

"Why would I do that?"

"I think you'd like to know if you're in love with

Katherine because she's, well, *Katherine*, or if the brooch is responsible."

"The damn brooch has nothing to do with loving Kate," he snapped.

"Then prove it," she demanded.

"You could toss the cursed thing in the Thames for all I care, but it belongs to Kate and she will be heart-broken when she discovers it's missing." He rose from the couch. "I'm going to Jessica's to get it back."

"She's not there. She's meeting you at the Palace." Pitty looked at her watch, then back up to Willie. "You have fifteen minutes, but I suppose you are fine in those slacks."

"You planned this right down to the minute, didn't you?"

Pitty shrugged but she couldn't hide her satisfied smile. "You're making a grave mistake by letting Katherine slip out of your life, but perhaps she wasn't meant to be a duchess after all. Try the pin on Jessica and see what happens."

"My grandmother's insane," he muttered under his breath as he left the room. "Absolutely insane." Now he had to put on a clean shirt and head to the West End. He would meet Jessica, find some excuse for taking the brooch and hurry to the St. Giles to return it before Kate realized it was missing. Damn Pitty and her bloody legends.

11

ANNE CALLED at seven-thirty. "I keep hearing about bomb threats at Heathrow," she said. "Is it safe for you to leave?"

"That happened a few days ago. It's been quiet since then," Kate assured her.

"Call me if you get delayed. Have you had a good time?"

How should she answer? Would the phrase "good time" describe falling in love with a duke? Kate chose her words carefully. "Yes," she answered slowly, "I had a good time." Then Kate explained she'd met a wonderful, handsome, kind Englishman who had showed her around London.

"Bring him back with you," Anne demanded. Her voice was loud and clear through the telephone receiver. "I want to meet him. So will the others."

"I'll ask him," Kate promised. "I don't know what to do, Annie. I've fallen in love with him."

"It's not a rebound thing from Jeff?"

"No. I thought it could be at first, and then I realized it wasn't the same feeling at all." She didn't add that he was a duke. Annie would never believe her. "He's a very special person. Very kind."

"I still can't believe you met someone."

"Well, I did." She also left out the part about spending the weekend at his house in the country. Her older sister would have a fit. "I think Aunt Belle's pin brought my heart's desire after all."

Anne chuckled. "You have quite an imagination, Katie."

"Not always." She decided to save the news about the brooch's worth. She wanted to see her sister's face when she told her that the oversize pin was worth a fortune.

"Are you seeing him tonight?"

"He's going to call. He's taking me to the airport tomorrow. He says it's his last chance to talk me out of leaving."

Anne sighed. "That's so romantic." Then her voice sharpened. "Be careful, Katie. You've only known him a week."

"I knew Jeff for five years, and look what happened."

"You have a point," Anne conceded. "But you can't be too careful these days."

"Don't worry," Kate assured her. "He is the nicest, kindest, most honest man I've ever known."

WILLIAM DIDN'T PAY attention to the play. He endured the first act and attempted to make his excuses during intermission, but Jessica met some friends. He bought a drink while Jessica disappeared into the ladies' room with Lady Taylor and Penny Southington for most of the intermission. He had no choice but to return to his seat and wait for her. She slipped in beside him as the theater grew dark, and then it was too late to leave. He couldn't very well unpin the brooch from above her right breast and run out of the theater in the middle of *Les Misérables*.

The brooch twinkled at him, as if mocking his predicament, but it didn't have the same glow as when Kate wore it. Maybe her coloring had complemented the stone better. He was a fool. He knew it. He could have been with Kate; instead, he was sitting in a darkened theater peering at his watch and wondering how many songs were left before the French Revolution ended. It had to be the longest musical in London.

At least he'd proved one thing: the ugly brooch had nothing to do with loving Kate. He shifted restlessly in the narrow seat and glanced at Jessica's chest to make sure the brooch was still there. He would return it, even though now it was so late he would have to wait until morning. Kate would be frantic if she discovered it was missing. Hopefully she hadn't noticed, and he could return it to her with no harm done, except the embarrassment of explaining Pitty's role in its disappearance. Then all he had to do was convince her to remain in London, with him—forever.

But would Kate stay? Not without a promise. Not without a few encouraging words of love. Well, maybe he could manage that. He loved being with her, loved making love to her, loved the way she laughed after she teased him. He loved her perfume and her hair and her eyes and her very luscious body. He wanted her to live with him, wanted to wake up with her in the morning and climb in bed beside her at night. Did all that add up to being in love? Was it enough to last a lifetime?

KATE FELL ASLEEP with the light on and the television repeating the evening's news. She'd packed and repacked, trying to find room for the souvenirs she'd bought. She even folded the paper bags from the gift shops and tucked them inside the suitcases, too. She couldn't bear to leave anything behind. The weekend caught up with her eventually, and she fell exhausted onto the bed and woke up at seven o'clock the next morning.

Would he ask her to stay again? She wanted to say yes, but what would happen after that? He wanted an affair; she wanted a marriage. She was in love with him and couldn't picture loving anyone else. The past nine days had been the most wonderful days in her life. Leaving England would be the most difficult thing she'd ever done, and yet she didn't know how she could stay.

Kate knew she had to make a decision before twelve-thirty. She could return to Rhode Island and settle into a new job and a new apartment. She could remember her time in England as a sweet interlude or she could take a chance and stay here with William, for however long.

The sun was shining, so she left her coat hanging on the back of the hotel door and, too edgy to pace inside her small hotel room any longer, headed outside into the bright morning air. She walked down Charing Cross Road, past the now familiar bookstores, toward Trafalgar Square. Unwilling to face bangers and bagels at the hotel, Kate bought a newspaper from the man on the corner of Leicester Square and stopped at one of the French *pâtisseries* that dotted the West End.

She ordered coffee and a giant jelly doughnut and sat down in the corner. Pretending she did this every morning, Kate drank her coffee and read the article on Heathrow and the terrorists; the situation didn't sound too serious. She skipped through the political scandals and paused at photos of royalty. Princess Diana had hosted a reception for the American Red Cross yester-

day afternoon. Prince Charles had given a speech
across town. Lady Helen Taylor, cousin of the queen,
had attended the theater as part of a friend's birthday
celebration. Lady Helen was a pretty blonde, Kate
noted, but the tall woman standing beside her looked
familiar. Kate looked closer. She was William's friend
from San Lorenzo's. And she wore the Thorne Diamond brooch pinned to the bodice of her dress.

THERE HAD TO BE A MISTAKE. It couldn't be the same
brooch—her brooch. Kate hurried back to her hotel
room, grabbed her coat from its hook and looked down
at the bare lapel. Then she realized she could have left
it pinned to her black sweater. She'd packed quickly,
after all. She might have missed it; she'd been so intent
on finding space for the coffee cups, teapot and various
boxes of bath gels. Kate tossed the contents of her suitcase onto the bed and pawed through the clothing,
then crawled on the floor and searched under the bed.

When had she last seen it? Kate sat on the floor and
tried to remember. She'd worn it on her coat in the car.
Her hair had caught on one of the prongs, and she'd
untangled it when she took off her coat at Thorne
House.

Thorne House. There had been no call from the Duke
of Thornecrest last night. There had been no word from
him this morning. He'd offered to buy the brooch; yesterday she had refused to sell it, once and for all. Had
he been pretending to accept the fact that it would not
be returned to his family? Had he been pretending all
along, about everything?

She blinked back tears. Crying would do no good.
Finding the brooch was the answer. Kate searched the
small room. She stripped the bed, checked between the

mattress and the wall and found nothing. She had to face the facts. The brooch was gone, transferred to the bosom of another woman, a woman Will had dated before he'd met her. He hadn't called last night, though he could have come over when she was asleep. If he'd knocked on the door and received no answer, he could have decided against waking her. But why hadn't he called this morning?

Because he was guilty? Because he'd finally obtained what he wanted all along? Kate didn't want to believe the man she loved would do such a thing, but she hadn't wanted to believe Jeff was calling off the wedding and marrying someone else, either. She'd thought he was joking.

There was nothing funny about losing something worth a quarter of a million pounds. There was nothing funny about believing she was loved, only to discover it was all a lie. She'd been foolish to insist on wearing the pin instead of storing it in a vault. She'd thought she was safe with Will Landry, too.

Kate slung her purse over her shoulder and grabbed the newspaper, folded so the photograph of the pin was displayed. She wanted an explanation, and she wanted it in person.

"I'M SORRY, miss, but His Grace is not at home at the moment." Mary wiped her hands on her apron and looked distressed. "I'm afraid I can't invite you in."

"Lady Thornecrest isn't home, either?"

"At the moment she's not receiving visitors."

Of course she wasn't. Why risk being confronted with the accusations of a furious American tourist? "Tell the duke that Katherine Stewart was here and will be going to the police about her missing jewelry."

She gave the little maid the paper. "Tell him the Thorne Diamond's on page thirty-one."

"I will, miss." The maid nodded politely and took the paper. "Will there be anything else?"

Kate hesitated, her anger and pain threatening to bubble over. Screaming on the duke's doorstep would accomplish nothing. She couldn't believe they were going to ignore her, but naturally that was exactly what they would do. Who would the police believe, a middle-class tourist on a budget tour or a respected member of British society? Pitty would back up anything Will said, of course, so it would be Kate's word against theirs.

She was having trouble believing it herself, but what else could she think? The pin was gone and entrance to Thorne House denied. Her love affair with William might never have existed, their days spent together a figment of a lonely woman's imagination. Kate blinked back tears and turned away from the elegant entrance of Thorne House.

She wished she'd never come to England.

"GONE? What do you mean, *gone?*" William leaned forward, unwilling to believe what he'd just been told. His fingers tightened around the paper wrapping of the roses he'd stopped to purchase on Oxford Street.

The young woman behind the counter shot him an affronted look and rifled through the pages on the counter until she found the one she wanted. "Miss Stewart has checked out, sir."

"Katherine Stewart? Are you certain?"

"Yes."

"How long ago?"

The woman frowned, obviously annoyed by his persistent questions. She looked back down at the paper before replying. "Sometime before noon."

Before noon? Will remembered to thank the young woman before stepping away from the reception counter. What on earth was going on? It was only twelve-thirty, and Kate had left without him. He returned to his car and picked up the phone. Maybe she had left a message with Pitty.

A few minutes later Will slammed down the phone and hurriedly put the Jag in gear. Pitty had babbled tearfully about a newspaper clipping and a visit from Kate and other things that didn't make sense. All he knew was that Kate was at the airport, preparing to leave him, and he had to stop her before it was too late.

"KATE!"

She heard the voice as she stood in the middle of the Body Shop, trying to to decide whether or not to buy a wooden comb. She didn't need a wooden comb, but she was trying hard to think of ways to keep busy, to keep from thinking of William and the way he'd betrayed her. She'd already bought a crossword puzzle, four packets of English chocolate and a bottle of unblended Scotch from the duty-free shop.

She must attract weird men, she thought, ignoring the voice calling her name. The voice couldn't possibly belong to William. He wouldn't come to find her, to tell her he loved her, to return her brooch and apologize. Things like that *definitely* did not happen to her.

"Kate!"

She felt a hand touch her shoulder, an achingly familiar touch. She drew a quick breath and turned around. He had the gall to smile. She stared up at him.

"You stole my brooch," she said, wishing she could

punch him in the stomach, but her hands were full of packages.

"No, I didn't."

"I want it back."

He looked uncomfortable. "I didn't steal it, Katie."

"Then you've brought it to me."

William looked down at her free hand. "Are you going to buy that comb? I'd like to get out of here and talk to you."

Kate dropped the comb back in the bin and held out her hand, palm up. "Give it back to me. I want to go home now."

"The brooch is still at Thorne House, with Pitty. She wants to talk to you."

"I'm through talking to either one of you," Kate declared. "I'm getting on a plane in an hour and when I get home I'm going to get a lawyer and find out how to get Aunt Belle's pin back. I know I don't have a snowball's chance in hell here, when you're practically a member of the royal family."

"That's not true," he protested. He took her hand and pulled her out of the store. "The brooch is safe and waiting for you. Come home with me. I'll return it to you."

Kate shook her head. "I don't believe you. You and your grandmother stole the brooch. You just had to have it, didn't you? Were you going to send me a check or were you just going to steal it outright?"

He gripped her hand tighter and led her past the ticket counters toward the exit. "We didn't steal it," he insisted. "At least, I didn't. Pitty was to have explained and apologized this morning, but she's a little under the weather right now." He slowed down as police scurried to bar the wall of exit doors. "What on earth is going on?"

"Another bomb threat," a British Airways employee beside them explained. "They're closing down everything until they determine whether or not it's safe to use runway two."

"For how long?" Kate asked. Her sisters would be frantic when they heard the news.

The man shrugged. "It's difficult to say, miss. It could be hours before we're cleared. No one can leave the airport and no one can enter until further notice."

William took her elbow and steered her away from the alarming scene. "Let's have some tea. There's something I want to—"

"I need to call Anne. She's the one picking me up tonight."

"Go ahead," he said, indicating a nearby wall of public telephones. "I'll wait here."

She noticed he didn't argue about her leaving. What had happened to the loving man who had asked her to stay in England and travel with him? Kate looked at her watch as she hurried across the wide corridor. Anne wouldn't be home, but she could leave a message on her sister's answering machine to let her know that there was nothing to worry about.

Kate glanced back at the tall man whose protective gaze was still on her. Oh, there was something to worry about, all right. The thieving duke still owned her heart.

"YOUR FLIGHT today is canceled," William declared, trying not to smile. He had conferred with the ticket agent after the announcement that the airport had been reopened. "You're not going anywhere tonight."

"You don't have to look so happy about it," she grumbled.

He tried to hide his satisfaction with the news. Five hours in this airport had crawled by like eight. Kate hadn't had much to say and neither had he. Which was fine. He didn't want to say what he had to say in the middle of Heathrow during an IRA bomb threat. "They'll start flying again in the morning and your flight will most likely be one of the first ones to depart. They suggest you return by six-thirty." He didn't add that he had other plans where her departure was concerned.

"Well—" Kate eyed the row of plastic seats beside her "—I suppose that won't be too bad."

"You're not staying here for the next twelve hours," he said. "And neither am I. You're coming home with me. Now."

"No." She sounded tired, and her eyes were suspiciously bright.

"Don't be an idiot. You can stay at Thorne House until morning. You will sleep in a comfortable bed." He stood up and picked up the bag by her feet. "Don't fight me, Katie. It's the least I can do after...everything that has happened."

"Will you give me the brooch?"

"Yes. Of course." He was doomed to spend the rest of his life regretting he'd ever set eyes on the damn thing. "After you've listened to what I have to say."

THORNE HOUSE was different. A faint odor of fresh paint still clung to the air, but the sheets had been removed from the furniture and the paintings were in their proper places. Kate longed to explore the downstairs rooms once again, but resisted asking Will for another tour of his home. She couldn't let herself be distracted from what she needed to do: get the brooch and leave for home. She could cry when she got on the plane. She was looking forward to it, in fact. But for now she wouldn't let Will see how much he'd hurt her. She had no intention of spending the night, either. She would pick up her pin and leave, no matter how many times the Duke of Thornecrest protested.

They took the elevator to the upper story, and Mary greeted them when they stepped into the foyer.

"How is Pitty feeling?" he asked the housekeeper.

"She's in the living room. I've prepared a simple dinner. You can eat whenever you're ready."

William thanked her and ushered Kate into the living room. Pitty, wearing somber knit slacks and a black sweater, waited for them in the wing chair. "My dears," she said, wiping her eyes with a lace-edged handkerchief. "I have been so worried about you."

"As you can see, we're fine. And you? Are you feeling a bit livelier now?" He sat on the couch with a grateful sigh and pulled Kate down to sit beside him. She attempted to pull her hand from his, but he held on tightly and pretended he didn't notice her efforts to distance herself.

"I'm better," Pitty sighed. "Much better."

Kate looked at the elderly woman's pale skin and couldn't help worrying about her. "Have you been sick?"

"Yes," she nodded, clutching her handkerchief. "A touch of that flu that seems to be plaguing the neighborhood, I suppose, but now that you're here..." Her voice trailed off as she looked at her grandson. "I'm still in trouble, aren't I?"

He nodded. "Kate would like an explanation."

"And my pin," Kate added.

Pitty nodded. "Of course. I must confess, I stole your brooch yesterday. Or rather, I instructed Mary to remove it from your coat."

"But why?"

"The legend," Pitty replied, looking toward William. "Explain it to her, dear."

William rested his arm on the back of the couch and, still holding her hand, turned to face Kate. "You're going to think we're all mad, I'm afraid." He smiled down at her. "But be patient, just for a few more minutes. My grandmother believes that the brooch— *your* brooch—brings happiness in the form of marital bliss to its owners. She is firmly convinced that the reason there have been unhappy Thornecrest marriages in the past four generations is because the brooch disappeared."

"Aunt Laurabelle said it would bring my heart's desire," Kate murmured. "I wonder if she knew there was something special about the pin. I can't believe she knew it was valuable, though. She kept it in her dresser drawer, with her other jewelry."

Pitty nodded. "It has always been passed down from mother to daughter, but unfortunately there have been no daughters in many, many years. I'd give a great deal to discover how it ended up with your aunt." She paused. "Do happy marriages run in your family, Katherine?"

Kate thought for a moment. "Why, yes, I guess they do."

Pitty gave William a triumphant look. "That proves it, you see. I was right all along."

He didn't look as if he wanted to agree. "Give Kate the brooch."

The old woman rose, went to the sideboard and picked up a small enamel box. She crossed the room and handed it to Kate. "Take it, my dear, and wear it with happiness."

Kate opened the box and saw the pin nestled securely inside. "Thank you."

William frowned at his grandmother. "Why on earth are you wearing black?"

"I'm in mourning," she sniffed.

"For whom?"

"All the beautiful children you'll never have." She sniffed. "When Katherine left, I thought you had lost every chance for happiness. I was distraught. I knew you'd never have a lovely little son to carry on the Thornecrest title."

"If you'll allow us some privacy," he told her, trying not to laugh, "I'm going to talk to Kate about that."

William waited for Pitty to blow them a kiss and leave the room before turning back to Kate. She returned the pin to its place in the box and set it on the table in front of her. "I think I'd better go," she said.

"Not until you hear what I have to say."

Kate waited, hoping against hope that he would say something that would make a difference. "Okay. You can start with why Jessica wore the pin last night."

He winced. "All right, but then we're not discussing that dreadful thing anymore. I realized yesterday that I had fallen in love with you." He tried to smile but failed. "I was such an idiot that I began to believe Pitty's superstitions about the diamond. She took the pin and sent it to Jessica to wear for one night. She suspected that I had fallen in love with you, and wanted to try it on someone else. It didn't work, of course. Which was probably her point all along. I think she wanted to prove that I was truly and deeply in love for the first time in my miserable life."

"You don't have to look so unhappy about it."

"I've wanted you from the first moment I saw you," he admitted. He touched her cheek. "It had nothing to do with the pin."

"I didn't want to fall in love with you, either."

"But you did?" He looked hopeful.

"Yes." Kate guessed it wouldn't hurt to admit it. She wondered if she had any pride left at all. "I certainly did."

"I can't tell you how relieved I am to hear that."

She twined her arms around his neck. "What are we going to do now?"

He leaned closer and brushed his lips against hers. "Well, I have several excellent suggestions. I had plenty of time to think of all sorts of things last night."

"For instance?"

"Pot roast," he said, kissing her briefly. "Apple pies." He kissed her briefly. "Children playing dress-up in the attic."

"Do you know what you're saying?"

"Of course not." He lifted his head and smiled down at her. "I'm under a spell. Will you marry me anyway?"

Kate's heart beat faster. She wondered if she'd heard correctly. "I thought you were against marriage and commitment."

"You've changed my mind," he said. "Say yes."

Kate opened her mouth, but no sound came out.

"I hoped you'd agree," he murmured, rummaging in his jacket pocket. He brought out a small velvet box and opened it. "If not, I planned to bribe you with jewels." Kate looked down as he removed an emeraldnd-diamond band. Set in gold and dotted with tiny pearls, it resembled the delicate antique ring she'd seen n Covent Garden. "It's not the same one, of course," he explained. "But I spent the morning hounding Eric at Antiquarius for something similar. Do you like it?"

"It's the most beautiful thing I've ever seen."

"Then you'll marry me?"

"Yes," she managed to say, then watched as he slipped the ring on her finger. "There's something I should warn you about."

Will stopped, his expression serious. "Whatever it is won't matter. We can visit your sisters as often as you like. And there is plenty of room at Thorne Hall for long visits. I've always envied friends with large families."

She smiled. "I think you should know that there hasn't been a boy born in our family for as long as anyone can remember."

"I'll change that," he promised with a very dukelike confidence. "We can start tonight."

"Uh-oh. How am I going to explain this to my sisters? They'll think I've lost my mind."

William wrapped her securely in his arms and bent to kiss his future duchess. He didn't care what anyone thought as long as he had Katie to share his life. "Tell them the fault belongs to Aunt Laurabelle."

Epilogue

"SHE HAS YOUR TEMPER," William noted, trying to distract eight-month-old Laura Anne Landry, who was intent on pulling his hair. He handed her a rattle, and she banged it loudly on the tray of the high chair. Sitting quietly in a high chair was not one of her favorite pastimes. She preferred to be carried around the house and the estate so she could observe everything that went on.

"He has your dignity," Kate, who held the chubby tenth Duke of Thornecrest in her lap, stated. She finished retying his left shoe before looking over at his twin sister. Little William smiled at his father, but made no move to show he was discontent with his situation. "Which may or may not be a good thing," she added, smiling at her husband.

"Fatherhood has taken away every shred of dignity I possess. Just ask Pitty." His daughter squealed for attention, so he scooted his chair closer and let her give him a hug. "See what I mean?"

"Ask Pitty what?" The elderly woman hurried into the dining room, a sheaf of papers clutched to the bodice of a fuchsia dress. Laura's eyes lit up and she banged the rattle with more gusto than usual. "Never mind. It's too exciting!" Pitty said, dropping her papers on the table. "After all this time I've finally discovered the connection!" She beamed at Kate. "With your sisters' assistance, of course. We've had ourselves quite a little treasure hunt.''

Will gently removed his daughter's fingers from his hair and glanced over at his wife. She shrugged, planted a kiss on little Willie's curly head and winked at her husband. William melted, as he did every day at the sight of his beautiful wife. She'd been a whirlwind of activity since their marriage. She'd redecorated Thorne Hall, cleaned out the attic and installed a gift shop in a stone cottage beside the cheese factory. She'd been delighted with pregnancy and motherhood, despite his fears for her health. Her sisters and their families had welcomed him as part of the family, and her nieces sent him letters and colored drawings. Not an hour went by that he didn't feel intense gratitude for the gifts he'd been given.

"William! You're not paying attention!"

"Sorry, Pitty." He gave Kate an apologetic smile and turned to his grandmother. "What are you trying to tell us?"

"Good news, my dears." She took a deep breath before making her announcement. "Katherine's ancestors were not thieves after all!"

"Well, that's a relief," Will replied, trying to keep a straight face so he wouldn't hurt the elderly woman's feelings. "What on earth are you talking about?"

"The brooch, of course. I've finally discovered the family connection. The diaries belonged to Alicia Landry, the third Duke of Thornecrest's daughter. It was her clothes you found in the attic last year. She eloped with a very unsuitable young man in 1814 and took the brooch with her. By rights it would have been hers, since her mother had died the year before. The Duke was so furious he disowned her, and her husband gambled all their money away."

"Poor thing," Kate murmured. "What happened to her?"

"They left for America. He must have died at a very young age, because there are no records of him at all." She flipped through papers until she found the one she wanted. "This is where you come in, Katherine. Alicia married a cattle rancher from Montana and had three children. One of them was your great-great-grandmother."

"So the pin really belonged to me after all?"

"Yes."

"And now it belongs to Laura."

William held up his hand. "Not yet, it doesn't. Not until she's...twenty-five. Or thirty. She's staying home with her father until then."

Pitty looked thoughtful and turned to Kate. "Would you mind if I wore it in the meantime? Thorne House is quite empty now that you spend all your time in the country. I could do with a little romance myself."

"Be my guest," Kate said, struggling to hide her laughter. "Will put it back in the vault in town, and you're welcome to it."

"That's right," William echoed, reaching across the table for his wife's hand. His son grinned at him again, and his daughter whacked him on the head with her chubby fist. "But be careful. That brooch does strange things to a man."

"I've noticed." Pitty sniffed, eyeing the happy family with great satisfaction. "Which is exactly what I intended all along."

HARLEQUIN® *Temptation*

It's hot...and it's out of control!

This spring, the forecast is hot and steamy!
Don't miss these bold, provocative, ultrasexy books!

INTO THE FIRE by Leslie Kelly
March 2002

Lacey Clarke never believed in lust at first sight until she set her eyes on the gorgeous stranger. How was she to know her perfect lover would turn out to be her worst enemy?

PRIVATE INVESTIGATIONS by Tori Carrington
April 2002

Secretary turned P.I. Ripley Logan never thought her first job would have her running for her life—or crawling into a stranger's bed....

ONE HOT NUMBER by Sandy Steen
May 2002

Accountant Samantha Collins might be good with numbers, but she needs some work with men...until she meets sexy but broke rancher Ryder Wells. Then she decides to make him a deal—her brains for his bed. Sam's getting the better of the deal, but hey, who's counting?

Don't miss this thrilling threesome!

HARLEQUIN®
Makes any time special ®

Visit us at www.eHarlequin.com

HTITF

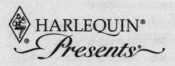

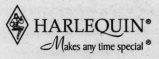

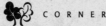

C O O P E R ' S   C O R N E R

In April 2002 you are invited to three wonderful weddings in a very special town...

A Wedding at Cooper's Corner

USA Today bestselling author

Kristine Rolofson
Muriel Jensen
Bobby Hutchinson

Ailing Warren Cooper has asked private investigator David Solomon to deliver three precious envelopes to each his grandchildren. Inside each is something that will bring surprise, betrayal...and unexpected romance!

And look for the exciting launch of *Cooper's Corner*, a NEW 12-book continuity from Harlequin—launching in August 2002.

HARLEQUIN®
Makes any time special ®

Visit us at www.eHarlequin.com   PHWCC

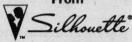